Praise for the novels of Leslie Glass

"This series [is] a winner!"   —*Mystery News*

"Detective Woo is the next generation descended from Ed McBain's 87th precinct."
     —*Hartford Courant*

"I'll drop what I'm doing to read Leslie Glass anytime."   —*Nevada Barr*

"Fast-paced, gritty . . . [April Woo] joins Kinsey Millhone and Kay Scarpetta in the ranks of female crime fighters."   —*Library Journal*

Continued . . .

More . . .

"Sharp as a scalpel. . . . Scary as hell. Leslie Glass is Lady McBain."
— *New York Times* bestselling author Michael Palmer

"If you're a Thomas Harris fan . . . looking for a new thriller to devour, you'll find it in *Burning Time*." — *Ft. Lauderdale Sun-Sentinel*

"A suspenseful story in which those who appear to be sane may actually harbor the darkest secrets of all." — *Mostly Murder*

"The plot is clever . . . and the ending is a genuine surprise. Woo is so appealing a protagonist that Leslie Glass can keep her going for a long time." — *Newark Star-Ledger*

STEALING
TIME

▰

LESLIE GLASS

A SIGNET BOOK

SIGNET
Published by New American Library, a division of
Penguin Putnam Inc., 375 Hudson Street,
New York, New York 10014, U.S.A.
Penguin Books Ltd, 80 Strand,
London WC2R 0RL, England
Penguin Books Australia Ltd, 250 Camberwell Road,
Camberwell, Victoria 3124, Australia
Penguin Books Canada Ltd, 10 Alcorn Avenue,
Toronto, Ontario, Canada M4V 3B2
Penguin Books (N.Z.) Ltd, 182–190 Wairau Road,
Auckland 10, New Zealand

Penguin Books Ltd, Registered Offices:
Harmondsworth, Middlesex, England

Published by Signet, an imprint of New American Library,
a division of Penguin Putnam Inc. Previously published in a Dutton edition.

First Signet Printing, February 2000
10 9 8 7

 REGISTERED TRADEMARK—MARCA REGISTRADA

Printed in the United States of America

PUBLISHER'S NOTE
This is a work of fiction. Names, characters, places, and incidents either
are the product of the author's imagination or are used fictitiously,
and any resemblance to actual persons, living or dead, business
establishments, events, or locales is entirely coincidental.

For my brother, Stephen,
and for Hallie, Lacy,
Marilee, Sara, and Tessa

ACKNOWLEDGMENTS

Thanks to all the psychologists in my ken, particularly everyone associated with the Glass Institute who contributes so much to the field and to my own life and work. I partake of your books and articles and wisdom daily, borrow your ideas with complete abandon, enjoy your company, and relish your every triumph. To my friends at the Middle States Commission of Higher Education I owe a debt of gratitude for enrichment of many kinds.

As always, special thanks to the thousands of New York City police officers who walk, pedal, ride, fly, swim, and cruise their particular beats, man the special units, supervise the uniforms, train and work the dogs and horses, crunch the numbers, and face the terrors of Comstat Wednesday and Friday mornings—everyone who works so hard to make New York City a safer and more enjoyable place to live and visit. I use bits and pieces of this enormous department, writing entirely as a novelist. I relocate important New York City landmarks and other geography, changing the names of streets and restaurants and even police policy and procedure at will. The errors I make may be intentional, or unintentional, or both, but they are entirely my own. Any resemblances to living persons working at any of the precincts I mention are pure coincidence. Thanks to the staff and trustees of the Police Foundation for all the good work they do, and to New York University Law School, especially the Criminal Justice Department, for a never-ending deluge of information and stimulation.

Special thanks to my agent, Nancy Yost, and editor, Audrey LaFehr, for believing in me (and for much more), and to all the people at Dutton/NAL in production, promotion, marketing and sales who work so hard to make the magic happen. And to Alex and Lindsey, my anchor, inspiration, and joie de vivre, three cheers!

Th' expense of spirit in a waste of shame
Is lust in action; and, till action, lust
Is perjured, murd'rous, bloody, full of blame,
Savage, extreme, rude, cruel, not to trust;
Enjoyed no sooner but despisèd straight;
Past reason hunted, and no sooner had,
Past reason hated as a swallowed bait,
On purpose laid to make the taker mad:
Mad in pursuit, and in possession so:
Had, having, and in quest to have, extreme:
A bliss in proof, and proved, a very woe;
Before, a joy proposed; behind, a dream.
All this the world well knows; yet none
    knows well.
To shun the heaven that leads men to this
    hell.

                —William Shakespeare
                Sonnet 129

CHAPTER
1

The morning Heather Rose Popescu finally resolved to set her life in order, she lost her baby, ended up in the hospital, and became the subject of an intense police inquiry. This result was no less than she expected because of the remedy she'd used to purge her troubled soul. And by noon, like a person condemned, she was already preparing for the end of her life as she knew it. In a state of terrified purpose, she set about her domestic tasks. For beauty, she put an arrangement of magnificent pink peonies on the table in the living room. For taste, she was preparing her husband's favorite dinner, roast duck. In her panic, she remembered the duck in the freezer and seized on it at the last moment as a possible appeasement.

She was well aware of the basic things that were certain to infuriate Anton, but there were also those other little things that she couldn't predict. She never knew what was going to set her husband off; and frequently, in the afternoons, she cast about helplessly for something to please or divert him so he wouldn't get started on her. Today, she knew the duck was a hopeless gesture, but it was defrosting in the kitchen sink, anyway.

The catastrophic event was triggered at half past two, earlier than she expected. She hadn't finished her preparations. She wasn't ready. When the doorbell rang, Heather Rose had just taken a broom from the closet to sweep the kitchen floor. She jumped at the deceptively innocent sound, terrified of what would happen when she opened the door. But, as with every-thing else in her life, she had no choice. She had to open the door. The difference this time was that, after years of the deepest suffering, she was finally doing what she thought was right.

The day had started just like hundreds of others in Heather Rose's marriage. She had awakened with the intense desire to atone, to address her shortcomings, and to finally receive the understanding and forgive-ness she craved. Above all, she wanted Anton to be kind, to accept and love her.

"How can I love you when you're constantly hurting my feelings, putting me down?" was his angry re-sponse. Daily, he told her that the punishments she received came as a result of her own failings. No mat-ter what she tried, she just couldn't get anything right.

For many years it had been Heather Rose's deeply held secret that one day she would somehow correct all the wrongs that Anton had done to her in the name of his hurt feelings, and somehow she would become whole again. Since he was more powerful and danger-ous, however, she did not know how she could possi-bly accomplish such a thing. And every morning, the will to exorcise the demons from her existence melted away with the four teaspoons of sugar she added to his breakfast coffee.

Like many people trapped in destructive relation-ships, Heather Rose had become convinced by her partner that she was a bad person. Anton had an end-less catalogue of her faults that he recited often. And the worst fault of all, the one that dogged her daily, resulted in the most painful disciplines, and shamed her most deeply, was that she did not love him as

much as she should. In her wedding vows, she had
promised that she would love him no matter what.
Anton reminded her of it continually and made her
pledge her allegiance over and over.

This pretense of unconditional love turned out to
be a greater ordeal than any she could have imagined.
He tricked her again and again, and the lies at the
center of their marriage were the poison that made
the burden of keeping her promise an impossible task,
a war she fought with herself daily but could not ever
hope to win. Often she had longed for a release from
life altogether.

At the sound of the doorbell, she glanced at the
clock. Two-thirty. Anton always rang the bell. Whatever time he arrived home he expected her to be there
for him, to open the door and greet him with a drink
and a pleasant smile. But he rarely came home this
early.

Oh God, now it begins, was her first thought. Anton
had a sharp eye. She hadn't changed her clothes; she
hadn't cleaned the last dirty diaper out of the pail.
What would he criticize first? She wanted to get the
diaper out of the apartment. But then the bell rang a
second time, and it hit home that today none of the
little things mattered. Trembling, she moved to open
the door.

"Hello, gorgeous."

She couldn't stop her eyes from registering shock.
"What are you doing here?" Reflexively, she stepped
back. But he moved with her, and she couldn't avoid
an embrace.

"Come to see my sweetie. Any reason why I shouldn't?"
Big smile on his face as he enveloped her in the Big
Hug.

"Hey, not today."

"Huh?" He drew back, looked at her with mock
suspicion, hugged her again, squeezed her bottom,

pressed her to him again, this time tangling his fingers in her hair. The whole ritual made her weak with terror. He wasn't a good man; he didn't like her at all. Everything was a sham. She'd be found out. Someone would be murdered. All this went through her head. Finally, he moved away and looked around.

"You look great. How's the baby?"

"Sleeping," she lied, knowing he knew.

"The place looks great," he said, following her as she fled into the kitchen. "You, too."

She didn't say anything. She was wearing tights and a sweater. Her hair was a wreck and she had no makeup on. She didn't look great at all. He knew everything.

"Hey baby, I missed you," he said to her back. "How about a quickie?"

The suggestion startled her. It was the last thing she'd expected. "Absolutely not." She turned around to be sure he understood, but before she could say anything more his arms were around her again, his hands taking inventory of her body in his very practiced way. His face was in her hair. She could feel his excitement.

"No." She tried to get away.

"Hey, don't do that. You're my honey."

"Come on, come on." She struggled in his arms, trying to cajole, trying not to panic.

"You smell so great," he murmured.

"No, don't, I mean it."

"With you no is yes. You want me as much as I want you. You're dying for me, baby. I can feel it." His fingers writhed their way into her tights.

"No." It was all she could think of to say. He knew, and he was angry. She could feel it.

"Yes." He drew back and found her lips, kissed her hard on the mouth, bruisingly hard. He tasted like beer.

The beery taste meant he was mad *and* drunk. Today, however, she wouldn't take it. She pushed him away. "I said no."

For a second his arrogance was replaced by surprise. He looked at her, amazed. Then he exploded. "Who do you think you are? You can't tell me no."

"I'm telling you no." She said it so softly she could hardly hear the words herself. She was almost afraid to breathe. Her back was pressed against the counter. Behind her the knives were stacked in their block of wood. The broom was propped against the refrigerator. She could see confusion in his eyes. He hadn't expected resistance. For a second he laughed, not believing she could act like this after what she'd done. But she didn't care. That morning she had resolved to be a good person, to draw the line in the sand and stop the lies, all the bad things that had happened since she'd married Anton with such hope and excitement—and been betrayed in so many ways.

This man was the worst. She could see his expression change from laughing at her, to disbelief, to anger. He was still, very still, as he considered her.

The first punch came as a complete surprise. He punched her in the stomach. She didn't have time to scream; she just doubled over, the air knocked out of her. Her falling down that easily made him mad. He thought she was faking, so he straightened her up and punched her in the mouth, then in the eye to teach her a lesson. When she finally hit the ground, he kicked her in the ribs. Luckily for her, she'd already passed out when he tired of using his feet and his fists and then saw the broom.

This event happened on a sunny spring afternoon when the temperature hit seventy-three degrees in Central Park and the sky was the color of cornflowers. When Anton Popescu called 911, he said he'd come home from work early and found his wife of five years bloody and unconscious on the kitchen floor and their infant son gone from their exclusive Central Park South apartment. The police arrived en masse within minutes.

CHAPTER
2

At the same time down in Chinatown, Lin Tsing, a newcomer to America, a seventeen-year-old illegal alien, lay on an old blanket under the living room window, as far away from the other occupants of the tiny tenement apartment as they could put her. She hadn't been well, and now she was acting spooky, like a woman possessed. She had come home early from work, spoken to no one, and wouldn't answer questions. She had a glazed and empty look on her face, as if she had entered another world since morning. And they didn't like it one bit. She lay there in a stupor, listening to them argue about her.

They were afraid she was sick; they wanted to put her out. She could hear them discussing this. The men kept their distance. The women hovered around her, covering their mouths and noses to protect themselves from whatever ailed her.

It was not so easy for them to get her out, however. She had enemies and no friends. Their problem was how to go about getting rid of her without bringing trouble from many directions upon themselves. No one made any effort to hide the nature of their dilemma. Lin could feel the women huddling together, not too close to her, afraid of everything, not knowing what to do.

Mei, with the shrill voice, said Lin was bad luck and they should put her on the street. This woman was shushed by the others for being so outspoken even though everyone, except the two aunties, believed that if Lin were put out on the street, an ambulance with sirens going and lights flashing would magically come and take her to the hospital. They were sure of this because they believed that the authorities in New York did not like to have sick people on the streets. The discussions intensified during the late afternoon when Lin would not speak and get up again, even to relieve herself. She could have been deaf for all they cared. The two aunties gave her a few aspirin, but they had no other medicine to give her.

Lin let herself drift, welcoming the emptiness in her head. She had been sick before and gotten well before. In the part of her head that was still aware and could think about things, she'd decided that being sick was a good way out. If she was sick, she did not have to work. She did not have to show herself on the street or have anyone ask her questions, threaten her, or get her in trouble. Now her troubles were over. She would rest, and she would recover.

In recent weeks she had been telling herself a story about survival: She was feeling bad because being sick kept her safe from other dangers, the real dangers that terrified her even more than having a slight fever. As long as she had a fever, she was safe. After her fever left her, she would get better and then she would escape. Today, she'd seen her stupid cousin Nanci Hua, and Nanci had hurt her again, hadn't even tried to save her. Still, she would do what she had to do. If she didn't get better in a few days, she would swallow her pride. Once again, she'd call that cousin who hated her, and who was probably hating her even more now that she knew how bad Lin really was. This was Lin's plan. All this time, she had avoided telling the stuck-up Nanci Hua her troubles. Now Nanci would come to this apartment and take her away as soon as she bowed low enough and swallowed the shame. Lin wasn't stupid. In the end she would bow. She would do what she had to do to survive.

When Lin heard the women muttering about the bad luck that would come to them from keeping her, she wanted to say something to stop it. But her head was separated from her. She was in a place where speaking made no sense. In the end, she didn't have the energy, and she didn't care.

She had been in this place with Mr. and Mrs. Wang and the two aunties for ten months and had never let Nanci visit once. Other people lived there on and off—two people, three people, whole families. They went to work, came back, cooked over a hot plate in the living room because the Wangs did not allow them to use their two-burner stove. They shared a toilet and sink in a dirty cubbyhole, and a tub by the refrigerator. For two months of her stay there had been three young children in the place, bringing the number of occupants in the two-room apartment to ten. That had been the worst. The children had cried often and been scolded. The scolding reminded Lin of her mother, who had died in a country hospital in China almost two years ago. The memories of her mother made Lin want to leave the apartment and go to Nanci, but the aunties said she owed them after all they had done for her. Lin had stayed, and later when she didn't feel well, she was afraid to go to a hospital where she was sure to die, just like her mother.

Lin faded in and out. There was no doubt she felt worse than ever before. Right now she felt worse than she had on the crowded buses traveling across China a year ago, worse than when she'd nearly starved on the tossing ship crossing the ocean. On both buses and ship she'd vomited so many times from the motion that she could not hold down even a sip of water.

Last year the two Lao women from her home village who'd been traveling with her for many months, the women who insisted they were her aunties, had several times thought she would die. Every time they thought she was about to pass on, they would take for themselves her few possessions and her little supply of money, sent by her rich cousin Nanci Hua in New York. They did this so no one else could rob her when the last breath of life finally left her wasted body. In the end Lin always surprised them by showing a strength no one expected she had. She always recovered. Of course, the fact that she lived on meant they had to return to her what they had taken, but each time she survived, they gave back a little less. Some of her money was always retained by them as payment for the care they had given her and their kindness in keeping her alive.

For them, it was natural that Lin stay with the old auntie and young auntie when they moved into an apartment with the Wang family and the three other people who had been there at the time. They argued that she owed them much more than she owed her cousin whom she didn't know at all, and who had waited all these years to bring her to the golden shores and never cared for her when she was sick. The two aunties told her this so often that Lin believed them. She believed them because the fear that haunted her dreams was not of dying, but of living on and on in a foreign place where no one understood or knew her and where the cousin who was so different from her scolded and disliked her and would certainly have abandoned her altogether if she had known the truth about her.

The two aunties had been friends with her dead mother. So Lin believed the things they said about their kindness and stayed close to them, sleeping on the floor on old blankets in the worst place in the fifth-floor apartment, under the window where the cold air came in around the frame and gnawed at her all winter.

Now she could hear the aunties whispering to each other about the blood she sometimes spat up. "Too much blood."

She also heard them arguing the case for letting her stay where she was so they could care for her themselves. They said her mother had been their friend. She was like their own daughter. They had a responsibility to their dead friend to help her daughter and look after her. She'd always been a sickly girl, they explained, sick all the time. But she was a good worker. Once she'd brought home a whole ham, already cooked. At other times, she gave them expensive food. She paid the rent, and sick as she seemed, this daughter of their friend always got better in the end. Lin believed she was safe.

CHAPTER
3

When Detective Sergeant April Woo, New York Police Department, reported for work at the Midtown North precinct at four P.M., the last thing she expected was to catch a kidnapping case. But then nothing about that Tuesday had been routine.

At five A.M., she'd seen the glow of morning spread from the living room, down the hall, and into the bedroom of the twenty-second-floor Queens apartment where her boyfriend had lived for six months and where no curtains concealed the drop-dead view of the Manhattan skyline. Punched out and highlighted by the dawn, the jumble of building shapes hung as if etched in the sky, a monument to the ingenuity of man, that great magician who used the raw power of steel and concrete in bridges and glass towers to dwarf nature and hide himself. Another day, and the city beckoned even before the cop was fully conscious.

April Woo was second whip in the detective squad of the West Side precinct between Fifty-ninth and Forty-second streets, from Fifth Avenue to the Hudson River. She was a boss who supervised other detectives and was in charge of the squad when her superior, Lieutenant Iriarte, was not around. She was also a person used to sleeping in her own bed. Having grown up in a Chinatown walk-up and living at the moment in a two-story house in Astoria, Queens, April was now in the highest place she'd ever spent the night. She yawned, stretched and let the soft drone of the news perpetually playing on 1010 WINS filter into her consciousness. A sharp detective listened for disaster twenty-four hours a day. Hearing a radio report of a crime in her precinct could get her out of bed even if she wasn't aware of hearing it. Now, April urgently needed a catastrophe story for her mother so she could claim she'd been working around-the-clock. She needed the story if she wanted to go home in peace.

Only three weeks ago, on April 25, April Woo had celebrated her thirtieth birthday, but you'd never know it by the way her parents treated her. It was particularly humiliating that instead of bringing her the respect she deserved, her rank in the department and the ripeness of her age served only to pick up the pace of her mother's tirades on the subject of her low-life job and lousy marriage prospects.

In the Chinese culture dragons can be both good and evil, can appear at any moment, and have the power to make or break every human endeavor. April called Sai Yuan Woo "Skinny Dragon Mother" because her mother, too, had the ability to change shape before her eyes and had a tongue that spat real fire. April was fully armed now, carried two guns on her person at all times, but she was still as afraid of her mother as she had been as a small and defenseless child.

Lately, Skinny Dragon Mother had upped the ante in her disapproval of her only child, calling April the very worst kind of old maid, a worm old maid with an undesirable suitor. The undesirable suitor in question, Mike Sanchez, was a Mexican-American sergeant, a colleague in the Detective Bureau. Unlike her, he was now assigned to the Homicide Task Force. Carefully,

April turned her head to look at him, lying on his stomach beside her, sound asleep. One arm was curved over his head; the other cradled the pillow that hid his face. The sheet covered his calves and feet. The rest of him was naked.

The clutch hit her above the heart and below the throat, somewhere around the clavicle. His legs and butt, the muscles in his back and shoulders, the fine tracing of curly black hair on the backs of his arms, more on his legs, seemed exactly right. His waist, though no longer exactly slender and boyish, was proportionately correct for his age and stature. He had smooth skin—in places it was as soft as a baby's—and the hard muscles of a trained fighter. His body was an interesting blend of hard and soft, dotted with a collection of scars from various battles. April knew the origins of only a few.

The tightness in her chest rose to her throat as she thought of his welcome last night. When she'd gotten there at half past one, he'd given her food and wine. Then, in the flickering light of a dozen candles, they'd made love for much of the night. The candles, she'd thought, were an unusually nice touch for a man. She shivered as the dawn slowly infused the room. The idea of her former supervisor as a thoughtful and compelling lover was so alarming that part of her wanted to get off the slippery slope and slide right out of there with the morning, never to return. Another part told her to relax and go back to sleep. She was wrestling with the conflict when Mike spoke.

"Want some coffee, *querida*?" The question came from the depths of the pillow. Not a muscle in his body had moved, but the sound of his voice told her he'd been awake for a while, knew where his gun was, and could roll over, hit the floor, and fire at the door or window in less than five seconds. She grabbed at the sheet to cover herself.

"No thanks, I've got to get going."

"Why? You don't have to be at work until four this afternoon." He rolled over, stretched his arms above his head, and arched his back, showing off his chest and stomach and the rest of the merchandise, which was fully restored after very little sleep.

April busied herself tucking the sheet around her neck, looking everywhere but at the goods. "You know my mother," she mumbled.

Mike laughed softly. "We're already acquainted, *querida*. It's okay to be naked."

"Not where I come from."

"Don't you like to look at me?" He nudged her with his knee.

"Yeah, sure." She mumbled some more, wimping out.

"So come on, take that thing off. We can look at each other in the light. Make my day." He reached out to tickle her, but she turned around to study the clock and didn't see the digits coming.

"Oh my God, it's almost six. Gotta go." She jumped when he touched her. "No, no, really."

He withdrew the offending fingers. "Aw, don't pull the guilty number on me. You know you don't have to go home anymore. You can stay here with me. We could have coffee, sleep a little more. If you don't want, I won't bother you." He lifted an edge of the sheet that covered her and pulled it over himself. The action got him closer to her. They were side by side now, touching from shoulder to knee, and the sheet did not succeed in hiding his intent.

She shook her head and laughed.

"What?" he demanded, his lush mustache twitching innocently.

"You know."

He rose up on one elbow to look at her. "Lucky

me, you are one pretty woman in the morning, *querida*. Give me a hug."

"Yeah, sure, I bet you say that to all the girls." By her calculation, Mike was the good-looking one—and he had a rep. He was like Sara Lee to the opposite sex: no one didn't like him.

"You're the only girl in my life." He said this with just the right amount of huskiness in his voice, not too hokey.

April swallowed the hook and believed him, but didn't want to get all teary about it. She scrunched down, put her arms around him, and laid her head on his chest. She was trying to go with the flow, but wasn't finding it so easy. From the things Mike said and did in bed, she was aware that her own erotic repertoire was somewhat lacking. It made her afraid that regardless of what he told her right now, he'd be tired of her before the week was out.

He was able to distract her from this pessimistic speculation for a while by kissing her all over and encouraging her to return the favor, which didn't turn out to be so very difficult. Then he got up, made coffee, and scrambled some eggs for breakfast. She was impressed by his domesticity. At nine he showered and dressed for the day, collected his gun and his keys from the table, and took off without saying anything about the case that was bedeviling him. April decided to put off going home. What difference could a few hours make, she asked herself.

Time made a big difference in everything, though. If she had gone home either sometime during the night or early in the morning, she might have avoided a whole lot of trouble with her parents. If she had been a few minutes earlier or later in to work that day, or if she hadn't started the evening tour on radio call, cruising around with her driver, Woody Baum, she might never have been involved in the Popescu case.

As it was she didn't go home. And when she reported for work, her boss, Lieutenant Iriarte, immediately sent her out on radio call. She and Woody had hardly settled into their gray unmarked unit when she got a call from the dispatcher to 10-85 the Midtown North patrol supervisor forthwith.

"Possible kidnapping, K," the dispatcher squawked. "Be advised the Midtown North patrol supervisor has also requested Crime Scene and Emergency Service units, K."

"10-4, Manhattan North detective supervisor on the way, K." April turned to Woody. "That's that fancy building at Seventh and Central Park South. Turn around."

Woody threw the bubble on the roof, hit the sirens, and made a gut-wrenching U-turn on Fifty-seventh Street, leaving tire marks on the pavement.

The address of the requested investigation was a glass tower that curved around the corner of Central Park South and Seventh Avenue, sweeping up as much view as it could along the way. A driveway to the building entrance curved out through the sidewalk. In front of the driveway was a tiny garden consisting of a burbling fountain, a Japanese maple full of red leaves, and a thickly painted patch of gold and purple pansies. The building was already locked down. Yellow crime scene tape was stretched across the entrance. Vehicles jammed the area. Uniforms swarmed everywhere. Three minutes from the 911 call, and the operation was already in full swing. The area was sealed off. The curious were clumped together outside police lines, talking, staring. The media was gathering. Traffic was stopped. Horns were honking. Drivers were screaming. The usual pandemonium.

"Park as close as you can and meet me inside." Adrenaline kicked in, and April was all nerves. It looked like something really big.

As Woody tried to pull into the driveway, a tall uniform with a mustache waved them to a stop. Woody jerked to a halt to talk to him as April took out her shield and clipped it to her jacket breast pocket. Before the uniform had a chance to wave them on, she jumped out of the car and joined the fray. She hurried toward the building, briefly looking up at two detectives on the roof. They were wearing vests, had double-barreled shotguns cradled in their arms, and were peering over the edge from above at ledges and anything else that protruded from the building.

Then she caught sight of a familiar face in the crowd of blue in the lobby and went to talk to the precinct patrol supervisor, Lieutenant McMan, a steely type with startling green eyes and no lips at all. He had called the special units in after receiving the call from the 911 dispatcher.

"Hey, Lieutenant. What's the story?" she asked.

"Hey, Woo. Woman's name is Popescu. It appears she was assaulted in her apartment. Her baby is missing."

"She still here?"

"No, she's in the ER at Roosevelt."

"Anybody go with her?"

"Her husband claims he found her." McMan shrugged. "I have two uniforms on him."

"Upstairs?"

"Four detectives trying to get the phones tapped in case there's a ransom demand. ESU's canvassing the basement, roof, elevator shafts, tops of the elevators, trash, trash compactors." He smiled grimly. "The building superintendent freaked out at the heavy tools and the floodlights. He didn't want them breaking down any walls or doors."

"Any sign of the baby?"

McMan shook his head. "Nothing yet."

"What about CSU? Wasn't the crime scene secured for their first shot?"

"Yeah, yeah, they're up there, too. Apartment 9E. You going up?"

"Just for a quick look-see. I want to go over to the ER to Q-and-A the victim right away. What's her status?"

"She was unconscious when she was taken out."

"Hey, boss." Woody bounded up.

"We're going up," she told him, nodding toward the front elevators, two pink marble-fronted horrors.

"Not those, we got people in the shafts. You'll have to go up the back elevator," McMan told her.

Uniforms were swarming on the back stairs as April walked through. One was also guarding the back elevator. The elevator operators and doormen were being questioned by detectives. Tenants unable to get home stood in a clot, having fits. April and Woody commandeered the elevator, stopped at the ninth floor, and tried to enter the apartment through the kitchen.

"Forget about it, I'm not even started here. You can look in and that's it," came a voice from behind the door. The unseen criminologist added, "I don't give a shit who you are," in case somebody planned to put up a fight.

"Sergeant Woo. We just want to take a look," April said.

"This is where it happened. One look, don't touch," came the warning.

"Fine."

The door opened a little and April and Woody got a partial view for all of three seconds of some bloodstains on a marble floor. Somewhere in the front of

the apartment another feisty crime-scene investigator
and more detectives were locked in a noisy conflict
over preservation of the scene versus the need to get
the phones up right away so they could tape all incom-
ing calls. She'd have to come back later.

April glanced at the garbage can by the back door
and repressed a strong urge to go through it. Victim
first.

"Okay," she said to Woody. She turned to leave
and realized he'd frozen the elevator on the floor so
she wouldn't have to wait when she was ready to go.
Good man, he was taking care of her.

Roosevelt Hospital was only a short distance away,
on Ninth Avenue at Fifty-ninth Street, just a block
down from the Manhattan branch of Fordham University. Woody negotiated the car through the streets and
April was lost in her own thoughts. Her antennae were
up, and she was bristling all over. By now there would
already be detectives from the Major Cases Unit. They
would move in and take over the precinct squad room,
maybe even her own desk. They'd be setting up their
easels and starting the clocks ticking on their chrono-
logical time sheets. It rankled that no one thought
precinct detectives could handle important investigations. From now, until this missing baby was found
dead or alive, the precinct squad would be doing the
scut work. No precinct squad detective liked it one bit.

What April always did was to work around the
members of the specialized units as if they weren't the
hotshots with all the muscle. Right now, she didn't
want to vent her feelings about how things were to
the new kid. She wanted to manage the case correctly
so the outsiders wouldn't make a mess in her territory.
And she'd do her best to ignore the frenzy of the
media, too.

"Leave it here," she said. Baum abruptly pulled the

car up to a no-parking zone by the emergency room entrance. Then she jerked her chin to indicate that Baum should accompany her inside.

They hurried into the ER entrance. Right away April picked out two uniforms flanking a nervous-looking man in a blue suit. She decided to take the time to stop at the reception desk before speaking with him. She didn't say anything to Woody. He didn't say anything to her. Good. The young detective, Baum, recently promoted and new to the squad, was following her lead.

At the desk a harried-looking woman with permed red hair saw the shields, then returned to her computer screen.

"Where's the assault victim? Po-pes—"

"Popescu. It's Romanian," the woman snapped. She kept typing and didn't look up.

"Thanks, that's the one. Where is she?" She didn't glance at Baum.

"She's in treatment in room three."

"I'd like to talk with her."

"She's unconscious."

"How about the doctor?"

"The doctor's with her."

"You have any idea when I could talk with him?"

"No." The woman returned to her typing, pleased to thwart. She filled out her uniform and then some, had angry eyes, and a patch of fiery red pimples on each cheek. After a pause, she added, "They've finished with the X rays. Shouldn't be too long now."

"Thanks." April turned back to the rows of seats, occupied by a motley bunch that formed a little pond of human misery in the waiting room. She didn't want to think about the bacteria and viruses circulating the room. She recognized Duffy and Prince. Both were white, five ten or so, beefy, a few years younger than she, and not much for taking initiative of any kind.

Duffy worked a wad of gum around his mouth without actually chewing. The two cops flanked the victim's husband in an informal kind of way. The obviously upset, dark-haired man sat on a chair between them, wringing his hands. She noticed that his tie had alligators on it, that his pink shirt had a white collar and the cuffs were stained with blood; and that his blue pin-striped suit looked expensive.

"Mr. Popescu?" she said.

His head twitched her way. "Yes."

"I'm Detective Sergeant Woo; this is Detective Baum."

He looked from one to the other. "Who's in charge?" he asked testily.

"I am," April said.

"What are you doing about finding my baby?"

"A lot of people are working on it."

"What about my wife? I want to see my wife," he demanded.

"The doctors are with her."

"I don't give a shit who's with her. She's my wife. I want to see her."

"The doctors are with her," April repeated. Then she changed the subject. "What happened?"

"I said I want to see my wife. You can't keep me from her." Popescu had a wide mouth and wide-set eyes as black as April's. The voice was cold, the eyes were on fire. He looked about to blow.

April felt sorry for him. It wasn't uncommon for people to get crazy when someone they loved was hurt. "The doctors are checking her out. No one can go in."

"But I don't *want* anyone to touch her without my being in the room. I'm her husband."

"I understand, but—"

"I won't have any emergency room doctor playing around with my wife." Popescu's panic screamed out of his voice. "I forbid them to do anything to her, working on her face—or, or . . ."

"Can you tell me what happened, sir?"

Popescu gave her a crazed look. "Somebody broke into my apartment and took my baby." His voice cracked. "He's only three weeks old."

"How did you find out?"

He looked surprised at the question. "I came home. I found her—"

"What time was that?" April had her notebook out.

"Three-thirty."

"Is that a usual time for you to come home?"

"What kind of question is that? I came home because I knew something was wrong."

"How did you know?"

"I called and called. When she didn't answer the phone, I knew something was wrong. And I was right." He pounded his fist against his hand. "I was right. Heather was on the floor. There was blood all over the place. At first I thought the blood was the baby's. Then, I realized the baby wasn't *there*—" His hands flew to his face. "Oh God, you've got to let me in to see her. I need to be with her."

"They have to clean her up first and X-ray her for broken bones. It's procedure."

"She's all right. I know she's all right. It's just a cut on her head. It bled a lot, that's all. These goons restrained me physically. That guy put me in a hammerlock. I almost choked to death." Popescu pointed accusingly at the offender.

April glanced at Duffy. He stuck the wad of gum in his cheek and gave his head a barely perceptible shake. *No way.*

"I don't want her to stay here. I want her to come home with me. I'm sure she's all right." Popescu was raving. April figured him for a lawyer.

She took some notes on her steno pad, frowned at

Baum to do the same. The first things people said were often important. The new kid on the block, Baum, dutifully followed her example.

Years ago, when April first joined the department and worked in Chinatown, she'd jotted some Chinese characters along with her notes in English on the steno pads the DAs called Rosarios. The DA on the case had gone nuts when he asked for her Rosario and saw the Chinese characters she'd written there. He told her nothing she wrote in Chinese counted and not to do it again. Now her notes were pretty much in English even though she missed the calligraphy practice. *Husband reports wife didn't answer the phone. He went home to check on her. When he got home at 3:30, his wife was unconscious and the baby was missing. The stains on his shirt are probably his wife's blood.* He would have tried to revive her, of course. Unless he'd injured himself and some of the blood was his. She kept her face blank; she didn't want to let him know she was wondering what kind of man kept such close tabs on his wife that he had to go home when she didn't answer the phone.

April and Baum saw the red-haired lady signal them. April tried to distract Popescu. "You want some coffee or something, Mr. Popescu? Officer Duffy could get you something while you're waiting."

"Where are you going?" he demanded.

"Detective Baum and I will be right back," she told him.

Popescu tried to follow them, but Duffy and Prince blocked the way. Their size and the clanking police equipment hanging on their hips convinced him to stay where he was. April didn't wait to hear what he had to say to them.

CHAPTER
4

Treatment room 3 was guarded by another uniform. A woman carrying a clipboard and wearing a white coat over blue scrubs came out before April could question him. Mary Kane, M.D., the woman's name tag said she was. The plastic picture ID clipped to her coat read the same. Dr. Mary Kane had a square jaw, blunt-cut wheat-brown hair, and the kind of eyes April's mother called devil eyes—washed-out blue without lashes or much expression. Dr. Kane looked about twelve, but April couldn't complain about that because both she and Woody did, too.

April showed the doctor her own identification. "I'm Sergeant Woo; this is Detective Baum. What can you tell me about Mrs. Popescu?"

Dr. Kane shook her head. "She's unconscious." She glanced quickly at Baum, then looked April up and down. "Maybe you can help."

"How badly hurt is she?"

"She has contusions, couple of cracked ribs. He must have kicked her. Lump on her head. Her skull isn't fractured. But she's bruised all over. Weird."

"What's weird?" Baum asked.

April gave him a look.

"Some of the bruises are fresh. Others look like

they're a few weeks old. And we have a chart on her. She's been here before."

"Did she have her baby here?" this from April.

Dr. Kane shook her head.

April pulled out her Rosario. "What was she here for on previous occasions?" she asked. Baum knew not to interfere this time.

The doctor checked the chart. "A third-degree burn. A cut—fifteen stitches on her arm. Sprained an ankle twice. She seems to fall down a lot." She recited the list with a face devoid of emotion.

April wrote some more. "Anybody call the police to check it out?" Heather Rose Popescu wasn't so lucky; but maybe April Woo and Woody Baum would get lucky and there'd be no kidnapped baby in this case. Maybe the mother hadn't been feeling well, had given the baby to a relative for the afternoon, and the assault had come from the husband.

The doctor's square face took on a belligerent expression. "I couldn't say anything about the follow-up. The chart indicates they were localized injuries—one site each time, nothing major. Not the pattern we would associate with abuse. I'm not aware of any requirement for reporting a cooking burn, a sprained ankle, that kind of thing. There's a note in the file that Mrs. Popescu has a neurological problem being dealt with by a private physician."

"Was it checked out?"

"Not if she wasn't admitted. Look, you're the detectives, we're ER. You want to try talking with her now?" It seemed as if Dr. Kane was one of those doctors who didn't like cops.

"In a minute. Is there anything else you can tell me?"

"I don't know." Finally she focused on April. "Maybe we've got a mental case here. If she's self-destructive, that would explain the previous injuries on her chart. She could have made up a story about a baby."

"Then her husband is a mental case, too. He says there was a baby this morning, and now it's gone."

"Maybe the baby was adopted," the doctor went on.

"They put it up for adoption? This morning?" April frowned.

"No, the woman here *adopted* the baby." The doctor was getting annoyed, as if April were really thick.

"Why do you say that?" Baum asked.

Dr. Kane pointedly consulted her watch, showing the two cops that she'd given them enough of her time. "She doesn't appear to have a postpartum body."

"Did you give her a pelvic exam?" April asked.

"For head injuries?"

April glanced at Baum. "What's a postpartum body?" she asked.

"There are changes that occur in a woman's body after childbirth." The doctor gave April an amused look.

April flushed. "What are they?"

Dr. Kane slapped her clipboard against her hip impatiently. "The breasts become engorged with milk. The skin on the belly is loose. The belly itself is soft, enlarged. Not all of the excess weight would have come off yet—a lot of things." She glanced at Baum. He was writing it all down. Probably didn't know a thing about women. But apparently, neither did she.

"And Mrs. Popescu?" April asked.

"No engorged breasts, no soft, distended belly. She either didn't have a baby, or she sure got her figure back fast." Clearly the doc didn't think that was possible. "Her body looks like yours," she added.

April was a little over five five, well-proportioned and willowy. She had an oval face with rosebud lips and lovely almond eyes, a slender neck but not the hollows and protruding bones of a truly skinny person. She also had clearly discernible breasts, though not really ample ones by American standards. Her hair came down to the bottom of her earlobes. When she was away from her boss, Lieutenant Iriarte, she hooked her hair back around her ears so her lucky jade earrings would show. Mike Sanchez kept telling her she was more beautiful than Miss America, and the thought of an Asian Miss America always made her smile.

At the moment, though, she wasn't amused. She didn't see how Dr. Kane could tell anything by *her* body, since it was covered by loose, nubby-weave slacks, a thin sweater, a silk scarf, and a cropped whiskey-colored jacket. Except maybe, if she was looking really hard, she could tell that April was carrying a 9mm at her waist.

"Maybe she'll come to soon and you can get something out of her," Dr. Kane said as she walked away. April would not have liked to be one of her patients.

"I'll handle this," she told Baum. Then she opened the treatment room door.

Heather Popescu was lying on a rolling hospital bed, covered up with a sheet so that only the shoulders of her blue-flowered hospital gown showed. The sides of the bed had been put up so she wouldn't fall off, but she wasn't going anywhere. One eye was covered with a cold pack. Her lip was split and already puffed. Her extremely long, inky hair spilled off the pillow. April was startled, then recovered fast. The unconscious woman, Heather Rose Popescu, was Chinese.

No wonder Iriarte had ordered her here immediately. Iriarte hated her. He'd never voluntarily give her a big case. He'd sent her here because the victim was Chinese, and it would look better to have a high-profile Chinese detective on it. April flashed to the husband standing out in the waiting room. A belligerent Caucasian. Oh man, was she in trouble. She didn't like this one bit. Skinny Dragon would think this was a warning just for her. She was going to shake her finger at April over this. "See what happens," she'd scream. "Mixed marriage, woman beaten to a pulp. That's what you can expect when you marry *laowai*"— shit-faced foreigner.

Oh, man. Suddenly April wished Mike, her mother's nightmare, were here with her now. He could take this case in hand. Woody Baum was too inexperienced to be of any help, particularly with the husband. If Popescu beat his wife, he wasn't going to like having April as his interviewer. April needed the expert partner she'd had in Mike, then lost on purpose because she hadn't wanted to mix business with pleasure. So much for integrity and scruples. She was on her own. Thank you, Lieutenant Iriarte.

April studied Heather Rose's battered face. Where were her parents, her protectors? "Heather? Can you hear me?" she said softly. "I'm April Woo. I'm here to help you."

No answer from the unconscious woman.

"Heather, we need to find the baby. Where's the baby?"

Heather did not stir. April felt the cold brick of fear in her belly. "Come on back, girl. We need your help here."

It was no use. Heather wasn't coming back.

April tried in Chinese. "*Wo shi, Siyue Woo. Ni neng bang wo ge mang ma?*"

No response.

Finally, April turned to leave the room. "Whoever did this to you, I'll get him," she promised.

Back in the waiting room, Heather's husband was standing in front of his chair. Baum was talking to him and writing down what he said.

"I want to see my wife."

April gave him a look. "She's unconscious."

"That's what you say. I want to evaluate her myself."

April studied him, this man who kept tabs on his wife and felt qualified to evaluate her himself. She made a note to herself to keep tabs on *him*.

Popescu's cheeks were gray, like a dead man's. He glanced at the two cops who'd stuck by his side since he'd come in. Duffy and Prince lounged against a wall as if they were used to hanging around for long periods of time with nothing to do. A baby on someone's lap on the other side of the crowded waiting room started to wail. She was trained to think like a cop: when faced with a mystery, think dirty. She was thinking dirty about Anton Popescu.

Then another brick hit her. If the baby wasn't Heather's, whose was it? Who was this man Heather had married, and why was he lying about why he went home at the early hour of three-thirty?

He caved abruptly. "Fine. If I can't see my wife, I want to go home now."

"We'll take you," April said. There wasn't anything they could do for Heather here.

CHAPTER
5

On the return trip to the apartment, Baum and April sat in the front seat of the unmarked Buick. Popescu sat in the back. At Central Park South, two uniforms were out directing traffic. Roadblocks were up on Seventh Avenue, and only one lane was open to cars. The noise of honking horns and cursing New Yorkers was phenomenal. It was now 6:45, the height of the dinner and pre-theater hour. Thousands of people in taxis and limos were stuck on their way to Lincoln Center to the west and Carnegie Hall to the south.

"Oh Jesus!" Popescu cried when he saw the jam of police cars, emergency vehicles, and press vans parked in front of his building, clogging Seventh Avenue all the way down to Fifty-seventh Street. The uniform at the neck of the bottle opened traffic for the Buick and waved it through immediately. Woody sardined the car in the driveway and turned off the motor. As April got out, a strong perfume from the garden confused her senses.

Looking dazed, Popescu emerged from the car.

Somebody among the crowd of media hacks and gawkers shouted, "Who's that?" and the press with cameras was galvanized. People ran at the car with minicams and still cameras, yelling questions over the blasting horns. Several uniforms came forward to contain them. Baum took Popescu's arm and hurried him toward the building. The cameras rolled and clicked for the late news deadlines.

"Oh shit. Oh Jesus." The blood had returned to Popescu's cheeks and nose in a rush. Baum propelled him into the lobby. He stuck up his hand to hide his face, and that was how he appeared later on the eleven o'clock news, his arm raised as if warding off blows.

Looking terribly important, Lieutenant McMan was talking on his radio to uniforms and detectives and managing the crowd of disgruntled tenants who couldn't get home. He wagged a finger at April as soon as he saw her. She moved toward him, glancing at the doorman, who was now back at his post. The man's name tag read Carlos. Carlos was a skinny Latino who had greasy hair and a thin mustache. Even with his fancy red livery coat with gold braid and buttons, he had the sly look of a gambler. April knew that look. Her father, Ja Fa Woo, had it.

"How is Mrs. Popescu?" Carlos asked eagerly as he opened the door for them.

Popescu ignored the question. He looked stunned by the throng of vocalizing neighbors—suddenly quieted by his arrival—and so many armed men sporting bulletproof vests and carrying rifles into his lobby. Two of them had huge German shepherds on thick leads. "What the hell—" The dogs really seemed to spook him. Baum touched his arm to restrain him when April crossed the lobby to talk with Lieutenant McMan.

"What's happening?"

"Nothing yet. A lot of people have different stories of what went down here today. No sign of the baby," McMan told her, keeping his eyes on the men and women moving through the lobby. "There are cameras on the front elevator. A log is kept of visitors coming up and down the back elevator. No cameras." He snorted. "No access to the back elevator from the front hall. Fire stairs only."

The units were finishing up in the building and trickling in, grim-faced officers and detectives with their blue-and-yellow POLICE vests. The Emergency Services people looked like the Airborne in their jumpsuits. April ignored the mounting tension. "How many building staff?" she asked.

"Five."

"Who's talking to them?"

McMan gave her a funny smile. "Major Cases. The CO and your boss are upstairs. What about the mother?"

"She's still unconscious." April glanced at Popescu, who appeared to be arguing with Baum.

"You figure the husband for a killer?" McMan asked, following her gaze for the first time.

"We're addressing the question," April said tersely. The elevators were operational again. She gestured to Woody. They were going up.

There was no operator in the elevator when the doors slid open and they got in. Popescu was still holding one hand up to his face as if to keep himself together.

"What's your baby's name?" April asked suddenly.

"Paul. His name is Paul." Popescu said nothing further.

When the elevator stopped without a jerk on the ninth floor, they were confronted by a group of important-looking men at the end of the hall.

"Jesus, who are they?" Popescu cried.

April saw the precinct commander, Bjork Johnson, and two other brass in uniforms, Lieutenant Iriarte and Detectives Skye and Creaker of the precinct squad. Her heart drummed in her chest as she hurried

toward them down a hall that didn't seem to curve
with the building.

Until a few years ago, she had worked in the 5th
Precinct in Chinatown and had never been in a building as luxurious as this. After working in the Two-O
on the Upper West Side and Midtown North for the
last two years, she no longer unconsciously held her
breath when she entered a rich residence. Heather
Rose's mother probably annoyed all her friends with
her bragging about the castle her daughter lived in.

The scene at the end of the hall was the usual. The
people of importance were standing around waiting
for something to break while the specialists tried to
get their work done. Iriarte and the CO had on their
angry-worried expressions, which meant they were unhappy that things had quickly moved beyond their
control. Before April said a word, her supervisor's
face told her he wanted her to clear this case immediately. He wanted the special units out of his territory.
How did he expect her to pull that off? Iriarte didn't
even know yet that the baby wasn't Heather's biological child. She introduced him to Popescu, left the men
together, and went inside the apartment with Woody
at her heels.

Apartment 9E faced the park, but April didn't have
time to admire the view. First, she saw the bloodstains
on the white carpet in the foyer. Looked like tracks.
The perp could have gotten blood on his shoes, or
Anton, or the EMS unit, taking Heather out. They
would have been working on the victim, not worrying
about crime-scene contamination. Fingerprint powder
covered every surface that could take it, in three unbe-
coming colors: white, black, and gray. She moved into
the living room, where two detectives were working
on the phones.

"Anything?" she asked. They ignored her.

She looked around. The furniture in the living room

was slick, shiny, and new, now messy with fingerprint powder. Here a Chinese influence was evident. Different-sized antique lacquer boxes were displayed on the tables. Silk brocade pillows with themes of old China were neatly arranged on the chairs and sofas. A green-and-white bamboo-patterned fabric covered the sofas. In the middle of the black lacquer coffee table sat a large bowl filled with real pink peonies. The smell of the peonies was strong enough to cover even the powerful odor of police sweat.

April realized with a start that the flowers had just recently been put there: only a few of the blossoms were fully open. A rack by the sofa looked as if it had been hastily stuffed with magazines. She could see no Asian ones. Heather Rose stocked up on *Vogue, Bazaar, House Beautiful, Bon Appetit.* They were current and didn't have address stickers. That meant she'd bought them on the stand within the last three weeks. Did brand-new mothers usually care so much about fashion and food? There were no magazines about babies.

"Guess she's not the *Good Housekeeping* kind of woman," Baum remarked. He'd noticed, too.

April caught sight of a wedding photo in a highly polished silver frame. Though not a classic Chinese beauty, the bride looked stunning in an off-the-shoulder, slim-fitting satin wedding gown with a long train. The groom, standing behind her, was not much taller than she. He was hidden from the waist down by the train on her dress. In the photo their cheeks were touching, and they had dreamy expressions on their faces, as if they were stoned.

April found the first signs of a baby in a room that looked like an office that had been halfheartedly turned into a nursery. A desk with a computer and papers (now gritty with fingerprint powder) sat against one wall, a swiveling leather desk chair in front of it.

Beside it, a bookcase filled with books for adults was covered with more powder. The white crib was placed by the window overlooking the park. The curtains on the window were office tweed; they hadn't been changed for the baby. Maybe she hadn't known it was coming.

The elaborate crib was new and clearly expensive. There was a changing table nearby, but nothing much was on it—an empty box of diapers, a container of baby powder. April opened the diaper pail. A strong odor of a poopy diaper jumped out at her. April felt the hairs rise on the back of her neck. She was all keyed up, the way she got when there was a homicide and all her emotions and adrenaline were charging up at once. Fear that she'd mess up and ruin her career and thus her whole life, anger at what had been done to the victim, passion for justice, for revenge against the perpetrator; the sight of a crime scene did that to her.

Heather Rose's being a victim didn't go down well with her at all. Chinese were good mothers, were famous for adoring their children except in certain circumstances—like extreme poverty, or if the babies happened to be girls—when they killed them. Paul Popescu, however, wasn't a girl, and the family was rich, not poor. And they weren't in China. And quite possibly the baby was adopted. There was no reason for a woman like Heather Rose to have killed him.

Suddenly April was aware of a small ghost in the room with her. April did not believe in ghosts the way her mother and other old-style Chinese—and even Mike's Mexican mother—did. She knew that ghosts were just an invention to scare people and make them honor their ancestors. All the same, something that felt like a ghost flew by her ear. Then it circled around and flew back, hovering in one place and beating at the air around her head to get her attention. April shivered as the ghost kept the hair raised on the back of her neck. It was telling her not to be intimidated by any of the bosses, not to be pushed into the background by the special units so someone else's career could get a lift. She was sure there was a ghost in the room, and the ghost was telling her that baby Paul had gone missing in her precinct on her watch. And further, since they didn't know who his biological parents were, she and the rookie detective, Woody Baum, who was all she had in the way of support, had better find Paul very soon.

CHAPTER
6

The hall was empty when April and Woody came out of the Popescus' apartment. "What do you see here, Detective?" April asked him.

Baum looked worried. "What do I see?"

"Yeah, what's going on here?" A hint of impatience crept into her voice. If Baum wanted to be useful and go somewhere, he couldn't answer a question with a question. He had to answer a question, period.

"Is this a test?" Baum was a preppy-looking guy; he wore a blue blazer and kept a second gun strapped to his ankle. His brown hair was so short it was hard to tell whether it curled. He rubbed at it with a free hand, as if trying to make it grow.

"Everything in this life is a test," she told him.

He walked along, chafing the stubble till they reached the elevator, where he punched the Down button. "The beating happened in the kitchen," he said finally. "This looks like a domestic case to me. Maybe they'll find some of the husband's blood in or around one of the puddles on the floor. Then we could nail him for beating his wife." He looked hopeful.

"What about the baby?"

Baum frowned at the second part of the equation.

"If he battered the wife, what do you think he did with the baby?" she elaborated.

"He didn't seem to know where the baby was."

"He could be lying, though. What else?"

"Isn't it your turn yet?" Baum hit the elevator button again.

"Are you some kind of smart aleck, Detective?" April wasn't amused.

"Nah, just a Jew," he cracked.

"Well, keep it in check, will you?"

"Yes, ma'am." Baum saluted.

"You have a problem with a supervisor who's going to run you over hot coals every day to teach you something?" *The way my supervisor did to me,* she didn't add.

"No, ma'am. It's just what my mother does."

"Good. So what about the baby?"

"The doc said it's not hers."

"So what do we do about that, Woody?"

"We question Popescu."

"Right. Now you just saw a crime scene where all the violence occurred in the kitchen. Was there blood on the back door?"

"No."

"Blood on the back doorknob?"

"No."

"Blood on the outside of the back door, or on the walls in the back hall, on the fire-stairs door, or on the fire stairs?"

Baum shook his head.

"There was blood in the front of the apartment. So what does that tell us?"

"The perp didn't go out the back way."

"What if he washed up first?" April demanded.

"He didn't wash up in the kitchen sink. There's a duck in a bowl of water in the sink, and there's no blood in or around the bowl of water. How long does it take to defrost a duck?" Baum wondered.

"Where I come from we buy the duck already

roasted. Would a frozen duck begin to soften in about two hours? It's fully defrosted now. We'll have to ask CSU how hard it was when they got here at what, four-fifteen? Might help with the time frame."

The elevator door slid silently open. They got in with a woman in a pink halter and purple pedal pushers who had a toddler in a stroller. The toddler was busy gnawing on a bagel.

"They talked to me already. The detective said it was okay to go out now," she said, looking at the badges on April and Baum's jackets. "Terrible thing. Terrible." She put her hand on her blond baby's head.

"Cute baby," April murmured.

On the main floor, the woman pushed ahead of them and exited the elevator first, pushing the stroller out into the lobby, then on out into the crush of cameras.

April wondered where the woman was taking her baby at this hour. Then it occurred to her that anybody could wheel a baby out, and no one would ask if it was hers. Everyone assumed that babies belonged to the people they were with. She turned to Baum. "You notice anything missing from that apartment?"

Baum watched the woman wheel the baby outside, then stop to talk to the reporters. "Wouldn't they have had a stroller?" he said.

"Yes. What else?"

"What, more twenty questions?"

"More like twenty thousand questions. What's the answer?" April clicked her tongue at his silence. "All right: when my cousins have babies, they have showers."

"So where's the stuff, right?"

"Exactly." She watched McMan signing off on the first of the teams. There was no sniper on the roof, no baby in the garbage, the incinerator, the elevator shaft. EMS was cutting out.

"So there was remarkably little baby stuff in there. Almost nothing in fact," Baum said.

"Right. Either Heather wasn't expecting a baby, or she didn't intend to keep it long."

They watched the young woman in the halter finish talking to the press and turn toward the park.

By 8:35 P.M., there was press activity at the precinct, too. The reporters were spreading like bacteria, and April didn't want to catch anything. When she arrived at Fifty-fourth Street and got out of the car, a woman in a pale purple suit, carrying a mike torch with the letters ABC on it, ran across the sidewalk to talk to her. The woman thrust the microphone in April's face before she reached the cover of the precinct.

"Hey, look, it's Sergeant Woo. How are you, Sergeant? I'm Grace Faye. I was on the Liberty case. Great job you did there. I hear you were in the hospital for two months."

April grimaced at the exaggeration. "I was in the hospital overnight." Well, for a few nights. "Excuse me."

"Hey, wait, what's your hurry?"

A second woman reporter April didn't know tried to push in front of Faye. "What can you tell us about the missing baby? What about the baby's mother? We had a tip she died on the way to the hospital. Is that true?" Faye pushed the other reporter back, and they had a bit of a shoving match.

April cocked her head for Baum to walk in front of her. "You're supposed to walk behind me except in instances where you have to clear the way for me," she muttered in his ear when he edged ahead.

Baum opened his mouth. "Clear the way," he said, using his elbows. "A spokesman will talk to you as soon as we have something."

"And I'll remember you at Christmas," the first reporter promised, cynically.

April didn't look at them as she went inside. What were they thinking? They knew she couldn't talk to them. She gave the desk lieutenant a little smile, then climbed the stairs to the detective squad room. Inside was the mob scene she'd expected. The phones were hogged by strangers, and the limited space was crammed with easels and flip charts. The noise and tension levels were high, and the room was filled with smoke. Lieutenant Iriarte was in his office with his three ugly henchmen. He gestured for her, but not Baum, to come in. April saw Baum flush with anger as he turned away to find someone else sitting at his desk.

She opened the door of the office. Creaker, Hagedorn, and Skye filed out. Iriarte pointed at a chair.

"Baum's not a bad guy. Who knows, he may even turn out to have some talent," she murmured, not wanting to let the insult go.

Iriarte had a really skinny mustache that came nowhere near his mouth. He squeezed his thin lips into a moue, then made them into a line. Working his mouth was how he thought. "I wouldn't bet on it," he muttered. "Why'd you pick him?"

"Baum's new. He could use some breaking in," April replied, neutral. And he didn't have any loyalties yet. She needed someone like that on her team.

"Look, April, don't take this opportunity to make a flaming mess of things." Iriarte blew air out of his mouth. April could tell he was unhappy.

"No sir, I won't," she promised him.

"I want our best people on this." He punched the air with his pen. "We got to stay in it all the way, you hear what I'm saying?"

"I hear you, sir. Do you have Hagedorn on the background stuff?"

"Yes, but four guys from Major Cases are on it, too. Let's see who scores first," he said fiercely. He stopped, shook his head at the intruders, then turned to his second whip. "And I want you out there until something breaks. All night, all day, as long as it takes."

"Yes sir, and Baum can drive me," she said after a moment. It was suicide. She didn't know why she'd said it. But without Mike she had no one. Creaker and Skye were Iriarte's boys; she didn't trust them. Baum was no detective, that was clear, but he was no worse than anybody else.

"Jesus, April, are you telling me you want *him?*" Iriarte exploded. Face turned red, the whole bit. He looked as if he were about to keel over on the spot. April hated getting him into such a state when he was already so upset.

Did she want Baum? Of course she didn't want him. The guy had no legs. He was a tadpole, but maybe he'd turn out all right.

"Getting the new ones up to speed is part of my job, as I understand it." She kept her face impassive. Even in bad times, when the pressure was on. Like this.

Iriarte smacked his desk with the palm of his hand. "Look here, I'm getting calls, a lot of calls about this."

"Yes, sir."

"So what do you have that I don't know already?"

"Baum and I talked to the doorman. He said Mrs. Popescu had a dicey pregnancy and wasn't seen very much before the birth of the baby."

Iriarte rolled his tongue around in his mouth. "Is that significant?"

"It sure is. At the hospital the doctor told us Heather Popescu had not given birth to a baby."

"*What?* But there is a baby, right?"

"Oh, yeah, there's a baby. Doorman said Mr.

Popescu left at eight-thirty A.M., as usual; the man's like clockwork. Mrs. Popescu took the baby out soon after that, a little after nine—"

"Did he see the baby?"

"No. He said he heard the baby crying. He knew it was the baby because newborns sound like kittens."

Iriarte rolled his eyes. "So—either the baby was alive this morning, or the baby was dead and the woman went out with a kitten. And, by the way, it wasn't her baby."

"Yes," April said.

"What about when she returned? Was there a baby or a kitten with her then?"

"No one remembers seeing her return."

"Did you talk to the relief doorman?"

"Yes. He didn't see her."

"What about the service entrance?"

"Security in the building is pretty tight. What I'm wondering about is the stroller. The doorman says it was more like a carriage, not one of those little fold-up jobs. She went out with it. It wasn't in the apartment when we got there. Where is it?"

Iriarte sat back and made a steeple with his fingers. "This whole thing sounds fishy to me. Let me see a picture of the baby." He held out his hand, wiggling his fingers as if he knew she had one.

Indeed, April had gotten a photo from Popescu before she left his apartment. She dug around in her purse and pulled it out. She glanced at it before handing it over to Iriarte. Baby Paul had a full head of dark hair and blue eyes. He was wrapped up in a blue blanket, caught by the camera with a serious expression.

Iriarte shook his head. "Cute. This baby doesn't look Chinese. The so-called mother, who is also the last person seen with it, is Chinese." He gave April a piercing look. "You're the primary on this case and I want you to clear it tonight."

April kept her face calm, but inside, panic rose like a flood tide. How could she do that?

"You hear me? I talked with Popescu. He neglected to mention the fact that the baby isn't theirs. You talk to him. Get a birth certificate. Find the birth parents. Maybe they have him."

"Yes, sir."

Scowling, Iriarte looked at the photo again. "They've got all the specialists in on this. And the baby may be out with a sitter, with a friend of the family, or with its real parents." He fixed his eyes on her as if she weren't paying enough attention. "You hear me?"

"Yes, sir. I'll get on it."

He dropped the photo on the desk, turned his palms up, and changed tack suddenly. "So who beat up the woman? Could she have gotten beaten fighting to keep the baby?"

"Anything is possible." April looked down at her hands.

"What do you think of the husband?" Iriarte gave a small whistle. "What's his problem? Is he the beater?"

"Anything is possible," she said again.

He handed her back the photo. If Paul Popescu had been a two-year-old or a five-year-old he'd have told her to blow up the photo and send it out on the streets. *Have you seen me?* But that was impossible with an infant.

Iriarte stared at the ceiling, musing.

"The doorman said she walked toward the park."

The special units were already headed there with their sniffers.

"Keep on the husband, and don't let anyone in to see the mother. You know." He shook his head. The last thing they wanted was for her to wake up and have her lawyer husband there to help her with her story. He swiveled away from her. That was it. He'd finished.

"Who's the ADA on this?" April asked.

"I don't know. Mayers, Meyers, something like that. Someone we don't know. Check out the legal aspects of this one." He consulted his watch and sighed deeply. "Find the baby alive and get a straight story. Otherwise you're out of here." Iriarte's color improved after he threatened to fire her.

Outside in the squad room Baum was holding up a wall, sulking over his notes and glowering at the fat detective who was sitting on the corner of his desk and dropping ashes on the phone. April came out of Iriarte's office and waved him over. "Let's go."

CHAPTER
7

Anton Popescu left Roosevelt Hospital after his evening visit, burning with humiliation. A nurse built like a Hummer had kicked him out of his wife's room. When he tried to talk her out of it, she cut him off mid-sentence.

"Hey, don't raise your voice at me. Sick people are trying to sleep here," she said softly.

"I didn't raise my voice," he insisted.

"You're yelling at me now."

"Oh yeah? You're crazy."

The cop, who'd been away from his chair outside Heather Rose's room when Anton arrived, suddenly came swaggering back. He hiked up his heavy belt with the gun and the club on it. "What's going on?"

"Mr. Popescu was just leaving," the nurse said coolly.

"I don't think so." Anton bunched his fist at her. He couldn't believe this was happening.

The cop didn't like the body language. "You heard the lady. Nobody goes in." He was a young, powerful Hispanic, heavily muscled, mean-looking, and not small enough for Anton to take on. He repeated himself a few times, then took a macho pose with the billy club.

"*Jesus!*" This was another in a brutal collection of

confrontations Anton hadn't been able to win that day. After six hours of incitements, he'd become a dazed bull, helpless and exhausted. A bunch of little people in uniforms had been pushing him around. In the ambulance, they'd kept him from Roe. In the hospital, they'd taken her away and wouldn't let him see what they were doing to her. When he'd complained, more cops restrained him.

Worst of all, the group of detectives, including a lieutenant and the Chinese sergeant, questioned him as if they thought he might somehow be involved. How could they think that? He, steal his own baby! Hit his own wife! What kind of person would do that? The fact that the police suspected him hurt him deeply. It enraged him further that the Chinese sergeant had been allowed into Roe's room and he had been barred. It was then that the sergeant told him about the Crime Scene Unit working at his apartment. He'd never given permission for criminologists to enter his apartment, they'd just taken over. *They'd tapped his phone.* Even now two detectives were sitting in his living room waiting for the phone to ring. And he couldn't find a way to protest. Not only that, two grubby-looking guys who looked like bums off the street had trashed his place. Crime scene! *They* were the crime, touching his things without his consent, moving them around, taking photographs of everything, vacuuming the carpets with their own portable vacuum cleaner. They cut a hole in his rug and took away the garbage cans. He actually saw them shine weird lights on the walls and floors—looking for what? They'd made sketches of the blood splotches on the kitchen floor and left gritty fingerprint powder everywhere. He didn't think the place would ever be clean again.

And all the while different detectives kept asking him questions, a thousand and one questions about his life, his wife, people she might have given the baby to or who might have come and taken him. He had no idea how to answer. The detectives were asking about private stuff that was none of their business. About the beating, they didn't ask very much. That really scared him. They'd taken his fingerprints and asked about his in-laws. But he didn't know what they were thinking. He had a right to know what angle they were following. That part was his business, his wife, his missing *baby*. He had a right to know what they were looking for. After most of the detectives left, two had stayed behind in the apartment to man the phones, and this made Anton feel doubly victimized. He and Roe were in danger now, and he no longer remembered why he'd gone to the police in the first place. Later, when he went back to the hospital, he was certain a plainclothes cop had followed him there.

Now, after visiting his wife again late in the evening and getting nothing out of her because she was still unconscious, he was tormented by another policeman taking an I-can-beat-you-up-if-I-want-to pose. He flushed purple. He wasn't leaving his wife there alone to be tortured by them as soon as she opened her eyes. He was going to wait until she awoke so he could talk to her himself.

But he couldn't get to her. Standing in the doorway of her room, the officer had blocked his way, staring at him in a threatening manner. The moment stretched into several long minutes as the cop silently challenged Anton to let go of all his restraint and pop him one. Anton debated his options. On the other side of the room in the hospital bed was his unconscious wife, with tubes in her arm and nose and a swollen eye and lip. He looked over at her, praying for her to wake up and help him. She hadn't stirred since he came in. But the Chinese could be a solid wall of noncompliance when they wanted to. They were supposed to be so weak and submissive, but that was a crock. He felt like shaking her. How could he talk to her when she was hiding out inside her head—the way she did sometimes just to spite him—but this time hiding in her head in the hospital, where he couldn't reach out and pull her back into reality. What if she lost her mind altogether and flipped out with the baby still missing? How could he save either of them then?

Come on, Roe, don't do this to me. He willed her to speak.

No answer.

"You want me to walk you to the elevator, sir?" Suddenly the cop dropped the aggressive stance and became helpful.

No, he did not want a police escort to the elevator. He wanted his wife to wake up so he could get her out of there and take her back home where she belonged. He was hungry. He was upset. He wanted his wife back, his baby, his happy life. His face contorted with pain as the cop escorted him to the elevator.

When he stepped off the elevator, it got worse. He'd forgotten about the reporters. Downstairs, by the hospital front door, a reporter took his picture. Anton was surprised and recoiled at the flash of light.

"Any word on your baby, Mr. Popescu?"

Anton was so stunned he couldn't even shake his head. Blindly, he pushed past the man and hurried east toward Central Park. The reporter followed him. Then a woman and another man ran to catch up.

"Is that him, Grady?"

"The police are saying there was no kidnap—" The first reporter dogged Anton's steps.

"Did she see her attacker?"

Why didn't the cop who'd been on his tail help him with *this?* Anton began to run.

"Can you tell us—"

He was like an animal looking for a bolt-hole. His wild eyes searched the sidewalks for a way out as first three, then four reporters came after him. There was no escape but the street and the oncoming cars. He ran into the street against the light. Cabbies leaned heavily on their horns as two drivers trying to avoid him crunched to a stop, barely missing each other. Anton spun around, swearing. "You stupid assholes!"

When he reached the other side of the street, he raised his hand. Another taxi stopped beside him. He got in, giving instructions as the driver took off. Then he saw two cops drive up in a squad car. He gave them the finger, but they stayed with him. When Anton arrived home, two more squad cars were parked across the street from his building, and Perry, the night doorman, was on duty. Perry was not one of Anton's favorites. More than once, he'd considered getting him fired. The man was a classic working drunk, never totally out of it, but always on the other side of vague. He had a big, puffy body and an enviable head of springy pale hair, and he kept several layers of smell over a solid base of whiskey and beer.

At the moment Perry had a forbidden cigarette cupped in one fist as he watched Anton get out of the cab. Slowly he doused the cigarette in the dregs of a take-out coffee, put down the container, then moved to open the door. He reeked of cough medicine and cigarette smoke.

"How's the missus?" he asked when Anton shuffled in. "She as bad as they say?"

Anton glared at him. "Get rid of that fucking cigarette."

"I don't smoke on duty. Must be all the cops. Could be anybody's smoke." The man's eyes were shrewd through his alcohol haze. He sucked his teeth and gave his head a shake. A shock of hair fell over his forehead. "Police up and down the street all night," he added with some satisfaction. "Talking to everybody and checking the garbage before pickup tomorrow morning."

Now Perry didn't look at all drunk, and Anton's pulse went crazy. "What are you talking about?" he demanded.

The doorman, in his red uniform that didn't fit, shrugged importantly. "The garbage gets picked up tomorrow morning, so they have to do their looking tonight. They're out in the park, too." He gestured with his chin across the street toward Central Park.

Anton's eyes narrowed at the lights clearly moving through the shrubs, illuminating the spring blooms on the taller bushes and trees. He made a noise in his throat as if he were choking. He couldn't seem to take in the full impact of the horrors being visited upon him.

"They're looking for the baby's body," Perry told him.

Anton saw a van cruise toward the circular drive in front of the building. It had a dish on top and a TV station's call letters painted on the side. Anton grabbed some cash from his pocket and thrust it at the loathsome doorman without looking at it.

"If you ring me upstairs for any reason or let any of those reporters in, you'll be out on the street picking through garbage cans yourself tomorrow." Then he ran across the lobby to the elevator and pushed the button. When the door slid open, he disappeared inside.

An hour and a half later his phone rang for about the fiftieth time, and for the fiftieth time, the two detectives in the living room tensed. Both were chubby and bald. Both wore headphones and drank a lot of coffee.

"You ready?" asked the one who had a mustache. That was how Anton told them apart. One had a mustache and one didn't. He hadn't bothered to learn their names.

Anton rolled his eyes and picked up. This one wasn't a crank call or a reporter. The soft voice of his brother, Marc, came on the line. "What the hell is going on? Some detective wants to talk to me about Roe and Paul. What happened? Is everything all right?"

"Go ahead and talk to the detective, Marc. It's for sure you can't talk to me. I'm under surveillance. And this phone is tapped for the ransom call."

There was a stunned silence.

"What ransom call?" Marc asked finally.

"Well, the police think there's going to be one."

"Huh?"

Anton hung up before Marc could say anything more. The two detectives turned their recording equipment off and looked at him. He gave them a grim little nod and reported the caller's name. They turned the machine back on and asked him to repeat it. While they were listening to the conversation, the doorbell rang. The detective working the phone paid no attention. Anton crossed the living room to see who it was. Through the peephole in the door he saw the Chinese detective and her sidekick.

"Jesus," he muttered. He was sweating and badly needed a drink. He felt like a squirrel caught in the middle of the road with cars coming in both directions. The doorbell rang again. He opened it, his heart beating at his chest like a hammer.

"Mr. Popescu?" The male cop spoke.

"Did you find him?" For the first time Anton's voice came out no louder than a faint whisper.

The two detectives traded looks. This time the woman answered. "No, sir. Not yet."

Anton clutched his chest. "Is my wife—?"

"No change. Do you mind if we come in for a few minutes?"

Anton took a deep breath and shook his head. "It's eleven o'clock; isn't it a little late for a visit?"

The Chinese gave him a strange look, as if that might be an inappropriate response. He didn't like her, and realized he had to watch himself.

"I'm Sergeant Woo. This is Detective Baum."

"I spent the afternoon with you. I remember who you are." He took a step back onto the white rug, which had a gaping hole cut out of it where one of Heather's bloodstains had been. The other stains were still there and already turning brown. Anton didn't look down. To see it would make him lose control.

The two detectives came right in. Anton hadn't had anything to eat or drink since lunch. He swallowed, surprised that he was hungry at a time like this. He really needed a drink. He didn't dare take one.

"I've already talked to about a hundred people. What do you want?" He looked wearily from one to the other.

The two cops looked at each other, then through the arch into the living room where the other detectives were still playing with the phones.

"There's a detail we need to take care of right away," the Chinese sergeant said.

Anton's expression became wary. "What's that?"

"It's about your baby."

Anton's jaw tightened. He didn't say anything. He stood in the small vestibule and waited for the bomb to drop.

"We need a birth certificate."

"What?" He genuinely looked surprised. "Why?"

"For identification."

"I thought you said you haven't found him."

"We'll need it when we do find him, and we believe it might help us locate him."

Anton stopped breathing. "What do you mean?"

"Mr. Popescu. The doctor told us that your wife has not given birth to a baby, so we know she's not the birth mother. We need to establish—"

"Oh, my God," Anton blurted out in an anguished voice. "Oh, God. I told you I didn't want them all over her. Oh, this is outrageous."

Sergeant Woo did not seem moved. "We have to have the facts of the situation."

Anton looked at the men in the living room and lowered his voice. "I don't want this to get around."

Detective Baum shifted his weight from one foot to the other, but Anton didn't continue.

"If the baby's adopted, we'll need to see the papers," the sergeant said.

"Oh, God." Anton rolled his eyes.

"We have to see the adoption papers," she repeated.

"I don't see what this has to do with it. It's our child, period."

"Well, that can easily be established." She kept at it.

"You're out of your territory here. It has nothing to do with getting my son back."

The two detectives exchanged glances again. "That's what we need to establish. Maybe the birth parents have abducted their own baby." The woman again.

Anton clutched his chest. "Oh, Jesus, that can't be."

"Why not?" she asked.

"I'm the baby's father."

"Who's the mother?" Deadpan Chinese face.

"She lives in another state." Anton gulped for air.

"We'll need to talk to her."

"I don't know where she is now."

"We know how to find people. Where did she give birth?"

"She had a home birth." He gulped again. "Look, this is complicated. I had an affair, okay? The woman was married. Let's leave it at that." Sweat was pouring

down his face. He wiped it with his starched white
shirtsleeve.

"Maybe she changed her mind and wanted the
baby, after all," Sergeant Woo wasn't letting up. She
didn't seem to be buying the home-delivery bit.

"No." It was an agonized cry.

"Did you beat up your wife, Mr. Popescu?" This
from Detective Baum.

"No!" Anton was reeling.

"Somebody beat her up," Baum said.

"I know, I know. It wasn't me."

"Mr. Popescu, you could save yourself a lot of trouble if you told us where the baby is," Sergeant Woo
said.

"I told you I don't know. Do you think I would
have called you assholes if I knew where he was?"

"Are you calling the sergeant here an asshole?" the
detective demanded.

"That's okay," the sergeant said smoothly. "I'll let
it go. Mr. Popescu, we're going to have to locate the
baby's mother. This is not optional. We have to do it.
We have to have the birth certificate. We can't investigate without it."

"It's not her. I know it isn't. She isn't even in the
country. I couldn't do it to her. Her husband would
kill her. He's a military man. And I just can't. My poor
Roe. You don't know what this would do to her."

"And I need the phone number of your wife's parents," Sergeant Woo said suddenly.

That really stopped him short. "They don't know
anything about this," he said, almost meekly now.

"They may know more about their daughter than
you think."

"Oh Jesus. I don't want them in this. They're—
emotional."

"It's procedure," the detective said flatly.

"I don't want them here, understand? I can't put up with wailing parents in my house. . . ."

"No one's bringing them here."

"They'll come here, believe me."

Anton couldn't help it. The weight of the situation broke him. He began to sputter and cry in front of them. Once he started crying, he couldn't stop. It was a whole big mess. There was no way he could contain it. He cried as if his fragile heart would break over the terrible things that were happening to him, and then he gave the two cops part of what they wanted. He gave them Heather's parents' telephone number in San Francisco. They stayed for a while longer, and then the detectives left. But the cops manning the phone stayed put. He could watch from the windows as the search in the park widened and went on. He couldn't leave the apartment. He couldn't communicate with anyone on the outside. And he had no idea what the police had found out.

CHAPTER
8

At half past one on Wednesday morning, the squad room of Midtown North was still jammed, noisy, and hot. April and Woody returned to the collection of small, windowless rooms on the precinct's second floor after talking with Anton Popescu and checking on the progress of the dozens of officers searching for the missing baby in the park. Before they went in she told Woody to go write up his notes and not to talk to anybody about what they'd learned.

The information they'd uncovered about the baby's parentage was for Lieutenant Iriarte's ears only. It was up to him to pass it on. Although Anton had not given them anything specific on the birth mother, he was beginning to crack in the first twelve hours, and would probably give it all up in the next twenty-four if they kept the pressure on. April hoped the child was still alive.

Feeling encouraged, she went into her very first office with actual walls and a door that gave her a little privacy and indicated her status in the department. At the moment it was occupied by a middle-aged detective she'd never seen before. He was wearing a black toupee, was wiry, and wired. He was talking on the phone, gesturing with his hands, smoking and scattering ashes all over her desk.

"This your seat?" he queried, putting his hand over the mouthpiece.

"Sergeant Woo," she murmured politely, indicating the nameplate in front of him.

"I was just leaving." He hung up without saying good-bye and went out to join his buddies squatting at other people's desks in the main squad room.

April put her purse down, fell into her desk chair with a sigh, and called Iriarte at home in Westchester. He was most interested in her report and said he'd call Hagedorn to start searching for the birth mother. After she hung up, April placed the difficult call to Heather Rose's parents in San Francisco, where the time was now a little after 10:30 P.M. A woman picked up after the third ring.

"*Wei.*"

April could hear Chinese TV on loud in the background. It was Mandarin, so she spoke Mandarin. "I'm Detective Sergeant April Woo, calling from New York. I'm sorry to bother you at this late hour, but I need to talk to you about your daughter, Heather Rose."

"Aieeeyeeee!" The woman started to scream before April could say another word. She screamed at someone in the room with her that Heather Rose was dead, she was dead in New York.

"She's not dead," April said into the receiver, but the woman was yelling, not listening. The TV was on, and April heard a man in the background trying to calm her down. It was just like home.

"She's dead, dead in New York!" Mrs. Kwan was screaming. "We have to go to New York. Call the airline. I have to go now."

The man took the phone. "Who is this?"

April had to start all over. She told him she was a detective in New York City and their daughter was not dead. But Heather Rose was injured and in the hospital.

"Ah." He conveyed that in Chinese to his wife. She continued screaming.

"What happened?" Heather's father finally asked.

April hesitated. "It's not entirely clear at the moment. Your daughter was assaulted in her apartment."

"Assaulted? By who—her husband?"

"Has it happened before?" she asked quickly.

Silence.

"She's unconscious. She needs your help," April told him.

"What can we do?" It was not a question. It was what people said when their children were involved in something they thought was stupid, but they loved them all the same. "What can you do?" they say with their shoulders climbing up to their ears.

"Their baby is missing," she added.

"Baby missing?" Now there was real pandemonium in the background.

"Hello, hello." April tried to get a word in, but the screaming in Chinese didn't stop.

"Baby missing?" This was more than Heather's father could deal with. He passed the phone back to his wife.

"Baby missing?" she cried.

"Mrs. Kwan, your daughter can't talk to me right now, and I need information about her and the baby. Can you tell me how the adoption was arranged?"

"Adoption?"

"Yes, didn't you know it was an adopted baby?"

"No, can't be. Baby is Heather's baby, my grandson."

"Certainly, but maybe not her birth child."

"Why are you saying this? He's her child, I know."

"How do you know? Did you see her pregnant, were you with her when she gave birth?" These were hard questions for a mother far away and in the dark about many things to answer. A pained silence followed.

"She sent me pictures," she answered after a long pause.

"Of the baby?"

"Yes, of course pictures of baby. But also pictures of herself pregnant."

It was clear Mrs. Kwan couldn't accept that her daughter was not the birth mother of her grandson and further that Heather Rose had tried to hide the fact by faking her pregnancy in photos. April felt sorry to be the one to pass on such dreadful news, sorry for the mother whose daughter had lied to her and cheated her of a grandchild she claimed as her own. And also sorry for herself because she was no closer to finding the baby's real mother than she'd been before.

"Tell me about your daughter, Mrs. Kwan," April went on as gently as she could.

"What is there to tell? She's good girl, beautiful girl. Smart girl. Went to best college, full scholarship. Marry very smart man, very rich man. She send many presents. Call me every week. Best-quality girl." She began to weep. What else was there to know?

April pressed on. Was Heather a sad person? Did she ever hurt herself? Was she upset when things didn't go well? How about her level of patience? Did she get impatient easily? Was she happy in New York? Did she ever set a fire when she was a little girl, ever hurt an animal? Did she ever get burned, or burn anybody?

"What kind of questions are these?" the mother demanded.

Routine, April assured her. She couldn't completely abandon the possibility that Heather might have found out her baby was her husband's with another woman and killed him in revenge. Such things were not completely unknown in history.

Mrs. Kwan knew what April was getting at, but insisted Heather wasn't that kind of child. Good child. Too independent, maybe, but good.

"How many months ago did your daughter tell you she was having a baby?"

Silence.

"Was she excited about it?"

"She's a good girl."

"When you talked to her after she got the baby, what did she say? How did those weeks go? Did she enjoy having a baby?"

"What kind of questions are these?" Mrs. Kwan asked again but this time in a way that indicated she knew very well what kind of questions they were. "Heather Rose good girl," she assured April again. "Best daughter in whole world. She call me every week. Never complain. Never." But Soo Ling Kwan must have heard something in her daughter's voice during those weekly calls.

She insisted Heather Rose had suffered no injuries, no accidents, had never hurt or starved herself. But she had also immediately jumped to the conclusion that any call from the police had to mean her daughter was dead. It might not be an unusual reaction, but still April wondered if a part of Mrs. Kwan had been expecting such an end for her daughter. She learned nothing else.

If it had been a quiet night, April would have been heading out about now. But this was the kind of case that made everybody nuts. Even if Iriarte hadn't told her to keep on it, she wouldn't have been in a hurry to leave. Nobody liked abuse and missing babies. They weren't the kind of thing you could go home and forget: have a nice night. Losing a kid was the worst. It was more than a career maker or breaker. It was personal. She glanced at the stack of pink message slips on her desk. Then her phone rang.

"Midtown North detective squad, Sergeant Woo," she said in nice even tones.

"*Hola, querida, que tal?*"

She smiled into the receiver. "Hey, Mike."

"Miss me?"

"Yeah," she admitted in spite of herself. Then she wanted to bite her tongue for revealing her feelings.

"*Yo también.*"

"How's the case going?" she asked, playing with a pencil. Mike had gotten a homicide two days ago, a real mess in a hotel on Lexington Avenue. All she'd heard were rumors that State Department, intelligence, and Israeli consulate people were working on it. For some reason he'd been holding out on giving her the details. Now he grunted.

"Victim was an Israeli. His business partner claims he had ten thousand dollars in cash and a sack of diamonds worth a quarter of a million when he was iced. ME's report says he was tortured and his crown jewels were hacked off while he was still alive. Poor bastard bled to death."

She knew Mike had attended the autopsy; now she knew the reason for his silence. Ugly, ugly case. She made a sympathetic noise, didn't envy him.

His voice brightened. "I hear you caught a big one, too."

"What do you hear?"

"Nothing—just you caught a big one. Need help?"

"No, thanks. You didn't ask for mine." April bristled; she wasn't good at inequality.

"You don't want to know about this one."

"Sure I do. And you just hate being left out of anything."

"Give me a break. Is it a sin to be supportive? I thought that's what every woman wants."

"Sorry. I'm a little touchy about this one. It's weird."

"Not as weird as mine," he shot back.

"Fine, it's not as weird as yours, but still it's weird." She gave him the gist of it, relieved to get it off her chest.

"Ransom note or call?"

"No."

"Anything on the phone tap?"

"Nothing yet, but I'd be real surprised if we get a ransom demand on this one," she said. "It's not her baby. But don't pass that around."

"No kidding."

"Get this: the husband of the victim says his mistress is the mother of the baby. She's married to someone in the military and has taken off for parts unknown.—Oh, and the victim is Chinese," she added suddenly. "The father's white. The whole thing makes me queasy."

"It has nothing to do with us," Mike said quickly, catching the subtext even before it came into focus in April's mind. Then he moved on. "I had a case once, man faked an abduction of his own baby. His motive was he didn't want a custody battle when he divorced his wife. Poor woman went around the bend when her baby disappeared. That's when he filed for divorce."

"What did he do with the baby?"

"Oh, he'd given it to his girlfriend in New Jersey the first day. He'd set up an apartment for her, everything. They wanted to get married and have a family right away."

Another girlfriend. And Heather Rose had no idea, her husband had said. April thought of the duck defrosting in the sink. People were out looking for a dead infant. She wanted to clear Heather Rose of any suspicion that she'd killed her rival's baby. "You voting for the husband as the kidnapper, then?" she murmured.

"Not yet. Remember those girls in New Jersey? One gave birth in the girls' bathroom during her high school prom, suffocated the baby, then went back to the dance. The other gave birth in a motel, killed her baby, and was back in her college dorm in time for her next class. Then there's the girl in Ohio gave birth and killed the baby while her mother was out to dinner. When the mother got back, they sat and watched TV for the rest of the evening—"

There went the duck-proves-innocence theory. "Those were young, unmarried teenagers, terrified of their parents. This is a mature—"

"Hell hath no fury . . ." he reminded her.

April had a stomachache. It had been bothering her for hours. She wanted baby Paul found alive and well, didn't want Heather Rose to be a killer or the father to be a kidnapper with a girlfriend in New Jersey.

Mike changed the subject. "You want to come over to my place? I'll make it worth your while."

"Can't, I'm staying with it," she said, and felt a guilty pang. Skinny was going to freak if she didn't come home two nights in a row—even if she had a good excuse. Then she thought if things quieted down, she might go home for a few hours, after all.

"Call me when you can."

"Sure." April hung up. Depression settled on her as she cleaned up her desk, picked up her jacket, and headed out into the field to see if the baby had turned up in the last fifteen minutes. He hadn't.

Three hours later, with no break in the case, April parked in front of the brick house she shared with her parents in Astoria, Queens, not far from Hoyt Avenue and the entrance to the Triborough Bridge. She got out of the car, locked up slowly, then stretched, feeling the space around her like a blind person picking out obstacles in the dark. All she wanted was to see her mom and have a quick nap before changing her clothes and heading back to work.

The street was quiet, but cop habits made her check for signs of trouble. Only a few lights in the surrounding houses were on this late. Some of the people who lived around here were old and had trouble sleeping. April knew everybody's routine. On this block all the houses were attached, single-family homes. A lot of Greeks and Italians, Brazilians and Indians, not that many Chinese. April's father, Ja Fa Woo, had chosen the place with the help of an almost-relative, the owner of Chen Realty in Long Island City. He'd chosen the location in spite of the ethnic makeup of the neighborhood because he was a commuter to Manhattan early and late and didn't want to travel too far at night when he was tired.

April's survey finished at her own house, and that was the only place something was wrong. The front light was off. She started up the cement walk. Though it was May, the air was still quite cold at night. Tonight it was in the mid-forties. She shivered in her spring jacket. A three-quarter moon hung in the sky, just above the block of houses, lending them an exotic touch. April figured the bulb must have burned out and her mother didn't have a spare one in the house to change it. She couldn't reach the socket anyway. For the ten thousandth time April told herself it wasn't easy having a mother who couldn't drive and didn't like going to an American store by herself. Sai knew the prices of things but couldn't read labels or signs. She also didn't like being in the dark. April thought it wasn't so easy being her, either.

She put "Get lightbulbs" on her mental list of things to do for her mother, then stood for a moment, drinking in the night, before going into the house. Sometimes she did this as a kind of restorative after getting home from a difficult tour of duty. Out in Queens, with no towering buildings nearby, there was open sky over her head, and the moon and stars felt like close friends. By their light alone she could see the hot-pink flowers on the azalea bushes that her mother had nagged her father so relentlessly to get. She had been right about them, at least. The shrubs lined the walk like runway lights, inviting her in.

April realized something else was wrong. No lights were on inside the house, either. She frowned and suddenly felt afraid. Her mother didn't drive. Her father didn't drive. Skinny always waited up for April no matter how late she was. This was a common cause of complaint, for April's hours were erratic at best. Skinny didn't care that crime didn't punch a time clock—she thought her daughter was inconsiderate. So where were they?

April opened the door with her key and went inside. No light shone from the kitchen where Skinny sat out her days and nights watching TV, waiting for her husband and daughter to return from their jobs. No light was on in the living room or the big bedroom downstairs that her parents had taken for themselves. Their door was closed. All was quiet. April frowned some more. What was this about? She'd never come home before without her mother there to nag her, plague her with ten thousand questions, or try to feed her a Chinese banquet in the middle of the night. The sudden freedom to climb the stairs to her own apartment and go to sleep in peace should have made her happy. Instead she climbed the stairs to her apartment confused and upset.

April's parents had always told her the Chinese treasured their children more than any other kind of people did. Heather Rose's parents had certainly been distraught at the news of their daughter's trouble, but they hadn't known she'd been injured before. They hadn't known she had not given birth. That meant Heather Rose had kept many secrets from them. She must have felt she couldn't turn to them for help. Tonight of all nights, April had wanted to talk with her own mother about her feelings for Mike and why he was a good man. And she'd wanted to ask Skinny Dragon, the authority on all things Chinese, if there was anything in the world that would make a young mother with a rich husband abandon or kill a baby, no matter where it came from.

On the other hand, parents could turn on a dime when they were thwarted. Maybe Heather's parents had turned on her when she married Anton. Maybe her own parents were turning on her because she was spending her nights with Mike. April figured her mother knew about this the way Skinny Dragon knew about all things, and she guessed by her parents' absence that the punishment was going to be severe. She reached the last step and unlocked the door that did not keep her mother out. She prayed that tomorrow Heather Rose would wake up and talk to her and that she'd find the missing baby alive and well in the appropriate maternal arms.

April got undressed and curled up in her single bed, certain she was too wired by Heather's situation and her own to ever fall asleep. She fell asleep within minutes, however, not with any insight into whether a wife might kill the product of her husband's betrayal, but with a certain sympathy for a grown child who might wish to kill its parent.

CHAPTER
9

Sai Yuan Woo and her husband, Ja Fa Woo, knew that the cycles of heaven affect the cycles of earth, and that imbalances in nature were the cause of all evils that damage and destroy human life. She had known her double-stupid daughter was taking the wrong step the day April decided to become a policeman. And she'd been right about the poor outcome. April had been burned in a fire, crushed nearly to death, thrown out of a window and fallen ten floors (at least), and lived to be promoted. This only child of hers was worse than a cat. When April was growing up, they'd expected her to make them rich, have a top job in a bank like Stan Chan, the boy who used to like her in third grade, or own a dozen restaurants all over the city like Emily, who married the Soong boy, or run an import company like Arthur Feng's daughter, Connie. That Feng girl had been the least promising of them all, Sai repeated often with bitter satisfaction. Connie had been big and fat, and much slower than April in school. Two years older and in the same class; no one had any hopes for her. But look at her now. Feng's parents couldn't stop talking about her. Connie Feng had red hair now and drove a Mercedes. She bought *her* parents a much bigger house than the Woos', and now the Fengs were telling

everyone about the important Hong Kong business-
man who wanted to marry her.

The Woos thought the least their daughter could do
was marry someone rich enough to support them, have
children, and be happy. Instead she was a policeman.
Bad was having a policeman for a daughter. Beyond
bad was betraying the entire Han people, whose history stretched back thousands of years. Sai knew very
well her daughter was lying about where she was when
she wasn't on duty. They knew she was doing monkey
business with someone who smelled too sweet to be
a man.

Ja Fa wanted to admonish and scold her out of her
foolishness, but Sai knew that scolding had no effect
on this bad seed. Something stronger than talk was
needed to save her daughter. They went into consultation with Chinese experts, one in Chinatown and one
in New Jersey, to find out what intervention would
work. The question Sai wanted answered was how
April had become vulnerable to possession by a
foreigner.

A highly regarded young man in Chinatown, recently arrived from China with much knowledge and
hair sticking straight up about three inches from the
top of his head, charged them a hundred dollars to
tell them about the energy flow in the spring cycle.
Spring was the cycle they happened to be in at the
moment, and this young homeopathic doctor was certain that energy flow was the cause of April's exces-
sive heat.

In very lofty terms he explained how the heart is
the root of life, the seat of both intelligence and the
shen—spirit. The heart's element is fire, he told them.
It is called the *taiyang* of the yang and is considered
yang. He explained that the lungs were the root of
the body's *qi*, and the storage place of *po*—courage.
Sai listened intently, trying to make sense of it. *Po*

was yang and yang was masculine. Masculine was assertive. Sai believed April definitely had too much of that. She nodded. Her husband smoked a cigarette and worried about the cost.

"*Po*," Sai said. Too much boldness, courage.

But the young doctor shook his head. He was not interested in *po*. He told Sai, because her husband had stopped listening, that only the wisest of wise men could diagnose someone who was not present, and he should be charging her more. This brought Ja Fa out of his smoky reverie.

"Already too much," he protested.

When the clever doctor realized no more money was forthcoming, he made a quick diagnosis. He said that in spite of the extremely reasonable fee and the absent patient, he was certain that April's trouble derived from the liver.

"The liver?" Sai frowned. Hadn't he said it was the heart?

"Yes, it's the liver. The liver is the reservoir of stamina. That is the place of *hun*—intuition. The liver is in the yin location of the abdomen. It stores blood and belongs to the yang element of wood; thus it is called the *shaoyang* of yin."

Sai nodded as if she understood every word. It was just that she didn't agree. She didn't think April's problem was yin. Yin was yielding, and April was not that.

"The trouble is in your daughter's heart. But the wood element of spring corresponds to the liver. So the problem arises from her liver."

Aieeyee! Sai's head swam. How did he know that? He looked so young. His hair stuck up like Elvis Presley's, or a movie star's. Sai could see there was hair spray in it. She wondered if a young master of classical medicine should be using hair spray.

The young master interrupted her thoughts. "There

are five elemental phases, five parts of the year: spring, summer, late summer, autumn, and winter. Each has its excesses and deficiencies."

Yes, yes, but what did that have to do with April's spending her nights with a Spanish man?

"In order to properly utilize the knowledge of the five elemental phases, one must calculate the arrival time of the season and observe normal and abnormal patterns. Since your daughter is ill in spring, we must calculate from the first day of spring on the Chinese calendar. If the first day of spring this year had not yet arrived but the weather was already warm—as it was this year—we must consider this an excess of fire. In your daughter's case the fire excess would humiliate the water element and damage the normalcy of the season. It would overcontrol the normal *qi* of metal. This is called *qi* yin or reckless *qi.*"

Ah, now they were getting somewhere. But then the young doctor of the Yellow Emperor's classic medicine started talking about the variability of heaven and earth, and Sai was confused again.

He said she must bring April to him so he could take her pulse. If she was in a truly advanced state of reckless *qi,* the radial pulse could be as much as five times as large as normal. At that point her yin will have collapsed.

"And if both the carotid and radial pulses are five times larger than normal, this condition is called *guan le* or obstructed. That means yin and yang have become extreme and stagnant. The prenatal and postnatal *ging* essence *qi* have become exhausted; the eventual consequence is death."

Sai swooned and nearly fell off her chair. Was April's heart beating five times as fast as normal? Sai had no idea. But then the young master reassured her again. For another hundred dollars she could obtain a powder that would slow down April's heart and save her life. This seemed an unavoidable expense. Sai figured if she could save April's life she could get the money back from her when she was well.

Neither Sai nor Ja Fa was entirely satisfied with this diagnosis, however. They felt they needed a second opinion and took the PATH train to New Jersey, where they spent Tuesday night with the Dong family and consulted another well-known Chinese doctor. This one inspired greater confidence in spite of charging a much lower fee. Me Nan was a bargain at only twenty-five dollars. She was one of the so-called barefoot doctors, also just recently arrived in this country, but she worked in a cleaning service during the week and had a boyfriend with only one hand. His other hand was made of wood and covered with a black glove that made him look very official when he opened the door of their apartment.

Me Nan gave Sai a cup of tea and asked many questions about April. She wanted to know the quality of her hair, its thickness and vibrancy. The color of her face and the tone of her flesh. She also wanted to know what else was going on in April's life, in addition to the Mexican police boyfriend, that might also be contributing to the impairment of her judgment.

"Uh, uh, uh," she commented as she listened to Sai's discourse on the matter.

"Good healthy hair. Pale face. Suspicious eyes, been that way from birth. Ugly, but not so ugly that she could not have a good man if she had a better disposition."

"Uh, uh, uh!" the doctor exclaimed. She gave Sai another cup of very black tea (the cheap kind) and asked if twenty-five dollars was too much.

Sai showed Me Nan the money and told of her sorrow that her daughter was a policeman and her pride that the girl was a good policeman. NYPD could not solve any important cases without her.

The doctor from China listened to the cases with interest and found in one of them the cause of April's complaint. "Liver. Yes, yes. It is the liver."

All this time Ja Fa Woo waited in the other room with the one-handed man. He did not want to hear any more theories. He wanted to spank his daughter. When she heard "liver" Sai thought of the hair-sprayed Chinatown doctor and nodded. "Yes, it had been warm and dry before the first day of spring."

"No, that is not it." Me Nan, the barefoot doctor, did not seem to care about the temperature before the first day of spring, but she made a great deal of the fact that April had been twice chilled and thrown out of a window back in January and had been given a large box of chocolates for Valentine's Day in February.

"When the evil wind invades the body it generally turns to heat and consumes the body's *qi, jing* essence, and blood," she said.

Sai frowned. That sounded bad.

"When the blood becomes depleted, the liver is not normal and malfunctions."

"But if it was not the warm air before spring, what could be the cause, a devil, a ghost?" Sai wanted to know.

"No, no, nothing as malignant as that. Cold invading the body in winter will incubate and manifest as febrile disease in spring because everything rises at that time of year."

Sai sighed with relief. April had caught a cold.

The barefoot doctor held up her hand. "*And* improper use of the five flavors. The chocolates in February made too much sweet taste and disturbed the heart *qi,* causing it to become restless and congested."

Sai thought back on the chocolates and marveled at her own robust state of health. She herself had eaten most of them, but then again she hadn't gotten her feet wet and chased criminals in the snow. "What is the cure?" she asked, thinking another twenty-five dollars was not too much to pay if April could throw off the Spanish love disease.

For only two dollars more Sai received a plastic bag of sour herbs that Sai must make into tea. The tea would both counteract the liver disease and make her daughter smell forever distasteful to the foreign devil.

"Ah, ah, ah." Sai listened with satisfaction. On the two trains going back to Astoria, Queens, she thought about the other additions she had to make to April's diet. Plums, chives, small beans like mung or adzuki. Dragon bones and dog meat. With a shiver, she wondered how far she would go to save April from this bad relationship. She hoped it would not be necessary to sacrifice her beloved French poodle puppy, Dim Sum, that had only just become reliable about holding her pee pee through the night. For this reason she was glad April wasn't there when they got home.

CHAPTER
10

Roosevelt Field was a huge place. Milton Hua told his wife, Nanci, it was the largest shopping mall in America. When she'd asked if it was anything like the ugly and foul-smelling shopping mall on Bowery in Chinatown, just at the mouth of the Manhattan Bridge that led out to Brooklyn, he'd laughed. No, no, this was a *Mall,* with a capital M. Big, really big. Bigger than Chinatown and Little Italy and Greenwich Village and SoHo and even Wall Street all put together. It was the mother and father of all malls. He was very proud.

Garden City, Long Island, next to Roosevelt Field, was where Nanci and Milton had moved last winter when it was still bleak and cold, and no green showed on the trees or on the lawns in front of the houses. Now they had a yard full of tulips and jonquils. They had moved to Garden City because a new section of Roosevelt Field was being built, and the pot of gold at the end of the rainbow had been offered to Milton because he was the smartest son in his family and the first to go out on his own. The pot of gold for him was a house, a car, and a brand-new Chinese restaurant to run in that business Mecca, Roosevelt Field, on the other side of the Queens line in Nassau County. What was in it for Nanci was the loss of the only home she'd ever known, the only job she'd ever wanted, and her independence. Outside, the taxi horn honked.

"You okay with this?" she called to her neighbor, who was reading a magazine in her kitchen and who had promised to stay until her return.

"No problem," Emmie called.

Nonetheless, Nanci was deeply troubled as she slammed the door of the brick house that was Milton's dream come true. The door was solid wood and the heavy thud it made shut out everything in her life she'd valued.

Everything was beautiful, from the little peaked roof over the front door, painted red for luck, to the pale tiles in the kitchen painted with all the herbs and vegetables prized in an Italian kitchen, to the stone fireplace in the living room, which Nanci would never use because of the fire that had killed her father in Chinatown when she was fifteen. It had everything; it was comfortable; and it was far, far from the apartment where she and Milton used to live, which also happened to be close enough for her to walk to her job at the Chatham Square Library even in the rain and snow. It was far from her cousin, too, and Nanci knew that her neglect was responsible for the problem she had now.

"Hey, lady, don't keep me waiting," the taxi driver yelled out the window.

She took a last look at the house, where her neighbor was keeping watch, and she hurried out to the car, which was the kind of wreck Milton would not want her riding in. Milton had a brand-new BMW. Nanci didn't know how to drive it, but even if she had, he wouldn't have let her take it into the city on this mission. He was angry; he'd told her to stay where she was. But Nanci's cousin Lin, difficult from the moment she'd arrived from China, had to be located immediately. Nanci kept replaying the events of yesterday in her mind: Lin calling her early in the morning and asking Nanci to come and get her; Nanci driving in with Milton and seeing Lin sitting on the curb in Chinatown like a homeless person, waiting for them with her possessions in a cheap plastic laundry basket; Lin putting the basket in the car without a word, then refusing to get in herself. And finally, Lin turning her back and hurrying away down the street.

"Oh, let her go," Milton had said, furious at the inconvenience and bad manners. "I have to get back to work." So she'd let him turn around and drive back to Garden City without a clue what had just happened, or why.

"Where to?" The driver was a big angry man with a baseball cap pulled low over his forehead.

"The station," Nanci told him.

"Which station?"

"Penn Station."

"I ain't goin' all the way into Manhattan."

"No, no. I want to take the train into Manhattan."

"Okay, little girl, what line?"

Nanci Hua was twenty-five. Nobody had called her a little girl in a long time. "Does it make a difference?" she asked angrily.

"Yeah, it does. Three stations, three fares. The trains go different times from each one and some you gotta change in Jamaica. So make up your mind, I can't sit here all day."

They were in Garden City, so she said, "Garden City station." She was in a hurry; she didn't have time for this.

He didn't say anything, just drove in a jerky stop-start way that made her feel carsick after the first block. In seven minutes he pulled up and braked hard at a station clearly marked "Mineola." She had no idea where Mineola was.

"That will be nine dollars," he demanded.

She gave him the money. At the station, there was an automatic ticket machine. She had to figure out the number of the station where she was going and the time of day she was traveling. It cost $6.50. At Penn Station, she had to go up a flight of stairs and find the subway. Another $1.50 for the token. She didn't know what subway to take, but the Canal Street stop was where she was going. Seven minutes after arriving in Manhattan, she got off there and climbed out of the tunnel into the light. It had cost her seventeen dollars to get home.

In the warming spring air, the Lower East Side was teeming with people. Nanci didn't have to get her bearings. The Bowery was on one side of Chatham Square; on the other side were East Broadway, Allen Street, Delancey, Orchard, Ludlow, and the rest of the Lower East Side that used to be all Jewish, then became Puerto Rican, and now more and more was Asian. The factory where Lin had worked when she arrived in America was on Allen Street. Nanci rushed past the library at 33 East Broadway, where she'd met Milton when she was twenty and they'd fallen in love. She wasn't thinking about that now. When she hit Allen, her heart started pounding. Soon she would have some answers.

Almost no one started out on top in New York. Everybody coming in worked in a restaurant or a factory, or cleaned houses. Nanci herself had come as a child and learned English within a matter of months. She'd never had to make bean curd or dumplings, wait on tables, sell things on the street, clean other people's houses, wash dishes, or sew in a noisy factory. Lin was older and not so lucky. Nanci and Milton wanted to place Lin in a store, but she couldn't read or change American money. She couldn't sell things on the street for the same reason, and she had no experience with flowers or dry cleaning or laundry. She knew nothing but how to sew. Nanci had been frustrated, trying to explain to her that she had to learn to read and speak English to get ahead in America. She had to go to school. But Lin had refused to speak the language of get-ahead ambition. Lin had refused to move in any direction. It turned out that her cousin, whom Nanci had tried so hard to help, did not like her, would not live with her. They had nothing in common, and now she'd entangled Nanci in real trouble. Nanci's stomach knotted with anxiety and fear. All the way into the city she had wondered how she, who had known and helped so many Italian, Latino, and Chinese children, could have been so helpless when it came to her own cousin.

At the address of the factory there was no name on the door. Nanci rang the bell. After a while a scratchy, heavily accented voice asked her through the old intercom what she wanted. She gave her married name, Hua, and asked if she could come up.

The voice switched to Chinese and screamed through the intercom that no one was there.

Nanci replied in Chinese that she was no one official, wasn't there to make trouble, she was just looking for someone. After that there was no more argument. The lock clicked, and she pushed the door open to a very small space with an unmarked door leading to the back of the first floor and a dark stairwell going up to another unmarked door on the second floor. The second-floor door opened just a crack. A pair of keen eyes in a wrinkled face looked down at her.

"*Ni hao, zumu, wo shi Lin Tsing Hua,*" she said politely.

"Okeydokey, come upstairs," said the voice behind the eyes.

It was an old building with a steep staircase. The steps sagged so badly they almost seemed to be tipping over on themselves. Nanci wondered how many times her cousin Lin had climbed these stairs and disappeared behind that door. She wondered if Lin was in there now. Nanci was used to climbing stairs. There had been three flights of stairs to her apartment. Still, these stairs were very steep, and she was short of breath when she hit the top. The old woman opened the door just wide enough for her to slip inside.

"Hello, Grandmother," Nanci said again. "I'm sorry to bother you in the middle of your important work."

The woman made a humphing sound that was not hard to interpret even over the roar of many sewing machines. Inside the door was a big room with more than a dozen machines and heads bent over them. Some heads still had the black hair of youth, and some were peppered with gray. Two heads of curly hair were pure white; the skin of those women was the color of butterscotch. And there were no men anywhere. A high chair with a rickety table, a chipped teapot, and a small cup marked the place of this woman, the woman with the sharp eyes.

For a second Nanci took in the cracked beams in the unfinished ceiling, the fat black-and-orange extension cords looping from one makeshift outlet to another high above, slats of some unidentifiable building material on the walls between a few patches of old plaster. By the windows were radiators, but not many. In May the room was already broiling with so many lungs sucking at the stale air and so many machines using electricity and acting as little furnaces.

There was no space for cutting tables here. The stacks of legs waiting to be sewn together suggested it was a pants factory. Some women were sewing the curve of the crotch, some just the zippers, some the waistbands. One older woman covered with thread was just cutting the threads from the finished garments. And in the farthest back corner clouds of steam were belching from the presser. All the activities, the noise, and so little air made Nanci dizzy; so did the dishonorable fact that she was so poorly acquainted with her cousin that she didn't even know what part of the garment Lin worked on. Rust and burgundy were the colors of the wool fabrics the women were putting together now. That meant they must already be sewing for fall.

Nanci felt that empty place of sorrows burn in her gut. It had taken her six years to save enough to bring her little cousin here, and now that Lin was here Nanci still could not reach her. She looked around and did not see her cousin.

"Everybody's here, and everybody's legal," the woman said in Chinese. "So who are you looking for?"

"Thank you for taking the time to talk to me. I am looking for my cousin, Lin Tsing."

The woman's eyes showed nothing as she shook her head quickly.

"What does that mean, Grandmother? I know she works here," Nanci said.

"No work here."

Nanci looked carefully at the bent heads again. "Maybe not now, this minute. But she did work here. If there's something wrong with her, please tell me."

The woman shook her head. "Never work here."

"Maybe she didn't give her right name."

"Know nothing."

"I have only one cousin. No one else. She may not be a good cousin, but she is all I have. She is my father's brother's child. My mother and my father and my uncle are gone. They would want me to take care of her. I need to find her. I have her things. It's very urgent."

"Bad luck," the woman said, but the shrewdness

didn't leave her eyes. "What things do you have—in case I hear of her?"

"Maybe you remember her. She's young, pretty, has short hair. She worked here for many months, you don't have so many people you could forget so fast."

"*Boo hao.*" The woman coughed up some phlegm.

Nanci ignored the disapproval. She guessed what was no good, but Lin had been sulky and secretive ever since her arrival, wouldn't even see Nanci, much less share her troubles with her cousin.

"I'd like to talk to the boss," Nanci said firmly.

"I boss."

"The owner, then."

"No here."

"When will he be back?"

The woman shook her head. Grandmother wasn't saying. Nanci paused at the table with the teapot on it. "If you see my cousin, tell her I have her things. I'm sure she wants them back."

"What things, in case I hear?" the woman asked a second time.

"Would you ask around and call me?" Nanci didn't want to tell her.

The old woman's hard eyes traveled to Nanci's purse. Nanci had never bribed anyone before. The idea of having to do so now made her nervous. She groped around in her purse, trying to count her money without appearing to do so. It would cost her another fifteen dollars, at least, to get back to Long Island. How much could she afford to offer? She gave the woman a ten. Was that enough? Apparently it was. A glimmer of recognition showed in the woman's eye.

"Maybe I'll look around for you," the woman suggested. "Maybe she has important things? Maybe you'll give a reward for her?"

Nanci's mouth went dry. "Yes," she said. "I have a reward."

"My name Annie Lee. How much?" she demanded.

Nanci frowned. How much was enough to get results? Now she was really frightened. Milton would be so angry about all this. She closed her eyes. She asked herself how much she'd pay.

"A thousand dollars," she said finally. "A thousand dollars if you can tell me where my cousin is."

The grandma nodded. "I'll ask around. What's your number?"

Nanci gave her the number. Then she walked back, crossed Bowery, and cut around to Elizabeth. On Elizabeth she walked back and forth in front of the police station a dozen times, asking herself if she should go to the police. What if Lin had done something criminal? What if Nanci were now an accessory to some crime? What should she do? The police were so dangerous. Her old friend, April Woo, the only representative of the police she'd ever liked and respected, wasn't there anymore. Nanci had seen her only twice since April started working uptown—it now seemed like a hundred years ago—and they never spoke on the phone or had lunch anymore. In the end she was too frightened to go into the station house and ask for April's current work telephone number.

CHAPTER
11

Lieutenant Iriarte had two characteristic expressions when things were not going well: fury at those beneath him for messing up and detached regret for those above him who could remove his head for it. Right now his face displayed the latter. "Nothing," he said flatly.

At quarter past eight on Monday morning Captain Bjork Johnson, the commanding officer of Midtown North, aimed frosty blue eyes at April Woo, the so-called rising star of his detective squad. Johnson was a man who looked as if he ate a cow for dinner every night and hadn't done any form of exercise since the day he stopped walking a beat more than fifteen years ago. The lack of discipline implied by his large, soft midsection, undisguised by his captain's uniform, gave him a somewhat dangerous air. His cold stock-taking of April told her he didn't think any more of her than Iriarte did. She wished that she'd had more than an hour's sleep.

Captain McCarthy, Johnson's second whip in the precinct, sat on the other side of the room, pretending to confer with his computer while waiting for the right moment to enter the conversation. He gave April an encouraging smile that did not actually mean he was on her side. Captain Johnson's eyes, however, made no attempt at nice. *What do you have to say for yourself?* they demanded.

April glanced quickly at her immediate boss. Iriarte was holding himself together with a studied air of comfortable authority. He sat straight-backed but relaxed, with both well-shod feet in their almost-pointy Italian loafers planted on the ground, like the gentleman he knew he was. He wore a carefully pressed Harris tweed suit with a purple silk handkerchief in the breast pocket. Under the jacket was a powder-blue shirt with his monogram on one white cuff. He was Puerto Rican and proud of it. April was trying to develop a similarly confident style. She stood beside him, not too close, and tried to appear professional—neither meek like the classic Oriental woman whom men of all races seemed to think they could push around, nor defiant like the butch American feminists who couldn't ever let go of their grudges. Thus she hung on to her tightrope balancing act, nervous as usual and right on the edge of a headlong crash into abject and groveling.

She was a boss now, but still so twitchy about the responsibility she could hardly stand still. A police department was most on the line in the "B cases"—the ones involving bombs and babies. Things couldn't get more intense or high-profile than this. She knew the department had a very good record with this kind of thing. With snatchings, detectives almost always came up with a scenario and a suspect within thirty-six hours. Same story with abandonment cases—young mothers who left their babies in parks or doorways or Dumpsters, either dead or alive. The babies were discovered quickly, and usually someone came forward with information about the mother. Of course, there were cases where women gave birth in secret and did away with their babies without anyone's finding out because no one, not even their mothers or

boyfriends, had known they were pregnant. Those
were the real perfect murders, and there were no sta-
tistics on how many of *them* happened in a year.

April tried to breathe evenly while three brass challenged her as if she alone, of all the detectives working
the case, had failed the mission. No baby had turned
up in the night. The papers were full of it.

Finally, Iriarte nodded at her.

"We had over a hundred people out checking garbage
cans in the area and searching in the park last night,"
she said. "We also had officers checking Dumpsters
parked outside a construction site two blocks away
from where the Popescus live. Came up with two dead
cats, that's it."

Iriarte made a face.

"You have a possible scenario for us, Sergeant?
You're a woman," Captain Johnson said.

"It's not the victim's biological baby, sir. I think the
most likely scenario is he was abducted by a brother,
father, even husband of the baby's mother. Even by
Popescu himself," April said, ignoring the implicit
snickers. "I don't think Heather Rose could have
killed him."

She got a cold stare in return. "Why not?"

"First, she was beaten up. That means there had to
be at least one other person involved. Second, the
baby's stroller is missing."

Captain Johnson chewed the inside of his cheek.
He didn't appear to understand the significance of the
missing stroller. All he wanted to know was how to
allocate the officers for the day. He glanced at McCarthy, then Iriarte.

"We know about the stroller. We didn't come up
with anyone who saw it, sir," Iriarte told him.

April jumped out on a limb. "Our guess is that the
missing stroller indicates the baby is still alive, and
someone has him."

Johnson seemed to like the idea. It would be better
for them if they could find the baby alive. However,
he knew it would be a poor idea to slow down the
search in case the baby's corpse was in the garbage
somewhere and they lost it forever. It would be next
to impossible to prosecute later without a body. He
wasn't sure what the best policy was here. He didn't
want anyone to think he wasn't proactive enough or,
on the other hand, that he was too dependent on the
judgment of his squad detectives. In cases like this the
squad detectives were supposed to direct the investigation and advise him of what they needed. He was
supposed to get the manpower and technical support
together, either from his precinct or from others in
the area. It had been his patrol officer, McMan, who'd
called for special units yesterday. Major Cases had
already overrun the detective squad and now that the
case was looking a lot more like a kidnapping, the
FBI wanted in, too. That meant even more people
hanging around, getting in the way, and confusing the
investigation. Iriarte was not a happy camper. Captain
Johnson, with only a few months in this job, was
clearly nervous. He addressed the more experienced
Captain McCarthy.

"The mayor's office just called. He wants to know
what we're doing to resolve this."

"Yes, sir." McCarthy smiled. It was an election
year.

Johnson struggled to figure out his position. Would
it look bad to abandon the search in the park, if they
were careful to assure the public they had promising
leads in other directions? Or would it look better if
they kept a visible presence in place to show how hard
they were working on the case? Finally he returned
to April.

"The mother's Chinese. You talk Chinese?" he
asked her.

"Yes." April's eyes dropped to her hands as if the change of subject meant the still-missing infant was her fault and hers alone. Then she wanted to smack herself for tipping over to meek.

"She speak Chinese?" Captain Johnson again.

"She's American-born, went to college," April said, trying not to flush.

"What's the culture on this? Didn't a Chinese couple kill their twelve-year-old daughter down in the Fifth recently? This a common thing among the Chinese?"

"This is not a Chinese thing, sir. The baby's father is Caucasian. The birth mother may well be, too." April knew he was pushing her buttons.

"So maybe having to take care of a white baby set her off," Johnson said, still going for the mother.

April became aware of Iriarte scowling beside her. His matchstick mustache twitched with anger. It was *his* privilege to torture his people. "I remember the case you're referring to," he said smoothly. "I believe it turned out there was no evidence that the Chinese family was involved in their daughter's death."

"I was talking to the sergeant." Johnson's eyes narrowed.

And he certainly had made his point. The culture question kept nagging at April. An ache in the pit of her stomach reminded her that when she'd checked the light outside the front door last night, she'd found the bulb had been unscrewed. Her parents had taken off without telling her. She felt anxious about what they were up to.

"So what do you want to do, Sergeant? It's your case." Iriarte slapped her hard with the responsibility.

"I think we have to look for Popescu's girlfriend and the missing stroller."

"You want to slow down the search in the park?"

April nodded. She'd be dead in the water if she was

wrong and three days from now someone found the abandoned stroller in a playground uptown and the baby's body floating among the rowboats in the Central Park Lake. "And hope Heather will wake up and tell us something."

"Fine, get going."

"Yes, sir." April exited the commander's office and climbed slowly up the stairs to the squad room.

In a dark mood, she opened the door to her office— it was empty at the moment—and saw a document was back on her desk unchanged that she hadn't approved a half-hour ago. She picked it up and marched into the squad room, still under siege and noisy, to find Detective Rudner.

His skinny butt was planted on the edge of Hagedorn's desk because his own was occupied, and he was calmly chewing the fat with the computer expert as if the last thing he'd ever do was try to pull a fast one. April jerked her chin at him.

"Hey, Charlie," Rudner said to Hagedorn, then shoved off the desk and followed her.

April shook her head and closed her office door. "Bertie, you try to use this in court, and they'll sentence *you*." She handed the form back to him. "I need to be able to visualize what happened here. What'd the guy do? Where was he positioned when he threatened you with a knife? Which hand held the knife? What size was the knife? Who was with him? The whole thing." The piece of crap he'd given her looked as if it had been written by a first-grader. Rudner was a detective with enough experience to know better.

"Aw come on, it's fine." He was a tall, lean blond with a red nose. The nose looked suspicious to her. Guy had red eyes, too. He was probably acting out because he was pissed at getting the scut work instead of the major case.

"Have a big night last night?" She glanced out the

window in the door at Baum, who'd just come into the squad room and was watching her with his antennae vibrating.

Rudner shook his head. "Allergy. All those trees and bushes in flower . . . man, it's really killing me." He sneezed to demonstrate how miserable he was.

"You taking anything for that?" Anything alcoholic? She was his supervisor. It was her job to be suspicious.

He shook his head again. "Nah, none of that stuff works."

"You sure that guy last night had a knife?" April was back on the arrest form. If it was a proper arrest, she didn't want to risk having the charges dropped because a lazy detective messed up the forms.

"Oh, yeah, we got it downstairs."

"Then fix this so it's crystal clear."

"I said everything; it's all right there."

"Yeah, for people who can read between the lines. Come on, fix it, Bertie. Make me happy."

"I'd have to do the whole thing over. And they're waiting to take the guy downtown." Rudner kept complaining as if he really thought she'd give up. He sneezed again for good measure.

"God bless," April said automatically. A hangover from her former supervisor, Sergeant Joyce, a Catholic. She wasn't going to give it up. She went to the door and opened it. "Do it again and show it to the lieutenant before you take the suspect downtown. You'll thank me later."

He certainly didn't thank her now.

Then, with her heavy purse swinging from her shoulder, she marched out into the squad room. "Come on, Woody, let's take a ride."

Baum jumped at the command.

CHAPTER
12

Anton Popescu's office was in an architecturally un-interesting glass and steel tower on Fifty-sixth Street and Broadway, within easy walking distance of his apartment. The law offices of Pfumf, Anderson and Schmidt were on the tenth floor, around the corner from the elevator bank. Imposing eight-foot mahogany doors separated it from a nondescript hall with gray stone floors and white walls. Anton's office had an Oriental rug in bright reds and blues and an expansive view of the building across Broadway.

On Wednesday morning he was a desperate and brooding man. His baby was missing and his wife was still unconscious in the hospital, where he could not bear to look at her through the window in her door, battered and out of it. After trying to get in to visit with her in the early morning with no success, he went to work as usual.

There, no one could take pictures of him. No reporter's voice could get through to him. He hid in his window office with the door closed and orders to the staff not to disturb him. But quiet was not to be his. Almost immediately his secretary Angela's Brooklyn voice came up on the phone. "Anton, you have some visitas."

He punched the speaker phone to reprimand her. "I told you no calls, no visitors!"

"They're from the police. What am I supposed to do?"

"I don't care where they're from."

"They say they won't take much of your time."

Anton made an impatient noise. "For Christ's sake, Angela. I've spent all night talking to the police. What more do they want?"

"The woman told me if you don't want to talk here, you can go to the station with them." Angela sounded as if she'd like to see that.

"Jesus Christ!" Anton's heart pounded. He let injustice envelop him with all its familiar incitements: fury's roaring heart, rockets of fire. Yesterday his whole life had fallen apart. The shock of betrayal was profound. The air around him seemed to stink of his vulnerability. He could feel the profound treachery reach deep into the core of his being to destroy his dignity, his love, everything that he'd held sacred. He could not look in the mirror without seeing the open wounds of his hurt and humiliation bleeding out of his eyes, drooling from the corners of his mouth. He could feel his ruin coming.

Anton was at his worst. He had not slept at all. Strangers were camping in his living room, waiting for a call that would never come. Now he was supposed to be preparing to take depositions in a very important case. He had people to talk to, the research of associates to supervise. He had a firm luncheon and meetings to run. He was a prominent lawyer. Look at the settlements and judgments he got in his cases, the hours he billed, the kind of money he pulled down. His hand curled into a fist around his fat Montblanc pen, one of the many indicators of his importance. The police had to go away. He could not bear the questions. Angela interrupted his thoughts.

"What do you want me to tell them?" she asked.

"Okay, bring them in here." He smacked the desk, a wide expanse of fine burled wood. The pen jumped out of his hand. He picked it up and stabbed the blotter. The point of the pen skidded, making a jagged line. Shit. Now he needed a new blotter. To hell with the blotter. It was not good to get excited like this. He blinked a few times to calm down.

The Chinese woman came in first. Anton could see by her walk she had the rank. He had trouble understanding how that could be. Her empty expression immediately gave him the feeling she was out to get him. The male, who seemed to be her lackey, followed her into the room and carefully closed the door. Popescu gave his attention to the lackey, with his conservative haircut and well-cut blue blazer. It was clear to him the buttons were real brass, so he knew the guy was no street cop. Maybe Baum was really the ranking guy, and they were trying to confuse him. That felt more correct to him. He scowled at the possibility of more treachery.

"Good morning, Mr. Popescu; you remember Detective Baum," the Chinese said, then closed her mouth.

"Yeah, what do you want?"

"We're real sorry to bother you."

"Well, you should be, coming here to my office and humiliating me like this." He stared at them belligerently, sure of his position.

"Excuse me, sir, humiliating you?" The cop swerved off the road, onto a tangent.

Anton eagerly followed him there. "You heard me, humiliating. Intimidating. Call it what you want."

"I apologize if you've gotten that impression." The young man gave him a chastened nod, which gratified Anton. He glanced at the woman. Her blank Chinese face stared back, cold as stone.

Baum nodded again and continued. "It was not at all our intention to give that impression, sir. Your wife and baby are our highest priority. The mayor is on it. The commissioner is on it. The whole city wants him found as much as you do." The detective spread his hands out, palms up.

Anton stabbed the air with his pen. "Okay, I accept your apology. But I told you everything I know last night. I have nothing more to say to you."

Detective Baum scratched his ear. "That's not how it works."

"Okay, I'll tell you how it works. You assholes had the chance, but you didn't get the job done. You didn't find my baby and you don't know who hurt my wife," Anton raged.

"Excuse me, sir." Baum cocked his head in the direction of the woman. "Are you calling the sergeant here an asshole again?"

Another curve ball. Anton made a disgusted noise. "Don't give me this shit. If you don't have something positive to report, I have work to do."

"Well, there's no need to be rude and insulting to the lady."

Anton recoiled in his chair as if he'd been smacked in the face. Rude and insulting! Weren't they the ones who'd barged in here, humiliating him in front of his whole office? His lip bunched. "I've never been rude to anyone in my entire life. Get out of here before I lose my temper."

"Is that a threat, sir?"

Anton half rose and smacked the desk again, stinging his hand with the impact. "Are you deaf? I told you if you don't have something to report, please exit this office."

"Well, the thing is, you came to a conclusion too soon about getting the job done. It's still early days, and we do have something to report."

Anton was interested. "Yeah, what's that?"

"Your fingerprints were on the weapon that battered your wife. If she dies of her injuries, you will certainly be indicted for murder. Maybe you'd like to save us all a lot of trouble and come down to the station and give us a statement now."

"What?" Anton's body clenched with terror. "No."

"No, what? No, your fingerprints aren't on the weapon, or no, you don't want to tell us where the baby is and what happened to your wife?" Baum stood in front of the desk. He looked to Popescu like some kind of storm trooper.

"No, everything. What are you trying to pull here? I had nothing to do with this." Now he was really scared. In a panic, Anton raked his memory for something that could be perceived by the police as a weapon. What was the cop referring to? There were no weapons on the scene. The man had to be out of his mind, had to be fishing.

"Just trying to establish what happened, sir." The detective looked apologetic again.

"I love my wife. I would never hurt her," Anton said slowly. "I told you that last night."

"You also told us about your relationship with the baby's biological mother. So, if there is such a person, she may have something to do with this. Any way you look at it, you're connected."

"Well, I had an affair, and I can explain that. It doesn't mean I don't love my wife." Anton clenched his jaw. "People have relationships. It happens all the time. One doesn't have anything to do with the other."

"Mr. Popescu, the FBI is very interested in this. Kidnapping is a federal offense. You don't want to play with those boys. They're a lot meaner than we are. And you mentioned the baby's mother lives across state lines. That also makes it federal. If you adopted the baby illegally, that raises other questions." Baum glanced quickly at the sergeant, who remained as silent and motionless as stone.

"Illegal adoption. The FBI!" Anton's eyes burned. His throat burned. His stomach burned.

"So, let's get to the point here. You say you had a baby with a married woman whose husband doesn't know and whose identity you don't want to reveal. And the baby is gone. We're not buying any of this unless you can prove it."

"Look, my wife doesn't know about it. I told you I don't want to hurt her." Anton bagged his rage, his fear. Suddenly the erupting volcano of his emotions was capped, cooled and stilled as if it had never gone off. He turned on a dime and smiled. He could never understand it when people told him or his partners he had a temper. He didn't have a temper. Baum was right; he didn't want to deal with the FBI.

"It's too late. She's already been hurt." The Chinese cop spoke up, almost kindly. "You can tell us the truth, she's beyond caring."

"What are you talking about, beyond caring? She's getting better. She'll be awake in a few hours. She'll tell you I had nothing to do with this."

"We need the baby's birth certificate," Baum said crisply.

Anton shook his head. "I don't have it."

"Last night you said it was in the office."

"I most certainly did not. I said I didn't have it at *home*. Don't start misrepresenting me or I'm going to have to get a lawyer."

"I suggest you do. The DA wants to talk to you."

"The DA! The FBI!" Anton let out a reflexive honking laugh, like the kind cops made at truly macabre crime scenes. "This is a joke."

"No, sir. We have to have the baby's birth certificate. And unless you know where he is and can verify his identity and his good health, we're going to pursue this case as attempted murder and kidnapping, which means local and federal agencies will be all over it."

"What about my wife?" Anton said softly.

"I don't know—with a good lawyer you may be able to get a separate deal on the prosecution of that. The DA's office is—"

"I didn't mean that," Anton said sharply. "I told you I had nothing to do with this. You're way off."

"Then cooperate."

"I can't," he said flatly. "I would if I could. But I can't. I don't know who has him, and that's the God's honest truth. Look, I appreciate the good work you're doing. I really do. If you refrain from torturing me in a cell, I'll commend you for your efforts." He glanced down and was suddenly pained by the sight of the jagged line on the blotter. "But you're going in the wrong direction. I want you to know this has been the worst night of my life. I've never suffered so much. I've been—hunted, *hounded* by media. My wife is in the hospital. I can't eat. The mess in the apartment— all the questions. It's been a nightmare." He paused for breath, then he smiled at them ingratiatingly. "I understand your problem here, but I'm as much in the dark as you are."

"Okay." Baum shrugged.

"By the way, what is that weapon I supposedly hit my wife with?"

"It was the broom, sir."

The blood drained from Anton's face. He closed his eyes to stop the pain. He didn't need this. He just didn't need it. Silently he cursed the woman he'd married with such hope and innocence. His own open wound bled out on the desk as he searched for an explanation for the broom.

CHAPTER
13

Good job, Woody, April thought as they left Anton's office. She was truly elated that the new kid she'd claimed as her own could actually think well on his feet. His free hand rubbed at his short hair as they walked down the hall to the elevator. He pushed the Down button and refrained from asking her if he'd done all right. He knew he had. She didn't look at him when the door slid open and they got inside. She didn't look at him as they went down.

Out on the street she told him, "I only let you do the talking because his wife is Chinese."

Grinning, he unlocked the car door. "Yeah, I kind of got the feeling there was some hostility there. So I went for it. When you didn't shut me up, I figured it was what you wanted." He punched the air. He was *good*, yeah!

"Transference," April murmured.

"What's that?" He cocked his hand to his ear before getting into the car and reaching over to unlock the passenger side for April.

April opened the door and climbed in. "This guy's mad at his Chinese wife; I'm Chinese, so he hates me. You could see it in his eyes." She slammed the door. They were heading for Roosevelt Hospital to have another crack at Heather Rose.

"Oh, that's deep. Transference, huh? And here I thought the hostility was because you're a cop, and you're trying to nail him."

"Yeah, Woody, *could* be that, or he could hate women. But I think it's because I'm Chinese."

"Maybe you're making too much of it." Woody gunned the engine and pulled out into the street without looking.

"Jesus, watch where you're going!"

"That fucker did it. His prints were on the broom."

April clicked her tongue. "Yeah? So, it's his house, his broom. When did the prints get there? Could have gotten there last week or last year."

"This jerko doesn't strike me as the kind of guy who regularly sweeps up after dinner."

"Prove he never touched the broom until yesterday; then I'll be impressed."

"It's him. He hit her. He took the baby."

"The baby was gone when we got there. What did he do with it?"

"So, it's a detail," Woody admitted.

"Come on, think. If he's protecting someone, who is it?"

"Himself. His prints are on the broom." Woody was back on the broom.

"Well, I can see other scenarios. A lot of them. What if the other woman showed up and told Heather Rose the baby's hers, she had it with *her* husband. The woman walked out with the baby. When hubby came home Heather confronted him. He beat her up."

"The woman takes the elevator from another floor," Woody embellished.

"The doorman would have seen her come up or go down. No one saw the baby go out. Try again."

"He knows where the baby is." Woody turned on the radio, listened to the dispatcher for a moment. Just a lot of static. Nothing new. He turned it off.

"I get the feeling he doesn't." April checked her watch. "We have to nail this today."

"I really got him going, didn't I? I thought he was going to pee in his pants over the FBI."

"Telling him she might die was a nice touch. I liked that. Let's hope we do better with her this time."

Woody parked in his usual no-parking zone in front of the hospital and locked up the car again. A few minutes later, they were upstairs, looking through the window into the room where Heather lay tucked up in her bed with her good eye half open. "Any change?" April asked.

The patrolman outside the room shook his head.

"Can I come in this time?" Woody asked.

April shook her head, entered Heather's room, and closed the door behind her. "Hi. It's April Woo," she said softly.

Some of Heather Rose's bruises were black. Some were purple and others yellowing. Her long inky hair lay in two loops on the pillow at either side of her face, like two nesting animals. The open eye didn't move as April stepped into her view, but April had an eerie feeling it was watching her. She took a step closer. Heather's arms were outside the sheet. Right below the elbow were several perfectly round scars that looked like burn marks. An IV was stuck in the top of her hand. April reached out and touched the hand. "You got beaten up pretty bad. Can you hear me?"

Heather's good eye didn't flicker.

"How are you feeling?" Stupid question.

April tried Chinese again. "*Ni hao? Wo shi* Sergeant *Siyue Woo.*"

Nothing.

April muttered on in Chinese. Heather's parents spoke Chinese, so it had to be the language of Heather's infancy. "*Wo shi* Sergeant *Woo.*" I'm Sergeant Woo. "*Shi zenme le?*"

April continued to stroke Heather's hand. The hand was cool and lifeless. " 'Heather Rose' is beautiful, but it's a mouthful. What's your Chinese name?" she asked in Chinese.

"*Chouchong,*" Heather's eyelid was hanging at half-mast; under it her eye was dead as a fisheye. The word seemed to come from behind her. April looked around. No one.

"Come on," April urged her. "Come back, I need you."

"*Tien na!*" The mouth didn't move. The sound came from the ceiling. Oh, no.

"You can hear me, can't you? You're okay now," April whispered back into the ether. "Come on, wake up." Heather had long slender fingers, and her hands would have been beautiful if the nails and cuticles and flesh at the sides of the nails hadn't been chewed and bitten to the quick. April stroked and squeezed the hand, got nothing back.

"*Chouchong.*" The eyelid hung at less than half mast.

"Wake up, Heather."

The next sound came from outside the window. It was a baby's cry. April's heart stopped as she listened. The sound came again. Now her heart was pounding.

"Come on, Heather. Don't go spooky on me. You're the only one who knows who did this. Wake up."

The patient looked dead, but the cry continued. Nothing April tried could make it stop. The baby's cry sounded as if it came from somewhere else. Finally April let go of the hand. More scary sounds and words filled her ears before April left the room. All Heather had told her of real significance was that her name was Insect. April's own mother called her Worm. They must be sisters. The rest was too frightening to think about. Shaken to the core, she hurried down the hall toward the elevator. Woody ran to catch up.

CHAPTER
14

Nanci Hua knew Lin's boss was lying to her, and she had her suspicions why. But whatever the story, she had to find Lin. She walked around the neighborhood asking people she knew, old friends and shopkeepers, if they'd seen Lin. Nobody had seen her since yesterday, when she'd been observed by many people, sitting on the curb with her pink laundry basket filled with clothes. After her brief encounter with Nancy and Milton, she'd disappeared. Nanci figured Lin must have gone home. Much as she hated to do it, she broke down and went to the apartment on Essex Street where Lin lived.

Only one ignorant Lao woman was there, and she seemed surprised to see Nanci at the door.

"Where's my cousin?" Nanci tried to go inside, but the Lao woman blocked the door. Not very polite.

"Not here."

"Where is she?"

"Hospital."

Nanci's eyes popped. "What hospital?"

The woman looked at her pretty jacket and skirt and didn't answer.

"What's wrong with her?" Nanci demanded.

"She has a cold." The woman looked at the dia-

mond engagement ring on Nanci's finger, at her gold
watch.

"She went to the hospital for a cold? You mean she
went to the clinic." Nanci calmed herself. The clinic.
She could find her there. "What time did she go?"

"Yesterday."

Nanci thought she must have misunderstood. The
woman's speech was slurred, and she looked frightened as she repeated herself.

"You mean today. She went today, this morning."

"Okay, today. She maybe very sick," the woman
offered shyly.

"Oh, my God. What hospital, Beekman?" Now
Nanci was upset because she was being made to stand
out in the hall. The woman wouldn't let her come into
the apartment and wouldn't tell her what hospital Lin
had gone to. She'd dealt with people like this many
times before and never gotten angry. Anger was not
helpful when people were ignorant and frightened.
Nanci usually had a lot of patience, but not now. Her
voice shook with fury. "Why didn't you call me? I'm
her only relative. You should know better," she
scolded. The woman kept looking stupidly at Nanci's
ring finger. Nanci wondered if there was something
wrong with her. "Who took her to the hospital?
You?"

The silence was thick; then the Lao woman shook
her head.

"Well, who then? Her boyfriend?"

"No have boyfriend."

"Yes, she did." But Nanci didn't want to argue the
point. The talking going on inside the apartment got
louder. Suddenly the Lao woman turned around to
join in the conversation behind her. Something about
her placating tone of voice made Nanci think she had
a boyfriend, too.

"A lady came and took her to the hospital," she said after some discussion.

"What lady?" Nanci demanded. She didn't believe a word of it.

"I don't know her name. Nice lady."

"Why?" Nanci was losing it.

The woman turned around again, conferred with someone behind her.

"Who was the lady? A young lady, an old lady, a social worker, a friend, who?"

"Yes, friend."

"What did she say?"

"Lin was sick at work again. Went home early yesterday. Nice lady. She want to take Lin to hospital."

"So she took Lin to the hospital?" The light went on. This must be Annie Lee the woman was talking about.

"Yes. Second time." Lao seemed to be nervous about this.

"She went to the hospital before?" Nanci was angry at herself for not knowing this. But there were a lot of things she didn't know. Of course, Lin had gone to the hospital. Nanci felt worse and worse. "She has more than a cold, doesn't she?"

"Just bad cold," the woman insisted.

"Okay, that's fine. You're not a help."

"Yes, I help. I took good care of her, save her life many times," the woman said indignantly.

"Then why didn't *you* take her to the hospital?" Nanci demanded.

"She had her friend. Her friend take."

"Okay, okay, and you don't even know if Beekman is where she went." Nanci was very angry. "And this is the second time. That's not taking good care."

"How can I find Lin? I don't speak English." Now the woman was ashamed. She hung her head. "Maybe you find," she said, hopefully.

"I'll find her," Nanci said angrily. "And I can tell you, when I do find her, I'll make sure she never comes back here again."

Deeply disturbed, Nanci went to look for Lin at Beekman Downtown Hospital. There was no record of her at the clinic, or the emergency room; Lin had not been admitted there today or yesterday or any other day. Now Nanci was really worried. With a sinking heart, Nanci Hua realized she was an evil person. She and Milton hadn't wanted to tell the police about her cousin for their own reasons. They should have called yesterday afternoon as soon as they got home, and they hadn't. Now she knew they had no choice; the Lao woman and Annie Lee at the factory were both lying to her. She had to involve the police. Finally Nanci went into the 5th Precinct and asked for Detective April Woo. The desk lieutenant sent her upstairs, where an ugly man wrote down April's number and even dialed it for her. The person on the line in whatever precinct April now worked said Sergeant Woo was out.

"Anything I can help you with?" the ugly man asked, staring at her hard as if he were trying to place her.

Nanci had met him before, but he didn't seem to remember. All Chinese must look alike to him.

"No thanks," she said. "I'll try her again later."

Nanci left the station and went down into the subway, boarded a train for Penn Station. On the Long Island list of stations Garden City was listed, so the taxi driver had lied to her about that. Today everybody was lying.

When she got off the train in Garden City, she was surprisingly relieved to be back there. And she was even happier to get out of the taxi at home. The house she lived in was like houses in the movies with lawns

and flowers and happy families inside. Now she understood why this was the American Dream, why it was
necessary for her to put her fears away and learn to
drive a car, be in control. It was almost as if she had
been cleansed of her fond feelings about her former
life in Chinatown, where old ways of thinking caused
so much trouble and kept so many secrets that it was
sometimes impossible to untangle all the lies.

Everything was peaceful at home, but Nanci was
not soothed by her nice neighbor, a plump woman
who didn't have much to do since her children were
all grown. Enthusiastically, the woman offered friendship and much advice about family life in the area.
She was clearly in no hurry to return to her own
kitchen. "Call me anytime," she said at last, when
Nanci escorted her to the front door, thanking her
profusely for her kindness.

When the woman was gone, Nanci sat down and
made a list of all the hospitals in Manhattan. She
called every single one. No Lin Tsing had come to
any of them. After that, with trembling fingers, she
punched out the number of the medical examiner's
office, the place to call if a person died in suspicious
circumstances and no one knew his name. There was
no young Asian woman in the morgue, either. After
that, there was nothing else Nanci could do for Lin
but wait for April Woo to get back to her.

CHAPTER
15

"What's going on, boss? You look upset," Woody said on the return trip to the squad room after the visit with Heather Rose.

April shook her head. Oh, man, she hated to see this. A Chinese woman, college educated, married to a creep. Okay, it happened. But there was more. Heather Rose might be one of those people who could do weird things. What she'd done just now was make her voice fly around the room like a ventriloquist. Called herself an insect, cried like a baby. "Nutty as a fruitcake" was the only explanation April let enter her mind. She got a tingling in the middle of her palm. Her skin crawled. And all this gave her a bad feeling. Iriarte was always threatening to fire her. Could be that, but it could be the woman was crazy. She had those scars on her arm. Perfect circles. In the twenty minutes April had spent trying to get Heather Rose to stop making crying noises from outside her body, a voice called April insect woman and predicted her death. It was creepy because the new sound had a toneless quality that almost made April think it came from the other side. *I don't believe in portents, signs, and predictions, and I'm not going to die,* April told herself. She also told herself she was a cop and hadn't heard this. No one heard this. But she was shaken all the same. Crazy people could do that to you. Now April had to reconsider this whole issue of the woman killing the baby, after all; and maybe the husband was shielding *her*. She shivered. One thing was clear: this woman was no longer unconscious, if she ever had been.

"You okay, boss?" Woody asked a second time.

April didn't hear him. At the precinct she left Woody to park the car and climbed the stairs to the second floor, fervently hoping to beat the odds and find her office free. Instead, there was a federal agent comfortably ensconced at her desk. She saw him through the glass in the door and didn't have to ask who he was. She knew he was FBI by the gray suit, white shirt, gray-and-white-striped tie. Mouse-brown hair a quarter of an inch long, features undefined enough to act like putty whenever necessary. No glasses, about thirty-five, medium height, slender build. This one was sharp, though. He looked down at the "Sgt. Woo" nameplate on the desk and up at her. Then he stood up behind the desk and waved her into her own office with three fingers. Showing her who was boss.

"Sergeant Woo, I presume?"

"Yes, sir. Special Agent—?" April got it all, the seeming politeness of his standing to invite her in, and layered under that, a putdown in the clear indication of his intention not to surrender the territory. God, she hated this.

"Gabriel Samson. Good to meet you, Woo." He held out his hand, challenging her to advance to the front of her desk. She advanced for the shake. She didn't have much choice in the matter. Then when she reached out for the bony hand he offered, she got her knuckles crushed.

"You must catch a lot of flak for the name," she

remarked, flexing her fingers. "Gabriel *and* Samson. Your mother must have had high hopes for you."

"I disappointed her in the music department," he said modestly.

"Only that? Then you're doing well. What can we do for you, Gabe?" April wasn't feeling as perky as she might, what with the crushed fingers, disembodied death threat and all.

His lips tightened. Oh, he didn't like a cop using his first name. He was a real FBI type. She felt a little better.

"There was no space outside, so the lieutenant offered me your office. I hope it won't inconvenience you too much." His smile lacked sincerity.

"Not at all. What's the deal?"

"The deal is we're cooperating. You tell us what you've got, we tell you what we've got, and together we clear the case."

"Great. What have you got?"

He laughed and wagged a finger at her. "April, your boss said to be careful of you, you're a pistol."

"I'm flattered." April laughed, too. They were having quite a party, but he hadn't answered the question, and she wasn't going to play nice and brief him on the case after Iriarte gave him her office without mentioning it to her and there were a dozen other detectives right outside the door who could brief him just as well as she could. And besides, right now she needed to use the phone. "Do you mind if I use the phone?" she asked sweetly.

"No, go ahead." He nodded toward the phone.

"I mean, privately."

"Oh, sure. How long will you be?" He was a pistol, too.

"Two minutes."

He checked his watch. "No problem."

April was impressed by his efficiency. The man was

actually going to time her. She wasted no time dialing Dr. Jason Frank's number. If she was going to consult with anybody outside the precinct, it was going to be Jason, and only Jason. He was a psychiatrist she'd met a while ago, when his actress wife was being stalked. Ever since April had called him whenever she had a head case. He was always busy with patients and rarely answered the phone, so she was astounded when he picked up now.

"Dr. Frank."

"Jason, it's April."

"Hey, April, my favorite police officer. What's up? I only have thirty seconds."

"Head case. I need a consultation."

"Could you elaborate a little?"

April peered out into the squad room where Gabe stood at the door tapping his finger at his watch. A real nice guy. She was tempted to flip him the bird. "In twenty seconds?" she asked Jason.

"Well, for you I have two minutes. What's up?"

She turned toward the wall in case Gabe could lip-read. Never underestimate a white shirt. "Got a creepy case, Jason. Missing baby. Possibly a battered wife. But the baby isn't hers. A lot of people are banking on the kidnap angle, but I'm not completely convinced this woman didn't maybe kill the baby, after all. I could be wrong, but I think this is a head case. Would you see her?"

"What's a head case, April?"

"You know what I mean. Wacko, crazy. By you, certifiable illness."

"Well, you know my credo on the subject: if they seem crazy, they probably are. Sure, I'll see her. You want to bring her to my office?"

"Sorry, can't do it."

"Oh, I don't know. I can't come into the station. I'm really socked in here."

"We'll come and get you. How's Emma?" April played the trump. She and Mike had saved Emma's life, and they both had scars to show for it. Jason owed her, and she would never let him forget it.

"All right, I had time set aside for jogging in an hour. Pick me up then," he said wearily.

"Thanks, I'll pay you back," she promised cheerfully.

"That won't be necessary, and Emma's fine. Thanks for asking."

April hung up, and Gabe walked right back in.

"Okay, have a seat. Let's do that debriefing now," he said.

"Sorry, I can't. Something's come up downtown."

He looked disappointed. "How about later?"

"Later's great." April picked up her purse and bade her office a sad farewell. She didn't plan to come back for a long time.

It was noisy out in the squad room, and chaos still reigned. Ousted squad detectives were trying to do their jobs in impossible circumstances, without their desks and phones. At the moment four of them were squeezed into Iriarte's office, having a conference. When Lieutenant Iriarte saw April through his window, he waved at her to join in the meeting.

"Whatchu got?" he asked, motioning for her to shut the door after her.

When no one jumped up to give her a chair, she leaned against the door frame. "I like our Feeb; he's a real charmer," she remarked.

"Oh, Gabe? He's from the New York office. We want to help out all we can, all right?"

"Sure. What's going on?"

Iriarte pointed at Hagedorn. "Charlie was about to give us some deep background on the Popescu family."

"What about the baby's mother?"

Charlie gave her a look. "Nothing on her yet. One thing at a time."

"Look, Charlie, if this guy Anton has a babe on the side, I want her name and address. When are you getting on it?"

"That was your job," Iriarte barked. "Go ahead, Charlie."

April shut her mouth. Charlie Hagedorn happened to be a first-rate hacker, good enough to go downtown to the Big Building with the big boys. Iriarte wouldn't let this happen as long as he drew breath. He saw computers as policing's future, and Charlie's talent for finding out things as his alone. He nodded for his favorite to begin.

Charlie gave April a smug look and let his chest puff. "The Popescu family came in from France in the thirties. The grandfather, Paul, and the two sons, Marcus and Peter. Had some money, set up shop on the Lower East Side. Marcus Popescu had one son, Ivan. Peter Popescu had two sons, Marc and Anton. Anton is the younger by twelve years."

"What kind of shop?" At the mention of the Lower East Side April got interested.

"Sounds like a sweatshop kind of thing. Any of your family in the sewing business?"

She shook her head. Her father was a cook. Her mother—though April found it hard to believe—had been pretty and popular enough to work in the front of a restaurant. A downtown hostess was a person who bossed people around. The job had been perfect for her. Skinny had screamed at waiters and argued with people who had problems with the bill or didn't like their food. The place had been old then. Now it was truly ancient. Thousands of holes-in-the-wall like it had come and gone in the ten years since Skinny Dragon had been lucky enough to stop working, but Doh Wa was still there, surviving the Chinatown trend

to white tablecloths and dishes like Grand Marnier
shrimp prepared with profoundly un-Chinese ingredients like mayonnaise and orange liqueur.

"But you came up in the Fifth, right?" Hagedorn
demanded.

April nodded.

"Born in Chinatown, right?"

April nodded again. "Born and bred. Any particular reason?"

"The Popescu family's been in the business for quite
a while. They've been shut down a number of times
over the years. The usual: fire code violations, inade-
quate wiring for the machines and fans. Building condemned, plumbing didn't meet standards—" He
thumbed his notes.

April snorted. Since when did plumbing shut anybody down?

Charlie looked up. "Problem?"

Only the usual societal complaints about exploita-
tion and poor working conditions. April shook her
head.

Charlie went on. "Illegal aliens. No record of trouble lately. Looks like they've cleaned up their act. Factory's on Allen Street, but it seems most of their work
these days is being done in China. Two sons to Peter,
as I said, Anton and Marc. Marc is in the business.
Anton is a personal-injury lawyer. Marc has been married twice, messy divorces. Has two children by each
wife. By the looks of their settlements, the business is
doing very well. Marcus's son, Ivan, is also in the business. He's married, has two children, house in Queens,
another one farther out on the Island. The father is
retired, lives—"

"Okay, okay. That's enough." Iriarte shut him up.

"They're raking in the money. I gather you don't
know them," Hagedorn kept at it. April ignored him.

"Any priors on the Brothers Karamazov?" Suddenly the tadpole Woody Baum kicked in. He was on a roll today.

April glanced at him in his blue sports jacket and blue button-down shirt. *Thank you, Woody.* No, she had not heard of the Popescus just because they happened to have a business in Chinatown. She didn't come from a sweatshop family. Her parents were skilled workers in the restaurant trade. The thought made her want to smile for the first time that day.

"Who the fuck are *they?*" Creaker demanded.

"Russian serial killers," Baum said with a straight face. "You never heard of them?"

"Fuck you, asshole."

"These guys are French. Get on with it." Iriarte was losing his patience.

"Popescu is not a French name. They must have just passed through," said Baum, happy being an asshole with legs and suddenly the self-appointed expert on passing through.

"Anton doesn't pay his parking tickets. And he's a speeder." Charlie gave Baum a dirty look. "Typical lawyer stuff."

"We need more on Anton. Where he went, who he hung with. Name of the girlfriend," April said. She was beginning to have her doubts about the girlfriend.

"That's your job," Charlie reminded her.

"All right. That's it. Check with the health department, see what you come up with on a birth certificate."

"You're not going to find that under his name," April told him. She had a feeling there was no birth certificate.

"It never hurts to check," Iriarte said. Everybody else filed out. He flapped his hand at April to stay, then gave her a little smile.

"Guess what, this guy Popescu wants to drop the whole thing." Iriarte shook his head. "Looks like he's gotten himself between a rock and a hard place on the adoption and wants out before it gets out of hand." He smiled cynically.

"What's your take?"

"This guy certainly has something to hide. Wife and a girlfriend. One baby between the two of them. Looks like the other woman has it. His wife in the hospital, beaten up. Let me tell you, the media would go nuts with this, so keep it to yourself."

"Has Popescu made an offer for some kind of resolution here?"

"Yeah, he says he won't sue us if we go away now. I told him that won't cut it. A baby's missing and a woman's assaulted. That's about as big as it gets for us, and we're not going away."

"I talked to Heather's mother in California last night. She had no idea the baby wasn't her daughter's."

Iriarte shook his head, looking impatient at all the lies. "Do you have any more thoughts about it?"

April did have another thought about it, but she didn't want to open a new can of worms to her boss just yet. What she hadn't verbalized, even to herself, was that the baby in the picture Anton had given them looked an awful lot like him and Heather Rose. Of course, she could be wrong. How much, after all, could one tell from the eyes of a three-week-old? She could easily put it down to just another creepy feeling. She wasn't seeing a white baby, she was seeing a Chinese baby with blue eyes. That didn't speak of an adoption from China, but of something closer to home. Oh, she didn't like this.

Iriarte changed the subject. "How you doing with Woody?"

"He'll be fine." April didn't want to say he could think but couldn't drive, so she didn't say anything.

"Oh yeah? That sounds tentative."

"He'll be fine," she assured him. "He's quick on his feet."

"Go find that baby." Iriarte flapped his hand.

"Yes, sir."

CHAPTER
16

Jason Frank was in front of his building at Riverside Drive and West Eightieth Street, studying his watch, at exactly two P.M. when the blue-and-white police cruiser pulled up at the curb. The police car took him by surprise.

"April?"

April leaned out the window on the passenger side. "Hi, Jason. Thanks for this—I know it's an imposition."

"No problem." Jason smiled at her. "You know I'd do anything for you."

"I appreciate it, really. This is Detective Baum. Dr. Frank." She introduced them.

"Hi." Jason leaned over and smiled at Baum, too.

The sandy-haired young man in the driver's seat raised his hand in acknowledgment.

"Well, get in, Jason. Let's go." April got serious fast.

Jason gave the car a doubtful look. "What's with the squad car?"

"The unmarked unit we usually take has a flat. You have a problem with it?" She gave him an amused look.

"Yeah, I have a problem. I don't want my colleagues and patients to see me driven away in a police car. It's bad for my image." He grinned as he said it, though, playing with her.

April grinned back. "Come on, don't make a political statement out of it, get in the car. We're in a hurry."

"All right, all right." Jason rolled his eyes and opened the car door. The outside was as clean as could be, but inside the car smelled as if the great unwashed had been living there for the entire millennium. Not only that, there was a thick wire screen between the front seat and the back. "What is this, your arrest car?"

"Yes." April turned around to talk through the screen. "Jason, I love you without the beard. When did you shave it off?"

Jason raised a hand to his chin, smooth for the first time in nearly a year. "This morning."

The car took off fast, throwing him against the backseat.

"Fasten your seat belt, it's the law," April ordered. Now she was playing with him.

"Whatever you say," he said, suddenly meek now that his life was at stake. "Where are we going?"

Woody sped down Riverside, hit the siren, and turned left onto West Seventy-second Street, plowing through oncoming traffic without slowing down. Jason had the uncomfortable feeling he was going to jail. No one relieved him of that apprehension.

He gasped when Woody braked suddenly. "Oh, God."

"Gee, I'm so glad to see you. It's been a while." April grinned some more again.

"Same here, I think. You look great, April." In fact, she looked gorgeous—radiant—in a red jacket, a navy skirt, and a white shirt with an oversized collar. In her ears were the jade studs she sometimes wore for good luck. His eye caught a chain around her neck.

"What's that?"

April reached to the middle of her chest for the medal hanging there. "Oh this? It's St. Sebastian. He's the patron saint of soldiers and policemen. Kind of like an evil eye, so I'm told." She said it deadpan.

"I didn't know you were a Catholic."

"I'm not." She smiled, shrugging.

"Boyfriend?"

April cocked her head in the direction of her driver. "Don't ask."

"Oh, I forgot how secretive you cops are. So what happened to Mike?" Jason couldn't help teasing, pretty sure the gift came from her old partner, Sanchez.

"He's in Homicide now." End of subject.

"Is Baum your new partner?"

"Jason, you're just full of questions, aren't you? We don't have partners in detective units. You know that. How's Emma?"

"Emma's great. She's taking a leave from the play, may or may not go back to it, depending." He grinned, didn't want to tell her why now. "So what's going on? What do you want from me?"

"I could have handled this myself if I had a few more days," she said airily. "But this is a right-now kind of thing. Sorry to haul you in on such short notice."

"Apology accepted. Now what's with the cloak-and-dagger?"

"Oh, God, will you look at that cutie?" April turned to admire a baby in a stroller stopped at a red light near them. Big fat cheeks, pink. Curls to die for. About twenty pounds, kicking feet in tiny red-white-and-blue sneakers. And a happy grin on her face that could conquer the world in a heartbeat.

"Adorable." Jason's eyes went all gooey.

"Jason, tell me about women who kill babies. And

I'm not talking about abortion here. I mean a full-term, three-week-old baby. Married woman, well-to-do, in her late twenties."

Jason clamped his jaws together to stop himself from showing his alarm at the way April always led him into things. He'd been through several investigations with her before, and each time whatever little problem she'd wanted his advice on had blossomed into a horror story that he couldn't wander out of. Baby killing! Nice of her to tell him.

"Someone with a character disorder," he said slowly.

"Does that mean a nutcase?"

"Someone who's insane? Not necessarily. A lot of high-functioning people have character disorders."

"Oh yeah? Maybe I know a few."

Jason smiled suddenly. "I'm sure you do."

"Okay—for Baum here, would you define the term?"

Jason went into teaching mode. "A lot of different kinds of symptoms fit under the umbrella of character disorder. Some people with character disorders relate to the world and other people only on the basis of how those 'others' make them feel. This kind of person loves whoever makes him feel good and feels angry at whoever makes him feel bad. Or her, as the case may be. Say you have a narcissistic mother with a new baby. If the baby cries and won't be comforted when the mother wants to console it, she might feel the baby was preventing her from feeling good about *herself.* She might think the baby was doing it purposely to hurt her. Narcissistic people have no conscience when it comes to hurting others. They are sometimes driven to punish people who they think are hurting them, to make the hurt stop." He paused for breath before going on.

"Another possibility might be a woman with a really extreme case of postpartum depression."

"Nope. Isn't her baby," April said flatly.

Jason groaned again. "It isn't her baby! Whose baby? Give me a break here, April."

She frowned at him through the wire. "What about revenge? Do you think a woman might kill a baby to get back at her husband who was cheating on her? I mean, if she was nuts."

Jason scratched the cheek where his beard used to be and wished he were back in his office where he didn't have to deal with baby killers. "Pretty extreme. Can you enlighten me a little further?"

"Did you listen to the news or read the paper this morning?"

"I heard something about a missing baby. Jesus, did you find—?" He couldn't bring himself to say the word "body."

"No, we don't have anything. We searched the building, the area. There's no evidence of an abductor. The woman who had the baby was beaten up. The baby is gone. In the emergency room we find out, it wasn't her baby."

Jason groaned a third time. "Why me, April?"

"You're my favorite shrink. Aren't you always telling me you have the best mind in the business?"

"That's a crock, and you know it. This isn't my field. I'm not forensic."

"No, but you're always telling me you're the best. So be the best."

"This is not my area. Can I refuse?" He knew he couldn't refuse.

"No."

He sighed and resigned himself. "Okay, so you're the detective, what scenario do you have in mind?"

"I have no scenario. It's not a clear picture. I was hoping for your input."

"What's the problem?"

"She may be a self-mutilator," April admitted.

"Hmmm." Jason raised his hand to scratch his beard again, remembered it was gone, and dropped the hand. "Is there a history?"

"She'd been hospitalized with injuries before."

"Has she been hospitalized for mental problems?"

"We're still checking into that."

"What does she say about what happened?"

"Er, we haven't questioned her too closely about it. We were hoping you could help."

"Who found her?"

"Her husband. He called the police."

"Do you think he would have called the police if his wife killed the baby, or if he assaulted her himself?"

"Yes, if he feared it would come out, he might want to be involved in the investigation. Sometimes they want to be the focus of the world's sympathy. Sometimes they just want to explain it away."

"There's something else you haven't told me, isn't there?"

They pulled up in front of Roosevelt Hospital. Baum stopped with a jerk, throwing Jason against the backseat again. "April, you didn't tell me she's in the hospital."

"Yeah, it's the first thing I said. I said, 'Jason, she may be feigning a coma.' "

"You never said it. And you can't feign a coma, April." Now Jason was really disgusted.

"She's Chinese. Let's go."

"What does that mean, she's Chinese?" Jason tried the door. It was locked.

"Woody." April reminded him to get the door. Woody got out, ran around and opened it.

Jason looked disgusted. He couldn't get out on his own. The door had a suspect-proof lock on the inside.

"April, didn't it occur to you that if the woman's unconscious, I'm not going to be able to help you?"

"You deal with the unconscious all the time," April said smoothly.

"*Unconscious* when the patient is *awake*," Jason said, suddenly feeling testy. "You're jerking me around, kiddo. I don't like that." Woody opened the door, but Jason didn't get out.

"Oh come on, unconscious is unconscious," April insisted. "You can do this, Jason. I told you I think she's feigning. She's not really out."

"April, you can't feign a coma," he said again, still not moving.

"Come and take a look at this. I know you can help. You always do."

"Oh shit." He got out of the car. He'd promised an hour. He'd give her an hour. "What's the baby's name?" he asked.

"Paul," she said. "His name is Paul."

CHAPTER
17

Jason looked through the window in Heather Rose's hospital room door before going in. Now he could see the reason for April's confusion. The patient showed some sign of movement. Two fingers moved back and forth across a small area of cotton blanket as if she were scolding or polishing it; and she almost seemed to be talking to herself. Apart from the moving hand, she was a bundle under the covers, an undefined shape, not very big. Jason's first thought was that Heather Rose was the size of a few standard pillows shoved together, not a fair sparring partner for a grown man.

The bed was cranked halfway up and the covers were pulled to her chin. Nothing of her could be seen but her face, which was a study of red and purpling bruises against the white sheets, the one arm that was outside the sheet, and her long, lush, inky-black hair. The way her thick and healthy hair fanned the pillow and framed her battered face was incongruous, shocking. The hair gave her a poignancy, an allure that seemed almost erotic even in the tragic circumstances and austere setting. It draped the pillow and looped over her shoulder, covering the curves of Heather Rose Popescu's chest almost to her waist. This surprised Jason, for hair so very long was an unusual feature for a woman living on the very edge of the twenty-first century. It was definitely a cultivated characteristic, like a huge mustache or a head shaved in patterns. It told Jason that Heather valued her tresses as one of her treasures, or that perhaps someone else, like her husband, valued a part of her that represented another time and place. In any case, the hair was a symbol, and like all symbols, had its profound meaning.

As Jason studied Heather Rose, the thick loop covering her left shoulder stirred just a little, like a snake shifting in the sun. It was as if her hair had an energy, a life of its own. Jason pushed the door open and went in.

"Hi, Heather, I'm Dr. Frank."

In the instant that the door opened and he spoke her body became still. No sound emanated from her. Her face was immobile in its swelling, and her uninjured half-closed eye showed no interest as he walked across the room, pulled up a chair, and sat close to the bed.

There were a thousand doctor things he could say and do: he could test her reflexes, talk to her, rub her hands, slap her wrists lightly.

Among all the possibilities, "Who's the president?" was what slipped out of his mouth first. It was something the doctors and nurses always said on rounds years ago when Jason had been an intern and a resident. It was what they said in emergency rooms and psychiatric hospitals. If a patient knew and could articulate the right answer, it meant he could hear, could understand, and was able to sort through the complicated circuitry of the brain and connect with reality.

Heather Rose did not tell him who was president, did not, in fact, respond to him in any clearly definable way; but he had not really thought she would. April had not been wrong about one thing, however. The woman on the bed seemed somehow to be present. He had the feeling that she had become watchful. Her two fingers stopped chastising the blanket. Now she seemed to be suspended on another level altogether, as if waiting for him to ask her the right question.

But Jason also knew it was not unusual for bedside visitors (even doctors and nurses) to have a wide range of feelings and beliefs about people who were unconscious. They seemed to be sleeping. They were sleeping, but sometimes they groaned, twitched, writhed, fought their tubes, and made other movements that could be interpreted as meaningful by those who desperately wanted evidence that their loved ones were still viable beings who could hear, could feel, and knew what was going on—and, most of all, that they could come back if only the open-sesame words, the correct stimuli, were supplied.

He said a few general things, then mentioned Heather's mother. April had told him Mrs. Kwan was coming from California. "Heather, you're not alone here. A lot of people are rooting for you. Your mom is on her way."

The hand with the IV in it twitched. Jason took it in both of his, examined the bitten cuticles and nails, turned it over and looked at the palm. Without realizing it, he had become like a cop. He was searching for some sign that she had resisted, had tried to fight off her attacker. Her nails were too short to be weapons, however. Her palm was soft and cool and the skin on it undisturbed. The arm above it told a different story.

"Look at these burn marks," he murmured, stroking her arm. "You've had a hard time. No one has to live this way. Come on back, Heather. Come on, talk to me. Your baby is out there."

Her eye flooded, but no tear spilled out. Interesting.

"No one can hurt you here. Not you, or anyone else. It's safe to wake up. If you wake up, we can protect you. We can help you get well. Whatever happened, we have to find the baby. He's a person. What happened to him can't be a mystery."

Jason squeezed her hand. It did not squeeze back. "Wake up now. It's over. You have to tell us about Paul. Heather, we need to find him. If someone took him, we need to know who and where he is. If something else happened to him, you can tell me. Please, wake up and tell me."

No sound, not a thing. He was having a solitary conversation, but he had the eerie feeling she was listening. He'd had that feeling with patients before. Sometimes he was right, and sometimes not. As a doctor he felt helpless more often than not. He wasn't being very doctorlike now. One look and he should have been out of there. Head case or not, baby killer or not, this was not for him. Still, he'd offer her the choice.

"I know you're coming up from a deep place. I know you want to come back. Come on, now's your chance to tell your side."

He squeezed her hand again. "Does your husband have Paul? Did he get mad and hit you? Is that what happened?"

Now a sound. Like a hiccup, a cough, a groan. Jason squeezed the hand. Still no pressure back.

"Here's your choice. There's the police, there's me, or there's your mom. Every minute you wait, everybody worries more about Paul. Give me a sign. If he's alive, squeeze my hand."

Nothing.

"Heather, I have to go now. I'll try to come back to see you later tonight." It was then he felt the fingers of Heather's hand tighten and release. Startled, he blinked. When he saw no change in her face and body, he wondered if he'd imagined it. In any case, he knew he'd have to come back.

CHAPTER
18

"Well?" April demanded when Jason came out of Heather's room.

He shook his head. "April, you know better than this."

"She's coming out, though, isn't she? Come on, Jason, don't hold out on me. This woman threatened my life two hours ago."

"What are you talking about, she threatened your life?"

"Well, predicted my death."

"That's pretty dramatic. What did she say?"

"Jason, I know she's not in a vegetative state," April insisted.

"People often attribute consciousness to people who are out of it." He gave her a sympathetic pat.

"Don't patronize me. I know what I'm talking about."

Jason sighed. "You always get me in trouble."

"And you always get me out of it. Please, pretty please? I have to nail down whether this baby is dead or alive. Come on. It's a police investigation."

"She didn't tell me what you want to know." Jason checked his watch, then started down the hall. "I have a patient waiting for me."

"Did she tell you anything?"

"No."

April scurried after him. "All right, maybe not this time, but she's not totally out of it, right?"

Jason blew air through his nose. "I'm not making a judgment call on this."

"But you'll try again later, right? Please, don't make me beg. A life is on the line here."

"Yeah, yeah, I'll come back later. Just take me home now. And don't come for me next time. I can get around on my own." They were downstairs, and Jason was looking at Baum as he spoke. April knew what he meant.

After they returned Jason to his apartment, she decided to have a little talk with Woody. They had been heading uptown, and she tapped her finger on the dashboard, checking for trouble and trying not to think about Heather in the hospital. The shrubs and fruit trees here were in pink-and-yellow bloom and the parks were alive with activity: babies in their strollers, dogs, people sunning themselves, running around. She didn't see any trouble on the street or in the parks.

"What did you think of Dr. Frank?" she asked Woody.

"Great guy. I liked him. Where to?"

"Fifth Precinct, Elizabeth Street."

"I know where it is." Woody made a sudden U-turn. He didn't hit the hammer as a warning when he was about to execute the change of direction, just dodged between oncoming cars. April inhaled sharply at a near miss.

"Woody, about your driving . . ." she said when her pulse slowed.

"Yes, ma'am." One arm hooked out the window, the man was now driving with one finger.

"What was your last unit?"

"I was in Anticrime." He accelerated, racing downtown as if he were in a car chase with a bad guy who'd just shot someone in a mugging gone wrong.

"I guess you did a lot of cowboys-and-Indians in that job," she mused.

"We had some fun," Baum admitted, slamming on the brakes at a red light.

April didn't doubt it. The boys (and the few girls) in Anticrime units dressed way down. They had unusual haircuts, tattoos, rings in their ears—whatever accessories they felt they needed to fit in with the scum they surveilled. Anticrime drove around in fast, battered, or flashy cars to appear badder than bad. Some never saw the light of day. Others looked like Con Ed workers. One Anticrime officer in a downtown unit drove a UPS truck. Another dressed like a pimp and drove a T-bird. Getting into trouble was what they lived for.

"I'll bet you liked the action," she said.

He gave her a sheepish grin. "It was fun for a while." Then he got silent.

"Yeah?" she prompted. "How long is a while?"

"Couple of years."

"You were on foot patrol before that?"

"Yes, ma'am. One-Nine."

That was the Upper East Side. Park Avenue. Madison Avenue. Lexington Avenue. Foreign consulates. Fancy restaurants, shops, and deluxe co-op apartment buildings. "Nice quality-of-life neighborhood," she commented.

"Yeah." He rubbed at his short sandy hair. That, apparently, was all he intended to say on the subject. April figured there was an incident in his past he didn't want her to know about. She made a note to check it out when things quieted down.

So the haircut was something new for the new job. Probably so were the button-down shirt, the pricey blazer, and the loafers. The pistol in the ankle holster was no doubt an old habit. Like the driving.

"So you want to be a detective," she said.

"Yes, ma'am."

"In that case you've got to do more than cut your hair and change your clothes, know what I mean?"

"Does it show that much?"

She shrugged. Out on the street cops had to process people and their body language in a special way, work on adrenaline and instinct. "Running on raw nerve and reflex is fine for the streets. Hey, slow down!"

"Sorry."

"No, I mean it. You've got to put that testosterone on hold. You can't live to scare people in this job."

"You don't like my driving?"

"In this job a lot of the time you're working with a different class of people."

"Is this about my driving?"

"I want to live to enjoy my next day off, so that's a yes," she confirmed.

"I've never had an accident off the job," he said earnestly.

"Well, how about improving your record and never having an accident *on* the job? If you hit somebody or scare one of my most important sources to death, it's on my head. Understand?"

"Oh, so the *shrink* didn't like my driving. He complain?"

"Nothing more than changing color a few times." She braced herself against the dashboard as Woody turned east without slowing down. This guy was going to be hard to train.

"Listen, about the case. Whatever you hear while you're on the job with me, you keep to yourself, understand?"

"Fine with me." Baum sped up through a yellow light.

Apparently he'd decided against the West Side

Drive, preferring to try to break the sound barrier going downtown on Seventh Avenue.

April had kept the snapshot of Paul Popescu with her. Now she took it out of her pocket and stared at it for a while, wondering again who and where he was.

CHAPTER
19

By 3:43 P.M., the temperature had gone up to a warm seventy-four degrees, but April felt cold shivers of apprehension as the car passed through the small area of Little Italy that hadn't yet been swallowed up by Chinatown. It slowed, then halted altogether in the traffic on Canal Street. At this hour the scene in Chinatown was wild, with kids out of school, merchandise blocking the sidewalk, residents shopping for dinner, tourists gawking. Life in Chinatown was a continual tide of humanity washing in, washing out. For many people, the neighborhood was only a port of entry, the hub where connections and arrangements could be made. It was a place crowded with a thousand dreams and schemes for every desperate newcomer. For tourists, simple hunger—delicious food for the belly—was an easier need to meet.

Baum parked the car half up on the curb, blocking a fire hydrant. He was going to get hassled for it, but April decided she wasn't going to play mother. He knew better, and when he got nailed it would be his problem. She got out of the car and was instantly assaulted by the smell of Chinatown and her past. Suddenly she was in her element, a fish in water.

The whole of her life was in her nose as she turned down Elizabeth. The complex mixture of odors brought

memories flooding back. She could feel her temples
smart from pigtails pulled too tight. Also the misery
of loving boys who hadn't loved her back; her cold,
cold face and feet from walking the home beat of the
O-Five late at night that first year after eighteen scary
months in Bed-Stuy.

April hurried down the block, past parked police
scooters and three-wheeled vehicles. She felt as if
she'd been away for years and years, and at the same
time it seemed only a few minutes had passed since
the last time she'd rushed down this street to work.
Today, she didn't see anybody she knew from the old
days passing by or standing in doorways, and that
made her sad. At the precinct, several uniforms, wrestling new-issue bicycles through the narrow entryway,
stopped to hold the door for her. And then the smell
of roasting duck and pork, frying dough, garlic, rotting
fish guts, and vegetable matter was replaced by the
dusty air of the precinct where she'd spent five good
years.

"Hey, look who the cat dragged in. April Woo, as
I live and breathe. What's a big shot like you doing
down here?" Lieutenant Rott was on the desk. He'd
been on the desk April's last day in the house, probably hadn't been home to New Jersey since. His hair
was grayer and his pink face was rounder, and he still
looked mean and big, and pretty high up at the raised
front desk, even though his squirrel eyes were trying
hard to be friendly.

"Hello, Lieutenant. How's it going?" April was a
sergeant now, so she put some warmth into her own
smile.

"Not too bad. You're looking good. Now we have
to read about you in the papers. That's how it goes,
you move uptown, make sergeant, and forget all your
old friends." He shrugged big shoulders in the blue
uniform.

"No, I haven't forgotten *you*, Lieutenant. You're always in my thoughts. This is Detective Baum. He's in the Midtown North squad with me."

Woody raised a hand. "How ya doin'?"

Rott fielded a phone call. "So, how can we help you?" he asked them when he slammed down the receiver.

April had never heard those words from the lieutenant before. Help? She was stunned. "Is Alfie still running things upstairs?"

"Yeah, he's still here. But we have a new CO since your time."

April nodded. Inspector Samuel Chew. She'd never met him. At one time she'd hoped he would somehow hear of her, show an interest in her, and bring her back home. In those days, she hadn't known how to get his attention, however, so it hadn't happened. Probably a good thing, as it turned out.

"You want to meet him? He's in there." Rott pointed across the linoleum of the lobby. April realized that she could now meet anybody she wanted. She turned her head. The door was closed.

"Maybe later. I want to see Alfie first; is he in?"

"Yeah, I think so. Want me to let him know you're coming?"

She shook her head. "I want to surprise him."

"Good to meet you, Baum," Rott said magnanimously.

"Likewise," Baum replied. Like almost everybody in a new position, Woody was having a great time standing around and only getting to speak when spoken to.

April went ahead of him down the hall to the center of the building. She could see there'd been a few changes at the 5th. Over several years in the previous administration, the crumbling Elizabeth Street landmark with its steep staircases had been poorly renovated at extortionate cost to the city. Now the quaint building, which harked back to the long-gone New York of Teddy Roosevelt, seemed to be in the midst of a second restoration, probably to fix the botched and unfinished repairs of the first. As April climbed the steps, she admired the work done on the magnificent banister and wondered if they'd gotten around to doing the women's room yet.

The real changes to the house, however, were not cosmetic. The commander's office, previously upstairs, was now just inside the precinct front door. When April got to the top of the stairs and headed back down the hall to the front of the building, she got a bigger surprise. The detectives had always had a big, airy room fronting on the street. But now a glassed-in enclosure was planted just inside the door. With the CO watching the front door downstairs and Lieutenant Alfredo Bernardino on watch over the detectives, it looked as if the O-Five had become a precinct on the lookout for trouble from within.

At the moment, the said Bernardino was in his glass office with his back to the door. Like a plant grown out of shape from straining toward an elusive ray of sunlight, the lieutenant was swiveled around in his chair as if striving to return to his previous place at the window, just above the precinct's entrance, where he could see everything going on in the street.

When April knocked on the glass, he swiveled back. His face was dominated by a huge nose that had been broken more than once, and his tough, wrinkled hide was generously pocked with the scars of teenage acne. As he swung around, his shrewd brown eyes were challenging and cold in their pouchy sockets. They lit up when he saw who was seeking him. April took in the aging ruin in the wrinkled gray shirt and wrinkled pink tie as if she'd never seen him before. His crude visage was still double-ugly, a face only a mother could

love. His stained brown leather jacket still hung on
the back of his chair as it did in almost every season;
a shoulder holster housed a .38 he'd only shot in action once, and a cigarette he would never light hung
out of his mouth. April realized with a jolt that Alfie,
a man nearly twice her age and ugly as sin, who'd
given her a start as a detective, who'd sparred with
her and taught her how to think—the irritable old soul
whom the people of Chinatown trusted and thought
had more than a few lives behind him—was the model
for Mike Sanchez, the handsome young man she
loved.

"April, *cara,* howya doin', sweetheart?" he exclaimed. His lean cheeks creased with pleasure and
his skinny hand reached out to take hers.

There it was, the "*cara,*" "*querida,*" "sweetheart"
bit. A surprised laugh escaped her lips. She wondered
if they'd all still be calling her sweetheart when she
made captain. She shook his hand.

"Alfie. Look at this, they got you in a box now?"
She went over and rapped on the glass. "This thing
bulletproof?"

"Nah, we don't go in for that sissy stuff. Who's the
friend? Come on in."

"Detective Baum—Woody."

"Woody Tree, that's a new one."

"Oh, you know Jewish," Woody said.

Alfie snorted. "Sure I know Jewish, Italian, Chinese,
Puerto Rican, Dominican—Fujian, Fijian, you name
it, I know it." He moved a few chairs around. "Come
in, sit, sit."

April took a chair that faced the desks and empty
holding cell. The desk that had been hers was also
unoccupied at the moment, but the shift changed in a
few minutes. Someone would come in and she'd see
who sat there now. Again she was flooded with memories of a life more simple than the one she had now.

The ghosts of all those shadowy longings she used to have for things she'd known nothing about now hovered in the air over her head, as the ghosts that she didn't believe in always did. The things she'd wanted so much had come to her at the price of her peace of mind and her innocence. She found herself almost overwhelmed with nostalgia for the time when she'd had no responsibility for the people below her and few choices about how to handle anything.

"Hey, it's great to see you, April. You made good, huh?"

Her chin dipped in a modest curtsy, acknowledging the compliment. It wasn't always easy to know what to do when people suddenly got nice. "How's Lorna, the kids?"

"Lorna's still Lorna, older. Kathy's an FBI agent. Bill's in law school."

"Looks like they got through college, after all. Congratulations."

"Could be worse," he said proudly. "What brings you down here? Still want my job, cutie?"

"Nah, you can keep it now. I have my own." April glanced at Woody with a smile. He was listening, probably thinking about taking *her* job.

"So what's up?" Alfie's eyes got shrewd again. "You won't believe this—an old friend of yours, remember Nanci Hua? She came in asking about you, oh not even an hour ago. Funny how things happen."

"Nanci? No kidding. What did she want?"

"She wouldn't say. She looked upset. She wanted you. I gave her your number."

"She still in the same place?"

He shoveled through the mess on his desk. "Uh-uh, out in Garden City. I have the number here somewhere, but I never thought I'd be seeing you. To what do I owe the pleasure?"

Alfie nodded at some people April had never seen

before, coming in for the afternoon tour, staring at the visitors with frank curiosity.

"Oh, just curious if you've heard anything about black-market babies," April asked.

"Black-market babies?" Alfie scratched his head as if she'd gone loony from working uptown too long. "From down here?"

April shrugged expectantly.

"We had a girl die last year of a botched abortion. Her family didn't want to risk taking her to the hospital, so she bled to death. We get a few of those." He was thoughtful. "Then there was the girl a few months ago. Only twelve. They found her in the water under the Brooklyn Bridge, but she was dead before she went in. Thank God the case wasn't ours." He shook his head, then tried out the words again. "Blackmarket babies. That's a new one on me. But you know how it is down here. What are you working on?"

"I caught the Popescu case."

"Yeah. I heard about that. I thought the story was the mother offed it." Alfie gave her a sharp look, waiting for enlightenment, just like the old days.

"Could be. Could also be something else. Keep this under your hat, will you? Turns out it wasn't her baby. So it's a mystery. You know how I hate mysteries."

Alfie frowned. "Couldn't it be a friend's baby? An adoption. How about from China, that play for you?"

"I don't know; the husband isn't forthcoming with papers. If the baby came in legally, there would have to be immigration papers. We got zip. That makes me think dirty thoughts."

"What's the mother say?"

"She's not exactly cooperating. She was hit on the head. She thinks she's an insect. But she might always have thought she was an insect." April shook her head. "And she might be out of it. It's complicated."

"You think she might have killed the baby?"

"If she did, she got rid of the body very efficiently. We haven't found anything."

"So what do you want from me?"

"You know everything that's going on down here, Alfie. I want you to put out a BOLO on a blue Perego stroller. Woody here checked the price of those for me. They cost a bundle. Not many people down here can afford an item like that."

"Any particular reason?"

"None at all. Call it wishful thinking."

Woody cut in. "What do you know about the Popescu brothers?"

April didn't cut him, but Alfie looked over at him as if *he* were an insect. "Noise," he said.

"Noise?" April echoed.

"Yeah, the Popescus are two big letter writers. Everything's a problem with them. Their latest beef is boom boxes. One of them threatened to get a gun and shoot the next asshole who pollutes the space in front of his building. Lot of people have been asking about them. How many people you got on this case?"

April lifted a shoulder. "Too many. What did you tell them?"

"You know me, I'm always helpful. I'll tell you the same thing. In the past we've had a lot of complaints about those guys. Anonymous, of course, and not from the Chinese. They used to have some Latinas in the factory, and there were some incidents then. No formal charges were ever made, though. They switched to Chinese workers years ago. They own the building, and the complaints these days all come from them. Noise, traffic, garbage pickup, stolen radio from one of their vans. They want a yellow line painted on the curb so no one else can park in front of their building. Every month there's something new." He took the unlit cigarette out of his mouth and threw it away. "Filthy habit."

"You been in there to see what they're so defensive about?"

Alfie pursed his lips. "They're a pain in the ass. I like to keep out of their way."

"Maybe that's what they want you to do," April said. "How about I go over and have a talk with them?"

He shot her a dark look. "I know them, I'll take a look." His interest was piqued.

April wanted to take care of this herself, but didn't want to offend her old boss. Suddenly, outside the glass house, she saw a Chinese male, a guy who looked older than she, sit down at her former desk. For a moment she was distracted. Then she said, "I don't want to put you out."

"Put me out. I'd love a walk."

"Fine, I'll go with you."

"Sure, cutie, anything you say." Alfie reached in his drawer for another cigarette he'd put in his mouth and wouldn't light.

She took a last look at the Chinese who'd taken her desk and wondered if he was smart. Then she nodded at Woody. "Make some friends, I'll be back in a while," she told him.

CHAPTER
20

Ivan and Marc Popescu were arguing and picking boiled beef and cabbage out of their teeth as they opened the door to their building after a late lunch. They found Lieutenant Alfredo Bernardino and a Chinese woman who looked like she might be from INS leaning against the closed door of their downstairs office talking with Annie Lee. Ivan pulled the toothpick out of his mouth and dropped it on the ground behind him. He gave his cousin a shove, but Marc was used to it and didn't respond.

"Come on in, Sergeant. Whatcha doing out here?" He was all smiles for the lieutenant, clapped him on the shoulder as if they were old buddies. "You here about the son of a bitch that stole my car radio?"

"Sure. He's sorry and brought it back when he found out it was yours."

"Ha, ha, I had no idea you were a funny man. Who's the pretty lady?" Marc opened the office door. Inside, the air-conditioning was on, and the room was nice and cool. When he flipped on the fluorescent lights, the old-fashioned office jumped into focus.

"What are you doing down here, Annie?" Ivan turned around to give the supervisor a tongue-lashing. "Didn't I tell you—?"

"Someone come—"

"Yeah, who come? I'll dock you a month's pay if you let people come in here."

Marc patted his cousin on the back, giving his shoulder a quick, calming massage. Ivan puffed out his stomach, straining the front of his silver warm-up jacket and looking hurt by the correction.

"This is Sergeant April Woo. Marc Popescu. Ivan Popescu."

April nodded.

Scowling, Ivan followed them inside. The front of the room boasted a cracked leather sofa and wooden office furniture from the year one. On the coffee table were a dying plant with a pink ribbon on it left over from Easter, and some recent fashion magazines. Behind it stood two messy rolltop desks covered with papers. Marc invited the detectives to sit down on the sofa. For a second the lights flickered, and Bernardino looked interested.

"To what do we owe the honor?" Marc asked the cop.

Bernardino continued to survey the room without sitting down.

"You won't light that up, will you? We have a no-smoking rule here," Ivan said.

"Oh yeah, this." Bernardino touched the end of the cigarette dangling from his top lip. "This is just for show. Fools me into thinking something's happening that isn't really happening, know what I mean?"

"Oh come on, don't start up. You know we're strictly legal here. Anyway, you guys aren't interested in our plumbing woes, or whether our girls have green cards. That's not your department." Marc's forehead furrowed as he looked over at the Chinese woman who hadn't spoken yet. The last thing he needed was someone nosing around the place.

"I thought you'd like to know we keep an eye on things around here." The cop kept looking around.

"Suit yourself, keep an eye on things. You know we're strictly on the up-and-up here."

"One of our Conditions boys noticed some wires hanging out the window upstairs. He wondered if the place was a hot spot. I said naahh, not my Popescu friends."

Marc gave Ivan a puzzled look. Conditions, what the hell was that? He could understand the two other detectives from downtown calling on them earlier to ask a whole lot of questions about Anton and his background, his associations, and his baby. That had been unnerving enough. But what was this Conditions thing about? "What kind of hot spot?" he asked.

"Oh, you know. With the mayor's new drug initiative, we have to check everything out."

Marc put his hand on Ivan's arm, but it didn't stop Ivan from exploding. "Are you nuts? What do you think, that we're growing weed up there?"

The cop shrugged. "Yeah, could be for lights. Could be you're converted into a happy dreams factory these days, cooking with gas up there. Could be unauthorized phone lines for drug buys. Could be a lot of things. I'd like to take a look."

Marc took it as a joke and laughed. "Could be we're a sewing factory and we run sewing machines. Listen to that rumble." He pointed upstairs. "Sewing machines."

"You're outta your mind. Get outta here before I punch out your lights." Ivan's face flushed as he took a boxer's stance in front of the detective. "Nothing here is your fucking business."

Marc was shocked. "Jesus! Relax, brother. He's just putting us on." He chortled. Good joke, a drug factory right down here on the Lower East Side, where everybody knew everybody's business inside out, sure.

"I'm not your brother, asshole." Even though he was wearing an expensive warm-up suit like an athlete, Ivan wasn't fit. He wasn't young, either. He looked

like a character trying to be a bad guy in a movie.
"Okay, you visited. You asked about the wires. Now
get outta here," he told the detective.

Marc cringed. Bernardino wasn't going to do what
Ivan wanted and leave when he was spoken to like
that.

"Well, let's just take a little look upstairs and in the
basement," the detective said easily.

"No way! Get a warrant if you suspect something."

Once again Marc closed in on him and put his hand
on Ivan's shoulder. "I'll take care of this. You need
to calm down."

"Don't tell me what I need to do. Don't you see
what this guy's doing?" He looked at the female, who
still hadn't said a word.

"You need to calm down," Marc snapped. "Cut it
out, are you crazy?"

"I swear I'll kill you if—"

"Who are you threatening to kill?" Now Bernardino was really interested.

Marc attempted humor: "It's just his digestion. He's
always like this after lunch. Come on, Sergeant, I'll
take you anywhere you want to go. You're welcome
to our rats. Maybe you can put in a good word to the
city about them."

"It's Lieutenant."

"Really? Congratulations, is that a new title?" Marc
jumped ahead of him to open the office door.

"Nope, it's been Lieutenant for a good fifteen
years now."

"Gee." Marc closed the door and led the way up
the stairs. "Now, tell me what can I do for you."

"You have any idea about those wires?"

"Uh-uh. You'll have to show them to me." Marc
opened the upstairs door. Only five of the sewing machines were going. Steam burst from the iron in short

blasts, but no one was pressing finished trousers. The heads bent over work were white and gray.

Annie was admonishing an older woman to work faster. Bernardino's teeth closed around the filter tip on his cigarette. Tobacco dropped on the floor. "Oops." He bent over to pick it up. Marc stiffened.

"You want to see the roof?" he asked. "The storage room?"

Bernardino sniffed. "Yeah, and tell me about your brother."

"What?" Marc was shocked. "Are you local cops in on this witch-hunt, too?"

"We're looking for a missing baby." The female spoke for the first time.

"Yeah, this is bad news." Suddenly, Marc realized Annie was listening. "Let's go for a walk, huh? It's hot in here."

"Yeah, you ought to get someone to turn that iron off when it's not in use." The female climbed the stairs to the storeroom, looked around, apparently didn't see what she was looking for, came back down.

"These girls don't have any respect for anything." Marc and the lieutenant both knew that the sewing machines and the steam presser had been abandoned by the girls who were working without green cards the minute the cops appeared at the door.

"Come on, Lieutenant, let's get away from my cantankerous relative. He doesn't always know the score, know what I mean? How about a walk? I'll tell you everything I know." Marc got the two cops outside without further trouble. They were heading north in the sunshine when the female hit him with a question he wasn't expecting.

"Did your brother always beat up women?"

"Oh, shit. Oh, come on. This is getting personal. Your friend here knows us. He knows better than to bug me about rumors involving my family. It's not true. My brother would never touch his wife, so don't follow that path with the rest of the scum." He shuffled his feet, kicking an empty soda can along the sidewalk.

"You don't look too happy with that line," she said.

"What's your name again?" he demanded.

"Sergeant Woo."

"Well, Sergeant Woo, I know my brother, and I'm telling you, he might get mad, but he'd never touch Heather. He adores her, same as I do and all the rest of the family."

"That's not what I hear. I hear he beats the shit out of her all the time."

"It's not true," Marc said gloomily. "I'll never believe that of him. Never!"

"So what about the baby?"

"I don't know nothing about that. This whole thing makes me sick."

"It's making a lot of people sick. Heather Popescu didn't give birth to a baby, so whose is it?"

"What are you talking about? Of course she did," Marc said vehemently.

"You know, the phone records show you guys are on the horn to each other every day. If you know your brother so well, and he claims he's the baby's father, then who's the baby's mother and where is she?"

"Whoa. Stop right there. Where are you going with this?" He stared at the Chinese sergeant. This was making him really angry.

"The Health Department doesn't have any record of any Popescu birth, and Anton says he's the father, so who's the mother?"

Marc whistled to cover his rage. "Don't look at me. This is new to me. I don't know nothing about it. Honestly, this is way out there." He whistled again. "That's what he said? He said he's the father?"

"That's what he said."

"Wow."

Bernardino cut in on the questions. "How come Anton isn't in the business with you?" he asked suddenly.

"He's a lawyer, he makes more than I do," Marc said sharply.

"No kidding."

"Yeah. Every family has to have one professional. In our family it was Anton. It was never in the plan for him to go into the business."

"Did he want to be in the business?"

They'd been walking slowly, but now Marc stopped. "I said it wasn't in the plan. He was the lucky one. He's uptown in a fancy office, eating caviar. We're down here in the slums, eating deli and working our asses off. What does this have to do with the price of tea?" He looked away, knew he was losing it. All this family crap was painful. He didn't want to talk anymore about it. He turned around to go back.

Bernardino shrugged and followed suit. "You tell me. I'm looking for a missing baby. This missing baby we're looking for doesn't seem to have a birth certificate. That means we don't know whose it is. So we're going to keep digging until we find out."

Marc made a rude noise. "I'm sure this can be cleared up."

"So, clear it up for us."

"Look, I'm not in the loop. I don't know any more than you do. I can ask, that's all I can do. The minute I hear something you'll be the first to know. Okay?" Marc didn't want to leave Ivan alone too long. He picked up his pace, eager to get back.

"Yeah, do that. Hey, and the next time you tell the girls to get out, you might remind them to take their garments out of the machines before they go."

"Oh come on. You didn't see anything up there. You know we're on the up-and-up with the labor."

"INS will be interested."

They came to a red light. Marc walked into the street anyway. "I *said* I'd ask around. But now I'll tell *you* something. These girls are pregnant, they're not sentimental. They get abortions. If they don't get abortions, they keep the kids. I know these people. They'd rather drown an infant like a kitten than give it away."

"Who said anything about giving away? I'm talking selling away. But whatever you're looking at—killing, selling—they're both against the law. Maybe you better think about having that baby turn up, huh?"

Marc tripped on the curb on the far side of the street. The lieutenant grabbed his arm to keep him from falling on his face. He made another of Ivan's noises. His fuse was slower, but he was sputtering now, trying to contain his fury and hang on to himself. He hated letting go the way everyone else in his family did. His brother and his cousin were the volatile ones. He'd always been the mediator, the gentleman. He wanted to keep it that way.

"I'll see you later," the cop said as he walked away.

CHAPTER
21

At nine P.M. on Wednesday Mike Sanchez closed the file on the castrated corpse he'd studied in the ME's office for the third time a few hours ago. Only a week ago Schlomo Abraham had been living in Israel with his wife and three children. By the wife's account, they'd been living a perfectly happy life. Their perfectly happy life had ended during a routine business trip to New York, when he was stabbed several dozen times in the chest and abdomen, presumably for the diamonds and cash he was carrying. This was a bad thing for this family, a bad thing for the Israeli Trade Consulate, and a bad thing for the city of New York.

Schlomo's tearful partner, Mickla, another Israeli, had told Mike that Schlomo always got himself a girl and suggested Mike look for prostitutes who worked the hotel. Today Mike had done just that, located the last person to see the victim alive. It was someone who worked the hotel on a regular basis, a hooker who called herself Helena. Turned out she was a guy. Real name Roberto Portero, always dressed like a girl, managed to stay out of trouble, had no priors—which was unusual because some customers got real upset if they found out they'd gotten a flavor they hadn't ordered. Some guys had simple tastes, though, and never

found out. Mike didn't know about Schlomo yet. He
shook his head, thinking about it. He always got the
queers. He'd talked to the he/she for three hours, trying to ascertain if the guy was their suspect. Helena
was really spooked, crying half the time, and all that
Mike had found out so far was his taste in clothes and
designer drugs. This particular boy-girl was clueless
about anything else, a real ditz. Afterward Mike had
gone back to the ME's office to try communing with
the body. Not everybody did this kind of thing. But a
couple of points kept bothering him: the wife's insisting everything was fine in the marriage, and the
fact that it took more than a ditz to slice a guy's dick
and balls off. After looking at the body again and
coming up with no new ideas, he'd gotten a message
that April wanted to see him and had gone home to
meet her at his place.

In the old days, before he'd fallen in love, Mike
would not have taken a break from a major case to
see a *chica*. He would have stayed with Roberto/
Helena and seen the *chica* later, if the timing worked
out. But here he was, waiting for half an hour in his
apartment before the doorbell finally rang. When he
opened the door, April was bedraggled and dripping
in the hall.

"I couldn't find a place to park. All the spots were
taken—Oh."

His embrace finished her sentence. He hadn't noticed it had started to rain, but rain always turned him
on, reminded him of all those times he and April had
been stuck in a car during radio runs and she wouldn't
let him touch her. At the moment she was cold and
wet. He figured he had to warm her up, so the kiss
took a while. She resisted for about a second, then
dropped her bag and her jacket on the floor and let
herself be swept away by it.

Her reactions always surprised him. They'd been in

some difficult situations, had their clothes burned off, witnessed autopsies of men and women in various states of decay. They'd seen violence, deviance, and death and had brought in nutcases exposing themselves, masturbating on the street. April herself had restrained a drunken security guard who'd shoved the barrel of his loaded pistol up his girlfriend's vagina. He was threatening to pull the trigger when April came in to deal with the situation. She'd also been the one to locate the severed head of a twelve-year-old who'd been decapitated in a five-car crash on the Henry Hudson Parkway. The girl might have lived if she'd been wearing her seat belt. Instead, her head landed in the woods, sixty feet away, and April had found it. Yet, after all that, she balked at leaving the lights on when they made love; she didn't want her mother or any Chinese ghosts to know what she was up to.

"Chinese are kind of puritanical about sex," she'd explained their first time together. "No one in my family ever mentions it. It's something you do only to get a doctor to marry you." She didn't elaborate.

It had been a big step to get her into the shower with him. But then, everything was a big step with her. She might have seen just about every horror imaginable on the job, but she'd been bullied and sheltered by her parents and hadn't experienced much pleasure. He liked opening her eyes to it, seeing her amazement.

Right now, she wasn't in the mood for fun, though. She stepped out of his embrace and shook her head. "I'm sorry, I'm having a bad day. I just needed a break."

He went to get her a towel. "I didn't mean to rush you," he said a little sheepishly when he came back.

"No problem." She toweled her head, then raked

her fingers through her damp hair. "Actually, I came because I wanted to talk to you."

"That's nice. Have a seat. What's on your mind?" He cleared his case file from the sofa, sat, and patted the cushion beside him.

"I don't know. Maybe I got used to you as a partner. And I don't like this new thing." She didn't want to sit down.

"Come on, sit down. I won't bite. What new thing?"

She lifted her shoulders. "You know."

"You mean *amor, querida*? You're having a little trouble with *amor*?"

"I'm not in love." She flushed as she said it, though.

"Okay, you're not in love. What's the problem, then?"

April sat down as far from Mike as she could get. "This case is really bugging me. Mixed marriage; *she's* battered and loony. The baby's missing. *He's* lying about everything. The family is weird and has this sweatshop in Chinatown that's mixed up in it somehow. His cousin is a maniac and, you know, the bottom line is I think the baby is dead. I really think so." Her eyes teared up.

"Oh, *querida*." He moved over and put his arms around her.

"It shakes me up. I never even wanted a baby myself, did I ever tell you that?" She said this into his shoulder.

"No, you never mentioned babies one way or the other."

She pulled away to look at him. "And now I'm seeing them everywhere. It just feels so bad. They're great, you know, really cute, like puppies." She shook her head again.

"You're so maternal." Mike laughed. "Nah, babies are better than puppies."

"Why would anyone kill a puppy?"

"It's not a puppy, *querida*. And it hasn't even been forty-eight hours. You may find him yet."

"I don't want to just find him. I want to find him alive." April rooted around in her bag for the photo of Paul. She found it and held it out to him.

Mike took the snapshot and studied the baby for a while. It was a pretty generic-looking baby, wrapped in a blue blanket. "He has blue eyes," he said finally.

"Anything else?"

"It's a cute little guy, what else is there?"

"Anything about the eyes?"

"You said it wasn't her baby."

"That doesn't mean it isn't a Chinese baby. The factory is in Chinatown. It's not nice, Mike. The baby could be one of those Little Italy-Chinatown mixes. Maybe somebody sold him to them. Could be something worse."

"Oh." Mike was silent for a while, thinking about what could be worse.

"You know what I have to do now?" she said.

"You have to hit every hospital in the metropolitan area looking for white-Chinese combination babies."

"Tristate area. The whole world, if I have to. Mike, I don't think I believe in mixed." That's what she'd come to tell him. She flushed some more.

"Mixed marriages, mixed love affairs, mixed drinks, what?" Suddenly he was angry.

"You know what I mean," she said softly.

"I know that's the prejudice that keeps all the wars going," he said evenly. "But sometimes you don't choose who you're going to fall for." He gave her a look to calm her down, but she wasn't buying.

"Don't give me that. It's not prejudice. I lost a friend. I lost my parents, everything," she cried.

"What are you talking about, you lost your parents? Are you nuts?"

"My mother's giving me the silent treatment. I went

home, no one's there. I call, no one answers the phone. Ever had your mother boycott you?" she asked.

"No, mine wouldn't know how. What's her beef?"

"You are." April put her hand to her mouth and closed her eyes. "I can't take it."

Mike sat up. He'd never seen that expression on her face before. "You going to cave for your freaking parents? That's *loco*!"

"I'm not making this up, Mike. She's wiping me out."

"Nah, she wouldn't do that."

"Yes, she would. She'd cut off her only daughter for face."

Face! You couldn't fight Chinese and their crazy concept of face. Mike chewed nervously on his mustache. "*Querida,* give me a hug. I'll help you with this. You want something to drink? Huh, how about a beer? You want to eat something? How about dinner?"

She shook her head again. "Sorry to throw off your sex schedule."

"Oh, don't do that." What was this? What was in her head here? Suddenly he needed a beer. He got up a little self-consciously and padded into the kitchen. In the refrigerator, he found a six-pack of Dos Equis. He came back with the tops popped on two and handed her one. She put hers on the floor without taking even a sip.

Mike swallowed some beer. "You want me to talk to your parents?"

"What can you tell them, that your intentions of ruining their precious Han daughter are honorable?"

"I could tell them we love each other and want to get married sometime within the millennium." Mike handed her back the baby picture.

"That's dishonorable. It would bring on World War Three."

"You told me World War Three has already started."

"It has."

"If they're boycotting you, how do you know something else isn't going on?"

"Like what?"

Mike shrugged. The Woos had a complicated variety of relationships with people they called sister-cousins, old uncles, young uncles, aunts, grandfathers, and grandmothers they weren't even related to but who nonetheless had the power of family members to one-up and torture them. Could be some crisis had come up with one of these nonrelative relatives.

"I have a feeling they'll get over it, *querida*. Why don't you ask me to dinner?"

"I can't do that, Mike. They're not at home. They're not speaking to me."

Most people were glad to get a little relief from their parents. But the silence seemed to unsettle April more than was absolutely necessary. He felt bad for her. "So leave them a note. Let me spend a little time with them. Trust me on this. They'll get used to me."

"Oh, they'll never get used to you. They're going to make me pay. You're costing me." A ghost of a smile played on her lips.

The sun was going to come out. "And the lost friend? Who might that be?" he teased.

"You. Chicks and guys can work together—I guess—but once you turn the corner into the other thing, God, it's babies and marriage and—nothing but trouble." She shook her head. "I hate this."

She loved it, but he wasn't going to argue. "You want to hear about my case?" he asked.

"Sure."

"Guess who was the last person to see Schlomo alive?"

"A queer. A transvestite."

He jumped away from her in shock. "Oh come on, who told you?"

She laughed suddenly. "No one told me. I was kidding. A transvestite, really?"

"He/she. Could be he castrated him for a souvenir, but it's hard to buy." Mike finished the beer and rolled the empty can around in his hands thoughtfully. "I'm looking for missing sex organs and you're looking for a missing baby. Your parents aren't speaking to you, and you're scared to death about race, sex, and friendship, in that order. Phew, this is a heavy week."

"Jesus. Somebody took his *cojones*? You didn't tell me that."

"Yes, I did. You weren't listening."

"You didn't tell me," she insisted.

He tickled her. "You weren't listening."

"Well, maybe they'll turn up. Look. I've got to go." She gathered herself together.

"*Bueno.*" Mike lobbed his empty beer can into a wastebasket across the room.

"What about you?" She finished the beer and put the can down on the floor.

"I've got to go, too." He stretched. "Anything else on your mind? I mean, other than breaking up."

She hesitated, then gave him a sly smile. "You want a last fling?"

He threw his hands up in the air. "Oh, no. You'll have to beg me now."

"I don't beg."

"Okay, then strip for me." He sat back with a grin. She rolled her eyes.

"Go ahead. Otherwise, we'll just end it now. Clean break. That's it."

"All right. *Bueno.* Turn off the lights. I'll strip."

"I'm not turning off the lights."

"Fine, I'll do it." April got up and unzipped her skirt. It fell to the uncarpeted floor. She unbuttoned her blouse, took it off slowly, and tossed it away from her. Then she gave him a shy smile and stopped.

Good enough for a beginner. He held out his arms. "*Venga.*"

CHAPTER
22

Jason finished his patient day, had dinner with his wife, Emma, then returned to Roosevelt Hospital late in the evening. April had left instructions with the nurses and the officer on duty to let him into Heather's room, so he had no difficulty gaining access. After talking to her nurse, he went in to see her, pulled up a chair, and sat close to the bed. She was in the same position on the bed and looked much as she had earlier in the day. He took her hand and squeezed it.

"Hi, Heather. It's Dr. Frank. The nurses tell me you're beginning to come around."

Her hand remained impassive, and she didn't say anything. There was an ice pack on her black eye, but the good one seemed to move a little in his direction. On the bed tray was a cup of water with a straw in it. "They tell me you asked for water." Jason offered the cup to her, but she didn't take any now. He went on.

"Somebody beat you up pretty bad. Do you remember what happened?" He massaged the hand gently.

Such a long silence followed that he'd almost given up hoping for an answer when the word "Clinton" came out of her swollen lips.

"What? Clinton?" Jason caught his breath. "Did

you say Clinton?" He waited for her to clarify. She didn't.

"Someone hit you on the head. The police say you were hit with a broom. Do you remember that?"

Then she said it again. "Clinton."

"Clinton hit you?" Jason's brow furrowed. This particular accusation was a first for the president. Heather must be pretty confused.

"Bill Clinton is president." She looked at him as she said it, not confused at all. Then her eye closed.

Jason's heart pounded. He realized she wasn't aware that any time had passed since his last visit. She was responding to the first question he'd asked her.

"That's right. Bill Clinton is president." Jason praised her. "Who are you?"

"I'm a piece of shit." She said this so softly that Jason had to lean close to hear her.

"That may be how you feel. It's not your name. What's your name?"

"Heather Rose."

"That's right. What day is it?"

"Tuesday."

"No, it's Wednesday night."

The eye popped open. "Wednesday? I must have—"

"You've been asleep for almost thirty hours. Heather, everybody is looking for the baby. Where is he?"

Her eye wandered around the room as if looking for him.

"He's not here. Where is he?"

"Paul?"

"Yes, Paul."

A tear formed and spilled over. "I told him I wanted to be good. I only wanted what was right for him." These words came out with great difficulty. Heather's voice was cultured but hoarse. She hadn't spoken for a while. It wasn't easy for her to speak now.

"What does that mean, Heather? Where is he? You can tell me."

Her hand came alive and gripped his. He could feel her trembling.

"Who beat you up, your husband?"

She shook her head.

"Someone else?"

She shook her head again.

"I'll make a deal with you. I'll help you if you help me."

Heather's eye traveled to the little window in the door. She became upset. Jason turned around and followed her gaze to a face peering in. When he looked back at her, her eye had closed and her hand had gone limp again.

"Heather? Heather? Come on, wake up." He squeezed and patted her hand. "Come on." The face in the window was gone, but so was she. Finally he got up and went out in the hall to find out who had frightened her.

The hefty nurse at the desk identified the densely built dark-haired man with a prominent forehead and soldier's rigid bearing. "That's the husband."

He was in deep conversation with someone of a similar stocky build but softer around the edges. This man had thick black hair sticking out here and there like a half-tamed fright wig. Unlike Heather Rose's husband, who was wearing a suit, the second man had several days' growth of grizzled beard on his face and was casually dressed in jeans, sneakers, and a sweatshirt.

"Thanks." Jason went to talk to them. "Mr. Popescu."

Anton spun around angrily and quickly evaluated

Jason from haircut to loafers. "How do you know who I am? Who are you?"

"I'm Dr. Frank, one of your wife's doctors."

Anton snorted. "You guys don't know fuck." He glared at Jason. His companion put a hand on Anton's shoulder, whistling softly under his breath. Anton shook off the hand. "Fuck you."

Jason didn't pick up the gauntlet. The silence forced Anton to go next.

"What were you doing with her? What did she say?" he demanded after a pause.

"I'd like to talk to you for a few moments, if you don't mind." Jason was coolly professional.

"What for?" Popescu took a challenging step into Jason's space.

Calmly, Jason retreated, taking a quick look at the man in the sweatshirt to see how he was reacting. He was now standing there with a vague air of detachment, looking away and scratching the extended belly under his shirt as if this was just another in a lifetime of Anton Popescu-generated embarrassing moments.

"Maybe I can help you," Jason suggested.

"Whose side are you on?" Anton said suspiciously.

Good question. "I have no stake; I'm just interested in finding the baby and helping your wife," Jason murmured. He turned toward a lounge area at the end of the hall, where there were some unoccupied chairs.

Anton stiffened. He glanced at his companion who offered a little shrug of encouragement. "Fuck you," Anton said again; then, to Jason, "So, what do you have to say to me?"

"I thought we might say a few things to each other."

"All right, all right." Anton marched down the hall to the chairs and indicated the one he wanted Jason to take.

Jason sat in a different one. "I can see you're very upset."

"Of course I'm upset. The police have fucked this whole thing up. There's someone watching me all the time. Look at that guy. They think I had something to do with this." He pointed at the uniform in front of his wife's room.

"It might be useful to get a little insight into what was going on in your life before this happened."

"I told the police everything I know," Popescu said, a little uneasily. He glanced quickly at his companion, then turned back to Jason. "What do you want to know?"

"There is some speculation that Heather may have harmed the baby—" Jason said.

"I know, I know. That's bullshit," Anton burst out.

"We need to rule it out as a possibility."

"This is making me nuts."

"You have some question about it?" Jason asked.

"No, no, absolutely not."   .

"She has a number of bruises and scars on her body that predate this incident—"

Anton nodded, gloomily. "Yes, she has some problems. This goes back a long way. She's a clumsy person." He shook his head. "It really worries me. Some people are just dangerous in the kitchen."

"What do you mean?"

"She just"—he rolled his eyes up to the sky as if only God could explain it—"knocks into things. Trips and falls. I swear to God, I've never seen anything like it. She could be humming along just fine, and suddenly—*bam*. She's on the floor, tripped over her own feet. I'm a busy man and I can't tell you how much time I have to spend mopping up after her. Icing her wounds." He made a noise. "But I don't want a medal for it. Somebody has to take care of her." He made another noise. "I swear the woman should have a nurse." He raised his shoulders, shaking his head fondly. "But what can you do?"

"Would you say you have a good relationship?"

"With Roe?" He laughed as if it were a ridiculous question. "Of course, she's my wife."

"What's she like?"

Anton shook his head some more. "She gets distracted."

"How would you describe that behavior?" Jason took a notebook out of his briefcase and opened it.

"It's damn difficult is what it is. The woman doesn't pay attention to what she's supposed to be doing and gets herself in trouble. I think she got kind of depressed when she found out she couldn't have children."

"What do you mean?"

Anton glanced at his companion again. Jason looked at him, too. The man started nibbling on his thumbnail, didn't say a thing.

Jason prompted. "You were saying—"

"She wanted children, couldn't have them. You heard me." He said this angrily, as if the infertility were Jason's fault.

"Was this an area of conflict for you?"

"What does that mean?"

"Do you fight about it?"

He looked surprised. "Fight, with Roe?" He laughed.

"What's funny?"

"Didn't I tell you how much time I have to spend trying to help her, nursing her damn injuries? I give her everything, anything she wants, and I take *so* much shit from her." He shook his head. "She wanted a baby, I got her one. What more could I do?"

"Do you ever get mad enough to pop her one?"

"Hell, no. I don't hurt her. She hurts *me*. Look at this whole thing she's—"

"You think she somehow engineered this?"

Anton shot him a look, raising his hands to his face.

"You mean these injuries could be self-inflicted?" He seemed interested in the theory.

So did his buddy, who now spoke for the first time. "Could be that."

"Shut up, Marc."

"She has some burn scars on her arms," Jason prompted. Anton shook his head, didn't want to talk about that.

"They look as if they must have hurt her pretty bad."

Anton clicked his tongue. "I shouldn't have brought her here. Now she's an exhibit, on trial. That has nothing to do with this."

"Who knows? Maybe the two are connected."

"What are you, some kind of shrink?"

"Yes."

"What!" Anton exploded. "Now I'm talking to a fucking shrink? I thought I was talking to a doctor. I shouldn't have to put up with this. Somebody kidnapped my baby."

"Since there aren't papers for the baby, I gather the police have widened their investigation. They're looking for the birth parents now," Jason murmured.

"I know." Anton shook his head some more. "Isn't this something?"

"What's the problem about telling them?"

"I don't deserve to suffer like this. I've given this woman everything. Do you know what her family is like . . . huh? You know where she comes from? These people are primitive. They didn't have a pot to piss in."

"Where did you meet?"

Anton's chest puffed up. "At Yale."

"She must be pretty smart to go to Yale."

"I wouldn't marry a dummy, would I?—This is my brother, Marc," he said suddenly.

"Hi," Marc said to Jason. "Heather's smart as a

whip," he added helpfully. "She's not just a dumb Chink."

"No one ever implied that. You told me there are some problems in the marriage, though, and Heather has scars on her body. Let's not beat around the bush here. Either she scarred herself, or someone else has been burning her repeatedly."

Anton looked at his brother, then dismissed it. "She fries things in hot oil. You know how they like fried food."

"You told me she's been depressed, you couldn't have children."

"I said she couldn't have children. But she was *not* depressed. She lives in luxury, gets everything she wants. I gave her a baby, didn't I?"

"Do you think she might have killed the baby because it wasn't hers?"

"No, absolutely not . . . I don't know." Anton lowered his voice.

"Is there anything else she might have done with the baby? Do you think she might have given him to someone, a family member, a friend—"

Anton interrupted. "Not possible. Her family is in California. She doesn't have any friends. I can't think. . . ." Miserably, he sought help from his brother.

Marc leaned over and gave him a reassuring hug. Anton pushed him away roughly. "Get off me."

"What other options do we have? How about the baby's biological mother?"

"No, she doesn't even know about—" His face purpled. "I've had enough of this."

"Well, thank you for talking with me." Jason rose from his chair and put his notebook back in his briefcase.

"What do you think you're doing? Give me that."

"Come on, Anton. Let's not fight with a doctor."

"He's a shrink. The man's a fucking shrink."

"Yeah, so what can he do?"

"Without your help, not much," Jason told them.

"What about my wife? What did she tell you?" Anton was nearly in tears.

"Oh, she's still unconscious. She hasn't said a thing yet," Jason told them.

CHAPTER
23

Milton Hua was not back from work at the restaurant when April Woo finally returned Nanci's call, soon after ten P.M.

"Hey, Nanci, I got your message. What did you do, go and move to Long Island?" April demanded when Nanci picked up on the first ring.

"April, oh God, thanks for getting back to me so soon. Yeah, Milton has his own restaurant now. We bought a house in the suburbs, can you believe it?"

"Sure, I believe it. Food any good?"

"You know it is." Nanci's voice dropped. "April, are you at work?"

"I have time for you, Nanci. We go back a long way. So there are big changes in your life, huh? You two breeding yet?"

"What?" The question startled her.

"Just wondering if you've started a family."

"Oh, that." She twisted the phone cord. "Funny you should ask that. No, not yet. You know Milton. He had to have every *i* dotted, every *t* crossed, money in the bank, the whole bit before he'd commit to family. How about you, married yet?"

"No, but I've been promoted. I'm a sergeant now."

Nanci could hear the pride in her voice. "Congratulations. That's—great." There was a lot of noise in the

background that stopped her from going on. April was
at work. Nanci couldn't help being afraid of the police.
Now she was nervous because April had a higher rank.
She wasn't sure how that altered the situation. Would
she be more sympathetic to the situation or less?

"So, you called me, Nanci. What's going on? You
have a problem?"

"Yes, I have a big problem. But we haven't seen
each other for a while. Things have kind of changed.
I don't know where to start." Nanci dropped the
phone cord and started twisting her wedding band
around on her finger.

"Nothing's changed between us. I've known you
since you were seven."

"And you were a real goody-goody twelve-year-
old."

"So give."

"Did I ever tell you about my cousin Lin?" Nanci
knew she probably hadn't.

"What about her? Is she the one in trouble?"

Nanci was ashamed of herself, ashamed of this
story. She was sitting in a comfortable house and her
cousin was sick somewhere and a lot of people who
should be taking care of her were lying about where
she was and what had happened to her.

"Yes, and she's all the family I have left. Except
for Milton, of course. She came in from China last
summer."

"Illegal?"

"You going to make trouble about it?"

"Immigration is not my department, you know that.
Go ahead, what's the problem?"

"You know how difficult sixteen-year-olds can be.
Lin got here, thought she was too old to go to school,
didn't want to live with us. Went to work in a factory.
I couldn't get a word out of her. I thought she might

have a boyfriend in the gangs and that was the reason for her being so secretive."

"What kind of secretive? Was she into something, flashing money around?"

Nanci sighed. "No. That was the thing. She was a mess, living in a dump. I didn't hear from her for a while."

"Could you hurry it up a little, Nanci? I'm working on something."

Nanci's voice got very small. "I know you're busy. But I didn't have anybody else to call."

"Hey, I'm sorry. I'm under a lot of pressure right now. Go ahead."

"Well, we had a fight. I wanted to apologize. So I went to look for her, but the people where she used to work told me they've never heard of her. The people where she lived say the lady from work took her to the hospital. I went to Beekman Downtown; she wasn't there. Then I called *all* the hospitals. She's not anywhere. I even checked the morgue. That's pretty crazy, isn't it?"

"I hope so." The noise intensified on the other end of the line.

"What's going on there? Did something happen?"

"Don't you read the newspapers out there on Long Island? We got a missing-kid case."

"Are you working on that, April?" Nanci said faintly.

"The mother's Chinese. ABC, but they thought she might not speak English. I got lucky."

"American-born, huh?"

"Yeah, she got herself beaten up. Nice mixed marriage. He's a lawyer. Looks like it's not working out. You're lucky you have Milton."

"I know." Nanci fell silent. "I'm sorry to bother you, April. Maybe I'm making too much of this."

"It's not a problem." April's interest seemed to

sharpen suddenly. "Give me some last-seens and I'll get on it. I have to go downtown tomorrow anyway. I'll make some time for it, okay?"

Nanci was doubting the wisdom of having made the call. She should be able to deal with this herself. Why involve the cops? She might even make it worse. "Could be she's just run off with a boyfriend," she said slowly.

"Could be."

"People lie all the time," Nanci said.

April agreed with her. "They do. But you're worried. I'll check it out. Where did she work? Where did she live? What's her name?"

"Tsing, same as mine was. Our fathers were brothers. Maybe I should give it another day, huh? Do you think I'm overreacting?"

April sounded impatient. "I'm not going to fight with you. You want help, you give me the info. I'll handle it discreetly, okay? Do you have a picture of her?"

"We just moved. Stuff is everywhere. If I look around, I might be able to find one. Can I let you know about all this tomorrow?"

"You can let me know any day. You have my number."

"Really, thanks. I appreciate it." Nanci hung up. She didn't even know where to look for a photo of Lin, and she knew April was mad at her because she was afraid to follow through. That made her feel worse. Even so, she decided to wait another day before pursuing it further.

CHAPTER
24

Thursday morning dawned bright and warm. The air was fresh in New York, and April drove into the city, breathing in the promise of a summer like no other. That morning, for the second time in her life, she'd had coffee in bed with a naked man. It happened to be some bitter Mexican brew, but the man was *suave* and *muy espresivo*.

Thinking about her travels back and forth from Queens last night ending with an unscheduled return to Mike's apartment for all of two hours before returning to work—instead of going home to sleep as she'd promised herself she would do—made April bold. She was determined to get out of the fog on this case and find the baby today, so she was full of purpose when she strode into the squad room of Midtown North at 7:48 A.M. The press was still all over the Paul Popescu case, and the squad room looked pretty much the same as when she'd left it late the night before. Three strangers were drinking coffee in the path to April's office. None of them said good morning to her. No one was in her office, however, and Special Agent Gabe Samson was nowhere to be seen. He wasn't her problem, though, and she didn't give his whereabouts another thought.

In her office, she filed her purse in a bottom desk

drawer and inspected the pile of complaint forms that had accumulated in the last few hours and now awaited assignment to a detective for investigation. Since becoming a supervisor, she had the power to hand over the shitty cases to guys she didn't like. She tried to avoid succumbing to that temptation, though, because they often did a shitty job in retaliation. Nothing major had come up, just the usual stuff: drunk and disorderly, a couple of muggings, a car theft, breakin. Assault. Now everybody on the squad had the shitty stuff.

Before dealing with the complaints, she spent a half-hour going over what they had so far on the Popescu case. The available paperwork included some preliminary lab reports on the crime scene, Hagedorn's background information on Heather and Anton, notes on the canvass of the comings and goings of people in the building and around the neighborhood that day, notes on as much as was known so far about the twenty-four hours preceding the incident. There were lots of pages but many gaps in every category. Most crucial of all: the baby's arrival in the Popescus' lives had not been dated, nor had his origin been discovered. April glanced up and saw her co-workers starting to straggle into the squad room with their containers of coffee.

"Hey, Sergeant." Baum walked by her door without stopping.

Hagedorn and several of the other detectives didn't bother to make eye contact at all. April wondered what it would take to make friends, wondered if she really wanted to, and knew in the bottom of her heart that she did.

Lieutenant Iriarte called his new gang of five favorite detectives into a meeting in his office at quarter past eight. For the first time since April had arrived in the squad, one of the three chairs had been saved for her. Baum had secured it and was now ignoring the snickers his action elicited. Iriarte raised his eyebrow at the preferential treatment.

"Okay, let's get the little stuff over with first. Tell me about this incident with Thomas," the lieutenant demanded. His face was showing the strain of having a high-profile case and dealing with the extra bodies it brought into his space. He wore a tan spring suit with a green shirt and tie. Canary-yellow handkerchief in his jacket pocket that clashed with his shirt. He was the kind of guy who didn't take his jacket off in his office unless he was alone. He had it on now, very formal. He gave April a little smile that told her he'd dump her first chance he got.

Creaker reported. "Carmen Montero, twenty-two—real good looker—driving a '96 Saturn. Officers Thomas and Crater observed suspicious behavior and told Montero to pull over. Officer Crater walked around the car for a look. Thomas approached the driver and asked for her registration. When she reached under the seat, he pulled his gun on her, cocked it, and ordered her out of the car. He held the gun to her head as Officer Crater patted her down."

"What did she do that was suspicious?" April asked.

"At 0300 she was in the Forty-second Street area, what else?"

"So why did she reach under the seat?" April asked.

"Apparently that's where she keeps her registration."

Six of them crowded in Iriarte's office thought about this poor judgment call. If the woman had been soliciting, she would have been used to being hassled and would not have complained if the officer in question had pointed an AK-47 at her. But Carmen Montero was not a hooker; she was a night nurse for a lawyer recovering from bypass surgery.

"Thomas says he thought she was reaching for a gun and was afraid for his life," Creaker elaborated.

"What does his partner say?"

"Guy's only a month on the job. His partner said he was a little shaky."

"What's ID doing about it?"

"Pulled to an inside job."

"Some people shouldn't be carrying a gun." Iriarte drummed his fingers on his desk. So much for that. In other years the incident might have gone unnoticed. Young woman scared by an officer new to the job, big deal. But now sensitivity toward the public was a big issue. The guy had to go down for shoving his gun in a woman's face. Iriarte quickly went through the other cases they had on the burner. Finally he was ready to discuss the one on all their minds.

"What about you? Anything new on the building canvass?"

Skye had been on that. He shook his head. "The tenants don't know the couple very well. The woman apparently doesn't talk to anyone, and they stick to themselves pretty much. Family members visit. That's about it. I get the feeling somebody on the building staff was out on break a lot longer than he should have been, or else knows more than he's saying. We'll keep at it."

"So, what's going on in the apartment?" Iriarte looked at Creaker.

"Popescu's mother was there last night, his brother Marc. His father; the cousin, Ivan. They all left at 22:07 except the mother, who spent the night. About two dozen crank calls on the phones. Nothing else."

"Charlie, what have you got?"

Hagedorn took out his notes. "A few interesting things. Anton Popescu lives a very regular life. In the morning he goes to his office. He has a temper, annoys his coworkers all day. He's a litigator, so he goes to court. He makes it a point to get home early in the evenings. He and his wife have most of their meals at home. They go out for dinner *maybe* once a week. This guy has no diversions—no golf, no clubbing, no drinks with his partners, no gym. When he travels, it's strictly business. Apparently, he's a devoted husband and did not like to leave his wife overnight. Associates said that on some cases he commuted back and forth daily to Philadelphia or Washington or Boston for weeks at a time to avoid spending a night away from her. He was lying about having a girlfriend. This guy didn't have time for a ten-minute Pop-Tart."

Iriarte glanced at April. "How about a surrogate mother?"

"Surrogate mother, on the sly? I don't think so. The guy's a lawyer. In a surrogate situation, wouldn't he be sure of securing papers?" April mused. "His wife would know."

"Yes, he'd want it down on paper. He'd have a birth certificate."

"Whatever," Hagedorn said. "The baby was born. There has to be a record of it somewhere."

April nodded. "Did any of the hotshots out there check on missing babies in other jurisdictions?"

"Meaning?" Hagedorn demanded.

"They could have bought it, could have stolen it, who knows? This was no spur-of-the-moment thing. Heather's mother thought she was pregnant."

"Maybe someone they knew had a baby she couldn't keep. That's an angle to look at." Iriarte pointed at Hagedorn.

"Friends with babies." He made a note.

"Okay, say they acquired a baby from an acquaintance, and the woman changed her mind about wanting to get rid of it. That would explain the birth certificate

question, but not the beating and not the 911 call,"
April said doubtfully. "And say they'd done something illegal getting this baby. Why would Anton bring
all this attention on them?"

"Yeah, but remember this guy loved her. He might
go nuts if someone beat her up."

"*He* beat her up." Baum downed the last of his
coffee.

"I like the surrogate-mother or pregnant-friend
angle," April said.

"This guy has connections. I'd put my money on
some illegal adoption maybe from out of the
country . . . China?" He raised his eyebrow at April.
"They have ties to China, right?"

"It's not so easy to adopt from China these days,"
she murmured. This had come up before.

"We're talking illegally."

"It's a big bureaucracy both directions, getting them
out, getting them in. You couldn't do it without people
knowing. Baby's only a few weeks old. More likely it
was born here."

"Someone knows." Iriarte drummed his fingers.

April thought of the baby picture. "You know what
puzzles me about this? The baby looks like them."

Iriarte heaved a sigh. "A mix, you mean. Not a
pure Asian."

"That's what I'm thinking."

Creaker rolled his eyes. "How much can you tell
from the snapshot of a three-week-old?"

"Something about the eyes." April shrugged. "It's
just a feeling."

"So, bottom line. What do you think? Is this kid
alive or dead?" Iriarte directed this at April.

She was busy studying the minute hand of her
watch, didn't want to go there. "I'm not the betting
type, sir. Just want to get it done today."

"Okay, do it."

April turned to Hagedorn. "Birth certificates three, four weeks ago. Charlie, that's you. You know what you're looking for. Get the list for the metro area, and we'll winnow it down from there. Names and addresses."

"What are you going to do?" Hagedorn demanded.

April shot him a smile. "I'm going to see a shrink about a head case."

Iriarte's scowl was transformed into a radiant smile as his door opened and Special Agent Samson barged in.

"Morning, Gabe," April said. "Let's go, Woody."

CHAPTER
25

At the time of April's meeting in her boss's office, Jason Frank was again sitting by Heather Rose Popescu's bed. Her face was still badly swollen, but despite the early hour, both eyes were open now, and she seemed aware of what was going on around her.

"Hi. I'm sorry to get you up so early," he told her. "I have patients all day. This is the only chance I had to talk to you until this evening."

"You didn't wake me up," Heather said softly.

"How are you doing?"

"The doctor told me I'll live." She swallowed hard.

"Do you remember what happened?"

"I was thinking about it when you came in. I remember the doorbell ringing. I went to open it. That's all. My mother came last night. She told me the police think I killed the baby. She's very angry."

"She and your father have been here all night. I spoke to them a minute ago. They're not angry at you."

"Are you a policeman?"

"No, I'm a doctor. A psychiatrist."

She looked up at the ceiling. "I'm crazy," she said softly. "I must be crazy." The fingers of one hand moved toward the scars on her arm.

"Some kinds of crazy aren't so bad," Jason said

smoothly. "The baby is missing. You want to tell me about that?"

"Everybody in the whole world thinks I killed my own baby." She turned her devastated face to him. "My mother told me."

"No one knows where he is, that's all. We have to find him and clear it up," Jason said.

"He's not my baby."

"I know."

"I lied to her and said it was. Now she's mad because she has no grandson. To her it's the same as killing him."

"Where is he?"

Heather ignored the question. "She was so mad at me when I married Anton. How could I tell her the baby wasn't mine?" Her eyes teared.

"Where is he?" Jason asked again.

Heather's head and magnificent hair moved on the pillow, but she didn't answer.

"Did you give him to his mother?"

"Didn't anyone tell you?"

"I don't think your husband knows where he is. Did he beat you up?"

"We couldn't keep him. It's my fault." The tears spilled over and ran down her cheeks.

Jason handed her the tissue box. "What's your fault?"

"I know I'm going to hell, but I'm already in hell."

"Why are you in hell?" Jason asked.

"Don't you know it's a sin to lie?"

"What's the lie?"

"That he was ours." Heather sobbed, wiping her face with tissues too small for the job.

Jason waited for a moment, then dug a little deeper. "Your husband mentioned that you've had some health problems."

She was quiet a long time. "Health problems?"

"Yes, he told me you couldn't have a baby and that upset you."

Her eyes filled again. "He said that?"

"Yes."

"He told everybody I couldn't have a baby?"

"No, only me. But isn't that true?"

"How could he say that?"

"Isn't it true?"

"No."

"When you were taken to the hospital your husband told the police the baby was yours. The doctors examined you and knew right away that you hadn't given birth."

She grimaced. "They examined me? He must have been upset." Again, she sought out the scars with her fingertips.

"Did he have a baby with another woman?" Jason asked.

Heather made an angry noise in her throat. "No."

"You know when something like this happens, the police check everything in people's lives."

"I don't have a life. I lost my life a long time ago." Heather's eyes returned to the ceiling.

"You want to tell me about it?"

"I'm dead now, just dead meat."

"Your husband doesn't have a girlfriend, and I don't think you have a doctor."

She blew her nose. "What difference does it make?"

"People with health problems go to the doctor, but my guess is you didn't. The doctors here have been wondering about the bruises and scars on your body—"

"What does he say about that?"

"I'm asking you. Do you hurt yourself, Heather, or does he hurt you?"

Jason's clock was ticking. He had a only a few precious minutes. He was in a hurry and asked the ques-

tion too soon. Heather broke down on the subject of
her injuries. This time she wept uncontrollably and he
couldn't calm her down soon enough.

"Just tell me where the baby is, and we'll work on
everything else."

"He's with his mother." That's all she would say.

The nurse came in with Heather's meds. Jason had
to leave. He called April from the hospital, but she'd
already gone out. All morning he screened his calls
waiting to hear from her, but she didn't phone.

At noon he left the double doors to his office
slightly ajar and waited for his eleven-fifteen appoint-
ment, a thirty-seven-year-old advertising copywriter
named Alison, to leave. He heard her sigh deeply and
knew she was stalling because of his lack of respect
for one of her periodic threats to jump off a bridge
that afternoon instead of returning to work. Alison
had been abused by her parents as a child; her goal
now was to elicit sympathy from Jason and avoid the
hard work of getting better. She had stopped dead in
the middle of the waiting room to consider her options. She might return to knock on his door with a
question, a demand that he do something, tears. And
then again she might not. She was a big tester; she
needed to reassure herself that Jason was paying close
attention to her. Because he knew she wasn't really
suicidal, he had to set limits for her.

His next patient, a physician named Albert, was
dying of AIDS that he'd contracted from someone
he'd met in a bar when his lover of a decade left him
a year and a half ago. It was a heavy morning for
human misery. While Jason waited for Alison to decide whether to go on with her day or torment him a
little more, he compared the time on his three newest
antique skeleton clocks. He couldn't help tinkering
with them between patients, adjusting things here and
there, cleaning the parts to see if he could get them

in sync with one another. His clocks, and the fact that time marched on regardless of the pain and suffering he witnessed, soothed him.

The tallest one ticked away on his desk, a magnificent steep brass triangle filled with complicated mechanics, a fine example of nineteenth-century man's desire to simultaneously harness, pay tribute to, and display the passing of time. Jason had last reset the clock when he'd come in this morning. Now it was five minutes slower than the others. Another skeleton clock stood on a side table, the third in the center of the bookcase in a position of dominance over a small collection of quite nice carriage clocks. By late afternoon the discrepancy would be increased by another minute or so. He wondered where April Woo was, and why she hadn't called.

A long ninety seconds passed before the door slammed and Jason stopped fussing over the clock. Then the phone rang, but it was Albert calling to say he'd been to the doctor and his T-cell count was way down. He didn't feel up to coming in. He sounded depressed. This meant Jason had a free hour now but would lose it later when he visited the dying patient in his home across town.

Instantly, the phone rang again. "Are you free?" It was Emma calling to ask if he wanted lunch.

"Yes, please." His early-morning visit with Heather had disturbed him deeply. Now he was thrilled at the prospect of an unexpected hour of peace with his wife.

He locked the office, walked the ten paces down the hall to his apartment, and opened the door to the sound of his home collection of clocks, some still chiming noon at seven minutes past the hour. He didn't pause to look at the mail on the table because he was puzzled by the sound of voices in the living room. Stepping through the open French doors, he saw Emma sprawled awkwardly on the sofa. Her eight-months-pregnant belly protruded so far that the knot of her navel showed through her cotton T-shirt. Opposite her, trying not to look at it, were April Woo and the young detective who was her new partner.

"How long have you been here?" he asked, taken aback by the unexpected visitors.

"Just a few minutes. We were hoping to catch you between sessions." April stole another look at Emma's belly, and Emma grinned, clearly pleased at the stunned reaction she was getting from the two cops.

"She's pregnant," April said, clearly shocked. "So that's why she quit the show."

"It was getting kind of hard to convince audiences I'd been a sexually repressed and spurned wife for ten years." Emma laughed, then beamed at her husband, clearly happy at last.

"Thanks for telling me," April grumbled. She was just crabby enough to make Jason wonder if she was a little jealous. Her eyes slid down to her own stomach, so flat the front of her skirt was undisturbed by it even when she was sitting down.

He smiled shyly. Yes, they were having a baby. His and Emma's lives had changed for the better. Heather Popescu's beating and the missing infant had come at a bad time for him. He glanced at Detective Baum, shifting uneasily in the comfortable club chair, and blew air through his nose in sympathy for the male embarrassment at fertility. Then he sat on the sofa next to Emma and took her hand.

"Here we are again," she said, squeezing his hand. "Just when I thought a normal life was possible."

"There's no such thing as normal life." Jason nudged her with his elbow because for April, barging in on people at inconvenient times with a lot of cop questions *was* normal life.

"Oh, I'm not mad," Emma responded, so quickly that Jason got the feeling that the two women, who'd met under the worst possible circumstances, were actually beginning to hit it off.

"Didn't you get my message?" Jason asked April.

"I wanted to talk to you in person. Are you coming home for lunch now that you're going to be a father? It would be a good thing to know." April was clearly proud that she'd found a way around his office and telephone rules by conspiring with his wife.

Jason couldn't help smiling at Emma. "You got me over here for them, didn't you? Sneaky."

"You beat me to the hospital this morning," April said. "By the time I got there the patient was out cold again. I talked to her mother and father, but she wouldn't talk to me. Thank you, Jason. Now I have to rely on you for my updates."

"Look, you asked for my help. You can't have it both ways."

"The nurse said you two had quite a talk. What did she tell you?"

"The baby is alive and with his mother."

April leaned forward. "Where? Who's the mother?"

"Didn't tell me. Heather Rose was very upset about Anton's lies. It's clear he lies, or she lies, or they both lie, about a lot of things."

"Poor woman," Emma murmured. She got up and left the room.

"It was when I asked her about the old injuries that she broke down. I still don't know whether they're self-inflicted. Either way, I can see why the husband would want to cover it up."

"We monitor domestic violence cases now. It's state law. Every time we're called to a domestic dispute we have to make a report on the incident and determine who the primary aggressor is. We have to follow up— a month later, two months later, six months later, depending. We have the computer data on all domestic

dispute cases, and we're supposed to keep letting people know we're watching them."

"So you're telling me there are no priors on this
couple."

April smiled at his use of the cop term. "Right. No
priors. Hospital visits, but no police visits. No *history*
of abuse. No follow-ups. That doesn't mean there
wasn't abuse."

"What do you think?"

"A woman like Heather Rose might not yell and
scream and call the police, or signal the neighbors to
call the police if her husband was hurting her. She
might think his violent behavior reflected shameful
things about her, like she was no good. He said she
couldn't have children. She wouldn't want anybody to
know her husband thought she was worthless."

"Do you think the husband beat her because she
gave the baby back?" Jason asked.

"The broomstick that hit her had her hair and traces
of her blood on it—and his fingerprints."

"Could the prints have gotten there on some earlier occasion?"

"What are you, a defense lawyer?" April asked irri-
tably. "Yes, of course they could have. But Popescu
doesn't strike us as the kind of guy who'd sweep up
the kitchen after dinner."

"What's your plan?"

"We're checking birth certificates of babies born in
the last three or four weeks to see what we can come
up with. We're also checking out the husband's family.
They have a factory in Chinatown."

"What's your thought?"

"In Chinatown people will do some unbelievable
things for money," April said slowly. "It's no secret
that immigrants pay twenty, thirty thousand dollars to
get here, and not on fancy cruise ships. They pay big
money to be hidden in the holds of the most dis-

gusting—well, never mind. Whole families pitch in to send a relative here. If they really have a lot to spend they can get forged papers and come on an airline. At the airport this precious and lucky relative—who might be the key to a whole family's future—might be met by a 'friend' of the person who arranged the trip. This 'friend' might kidnap the relative. Then a lot more money is extorted from families desperate to protect their investment and save their loved one. Sometimes the victims get a few of their body parts cut off. Sometimes they're kept in slavery even after they're ransomed, so they never get their money back."

April said all this matter-of-factly, but Jason could tell it was a subject that upset her.

"Greed is one of the seven deadly sins. It's not a uniquely Asian thing," Jason told her. "Kidnapping is common in a lot of countries these days."

"Yeah, but in other places it's the rich who get nailed," April pointed out. "The ones who have the money to pay. These people are the poorest of the poor, and they have no one to help them. They're as afraid of the police as they are of the people exploiting them."

Emma came back into the room with a tray of fancy open-faced sandwiches, a glass of milk, and some cans of Coke. Jason did a double take: the love of his life was serving lunch. Then he got a better look at the two combinations: grilled peppers, eggplant, mozzarella, and anchovies and blackened chicken, provolone, avocado and sprouts. Honey-pepper relish on the side. Very creative. He hoped they wouldn't have the leftovers for dinner.

"So, I'm wondering if someone didn't get the idea of extorting a newborn from some poor woman, then selling it to an uptown couple for a lot of money," April was saying.

"Oh, my God." Emma flinched, almost dropping the tray. Baum jumped up to take it from her. April gave him an approving look as he set it down on the coffee table.

"Honey, you okay?" Jason put his arm around her. "You don't have to listen to this."

"I'm not an invalid. I made lunch; eat up."

Jason glanced at the tray of food without seeing it. April was staring at Emma's protruding navel again. "You sure you're okay? Aren't pregnant women supposed to think only happy thoughts?"

"Eat something. I have to feed people now. I'll get my happy thoughts from that."

Baum raised his eyebrows at his boss. *Could he take a sandwich?*

"Take one," Emma insisted. "I need reassurance, really."

"Take one," April told him.

Jason took a sandwich and examined it. He knew he was going to have trouble eating it but didn't want to ask where the top of the roll was or when she'd made it. "Thanks, Emma. This is terrific."

Emma nodded at him proudly. *See, I'm going to be a good mother.*

Jason liked very simple food, like tuna fish and chicken salad. As he struggled with the Cajun chicken paired with Italian cheese and soapy avocado, he wondered how wild Emma was going to get in the coming years with her cooking and if she knew that the sudden urge to supply food at regular intervals was part of nesting. But he couldn't complain about the impulse or the result. At thirty-four and forty, they were ready for domesticity. It had taken them both a while to grow up and settle down enough for children. Now they were truly exuberant parents-to-be. The baby they were expecting in just a few weeks had become the focus of their lives, and along with that, apparently, came lunch.

As for the case at hand, Jason had mixed feelings about Anton Popescu and felt terrible for Heather. The truth about their relationship had yet to come out. Depending on which of the clocks all around him he consulted, he had between five and twelve minutes of his free hour left. By the time the first one started chiming, the exotic lunch was over and the two detectives were gone.

CHAPTER
26

After their gourmet lunch at the Franks', April and Woody checked in at the precinct to brief Iriarte. He was alone in his office, talking on the phone, when they got there. He put his hand over the mouthpiece. "Yeah?"

"We lucked out with Heather Rose, sir," April told him.

He hung up without saying good-bye. "She give it up?"

"Some, not everything. She didn't nail her husband as a beater, but she did tell Jason the baby is with its mother."

Iriarte heaved a great sigh. "Sometimes I think there is a God. Who is it?"

"She didn't say."

"What do you mean she didn't say?" Iriarte erupted again.

Hagedorn appeared at the door, rapped on the window, then plunged in without waiting for an invitation. "Ten," he announced.

"Ten what?" Iriarte looked at him expectantly.

Hagedorn held up a file. "Ten mixed babies." He stood there, grinning, one hand raised and his pudgy body frozen in the pose of triumph as he offered, like a precious trophy, the regurgitations of his computer.

Iriarte blinked. The blink meant he didn't really care ten what, and furthermore he didn't want to know. But for Hagedorn, his favorite, the lieutenant had the tolerance of a saint. "Go ahead, Charlie."

Hagedorn gave his boss another shit-eating grin. "I checked them all out. Guess what?" Excitedly, Hagedorn pushed his lank hair back from his pale forehead.

"What?" Iriarte asked nicely.

"One hundred forty-two babies born in downtown hospitals during your time frame, Sergeant." He nodded at April.

"Uh-huh."

"Eighty are black or Hispanic or mixed. Fifty-two are pure Asian." He looked up. Here was the triumph. "Only ten others are mixed Asian and other."

"Good work, Charlie." Iriarte looked impressed.

"Do you have home addresses for them?" April asked. Only ten was too good to hope for.

"Yes."

"Let's go, Baum." April reached for the file.

In four minutes, she and Baum had once again evaded the specialists and were on their way down to Chinatown to start checking them out. April was too preoccupied thinking about Emma and Jason having a baby, and of the 142 other couples engaged in productive monkey business nine months earlier, to worry about Woody's driving.

She wondered how many of those fornicating couples wanted the babies they got. Were all the parents still together and able to keep their offspring? Had one or more of the infants been sold or given away? These were not terms in which April thought very often. Usually, she tried to avoid thinking about normal people getting married, having babies. She was still reeling from the sight of Emma's protruding belly with a human being inside of it. It was disturbing.

She braced a hand against the dashboard as Woody

braked suddenly for a pedestrian. But she was excited
about the case now, keyed up for the hunt and undaunted by the fact that searching for an infant born
almost four weeks ago might turn out to be like looking for a lost item in a landfill. Chinatown was a maze,
but people were connected there; they knew things
about each other, even if they didn't tell. Somehow
she didn't think this was going to be a hard one.

Upbeat and optimistic though she was, April was
surprised when she stopped in Bernardino's office in
the detective squad room and he punched the air at
her accusingly.

"I've been trying to get hold of you," he said.

"No one told me. What's up?"

"We found your stroller," he announced.

"No kidding? What was in it?" Now April was
really excited.

"Groceries. Sit down, make yourself comfortable."

April took a chair and nodded at Baum to do the
same. He sat. "Groceries?"

"Madison spoke with her. Ah, thanks, Madison."
The Chinese detective April had noticed yesterday,
with the serious narrow face and the receding hairline,
came in and handed Lieutenant Bernardino a cup of
coffee.

Bernardino made the introductions: "Sergeant Woo,
Detective Madison Young, Detective Baum."

Young nodded at Baum, then at April. "Good to
meet you both," he said.

"Same here," April said.

"Ask the sergeant if she'd like some coffee," the
lieutenant prompted.

"Would you like some coffee, ma'am?" he asked
politely.

"No, thanks," April told him, noting again how the
situation had changed for her. Now guys were getting
her coffee.

"Madison, you found the stroller. What was the woman's story?"

"I caught up with her this morning at quarter to noon on Pike Street. She was pushing the stroller in question. Light blue Perego, brand-new, right?"

"Right."

"Turns out she's an older woman, a grandma. She had the thing filled with groceries and was carrying a child."

"Ah, how old a child?" April asked excitedly.

"More than a year old. She put the child down while we were talking. A little girl. She toddled around."

"You have an address on them?"

Madison nodded. "They live in the projects. The kid's her daughter's. She takes care of it during the day while her daughter works in the Hong Kong Supermarket."

"Is there a younger baby in the family?"

"No, a son in kindergarten. The way Grandma tells it, a well-dressed woman with a long ponytail got out of a cab on Tuesday morning."

"What street?" Baum asked.

"Allen Street."

"Allen?" April said. This was sounding good. The description fit Heather Rose.

"The Hong Kong Supermarket is on Allen," Madison explained.

"Go on. What about the woman with the ponytail?"

"She had two shopping bags and was holding a baby. The grandma says she looked around for someone. The stroller was in the trunk of the car. The taxi driver didn't want to help her get the stroller out of the trunk. She was upset with the driver because he just stood there, wouldn't help. While they were arguing, another woman came up to her, and they talked for a moment. The second woman took the baby and the shopping bags, but she didn't want to take the stroller, said she didn't need it. She took the baby and the shopping bags and walked away, leaving the woman with the ponytail crying." Madison shrugged. "That's it."

"How did Grandma get the stroller?"

"Oh. She figured the crying woman didn't need the stroller anymore, and she didn't want the man with the turban to have it, so she walked over and asked if *she* could have it."

"The driver was a Sikh?" Baum remarked.

Madison nodded.

"We're looking for him," Alfie told them. Hundreds of New York cabbies were Sikhs.

"How reliable is this grandma of yours?"

"She was pretty slick, told me right off the bat she didn't steal the stroller. The woman with the ponytail gave it to her. She got kind of defensive about it, knew how much it was worth."

April was excited. "Okay. Now we know Jason had it half right. The other half is that Heather herself gave the baby back to its mother. It wasn't kidnapped by anybody. Good work, Madison."

"Who's Jason?"

"Oh, he's a shrink I know. He talks to head cases for me." April grinned at Baum. They had the pieces now. They could crack the case.

"So, sweetheart. You wanted to come home. Here you are." Alfie smiled. "We don't do shabby work here."

"No, sir. You did good. But what did she mean, she didn't need it?"

"Who?"

"The baby's mother. Why wouldn't she need the stroller?"

"That's the next question. By the way, what do you have for me?"

"We ran a birth certificate check. I have some addresses of possible mothers. You mind if Madison
takes a few?"

Bernardino shook his head. "Not at all. What about
the Popescus?"

"What do you say we bug them later?"

"Later's fine." Alfie grinned at her. "Welcome
back."

CHAPTER
27

Nanci Hua was struggling with her conscience when April called her again Thursday afternoon.

"Did you find your cousin?" she asked.

"Who is this?" Nanci demanded, startled because she was still hoping the enticement of a thousand-dollar reward would inspire Annie Lee, the lady in the factory where Lin worked, to call.

"It's April—who do you think it is?"

"Oh, April, I wasn't expecting you," Nanci said guiltily.

"I'm sorry I was short with you yesterday. You know how it is." April's voice trailed off as the noise in the background picked up.

"Oh, I didn't take it personally. I know you're busy."

"We go way back. You can count on me. Have you heard anything new?"

"No," Nanci said. This was the truth. She'd tried the hospitals again. Still, nobody had heard of Lin Tsing. In her most optimistic moments, Nanci tried to imagine Lin getting in trouble with a boyfriend and running away somewhere with him. In her less optimistic moments, she had darker fears.

"You want to tell me about it?" April said in her crisp cop voice.

"Tell you about what?" Nanci said warily.

"You didn't give me the whole story yesterday. If I'm going to help you, I have to know it."

"You already said this. I told you I feel guilty about bothering you."

"Get off the guilt trip. I don't have a lot of time to chew the fat, is all. I didn't mean to be impatient. Look, I'm down in Chinatown right now. I'm hoofing around, and I can ask some questions for you if you want me to."

Nanci hesitated. "How's the case going?"

"It's coming along."

"What does that mean? Did you find the baby you were looking for?"

"We have some leads."

"Yeah?"

"Yeah, we'll find him. About your cousin—"

"It's a boy?"

"Yeah, Nanci, it's a boy. Blue eyes, we're guessing half Chinese. If you know where he is, it would be a big help if you passed it along."

"How would I know?" Nanci bristled.

"Just kidding." April laughed on the other end of the phone.

"Why are you talking like this? I really resent it. Why do you always have to act like a cop?"

"I *am* a cop, Nanci. That's why you called me," April reminded her.

"I called because you're an old friend," Nanci retorted defensively. "I didn't expect you to start accusing me of things."

"Hey, I was kidding. I called to make up. So, give me some facts. I'll check into it. Where does your cousin work?"

"Um . . ." Nanci stalled. She wanted to talk to the boss in the factory herself.

"You said you went there," April said.

"Did I? Maybe I did."

"So. What's the name and address?"

"I'm trying to remember." Just like yesterday,
Nanci got to the place where she couldn't go any further. Cops always acted like this. She remembered the
police coming and talking to her after the fire that
killed her father. They kept asking her the same questions over and over about what happened that day,
and who was in the building. On and on, as if it were
all her fault and they were going to find out and punish her. She'd been fifteen then, not much younger
than Lin was now. She'd been stunned and frightened,
having lost her only relative in America. And it
seemed to her that the police just would not believe
her. Proof of all this came a few days later when she
had to go into the police station and say the same
things all over again to different people. Friends of
her father took her in because she was underage and
the city social workers would have taken her away,
sent her back to China. At the time, April had already
taken her police department test, but she had not yet
been acccepted. April hadn't been able to help her.

What happened the day Nanci lost her father was
the same as what happened every other day. She'd
come home from school. She'd done her homework
at the table where they ate their meals. Always, she
waited for her father. When he came home from the
noodle factory where he worked, he gave her some
money and sent her to buy food. No different from
hundreds of other days. After they ate, she went to
the library for two hours. Same as every day. But that
day, when she came back with three oranges and a
fish, the building was full of smoke and fire. Her father
and a little boy were dead, and her life was changed
forever.

"Nanci? I've got to get moving."

"I'm trying to remember. I think it's on Orchard Street, or maybe Ludlow."

"What kind of factory did you say it was?"

"I didn't."

"So what kind of factory is it?"

Nanci stalled again. "Um, Lin can really sew. I don't know the name of the place."

"Nanci, you want to get hold of the company's name for me? I want to check it out, all right?"

"Okay, okay. I'll get it. I'll call you. You're still the same old bully."

"And you're the same old brat. I'm on your side, remember?"

"Thanks, April. I know you are." Nanci wasn't so sure, though. She felt sick in the pit of her stomach. The way April was talking to her made Nanci think her old friend also knew more than she was saying. Why else call and nag her, when April was so busy and Nanci clearly wasn't sure she wanted to talk about it? She dialed Milton's number at the restaurant to tell him about this new development, but he wasn't there.

CHAPTER
28

"You bad girl, too much trouble," Annie Lee complained in Chinese as she came upstairs Thursday morning before the workers were in. Too much work, had to take care of sick girl in the old cedar closet upstairs, had to get her water and give her pills. Annie was mad. This wasn't her job. She grumbled about the dark, angry about that, too. She must have turned the light off when the police came yesterday and not turned it on again when they left.

She reached for the string and turned on the light in the closet, clicking her tongue at all the trouble. She was too old for this, almost ready to retire and be cared for herself. She felt put upon as she quickly examined the heavy-breathing girl. She squatted and mopped her face with a wet towel. Lin moaned softly.

"Good, wake up. Let me see you."

When Lin opened her eyes, Annie forced another pill down her throat with hardly any warning. The unexpected foreign object started the girl coughing again. Annie made an impatient noise. This was the fifth antibiotic she'd given her. Wasn't she supposed to be getting better now? Annie worried about this.

"Why you not better?" she said angrily, as if Lin had a choice in the matter. The bad girl was looking very sick, so she relented. "All right, here's some

water." She held out a chipped cup with a spoon of
honey in it.

Lin allowed Annie to wet her tongue, but closed her
mouth when Annie tried to force her to swallow some.

"That's not enough. More," Annie scolded. When
it was clear Lin wouldn't take any, Annie made more
disgusted noises. "What am I going to do with you?
Can't keep you forever. Maybe you tell me now and
go," she suggested.

Lin moved her head. Yes, she wanted to go.

"Go where? Those people are no good," Annie
said scornfully.

Please, Lin begged with her eyes. She wanted to go.

This annoyed Annie even more. All this trouble and
the girl wasn't grateful. She gave her a cough drop.
Lin spat it out. Annie clicked her tongue. She didn't
like to listen to Lin's cough. The sound was deep and
phlegmy. The hack and rattle were so persistent, the
girl couldn't stop once she started. She also refused
to respond to the Robitussin and other medicine
Annie gave her. Didn't like tea, didn't like honey
water. That made her obstinate and stubborn beyond
reason. More than two dollars every pill for the antibiotic. Ivan told her it was the best you could buy.

Lin managed to say please in a begging tone, but
Annie was not appeased. "You tricked me. You didn't
tell me you had a cousin," she said reproachfully.

Lin's eyes were glassy, but she looked upset that
Annie knew. That gave Annie some satisfaction. "Oh,
yes, I know everything. Before, you tell me all your
family is dead. Now you have rich cousin. Why lie?"

Lin's answer was another long and irritating fit of
coughing. Lin's glassy eyes stared at her.

"Stubborn girl," Annie muttered guiltily. The girl's
eyes told Annie she didn't forgive her for what had
happened and now she wouldn't cooperate and help

Annie solve this problem so she could go home and forget about it.

"Not my fault. Take some water," she demanded. Lin wouldn't take any water. Roughly, Annie opened her mouth and poured a little in, scolding some more. The honey water dribbled out. This time Annie ignored it.

"Your cousin came looking for you yesterday." Annie made another disgusted sound when the glassy eyes filled with tears. "Too late for tears."

"I'll go." Lin coughed. "Tell her. I'll go with her."

"What do I get, ah? Big mess." Annie shook her head. "What am I supposed to do?"

"Call Nanci."

"It's not for you to say." Annie thought a minute. Lin's eyes closed. She didn't answer.

Annie grunted. The stingy Popescus hardly gave her anything for all her trouble. A few dollars, nothing more. She couldn't help thinking about the money Lin's cousin had offered her. If a thousand dollars was her first offer, she had more to give. Maybe five thousand for a cousin was not too much to pay.

She thought about all the bad things happening— Lin lying to her for so long about the cousin and giving her such a hard time now. Annie wasn't paid to be a nurse. Why did Lin have to be sick in this storeroom and make all this trouble for poor Annie Lee for so many months when all along she had a rich cousin who should have done this?

Annie didn't know what was worse: Lin, who wouldn't cooperate; or Lin's cousin, who turned up offering Annie enough money to make Annie worry that this cousin was an important person who could find out what had happened to Lin and make more trouble if Annie didn't help her now. It was all a big mess.

Annie didn't like the sick girl looking at her with

those pleading eyes. The rich cousin had those same pleading eyes, as if all this were her fault. This was not her fault. For five thousand dollars, Annie was beginning to think, the right thing to do was call the cousin to come and get Lin and be done with it. The rest of it was not her business.

Annie poured some more water into Lin's open mouth, then held her mouth closed so she had to swallow. Then she turned off the light and went downstairs.

Annie Lee knocked on the boss's office door.

"What do you want?"

"Lin very sick," Annie said, easing the door open.

"Did she say anything?"

"Said she want to go."

"Did you tell her she could go as soon as she cooperates?"

Annie wrung her hands. "Very sick," she said. "Needs more medicine, needs docta."

"Tell her she'll get a doctor when she cooperates."

Annie looked at the two bosses. Sometimes they were mean, sometimes nice. Now not so nice.

"Why you no give me something?"

"Sure, we'll give you something. We'll give you a hundred dollars on top of what you've gotten already. You've been a big help," Marc said grandly.

"And that's it." Ivan popped a beer.

"Only a hundred dollas, why not thousand dollas?"

"A thousand dollars? Are you crazy?" Ivan laughed. "She wants a thousand dollars."

"Lin very sick. No remember anything."

"Well, make her remember," Marc said gently. "We don't want to have her here any more than she wants to stay here."

"I'll make her remember," Ivan offered.

"Oh, shut up, Ivan. You're not going to touch that girl."

"She has a cousin. Maybe cousin knows."

"Ahh, now we're cooking." Marc smiled. "Good work, Annie. Now find out where she lives."

"You give me a thousand dollas, I find out."

"Jesus, I'll find out for nothing. Get out, Annie."

Annie worried about this problem all day. She decided when she got home to 110th Street and Third Avenue, where she lived with her retired husband, they would talk the situation over. Maybe they'd call Lin's cousin from there and offer to give her back for the right price.

CHAPTER
29

Annie Lee called Nanci Hua in Garden City just after six on Thursday evening. "You Lin's cousin?" she asked in Chinese.

"Yes, who's this?" Nanci asked, though she knew right away who it was.

"Never mind who. I know where she is. You want to know?"

"Yes."

"You give me five thousand dollas?"

"Five thousand dollars!" Nanci was shocked.

"Yes, she's your cousin. You owe it for her."

"The money is for her? I don't understand. Where is she? They said you took her to the hospital."

"No hospital, who said hospital?" Suddenly the voice became uncertain.

"A woman where she lived told me her friend from work took her to the hospital. You're Annie Lee, the friend, right?"

"You'll give me five thousand dollas?"

"What do you need five thousand dollars for? What is this? Are you holding her for ransom or something?" Nanci's voice shook with anger.

"Okay, three thousand."

"This is bribery. You can't do this."

"Very important men maybe hurt Lin," Annie Lee said cagily.

"You can't scare me. Who are these men, your bosses? The president of your company, the owner of the company? The king of the world?" Nanci was furious. "Lin is only seventeen years old. She's a baby. Whoever hurts her could go to prison. Do you understand me?"

"Lin very sick." The tone was accusing.

"Tell me where she is, or I'll call the police right now."

"Two thousand dollars and no trouble. That's my last offer. You give me tonight, see cousin tonight. No give me, maybe Lin die."

"What are you talking about? I want to talk to her. Let me talk to her!" Nanci cried. Oh, God, she didn't know what to do. It was dinnertime. Milton was busy at the restaurant, and she wasn't sure what was right. Call April Woo or give the woman the money? After all the expenses with the new house and the down payment on the new car, Nanci wasn't sure they even had two thousand dollars. Her mind raced. But they could get it from the restaurant. Maybe even tonight.

"You have the money?"

"Maybe. I'll have to let you know. Give me your number."

"No, I call you back. Ten minutes."

The woman she knew was Annie Lee hung up. Nanci called Milton at the restaurant. She was sure there would be more than two thousand dollars there. She felt very bad about Lin, bad enough to give Annie whatever she wanted. This was her fault. All her fault. The assistant manager at the Golden Dragon said Milton would call her right back.

CHAPTER
30

At 6:17 P.M. the phone rang in Jason's office. He was just going into a session but took a moment to pick up. "Dr. Frank."

"Hi, Jason, it's April. Thanks for the delicious lunch."

"You're welcome," he said, knowing this was not a social call.

"You didn't tell me Emma was pregnant." Her voice had a bit of an edge to it.

"You never asked."

"Ah well, always the shrink. It doesn't matter. You're together. She looks happy; you look happy. That's all that matters. I'm glad for both of you." He heard a sigh.

"Thank you for saying so, April. I have thirty seconds. . . ."

"Have you been back to see Heather?"

"I've been with patients all afternoon."

"Will you go and have a chat with the husband for me?"

"I have to go, April."

"You know Heather has been abused. The husband's fingerprints are on the broom that bashed her on the head. He's involved, but we can't take him down on this unless we know more about them, and of course she has to cooperate."

"I thought this was a missing-baby case."

"We're working both angles."

"I don't know what you want me to do." Jason had already told her that intervention was something he did only when people called him. This case was not like the others he'd worked with April. In those, the principals had already been personally involved with him. This time Jason was an outsider. He didn't know the victim, didn't know the suspected perpetrator. He knew nothing about either of them. They were strangers. The ethics of the situation were complicated. He had no authority in the matter. April was asking him to act as an agent of the police department. It was pretty nearly certain that he'd be asked to testify in court. He didn't have the time or the heart for it. He felt cruelly used. He didn't just barge in on people no matter how exteme their crises, but April didn't care about that.

"Just talk to each of them once more." She was pushing hard.

"Don't you have your own police psychiatrists for this?" Jason asked.

April didn't answer.

"Shouldn't there be a DA involved here? Aren't they the ones who determine the course of an investigation like this?"

Yes, yes, and yes. But she wanted *him*. "This is a favor, Jason," she said finally.

"I'll think about it," he replied. Which meant he would stall.

"Look, I spoke to Heather's mother. We can get somewhere on this case if you'd just scare the husband a little. You know how fast bullies crumble with the right inducements."

"April, I'm a doctor. I'm not playing bad cop for you."

"Come on, you played the *good* cop on the last case," she joked. "You can't expect to be the good cop every time."

"But I'm not a *cop*," he reminded her. He heard the waiting room door open and close. His next patient was there.

"You promised you'd help," she reminded him.

"I never made such a promise."

"Please." Oh, great, now she was begging.

"By the way, April, I was wondering. Did your people come up with any other fingerprints in the apartment?" he asked.

"Well, sure, tons of them. The Latent Print Unit at headquarters is still working on it."

"What are you doing about making a match? Come on, all those experts. You should know something by now. I'm getting the feeling there's more to your request. What's your motive here?"

"Oh, now you're really hurting me, Jason. Good call. We don't have identification yet on some latents that turned up in a number of places in the apartment, including the kitchen and the baby's room," she admitted. "Why do you ask?"

"I've been thinking about this and it doesn't add up. Anton Popescu doesn't have the profile to hit his wife in the face where it would show, you follow me?"

"So what are you saying?"

"You asked me to get to know them. So, I'm telling you I'm not at all convinced Anton was the one who assaulted Heather. He can be rough and nasty, but he's not the kind of guy who'd want to be known for messing up her face. And now you're telling me there are other prints in the place. So you think there's more to this case, too."

"Yeah, I do. One more try with them to prove your hunch is right. How about it?"

"I'm a psychiatrist, April. I don't have hunches. Gotta go." He didn't say he would call, but at eight, right before he was scheduled to go home for his dinner, he dialed the Popescu apartment.

Anton picked up after the first ring. "Yes, who is it?"

"It's Dr. Frank," Jason said.

"Who?"

"We met in the hospital."

"How did you get my phone number?" Anton sounded angry.

"How's Heather doing?" he asked.

"What fucking business is it of yours?"

Good point. "I'm a doctor. She's hurt and upset. I think I can help."

"He thinks he can help," Anton said sarcastically. "I'm her husband. I can handle this."

"You have a lot to be upset about, too."

"Fucking A, I do. I'm suing you for malpractice."

Oh, shit. Anton Popescu just loved dirty words. Jason didn't think the man could sue him if Anton hadn't hired him in the first place, but he wasn't absolutely sure. April was asking him to do things psychiatrists weren't supposed to do. He wondered if he was a coward. Anton pounced on the silence.

"Ah, I see that got to you. I'll bet you've been sued for malpractice before. It's something I can find out. I'll sue you from here to hell and back," Anton crowed.

Jason started thinking that it wasn't a good idea for a therapist to be *totally rigid*. One had to be innovative from time to time, in dire emergencies. And besides, this guy was pissing him off.

"Mr. Popescu, you're a lawyer. You know much better than I do the legal implications of your case.

You had a baby, but no papers for the baby. Your fingerprints are on the weapon that injured your wife."

"Shut up. How can you say this? Who told you this? This is a pack of lies. I have all the appropriate papers. Anyway, I don't have to produce any fucking papers. And I didn't hurt my wife. I've never touched her in anger. I would never, absolutely never, never hit my wife with a broomstick."

"Who said it was a broomstick?"

"It was lying on the floor next to her. It was a fucking broomstick. You think I'm stupid? The thing had blood all over it and I picked it up. Jesus." Anton's voice broke. Jason could hear him crying. "Jesus. I picked it up. Okay, maybe I was stupid to touch it. It doesn't mean I hit her with it. Jesus, I never thought anybody would think *I* hit her with it."

"Somebody did."

Anton's voice got very low. "I saved her fucking life. Don't you understand, I save her twice. She was a nothing, and now she's ruined my whole life."

"Mr. Popescu, I'm glad you shared this with me. I'm concerned that when Heather recovers, she may be at risk for suicide. You did tell me she'd hurt herself in the past."

Anton sucked in his breath. "Yes."

"Why don't we get together and talk? Maybe I can help you."

"I don't need help." Anton wasn't an easy person to talk to.

"The police aren't going away until the baby is found. Don't you want to find Paul?"

"I don't see how—"

"How about my office?" Jason suggested.

"I'm not a nutcase. I'm not going to any fucking shrink's office."

"If you come to my office, no one will see you. We'll be able to talk privately."

"The cops have gone. They left an hour ago."

"What cops?"

"They tapped my phone. It's probably still tapped. Better watch what you say."

"I have nothing to hide," Jason said, but he was shaken by the idea of cops taping the call. He wondered if the Popescus' apartment was bugged as well. He wouldn't put it past NYPD.

"This has to be confidential," Anton was saying.

"Of course," Jason assured him. Too bad, April.

"Oh, shit, just come to my apartment."

"No problem. I'll be there in fifteen minutes." Then Jason called Emma to tell her he'd be late.

Fifteen minutes later a short, fat woman opened the Popescus' front door, looked him over with a sour expression, and disappeared without a word. Jason stood in the foyer until Anton's voice directed him.

"Come in here."

Jason followed the sound into the living room, which had the look of a professional decorator. Anton was sprawled on one of the green-and-white chintz sofas with his shirt collar open. He looked bad. He picked up the bottle of scotch sitting on the table beside him and refreshed his drink, making a point of not offering any to Jason. "What do I call you?" he demanded.

"You can call me Dr. Frank," Jason said.

"Dr. Frank," Anton mimicked. "I hate fucking shrinks, did I tell you that?"

"I didn't come here to be abused." Jason looked around for a stereo to turn on. He didn't see one, decided not to worry about a bug.

"I'm a nice guy. I don't abuse people," Anton was telling him, not for the first time.

"You've said that before." Jason sat in a club chair without being asked. Already he was regretting the visit. Anton had clearly downed more than a few and wasn't in the mood to cooperate.

"My mother-in-law is here," he said bitterly. "Twenty-eight years in America and she still speaks only about three words of English. It freaks me. The father burps and drinks like a fish. This is the family I married into."

"Are they staying here with you?"

"They're not here yet. But yeah, I'm sure. Can you believe this? I didn't say they could come. If I weren't such a nice guy I wouldn't let them stay here, now would I?"

"How's Heather?"

Anton drank some scotch. "I'm so tense. I want my son. What's anybody doing about it? Nothing."

"How's Heather?"

"I don't know. They won't let me see her," he complained bitterly. "I just don't get it. They say she's all right, but they won't let me in. It's the fucking cops. I'm going to sue the city for this."

Jason didn't say anything.

"You want to know if I hit her, don't you? Well, I didn't hit her." Anton looked at Jason. "Want a drink?"

Jason shook his head.

"I'm offering you a drink. Have a drink," Anton insisted.

"I'm fine," Jason assured him.

"What's the matter, isn't my scotch good enough for you?"

Jason acknowledged the expensive, unpronounceable single-malt label. "It's a very good scotch."

"Damn straight. So don't insult me, have a fucking drink," Anton insisted.

"You like to get your way," Jason observed mildly.

"What are you talking about? I'm being nice.

You're being an asshole. How do you expect me to talk to an asshole?" He glared.

"What if I don't want a drink?"

"That's not the point."

"To get along with you I have to do what you want me to do, is that the deal?"

"What are you talking about?"

"You have an aggressive way of getting your points across."

"What do you want from my miserable life? I didn't hurt my son. I didn't hit my wife. I could kill the bastard who did this to us."

Jason shifted in his chair. "Who *is* the bastard who did this to you?"

Anton looked uncertain for a moment, then shook himself. "How would I know?"

"Okay, let's go backward a little bit. Let's talk about you and Heather in happier times."

Anton relaxed a little. "What do you want to know?"

"What attracted you to your wife in the first place?"

"What kind of question is that?"

"It's a background kind of question, exploring your feelings about each other, your issues."

"She adores me," Anton said, playing with the pants crease along one thigh.

"How did you two get together? What did you like about her? You went to Yale, right? There must have been a lot of girls to choose from. What made her special to you?"

"Well, that's a good one, isn't it?" Anton looked out the window. "Oh, God." He shook his head. "She was there, wasn't she? That meant she had to be different."

"Different from—?"

He jerked his head as if anybody should know. "The JOBs."

Jason frowned. "The what?"

"Just off the Boats. Everybody calls them that."

"She was an educated Chinese girl, born here, is that what you mean?"

"Yeah, she talked like us. I thought . . . you know, she was like us."

"How did you meet her?"

"I don't know. I don't remember. Yeah, I do. She was a freshman. She had a class and she was wandering around lost. I gave her directions."

"You liked her looks."

"Well, she had that blunt dykey haircut a lot of them have, but, yeah, I thought she was kind of cute."

"Was she your first Chinese girlfriend?"

Anton balled the fist that wasn't holding his drink. "What's that supposed to mean?"

"The choice of a mate has meaning, that's all. I just wondered what the meaning was to you."

"My family. They're all bigots, you know. I was the smart one, had to get out of the family business. There wasn't room for three of us in the business, and, like I said, I was the smart one. So I went to law school. Hell, I wouldn't want to do what they do, anyway. They work with shit; everything they touch turns to shit."

"What do you mean?"

"They're my relatives, but let's face it, they're fucking morons. Look at this mess."

"Tell me about the mess."

"The police took my fucking fingerprints! Even you know about it."

"So why are you upset about it?" Jason asked.

"I don't like being accused. It makes me angry. I'm not like them. I don't use people. I always liked the Chinese girls; they weren't nasty like the girls in school. You never had to do anything to impress them. They just liked you, know what I mean? It didn't matter to them if a guy wasn't perfect. I never used them." He pulled on his fingers, wringing his hands. "I'm a good person. That's why this whole thing burns me so much. Did you see my wife's face? She's a mess. This is too much." He dropped his hands to his lap and let his chin fall to his chest as if depleted of all his energy.

"Do you think Heather will tell her mother the whole story?"

Anton raised his head slowly, as if considering it. "I don't know her anymore. I don't know what she'll do. Do you think she's crazy, I mean really crazy?" He asked it with his eyes wide, innocently.

"You suggested it yourself the first time we met. And again tonight."

"I know, but there are other factors," he said vaguely.

"You mean somebody hit her on the head with a broomstick."

"Not me," Anton insisted.

"Who?"

Anton pushed air through closed lips making a farting noise.

"How could I know? I wasn't there."

Jason didn't like the guy, but oddly enough he believed him. Half an hour later, when Anton nodded off in the middle of a sentence, Jason went home for dinner.

CHAPTER
31

By evening Mike was beginning to worry about April. It had been a big day. He'd received a call from the Tel Aviv police in the morning with some information that broke his homicide case. He tried to reach April with the good news, but she didn't respond to his page. This prompted him to stop in Forest Hills on his way home to buy two cell phones. April still wasn't responding to her beeper when he got home at half past seven. Mike paced around his apartment for nearly an hour, then was astounded when she arrived with two shopping bags at quarter past nine.

"*Querida,* where have you been all my life?" He took the shopping bags from her, drew her arms around his neck, and gave her a lingering kiss that threatened to go on for a long time.

She let her arms slide down his sides and around his back. Her fingers felt around in the waistband of his trousers. Still kissing him, she raised her knee up the inside of first one leg and then the other, like a spy on assignment, looking for a weapon.

He realized what she was doing and laughter bubbled up from deep inside. April was feeling him up and patting him down, arousing and teasing him at the same time. His pants were suddenly unbearably tight. Then, with sleight of hand worthy of a magician making tigers appear and disappear, April had his trousers unzipped and around his knees. He stopped trying to kiss her because he was laughing too hard.

"Ha ha ha ha."

She sure knew how to disarm a guy. "Ha, ha-ha, ha!" He was laughing, and then she had him nailed.

"Look at what I found," she murmured. "Sir, did you know you're carrying a concealed weapon?"

"No, ma'am. Nothing concealed about that."

"Oh, yes, it was concealed until I revealed it. You have a license for this?" she asked, giving him a friendly squeeze.

"Ahhhh uhaaaa."

"You wouldn't want me to take you in for this. This is big. What is it, a semiautomatic you've got here?"

"No, it's completely automatic. Ahhhaaah—" He made some more noises, not laughing anymore. "Oh, my God. Okay, okay, you win, *querida*. What do you want?"

April stepped away, appraising him with a raised eyebrow and a smile the way men did so often with women. Then she patted him on his bare bottom and let him go. "I need a few minutes, *mi amor*. I have to call my mother."

Then she turned to look for the phone. And his heart, pumping away at his lifeblood, wouldn't let him calm down. She'd turned the tables on him. Once again he was on fire and didn't know whether to take his pants off or put them back on. Whew. The woman knew how to even the playing field, and she had a mind of her own. It was going to take some getting used to.

April dialed the phone in the kitchen and waited a long time. Then she dialed again. He could hear her hang up. She came out of the kitchen shaking her head.

"What's going on?"

"I'm making dinner," she said, a little distracted. "I was in Chinatown all afternoon. I couldn't help shopping."

"But how'd you know I'd be here?"

April gave him a look. "Where else would you be?"

"I could be out on a homicide, could be anywhere." He pulled at his mustache, trying to figure her out. Why hadn't she just let him know she was coming so he could have been happy and anticipated the pleasure of seeing her, trying out her cooking. "I broke the case."

"That's great," she said.

"Yeah, I got Schlomo's killer."

"Who was it?"

"Another Israeli. Get this, the victim's wife received her husband's private parts by Federal Express this morning. Guess there wasn't any problem with customs. Scared her so much she told Tel Aviv police she and her husband's partner had been having an affair for some time. When she decided to break it off and go back to her husband, the partner made good on his threat that the next time she saw the gonif's dick it would be in a box."

"Wow." April still looked distracted.

"This guy was in trouble over there a number of times dating back to his army days, so they were eager for us to keep him. Guess where he was?"

"Do I have to?"

"He was doing business in his office as usual, selling the diamonds he'd stolen without the slightest fear of getting caught." Mike laughed. It was constantly amazing to him how people did the stupidest things and thought they could get away with it.

April started unpacking her shopping bags. "Well, you had a better day than I did. All I did was check out a lot of people who had new babies, none of which was the one we're looking for. Bugged the Popescus some more, didn't get anywhere with them. And I went shopping." She took two jars of nasty-looking stuff with Chinese labels out of the bag; then came garlic, ginger, scallions, and something that looked like green beans but were way too long.

Mike recognized cucumbers and dried mushrooms but couldn't identify some leafy things or the black bulbs in a plastic bag. A bottle of mushroom soy sauce emerged from its wrapping in a Chinese newspaper.

"I needed a break," she said.

"Hmmm . . . This cooking and break thing is new with you. What am I supposed to do, hang around here just in case you decide to come over on the spur of the moment?"

She gave him a mischievous smile. He leaned against the counter close to her, trying to be cool and not grab her again. "What are these black things?"

"Fresh water chestnuts. We're lucky. You don't see them every day." She finished unpacking the bags, finally taking out a whole roast duck. This she left on the counter. "Want to fool around?" she asked, touching the buckle on his belt.

The invitation threw Mike off balance again. He hadn't wanted to rush her and be corrected again. He took a teasing tone. "Right now? Don't you want to call your mother, hear more about my day, tell me about yours?"

"No." April put her arm around him and drew him back into the living room and sat on the sofa. She checked her watch, then took off her sweater. Under it she was wearing a lacy bra he hadn't seen before. "I've been here five minutes. You want to fool around now?"

"You sure we've been civilized long enough, *querida*?" Mike teased, finally on solid ground.

An hour later April was still drunk with love. Gone was the gun at her waist; gone was her heavy shoulder bag with all its necessary supplies like her second gun, notebooks, beeper, Mace, flashlight, rubber gloves, tissues, breath freshener, plastic bags, wallet, and keys; gone were her sweater, jacket, tights, and boots. Without all the paraphernalia of life as she knew it, weighing down her every breath, both her soul and body felt light. She felt as light as a leaf, as light as a butterfly perched on a flower. She felt like a bee, a honey-seeker in her lover's thrall. The curtains were open in the living room, and from where she lay in Mike's arms April could see the skyline of Manhattan. They were so high up, and there was no building in front of them; even if the lights in the apartment had been on, no one could have seen them. Mike's lips caressed her arms and her fingers, distracting her. He was a lover whose enthusiasm did not diminish when the main event was over.

"*Tienes hambre, querida?*" he murmured.

"Mmmmm."

"Is that a yes or a no?" He nibbled on an earlobe.

"*Hambre sí,*" April said. *Inamorada, sí también.* She didn't want to say she loved him.

"*Te amo,*" he murmured. With a finger he traced the curve from her shoulder to her ear. He lifted the hair from her neck and blew gently. "*Me amas tu?*" he asked, nudging her with his chin.

Did she love him? What kind of question was that? How many people did she cook for? "Maybe," she teased. She shifted in his arms, turning over, grazing his stomach with her lips. Then she slid off the sofa, stood up, and stretched. Never had she spent so much time without any clothes on.

"Come back."

"Uh-uh, I've got to get going." She reached for his shirt and put it on without buttoning it.

"Going where, *querida*?"

"I have to clear a few things up."

"I thought you were making dinner."

"I'm making dinner; then I'm going home."

"That's a really bad idea."

"Bad or good, I've been putting it off too long. I have to do it." She moved into the kitchen, washed her hands, then carefully washed the vegetables. When Mike came in she was examining his knife collection.

"Pathetic," she remarked, testing the bigger of the two blades with an index finger. "How am I going to hack the duck with this?"

"Why do you have to hack it?" Mike put his arms around her. She was wearing only her panties under his shirt. "*Te amo,*" he said again, patting her bottom.

"Hacked duck has to be hacked; any idiot knows that. Never bother a woman holding a knife." She opened a cabinet, found a frying pan, examined it for dust, rinsed it anyway. "Can you peel the water chestnuts, garlic, and ginger, and shred the scallions and cucumber?" She was all business as she opened the jar of hoisin sauce. "I like a man who's useful in the kitchen."

"Uh, I can be useful in the kitchen." He patted her bottom again.

"We did that already," she said. With one stroke of the poor-quality knife April split the breastbone of the duck, then pressed down on it with both hands, cracking the rib cage and loosening the meat. He watched her for a minute, then set about the task she'd given him. Even though he didn't have much in the way of equipment, and two very poor knives, he knew his way around the kitchen. In twenty minutes she'd finished making the crispy hacked duck with five flavors and the Buddha's delight with pan-fried noodles. At quarter of eleven they sat down at the table by the window with the view to eat the feast off unmatched plates.

"I like this." Mike struggled a little with the red-lacquered chopsticks April had put by his plate. Finally he stabbed a piece of duck and dipped it in the hoisin sauce before putting it in his mouth. "I like this a lot. This is sexy."

April laughed. "Not like that." She rearranged the sticks in his hand. "You have to make a hinge with your finger. You know how to do this."

"I like it when you make the hinge with my finger. Will you still be cooking like this for me when you're old and gray, *querida*?"

"Probably not." She frowned, thinking of her mother, who dyed her hair, and of Mike's Mexican mother, plump and very Catholic, who probably dyed hers, too.

"Oh, come on, *querida*, don't fade on me. This is good, this is more than good. I cook for you, you cook for me. You don't nag me about my day, or tell me about yours. We can do this, *querida*. You can tell me about your case. Maybe I can help you."

She ate some noodles. "You like my cooking?"

"Yeah. I told you I did."

"I hope we find this baby alive and well."

"I know you do."

"You know what Woody told me?"

"Who's Woody?"

"Didn't I tell you about Woody?"

Mike shook his head.

"Yeah, I told you about Woody. He's the new guy in my squad." She made a face. "He's from Anticrime, drives worse than you do. I'm lucky to be alive."

"Good-looking guy?"

"Nobody's as good-looking as you." April smiled.

Mike raised an eyebrow, pleased with himself. "I don't like him anyway. What'd he say?"

"He thinks Anton is the one with the problem and that's why he beats her up. We found the stroller in

Chinatown. So we're thinking the baby's down there. Don't you like my cooking?"

"Yeah, yeah." Mike shook his head and picked up the chopsticks. "Am I going to have to use these every day?"

"Get used to it." They ate quietly for a while. Then she touched his hand. "Gotta go. I have to be in early tomorrow. Maybe I'll get lucky and break the case. That would make it a good week for both of us."

"It's already been a good week for us, *querida*," he reminded her.

"True." April put on her clothes and left Mike with the dishes, promising to do them next time. Just as she was heading out the door, he gave her the cell phone so they'd always be in touch. She thought it was so unbearably romantic she actually cried in the car on the way home.

CHAPTER
32

Lin Tsing hadn't been feeling well on Tuesday. But she hadn't felt well in so long she'd almost forgotten what it was like to have no sores and no pain. That morning she'd been hotter than usual and knew she had a fever again. The aunties always scolded her when she was sick and made her go to work anyway. She was sitting at the sewing machine, on the stool that was backless so she couldn't slack off or fall asleep, when Annie Lee marched over to her, face frowning.

Right away Lin knew more trouble was coming to her. This certain knowledge that her troubles were not over made her homesick for China, where she'd lost her mother and almost starved to death more than once. To save her life, her cousin Nanci had paid for her to come here to this land of golden opportunity, but it hadn't been so golden for her. Lin knew everything that happened after she got here was her fault, but fault or not, Lin did not know how she could have done anything any other way. She had traveled with the two aunties, who were at least as old as her mother would be if she had lived, more than thirty-five. Lin was half their age and by far the prettiest of the three. She had worked in a factory before, and knew that she could not do any of the jobs her cousin expected of her. She'd been convinced by the two aunties that she could get a good job right away even though she didn't speak a word of English, and further that she was obliged to do this for them to repay for the care they had given her after her mother died.

The aunties' confidence in Lin was rewarded by immediate good luck. Some people in the apartment where they stayed told her of a job that paid ten dollars a day and required no English. Lin could have it right away. She went to the place at eight in the morning. A Chinese woman, who turned out to be Annie Lee, talked to her and made her sew a seam to prove she could use a Singer machine. Within half an hour she was hired and had the two aunties claiming to be her dependents. Still, Lin had considered herself lucky to be independent of the cousin who made her feel stupid, told her so many lies about her future, and frightened Lin with her certainty about the bad things that could happen to her if she didn't listen.

But Lin hadn't believed her cousin, and she got in trouble right away. The very first day, after she'd sewed all her pieces, the Chinese boss, Annie Lee, asked her to get more work from the space upstairs. Lin went where Annie told her to go and picked up a stack of unsewn pattern pieces, balancing it on her head. The stairs were narrow. When she started to come down again, the big foreign boss was down at the bottom, blocking her way. He said something and laughed. She thought he wanted her to move away to let him pass, so she backed up a few steps into the space upstairs where broken furniture and rubbish were stored, along with the cut garments to be sewed. The pieces came in thick stacks and were tied up with long strips of the same fabric. She still remembered what the fabric was that day: yellow-brown corduroy the color of sesame-seed candy.

It had been August then and the air was stifling up

in the attic space. The bundle of heavy fabric on Lin's head weighed her down. The red-faced man said something she didn't understand. He pointed to her head. She could see his mouth laughing. She didn't know what she was supposed to do, come up or go down. It was three o'clock. She'd been there only since the morning and didn't want to do the wrong thing, anger the boss, and lose her job after she had been so lucky to get it.

On the floor below, eleven sewing machines roared, chewing up the miles of seams like hungry animals devouring easy prey. The red-faced man came up the stairs and Lin stepped back, frightened that she would be fired and the two aunties who depended on her would be angry and they would all have to leave the place they lived. All these fears crowded into Lin's head. Her heart hammered in her chest as she searched behind her, looking for a place to hide from the man's view so he would not try to talk to her.

She did not think this was like the moments she had known before, when rough bosses in China teased the girls and did things to them that were not allowed but not prevented either. She thought the red-faced man wanted her to do some work she did not know how to do because she was so new in the golden city. But when the boss reached the top of the stairs, he did not seem angry. He pointed and laughed at the bundle on her head. He closed the plywood door on its squealing hinges and waved his hand at her to come with him to another stack of cut fabrics across the attic space. She let her breath out; she must have taken the wrong pieces. When she came to where he pointed, he reached over and lifted the bundle off her head. This caused her to let her head drop the way she'd been told by her mother and the aunties to do when men were talking to her. She'd been told not to look in their faces and tempt the devil. Later, whenever

she had a fever, she saw herself like this, with her
head turned away from trouble, then trouble coming
after her anyway. She was busy warding off shame
when his hand reached out and squeezed her breast
as if it were a piece of fruit in the market. The vibration from the sewing machines roaring below was like
her heart sinking to her feet, then beating helplessly
on the floor as he took his other hand and seized her
other breast. Time stopped.

It had been so hot that August day; all Lin was
wearing was a thin T-shirt and cotton pants with an
elastic waistband. She was seventeen and had never
owned a bra. He was an old man, a heavy man, smelly
and red-faced, the big boss and source of her lucky
job. He pushed his hands with spread fingers against
her breasts, flattening them, then opened and closed
his fingers around her nipples, pulling up the T-shirt
so he could look at her stomach. He pushed the waistband of the pants down, so more of her stomach
showed. He pinched her ribs. Then he said something
in English and she was so terrified she thought she'd
pee in her pants.

Her eyes were on the ground, her chin was glued
to her collarbone. Her tongue was frozen in her
mouth. She could not look up. He had to pull up her
chin to get where his mouth and brown teeth and big
tongue wanted to go. He was in a hurry. He bent his
knees to get lower, shoved his chest and hips at her.
She was small and thin, undernourished, and so
shocked she was shaking all over. He dragged her
pants down to her feet, pulled her legs and her but-
tocks apart and held her up like a dummy for public
ridicule then stabbed into her with deep, determined
jabs like someone who was used to entering closed,
unwilling places where nothing had ever been before.
He hurt her so much she thought her body would split

apart, but she did not dare to make a sound. She didn't want anyone to know.

When the man was finished with her, he let her go. Her legs wouldn't hold her up; she fell to the floor. He let her sit there a few minutes and then made the motions for her to go back to work. When she went downstairs with the stack of unsewn garments, Annie Lee did not look at her. No one looked at her, and she looked at the floor. She did not tell the aunties. She did not tell her cousin, who was married to a rich man and would be angry because Lin hadn't listened to her. She could never go and live in their house, never look at either of them. She could not tell anyone, and she could not leave this place because she had no place to go. Her life was over.

After that the red-faced man had no need to speak to her. He told her to go upstairs with his chin whenever he felt like it. One time only did she shake her head, and that week she got no fifty dollars to give the landlord and to pay for food for the aunties. When the old man tired of one way, he made her lie down, or mounted her from behind. He also pushed her down on her knees and put his thing in her mouth, then made noises as he pushed up and down her throat, until the white fluid pulsed out in her mouth. The only time she cried was the day he stuck it in her behind. That day, with a big smile, he gave her a ham as a present. Another day he gave her half of his big meat sandwich. Then he gave her some sweatshirts and some pants to hide her body when it swelled and hardened. He gave her some pills to stop her from throwing up. And he kept doing the same things to her until two days before the baby was born.

Annie Lee was the one who shocked Lin with the news that she was going to have a baby. She didn't know what was wrong with her. She'd thought she was sick with a tumor, a cancer like her mother had died from. In the past she'd missed her period for months at a time. She was so irregular that she missed it more often than she had it. She didn't connect the sickness she felt and the swelling with having a baby. And she was not relieved to hear that she didn't have cancer, she was having a baby instead. She considered hanging herself, the way a young girl from Lin's village had done when Lin herself was very small. That had been a big event because the girl was only thirteen and no one would say who did it to her. Everyone had come to see the dead girl's bloated body and black face, Lin and her mother included.

Annie Lee was the one who reassured her and told her she was a lucky girl. She promised she would not tell anyone and would not throw her out. It would be their secret. She would let Lin keep her job and she would help her when her time came. She said nothing about the red-faced boss. The father of Lin's baby was of no interest to Annie Lee. She also said nothing about what would happen to the baby after it was born. Lin didn't think about it. She was just grateful because her Chinese boss was as good as her word. Lin had been able to keep her job and hide her condition, and when her time came she did what Annie told her to do. She gave birth to her baby in the storage room of the factory. And when the baby was born, and she did not hear it cry, she was not unhappy when Annie told her it was born dead. It seemed to her only fair. The birth was one month ago. One month ago she'd thought her troubles were over.

But on Tuesday when she still wasn't feeling well, Annie Lee came over, scowled angrily at her, and told her she'd made a mistake when she said the baby had died. The baby hadn't died. A lady had taken it away, but now the lady had changed her mind about keeping it and was bringing it back. And by the way, *gongxi, gongxi,* it was a boy.

Congratulations! Lin was so stunned she almost fainted on the spot. She didn't know what to say.

Finally she asked, *"Weishenme?"*

"None of your business *why,* you stupid girl," Annie snapped. "Just take it away. Your fault, your problem."

"Take it away?" Lin panicked. "Take it where?" She was whispering. She still didn't want anyone to know. She didn't want the aunties to know, nobody. She didn't know what to do with it. Throw it away in the garbage?

"Take it away during your lunch break, then come back to work or you'll lose your job. And don't tell anyone."

Her lunch break was ten minutes. She wasn't supposed to leave the building. What could she do with a baby in ten minutes? She didn't want a baby. She'd never wanted a baby. But why didn't the woman who took him want him, either? Lin couldn't understand why this was happening. Agonized, she finally asked, "Is something wrong with him?"

"Nothing's wrong," Annie said coldly.

"Why?" she couldn't stop asking the question. It was the only one she could think of. Why was the bad luck coming back to her? Why was this baby not dead and gone as Annie had told her it was? Must be a no-good baby. She thought of running out and putting the baby in the garbage. Then she and the aunties could disappear. They would cross the river and move to New Jersey where no one would ever find them.

But that didn't happen. She didn't wait for her lunch break. She left the factory right away. She stood on the street for more than half an hour, waiting for the woman to bring the baby no one wanted. Lin watched her get out of a taxi; she was a rich woman. She was crying when she handed him over and told her more

than once that he was a wonderful baby who deserved
to be with his mother.

Lin was too frightened to ask why give him back if
he was so wonderful.

"He's a good baby. Take good care of him," she
said one last time.

Lin didn't even look at his face before she got rid
of him. By eleven-thirty, he was out of her life. Then
she went home and lay on the old blankets, refusing
to say anything about anything to anybody. And the
quarrels about what to do with her floated around her.

Seven women lived in the apartment. They didn't
like her taking up space on the floor for twenty-four
hours a day, not taking turns as she was supposed to
do. They talked about her bad cousin with no sense
of family responsibility, who would probably not even
come to take the corpse off their hands if she died.
No one in the apartment thought Lin had a simple
flu. She heard voices talking about taking her to the
hospital. The aunties gave her special tea and tried to
reason with her. But nothing they said helped Lin
Tsing get over her fever. That same day Annie Lee
from the factory came to talk to her, but the aunties
hid her and said she wasn't there anymore, because
they didn't want Annie Lee to find out that Lin was
sick and fire her from her job.

The next day the aunties agreed that something had
to be done about Lin, but they weren't sure what.
They did not want to leave Lin on the street in the
hope that an ambulance would come for her, because
even if such a lucky thing were to happen, the girl
would disappear into some hospital and they would
not be able to find her again. Or she might be put in
jail or deported without their ever knowing. If she got
well, she might tell who her friends were and have
them all deported. Early Wednesday morning Annie
Lee came to ask about Lin a second time. This time

the white-haired woman was so worried and concerned about the girl, so far from angry about her being sick, and so eager to care for her, the two aunties were happy to accept the fifty dollars' goodwill money and let the good-hearted woman take Lin away for medical treatment.

But Annie didn't take her to the hospital. She took her upstairs to that closet. Annie Lee promised she and the boss would take Lin to the doctors as soon as she told them what she'd done with the baby, but Annie had lied to her when the baby was born, and now Lin did not trust her anymore. She was as afraid of doctors as she was of the red-faced boss and Annie Lee, so she did not tell them what they wanted to know. She had no idea how long she had been in the closet when the boss came up to talk to her himself. He had forgotten that she couldn't speak English and didn't know what he was shouting at her. If she had been able to answer he wouldn't have known what she was saying. All she knew was that he was very angry. Then Annie Lee came back and made him stop. A little while later, the hitting and shaking started. She was pulled off the mattress and taken out into the attic room where the red-faced boss had raped her so many times. Her head was slammed against the floor and against the wall until she had no feeling. And still it went on.

CHAPTER
33

I think you should call April," was Milton's first response to the problem of Lin's ransom. It was late Thursday evening, and he was still wearing his restaurant uniform of black jacket, black pants, white shirt, and black tie. His handsome face looked unusually stern and serious. Annie Lee had not called back, demanding the money again. Nanci was even more worried than before, and now it was clear that somebody had to go into the city in the morning to deal with the situation. No more putting it off. She balked at the idea of calling April, though.

"What's the matter with you? This is something for the police to deal with." Milton was getting impatient with her, even angry, and this was something that rarely happened.

"I know." Nanci looked down at her hands, twisting a napkin around her fingers. How could she tell him she'd lied to April about everything? April would be mad if they called her now, and there'd be consequences, no question about that.

"So let's call her."

Nanci shook her head. "You know what would happen."

"Nanci, we have to deal with this," Milton said.

"I know." She wouldn't look at him.

"Then let's call her."

How could she tell him again about what happened when her father died, how much harder the cops had made the tragedy for her with all their questions? Even though she'd known at the time that they were just trying to find out what happened, they'd sounded so accusing. She'd felt it was her fault, and she'd been so frightened of the social workers and having the city take her away to a foster home, even deport her to China where she had no relatives who could take care of her. It was hard to explain these things to Milton, who was born here, had a big family, and didn't understand about money worries. April used to be a friend, but she was all cop now. Nothing but trouble, just like the rest of them.

"Let's just give her the two thousand and get Lin back," Nanci said.

They went around and around on it, and finally Milton suggested something that appealed to Nanci. He had a shady friend from Catholic school, Frankie Corelli, who knew Chinatown and Little Italy better than anyone. He and Milton had started out in high school as opposites and sworn enemies, but had ended up unlikely friends. Milton had been responsible, got good grades, and had ambition. Frankie was a troublemaker then and had been in and out of trouble ever since. Milton hit on the idea of using Frankie as an intimidator to frighten the old-lady extortionist into giving Lin up without a bribe. Nanci liked this idea. It was always better to use local muscle. So Milton called Frankie, and Frankie was all excited: this kind of favor was right up his alley.

"Two thousand dollars is what she wants," Milton told him. "If you need the money, I have it. I could even bring it in now." He looked at his wife, who was still torturing the napkin.

"Don't worry about the money. This is nothing. I'll

walk over to the place with Joey, you remember Joey Malconi? We'll have a little talk with the lady, get this thing straightened out. You'll have your cousin by noon. How about that for efficiency?"

They had Frankie on the speaker phone so they both could talk to him. Nanci had listened to Milton explain the situation without comment. And she had heard Frankie's enthusiasm as he picked up the challenge to intimidate an extortionist and save a female in distress. He responded too eagerly, which made Nanci stay awake half the night worrying about whether Frankie was up to taking care of much of anything. Nanci knew some of Frankie's friends were rough. She knew she and Milton ought to be calling the police, but, once again, she just couldn't do it.

CHAPTER
34

It was almost one o'clock on Friday morning when April parked in her usual spot in front of the brick house in Astoria, Queens, that no longer felt like her home. Sharply etched in the sky just above the house was a crescent moon. As she glanced up and down the block, checking the lights in the neighbors' houses, the night air felt like warm breath on her face. She could almost feel the flowers in their neat little plots reaching up through the softening earth. All looked quiet and safe. But April knew this sense of peace was false. She touched the flip-down cell phone Mike had given her. It was small enough to live in her pocket. For the first time in her life she felt loved. She dawdled under the stars, taking her time getting into the house that had been big trouble for her from the very beginning.

Soon after she'd settled into her first precinct, in Bed-Stuy, her father had picked out this house without breathing a word. He was a great reader of Chinese newpapers but not much of a talker. After much silent consultation with himself, he decided that he'd been living in a Chinatown walk-up for twenty-five years, saving every spare penny. Now he was ready to move up. Also, he'd been waiting for his girl child, Siyue

Woo, to marry a rich man and or get a good job. The job had materialized before the rich man.

April had been summoned to the National Bank of New York without any idea what for. Judy Chen, one of her oldest friends, was there with her father, Ronald Chen of Chen Realty, along with April's parents, both in their best clothes. The four of them made a nice family picture around April when the mortgage agent from the bank handed her the papers to sign. They jabbered at her for a while in Chinese, and that was the first she heard of their expectation that she would hand over her life savings (from working since before she was fourteen, washing hair in a beauty shop, selling groceries in Ma Fat's supermarket, and teaching English to people who were too shy to go to real classes) for the down payment. Ronald Chen argued that April's old father might not be able to work much longer and needed his own life savings in case of war, famine, or possible retirement. On the other hand, anybody could see that April was young, not ugly, and had many chances to get ahead, with her whole life in front of her. Old Father, all of fifty-one, had nodded his agreement to all this. Old Mother had noddded, too.

The mortgage was another shocker. Ronald Chen spoke for the Woo parents. If the mortgage was in April's name, then the venerable old parents wouldn't ever have to worry about their future. This little meeting more than six years ago had doomed April to endless worry about getting ahead in the department and securing enough overtime to cover her expenses.

It wasn't until some weeks later, at the closing, that April found out the house wasn't in her name. For her parents, this, too, had made perfect sense. This way, if April were a bad daughter or disgraced them in any way, they could have their cake and eat it, too:

They could throw her out of their house and still have
her pay off the mortgage.

With the facts of her life well in mind, April opened
the front door and was immediately assaulted by a
strange odor, hot and intense, as if something rotten
were baking in the oven. The smell enveloped the
house like a deep fog from which there was no escape.
When April closed the door with a sharp clap, there
was no response from her mother's poodle, Dim Sum.
This worried her. She wrinkled her nose, fearing what
Skinny Dragon was up to.

The living room was dark. Beyond it, the kitchen
door was open. Flickering light in there suggested that
Skinny Dragon had the TV on with the sound off. If
April had felt like hiding, she would have been grateful for the chance to run upstairs unnoticed, but tonight she wasn't hiding.

"Hi, Ma," she called softly. "What's up?"

April found Skinny sitting at the kitchen table, an
old linoleum number like the ones in the restaurant
where she'd worked for so many years. She did not
raise her eyes from the gruesome scene on the TV
screen in front of her. April's mother was watching a
body covered with green sheets. The chest cavity was
open and something really terrible was going on. It
appeared that Skinny was passing the time waiting for
her daughter to come home by avidly watching a heart
transplant. The combination of the smell of the steam
rising from a pot on the front burner of the stove and
the green tent over ribs cracked apart with several
people huddled around the cutting away of a defective
heart chilled April as much as anything she'd ever
seen on the street.

She attempted a little smile. "What's going on,
Ma?"

Skinny Dragon refused to look away from the TV.
When April was little she used to amuse herself by

counting the different meanings of her mother's silences. She'd calculated a hundred different kinds of silence, including Skinny's crowing satisfaction when she shoved something truly disgusting—that April *really* didn't want to chew up and swallow—into April's mouth when she was little and defenseless. The silence now was number 23 silence. Number 23 contained the message: *You've been gone too long, you've been up to no good, and whatever you tell me will be a big lie.* Although most silences were no-win silences, silence number 23 was particularly no-win.

"Where have you been? I must have called a dozen times in the last few days," April began.

"Where I, where you?" Sai demanded. Her first words were a battle cry already rising to a shriek. "I here."

April shook her head. "No, you weren't, Ma."

Sai's jaws clamped together as she remembered that she was supposed to be silent. Her eyes traveled to the steam rising from the roiling pot. April's eyes traveled there, too. The contents seemed to be some kind of thin stew, but the liquid was black and smelly beyond belief. She didn't know how her mother could sit in the same room with it. Skinny must be really angry. April had the disconcerting thought that her mother might have killed a rat, or a raccoon, or even Dim Sum because the dog had been April's gift to her. The thought of her mother killing the adorable puppy made her feel even sicker.

"I was worried about you," she said. "It's not like you to take off without telling me. Where's Dim Sum?"

Silence.

"Ma, where's the puppy?" April looked around the kitchen. No dog under the table. No dog in her father's chair.

Silence.

"Ma, what's in the pot?"

"Save your life, that's what." Now Skinny's eyes were sharp as she avidly studied her subject.

April had thought she looked pretty good when she left for work the morning before. But Thursday had started in Mike's bed, ended there, too, and April knew by her mother's expression that the poison in the pot was for her. She coughed and tasted bile, wishing she'd delayed her return another few days. With the cough, Skinny came alive.

"You very bad," Sai said ominously in Chinese.

"Yeah, well, whatever you're doing there is really making me sick. I better talk to you tomorrow, Ma." April backed out of the kitchen. She was now pretty sure there was decayed animal matter cooking in the kitchen. She decided that wherever her mother was headed with it, Skinny Dragon had to go there alone. April wasn't visiting this particular hell with her.

"No, no, no." Sai jumped out of the chair with amazing nimbleness for someone who did nothing all day but watch TV and brood. She grabbed her daughter, restraining her with an iron grip that transported April back to the time when her mother used to dig all ten fingernails into April's upper arms to break the skin, or her daughter's will, whichever came first. Skinny didn't dare do that now. But she held on, stopping April from escaping out the kitchen.

"No, Ma," April said firmly, prying off her mother's fingers. "Let go. We're not playing doctor tonight. I'm fine."

"You sick," Sai hissed. The top of her head with its crown of frizzy dyed-black hair came up to April's chin. April could have wrenched away, could have taken her mother down with the twist of her wrist. But she didn't. She let Skinny reach up a scrawny paw and clamp it on her forehead to prove she didn't have a fever.

Many times in her life April had longed for a hug, not a poke or a shove, but Skinny Dragon believed that the best mothering was achieved through tyranny, threats, and deprivation.

"Hot," Sai said with satisfaction.

"No." April moved out of range. No matter what, none of that stinking brew was going down her throat.

"Hot," Skinny insisted.

"I'm going to bed now, Ma."

"Liver very bad," Sai said knowingly.

"My liver's great."

Sai's face twisted with Chinese opera as the charges poured out. Worm daughter's face was a no-good color. Worm's pulse was racing. Pulse was elevated to ten times its normal rate. This was a sign of imminent death. Sai screamed that she personally didn't care if *boo hao* daughter bit the dust, but such a death was an insult to *her* father and mother, to their Han ancestors dating back to the beginning of time.

"My pulse is racing because I'm tired and you're screaming at me."

"No screaming!" Sai screamed.

"What's the matter with you, Ma? You've got to calm down. You're going to have a heart attack."

"No care about me. No care about your father. Only care about yourself." Still in Chinese. She gripped April's arms again.

"Oh, God." April detached herself a second time. "It's one o'clock in the morning. I have to go to work in a few hours." She stepped across the room and turned off the burner on the stove.

"Okay. Go to work. Never come back. But take medicine first."

"I'm not taking it," April told her. For the first time in her life April was absolutely determined not to take any smelly medicine.

"Yes." Sai was acting the peasant in her black pants

and jacket, trying to deceive the gods about her pros-
perity. But the peasant guise was ruined by the natural
disaster occurring on her face. Rage like a tornado, a
hurricane, blasted her because she could manage any
demon but her own daughter.

"No, I'm not taking it. I'm throwing it out." April
reached for the pot handle.

"Nooooo!" Sai screamed. This sustained shriek was
so loud it woke the dead. A loud protest came from
the bedroom, and April's father shuffled out.

Ja Fa Woo was wearing shorts and a white T-shirt
on his skinny body. His tongue was probing the place
where two important gold teeth were missing from his
lower jaw. His face was bleary with sleep. The top of
his head was bald; the sides, where hair grew, were
clipped down to the skin. He was even bonier than
Skinny Dragon Mother, his head hardly better fleshed
than a skull's. He fumbled with his black-rimmed
glasses, got them on, and rubbed his flat nose, looking
out at wife and daughter from eyes narrowed with
pain and suspicion. He spoke with the powerful number 12 silence: *What is the meaning of this disturbance
to my important sleeping self?*

His wife replied with the non sequitur of silence
number 42. *I told you so.*

"Hi, Dad," April said.

Ja Fa Woo sniffed at the pot, scowling with silence
number 3: *You did it wrong.* About the medicine.

Skinny's stony face replied: *I did not.*

They fought on in this vein for a while.

"What's going on?" April was the first to speak.

"Your mother thinks you're not in harmony."

"I'm in perfect harmony," April said, touching the
phone in her pocket.

Sai glared at her husband.

"Spanish boyfriend bad for liver," Ja Fa spat out.

"Huh?"

"Doctor said."

April shook her head. "No real doctor could have said my boyfriend is bad for my liver." She backed out of the kitchen. "If I had a boyfriend." *Which I do,* she didn't add. Both parents followed her into the other room. She felt on safer ground in the living room, turned on the light. Ah, normalcy.

Her father moved toward her suddenly, in slippered feet, and clamped his hand on her forehead as her mother had done. "Hot," he announced, as she had.

"That's because your hand is like ice. Sit down. I want to talk to you."

Sai sniffed at the air around her daughter. "Smell like monkey business."

"I'm thirty years old."

"Old maid," Sai muttered. "Double-stupid. Boyfriend no good."

"He's good."

"Why not captain?"

"He's almost the same as a captain."

"No-good Spanish," Sai spat at her.

"I won't hear that." April was ready to spit fire herself. Her mother was not even five feet tall. Her father was not more than five two. She suddenly realized they were not the giants she'd thought. She let her voice show her anger. "I will not hear that. I will not let you say that. Mike is a good man. He is a better man than anyone I've ever met. I love him."

"You marry?" Sai screamed.

April flushed, unsure. "Maybe."

"No marry you, not good man," her father said.

"He wants to marry me. I'm the one who's not sure," April clarified.

"Ayiee!" Sai screamed. Worse and worse.

April threw up her hands. What did they want? There was no pleasing them. "I'm going to bed now," she announced.

"You eat something." Sai tried a new tack.

"I ate."

"You take medicine for your heart." Skinny followed her to the stairs.

"I thought it was my liver."

"Heart," Sai insisted. "Heart fever."

Whatever. April had reached the first step when a high-pitched wail rose from outside. Sai charged out into the kitchen. "Sollie, sollie, sollie," she cried.

"What's that?"

Ja Fa Woo shook his head as Dim Sum charged into the living room barking excitedly, jumped on April, and hugged her leg with her front paws. Sai must have let her out and forgotten her. She continued to apologize to the dog in the dog's native language. "So sollie, so sollie."

April squatted down to let the beautiful apricot puppy cover her face with kisses. Her own heart beat as frantically as the dog's. There was no question that her parents' house was an insane asylum. And now she had to admit she *was* feeling a little hot, a little overwrought herself. Her parents were crazy; that point was not in doubt. But now it seemed, so was she. She'd actually thought Sai would kill her own beloved pet and make her eat it just to spite her. That proved she was as nuts as they were. "I love you," she murmured to the dog.

"Who love?" Skinny screamed.

"I love you, Ma," April said dutifully. Then she gave Skinny a smile that contained the hardest silence for a mother to bear, silence number 101, a brand-new silence and more powerful than all the others put together: *But don't push me, because I love my boyfriend more, and I'll marry him if I decide that's the best thing for me.* Skinny made a wise decision and backed off.

Half an hour later April's pulse was beginning to

slow and her eyes were closing, when the phone by her bed began to ring.

Sleepily, she fumbled for it. "Sergeant Woo."

"Hey April, sorry to get you up."

"Alfie?" April's eyes popped open.

"Yeah."

"Jesus. What's up?"

"We got a suicide you might be interested in. Young woman. Chinese. Looks like she might be your little mother."

"Oh, God, where are you? I'm on my way."

"Too late for that. The body's already been removed. I'd like to see you tomorrow, first thing."

"You have a COD?"

"Looks like she went out of a window. Guess where."

"I'll bite. Where?"

"The Popescu building. Eight o'clock in my office, okay?"

"Oh, Jesus. I'll get there as soon as I can."

"You brought me this one, April, you better help me clear it."

"See you, Alfie."

April was sure she didn't close her eyes or sleep at all. She had bad dreams and was up before six, bothered by the horrid rotting smell, which had moved upstairs during the night. But she had slept and when she opened her eyes, she was stunned to see the electric kettle from the kitchen plugged in by her bed, steaming her mother's evil brew directly into her brain.

CHAPTER
35

When they met just before eight o'clock Friday morning, Lieutenant Iriarte was in high spirits. "Well, this is good news. Very good." He clapped his hands and rubbed them together.

"How's that?" April didn't get the reason for her boss's pleasure at the news of a young woman's death in Chinatown. But then she wasn't feeling up to par herself, and therefore was maybe a little slow on the uptake.

"We're out of it now." Iriarte waved his hand for her to sit down. "And that's good, because you messed this one up, Woo."

April's eyes burned, her throat hurt, her head was reeling, and she seemed to be having some trouble breathing. One young woman had a concussion and was covered with bruises and burn marks, a baby was still missing, and another young woman was dead, and Iriarte was congratulating himself because he thought they were out of it. "Can I go now, sir?" she asked, not wanting to hear how she'd messed up.

"Go? Go where?" The lieutenant's face registered annoyance again.

Green spots jumped in front of April's eyes. She'd just explained that Lieutenant Bernardino, her boss for five years down in the 5th, had asked her to come down there to question Annie Lee, the old woman from the Popescu factory who claimed she'd seen the dead woman jump from a window. "Downtown, sir."

"No way. You let a lot of things slip here. You gotta get back on track. Right here. I want you all over Popescu. Shake him up. I want to know where that baby came from." He picked up a complaint from the pile that had collected since last night.

"The baby came from down there," April told him. "We haven't found him yet. I thought finding the baby was our highest priority—"

"And what's the matter with you? Why haven't you found it yet? You getting soft or something?"

April flushed.

"What does your shrink friend say?" Iriarte went on to another tack.

Soft, was she getting soft? And now that he mentioned it, she'd forgotten to call Jason. Was she losing her edge? She felt clammy and scared. Soft? Really? "I'll call him," she promised.

"Good, call him now." He flapped his hand for her to leave. She didn't move. Iriarte and Hagedorn exchanged glances. "Is there something wrong, Sergeant?"

"Bernardino needs a translator for the witness," April said firmly. She wasn't going soft. She was going down to Chinatown to find out what happened to that woman and her baby.

"So? Chinatown is filled with translators."

Now her head was getting hard to hold up; it was as heavy as a boulder. She was torn between her former boss and her present boss and couldn't think straight.

Iriarte sniffed the air. "Do you smell something funny?" he asked Hagedorn.

"Yeah, what is that weird smell? Ugh." Hagedorn's eyes circled their sockets.

Both men focused their attention on her. "April?"

What was this about? She sniffed, horrified, wondering what it could be.

"What is that smell?"

She wrinkled her nose. Yes, there did seem to be a weird smell, and it did seem to be coming from the white shirt she was wearing under her navy jacket. Or maybe it was coming from the red-and-gold scarf tied around her neck. "I have no idea, sir."

Hagedorn not so discreetly sniffed the air around her. Suddenly she knew what it was. Sweat broke out on her forehead. Her bottom slid forward on the chair. The steam from the kettle had gotten inside her and was now coming out of her pores. Her face was red, and the boulder that was her head threatened to explode. Oh, she was in trouble, and there was a dead woman in Chinatown who needed her attention.

"And they found the missing stroller right on Allen Street. I know we can clear this up today, sir," she promised.

Iriarte wrinkled his nose, then flapped his hand at Hagedorn. Hagedorn nodded, jumped up, and moved out the door, closing it behind him. "Are we going to have a problem, you and I?" Iriarte demanded.

Dizziness overcame her. "No, sir."

"Then don't make assumptions. Do what you're told."

"Yes, sir." She tried to sit up, felt horrible, wondered if her mother would go so far as to kill her to stop her from marrying a Mexican.

Iriarte grimaced, grit his teeth, stroked his skinny mustache with two fingers, then punched out his words, enunciating clearly. "Find the baby. That's your job here."

"Yes, sir."

"And whatever you do, get back here before lunch."

April smiled weakly. "Thank you, sir."

"And April—"

"Yes, sir?"

"Are you sure you're all right?"

April touched the cell phone in her jacket pocket. "Oh yeah, I'm fine."

He raised his eyebrows. "Okay, then take the dunce. Maybe he can do something useful."

April pulled herself out of the chair, mustered what she could of her dignity, and left the office. "Woody," she called into the squad room.

Baum was sitting at his desk, eating a bagel. "Morning, Sergeant. Ooh, what's that smell?"

"Let's go," she barked.

"You all right?"

"Now."

"Uh, any chance of finishing my breakfast?"

"No." April was angry and hurt. She'd been poisoned by her mother, and her boss was calling her soft. She scowled at the bagel crumbs proliferating on Woody's desk. She'd be damned if she'd let herself get soft. She felt worse and worse. She hadn't spoken to Mike this morning. If she died now, he'd never know what happened.

"Okay, okay, if it's that important." Woody brushed the crumbs onto the floor.

April stopped by her office to get her purse. Message slips indicated that during her meeting with Iriarte, Jason and her mother had called. Nothing from Mike. On the other hand, if she died suddenly, Mike might well investigate. He might figure out what happened and send Sai Yuan Woo to jail for life. That would be a fitting end for the Dragon.

April left the precinct without returning her calls. She didn't notice Baum's driving and didn't hear a word he said, though he chattered all the way downtown.

Bernardino's first words when she entered his glass

office were "You look bad. What's the matter with you?"

April sniffed her hand. "Don't worry about it."

"Who said I was worried? You just look green, honey pie." He called out into the squad room, "Madison, would you get the sergeant here some coffee? Baum, you want some coffee, too?" he asked Woody.

"Sure, why not?" Baum said.

Alfie returned to the subject. "You, ah, smell like a—"

"Swamp?" April helped him out.

"And you're green."

"So people have been telling me."

"You coming down with something?"

"Where's your witness? I haven't got much time."

Alfie regarded her uneasily. "You want me to get you a doctor?"

"No."

Madison came in with a single cup of precinct coffee and offered it to April. She took it, nodding her thanks. "Woody, you want to run up to the Popescu apartment and get hold of a photograph of Heather Rose?" she asked him.

"You want me to go up there now?"

"Yes. Don't call first, and don't say what you need it for. Is it okay if Madison brings the grandmother in here to ID Heather Rose?"

"Where are you going with this, April? We got a death to deal with."

"It's all connected. Madison's grandmother with the stroller saw Heather Popescu give the baby to a young woman. If we can get her to ID Heather, and ID the woman she saw Heather give the baby to as our dead girl, bingo. I just hope we don't turn up a dead baby down here."

"You think she may have killed the baby before she killed herself—or was helped along?" Alfie asked.

"Anything's possible," April murmured. She put her hand to her mouth and waited until Baum was out in the squad room. "I want to see where the body was found."

"I'll go with you."

"Then I want to see her."

"Annie Lee?"

"No, the body."

"Whatever you need, but I want you to talk to Annie."

"I only have until noon," April warned.

"What happens then, do you turn into a pumpkin?"

"Probably."

Alfie laughed. April didn't. They trooped downstairs and got into an unmarked vehicle parked down the street. A few minutes later they'd crossed the Bowery and were cruising Allen. The two-way divided avenue that bore the unassuming name of Allen Street had seen many changes over the years. Now, in addition to pockets of five- and six-story tenements from the turn of the century, and even smaller buildings like the one owned by the Popescu family, there were twenty-story apartment buildings with terraces and the large Hong Kong Supermarket where the daughter of the blue Perego stroller's new owner worked.

April stared out of the backseat window at the Popescu building. It hadn't been much to look at when it was built and was now lost in time, unexceptional in every way, just waiting for the wrecking ball. Nothing gave away what the property was used for. No air conditioners were installed in the blackened front windows. No signs identified the business. No brass plate named the tenants. And there were no yellow crime-scene tapes on the sidewalk where she assumed the dead girl had been found. April didn't believe for a moment that the girl had jumped. She guessed that the girl had killed the baby after Heather gave it back to her, and that one of the Popescus had thrown her out the window in a rage.

"Where's the scene?" she asked suddenly.

Alfie turned around and flashed her a look from the front seat. "Didn't I tell you? She was found in the alley."

No, he had not. April felt really sick. The uniform driving them killed the motor. April grabbed her purse and got out of the car slowly. It was her fault for not tumbling to this yesterday. If they'd been more agressive, maybe both mother and baby would still be alive. What were the chances of finding the baby alive now? She was afraid that the god of messing up had bewitched her last night. That faceless demon was responsible for making her think of shopping, of food. And yes, for making her so hot for love that she'd thought more of Mike, more of Emma and her pregnancy, more of searching birth records for a live Eurasian baby, than of pressing the Popescus about their employees. She'd followed the tangent instead of the lead, and now a woman was dead and had been thrown out, another piece of useless garbage.

Her face flushed. Drops of cold sweat sprouted like seedlings on her forehead—whether from sickness or shame, she didn't know. But she did know she couldn't just run away, just return to Midtown North and obey Iriarte's command to avoid involvement in this death that had occurred way out of her precinct. Alfie's concerned face told her that Madison Young had not taken her place in his estimation. She didn't have a choice. She had to stay and find out what happened to make that poor woman end up in an alley. She checked her watch. Now she doubted her wisdom in sending Baum uptown to get a photo of Heather. He'd been gone for more than forty minutes. Even with his driving style it would take upwards of two hours to get uptown to Fifty-ninth Street, wheedle a picture from the Popescu apartment, get back to show it to the stroller grandmother, and make a positive ID on Heather Rose. They also needed a photo of the dead woman for Heather Rose to see. April's gut clenched. She was getting soft. She was doing it backwards. And of course she needed to talk to the supervisor who'd said she'd seen the dead woman jump. It was already a quarter of eleven. No way was she getting back to Midtown North by noon. She looked around for a phone, thinking she should call her boss, had forgotten she now carried one in her pocket. Her right leg felt strange, weak, stuck with pins and needles. Another needle was lodged behind her right eye, stabbing outward. She wondered if this was what dying felt like.

"*Hshh, hshh, hshhh.*" Alfie was making the kind of sniffing noises in her direction that excited dogs make when they're close to dead meat. April's heart accelerated in a sudden surge. She could feel the *thud thud thud* as the crucial muscle kicked into gear, shooting boiling blood through her veins. She didn't want to die.

"You okay?" he asked.

"Yeah, let's go."

They crossed the sidewalk and passed through a chain-link gate into a junk-filled alley festooned with the yellow police tape April had somehow thought would be out front on Allen Street. Why had Alfie given her the impression the girl had gone out the front windows? She shook herself.

"What?" Alfie read her mind.

The cracked pavement around where the body had been found had been picked clean, possibly swept up or even vacuumed by the Crime Scene Unit. Only a few spots of dried blood were visible. April looked up at the sky. The eyes of dozens of uncurtained windows stared down at her. The alley streaked west across

rows of building backs on the two blocks perpendicu-
lar to north–south running Allen Street. On the side
streets moving west most of the buildings were small
and had laundry strung out the windows. But directly
opposite, with an entrance on Allen, was a modern
apartment house, more than twelve stories tall. One
side of this building had ringside seats on the backyard. Alfie followed her gaze and read her mind once
again. "Yeah, we have people in there now."

April's pocket burbled, unnerving her with the unexpected vibration. After a few pulses, she managed
to pluck out the plastic flip-down and gingerly punch
the Talk button. She was upset and distracted by the
interruption. In a normal and healthy state she would
have grumbled and snapped. But now her voice came
out like warm honey.

"Where are you, *chico*?" Oh, she was in trouble.

"I have a prelim on your Jane Doe," Mike said
without introduction. "Guess what?"

"What?"

"Guess."

"How do you know about this?" she asked.

Mike made a sound that managed even on the
phone to sound arrogant and impatient at the same
time. "The woman was already dead when she hit
the ground."

April's eyes swept the few spots of blood on the
cement.

"Tell me something I didn't know."

"Okay. She was young, a teenager, a seamstress
from the looks of the calluses on her thumbs, index,
and pinkie fingers. She was undernourished, dehy-
drated, and had some real bad pelvic infection. The
doc said she also had herpes and pneumonia. She was
not a healthy lady."

April's spirits sank. "Anything else?"

"Yeah, she'd had a baby."

"Uh-huh."

Alfie scowled at her, tapping his foot impatiently. "What?"

April held up a finger to silence him.

"Might be the mother you're looking for."

"Uh-huh."

"*What?*" Alfie punched her arm. She ignored him.

"What was the COD?" April asked.

"Someone bashed her skull in."

"Oh, God." More green spots drifted across April's field of vision. She had a brief vision of Anton's angry face and wondered if he was the killer. Maybe he'd retrieved the baby already and had hidden it somewhere. April wanted to tell Mike that she was sick, that people around her were sniffing her as if she smelled of death. She knew that sick smell and was scared of it. She'd been so out of it when she left home that morning she hadn't known the putrid odor was clinging to her. She didn't know how to tell him any of those things on the phone.

"You don't sound good. Is something wrong?"

"Yeah. What's your involvement in the case?" she asked weakly.

"I'm in. Where are you?"

"Allen Street. Maybe there is a God," she murmured, surprised she was so relieved.

"*What?*" Alfie demanded again.

April handed the phone to him. "It's Sergeant Sanchez of Homicide. He seems to know all about it. Talk to him yourself."

The two conferred while April swayed on her feet. I'm dying, she thought. Then, Better find the baby first.

Alfie hung up and handed her the phone without turning it off. It took her a few seconds to hit Power, flip it up, and put it away.

"What's the plan?" she asked.

Bernardino turned to a detective smoking a cigarette at his side. "Annie Lee?"

"Okay." April wondered where Mike was and when
he planned to join her.

Now she was irritated as well as faint. Baum hadn't
come back from uptown yet. Mike had hung up before
she could tell him she was seriously sick. She didn't
remember his cell number so she couldn't call him
back. She might have beeped him if she'd thought of
it, but she didn't think of it. Instead she gazed bale-
fully at Alfie, who was being high-handed just like the
old days. Only one person knew how long her legs
would hold up; her mother. She wasn't going to call
Skinny Dragon.

Alfie approached her, stepping over some soiled
rags to get there. He put a solicitous hand on her
shoulder. "You're not looking too good, April. Come
on, I'll take you back."

Back where? April heard thunder, but the sun was
out, shooting blinding white light into the Ming-blue
sky. She looked up at the blacked-out windows in the
Popescu building, her brain scuttling like a rat in a
maze. They were going to talk to Annie Lee, but why
weren't they going up there to examine the rooms
behind the windows first? Her vision clouded and her
brain shut down before she had a chance to ask.

CHAPTER
36

Heather Rose was discharged from the hospital early Friday morning. The doctors had given her the green light and there was no excuse to keep her any longer. The day before, when she'd finally awakened from her protective sleep and been fully aware of what was going on, she had at least three guards around her at all times. There was a policeman outside her door. And finally, unimpeded by the opposing will of her husband, her parents had come from San Francisco to be alone with her for the very first time since she was married nearly six years ago. These two hard-working, gray-haired people, who had labored eighteen hours a day in a dry-cleaning store so she could fulfill their dreams and attend the number one university in America, climb the ladder of success, be rich, and live in splendor the rest of her life, were there to see her shame. They sat by her bed, solemn-faced, talking quietly in Chinese and eating the food they brought in from a Chinese take-out place across the street that was not first-rate. They did not leave her room unless the nurses or the doctors or the police came and told them to go out into the hall. They left the hospital only one at a time, and only to get food and return to their post.

If Heather Rose could have hung her head, her

forehead would have been knocking the ground. She knew that they, and everyone else, could see she was a walking piece of human shit. And no longer even walking. Just a lump of human shit in a hospital bed. She knew that she did not deserve to be alive. Better to have been drowned in the bathtub, better to have been pushed under a subway car. Better to have died of poisoning. Anything would have been better than the eye swollen and purple like a bursting plum, her lips deformed, her scalp split and her ribs aching so that she could hardly think straight, and the burn marks on her arms and inner thighs—all revealed for her parents and the police and the doctors and nurses to see.

Luckily for her, her parents were the only ones who did not ask what had happened to her. And she knew that as long as they lived, they would never ask her. They might see her every day, feed her and scold her and advise her to do any number of things, push her this way or that way. But they would not ask what had happened after she married Anton and went to live the rich life with him in New York City. To ask, and to receive the answers, would mean they would have to swallow her pain and be destroyed by it, and they would never do that.

When she was little, Heather's mother used to tell her that in China people would eat anything. They would eat lice and maggots and rats, scummy things from ponds and seas, crusty things from trees and fields, even stones and earth and bones. They would dry and pound into powder whatever was dreadful, frightful, or dangerous to them. They would ingest it, and in this way they would both consume their fear and acquire its power. They believed that horrors could be eaten; but sadness could not be so easily conquered and exterminated. The many sad parts of life had to be the most deeply held secrets, unvoiced and rigidly contained in an iron box of a soul. To give sadness a name was to make it unendurable for others, so the highest form of love was to say nothing. And so Heather Rose's parents prepared for her release from the hospital, bought her a ticket to return with them to San Francisco, and asked her no questions.

She was sitting up when the psychiatrist Jason Frank came to see her, very early, at a quarter past seven. Her parents quietly left the room. As soon as they were gone he said, "You're looking a lot better."

She blew air through her nose. "Today is Friday; Clinton is still President, but maybe not for long. My name is Heather Rose Kwan Popescu, I don't hear voices from outer space, and I don't think the devil lives in the television set."

The doctor laughed. "Well, that clears a lot of things up. I gather they've been asking you those questions to see if you're disoriented, or hear things that may not be there for anyone else."

"Dr. Frank, the psychiatrist, right?"

"And you have an excellent memory. Yes, I'm one psychiatrist. Have there been others to see you?"

"I'm told this is a coming attraction for me. I'll miss it, though."

"Oh, how will you manage that?"

"I'm going home in a few minutes."

"Really, are you feeling that much better?"

"Yes. They gave me brain scans and everything. I guess I'm lucky—just a concussion." She gave him a look. "I'm not a suspect. I'm the victim. If I don't know who assaulted me, I can't help the police. They, in turn, can't keep me here. Anton wants me to come home. My parents want me to go back to San Francisco."

"What do you want?"

She rubbed her arm. "Do you think I'm crazy?"

"There are many kinds of crazy," he said, as if being

crazy were no different from having red hair. "Some kinds of crazy aren't so bad."

"You said that before."

"Must be because it's true." He gave her a little smile. "We were getting somewhere last time, and then all of sudden I lost you. Something really scared you, and you went out like a light. My guess is you're terrified of your husband."

"Have they found the baby?"

The shrink shook his head. "Not that I know of."

"Oh God. I hope she didn't hurt him." Tears filled Heather's eyes. "I thought giving him back to his mother was the right thing to do."

"Yes, you implied that; but you didn't tell me who she is. That's why they can't find her."

"I don't know her name." Her tears were falling harder now. "Everything was arranged through Annie."

"Annie?"

"Annie is the family's Chinatown connection. She works in the factory, kind of manages the personnel side of the business. Annie told us about the baby in the first place. She arranged it when I decided to give him back to his mother."

"Did you tell your husband?"

"No," she wailed. "I couldn't talk to him about anything. I just did it. I don't know what I thought would happen. I just had to. . . . He's an angel baby. Oh, God, I hope he's all right."

"How did you get involved with your husband?" the doctor asked her suddenly.

She blew her nose and pulled herself together. "We met in college."

"Where was that?"

"Yale. Only number two," she said softly.

"Number two?"

"For my family there's only Harvard. After that,

forget it. I'd failed. You asked about Anton. He was
a senior. I was a freshman. I'd never been away from
home before."

"San Francisco, right?"

"Yes. You saw my parents: very strict. I couldn't go
out at all. I'd never had a boyfriend before. I guess
you could say I've never had a boyfriend."

"What do you mean?"

She moved her head on the pillow.

"Did your parents approve of your husband?"

"No, of course not."

"Why not?"

She shook her head again. Any idiot should know
why not.

"What did you study?"

"Oh, I had to choose business, medicine, or
science."

"I thought Yale offered many more choices than
that."

"Those were the choices I had." She found that she
had been holding her tongue for so long it was easy
to speak now. Someone wanted to know, so the words
came out.

"Who gave you the choice?"

"My parents did. Will you tell the police to ask
Annie about the baby? She must know where he is."

"Yes, I will."

"I loved him; I would never hurt him. He was the
sweetest thing—the best thing that ever happened to
me." Her throat closed, taking her breath away.

"Why did you give him back, then?"

"I found out he wasn't really adopted. I thought it
would be better for him to grow up poor with his own
mother than be hurt by those people."

"How did Anton hurt you?"

"Anton was my first boyfriend. No one had ever
asked me before. . . . I was homesick and alone, and

he made it like the movies, like a dream come true."
Heather looked at the doctor with her eyes streaming.
"Like a dream come true."

He handed her the tissue box. "From the looks of
your arms and your head the dream didn't come true."

"He never touched me."

"He didn't burn you?"

Heather's head ached. "I mean, it wasn't like the
movies where there's all that kissing, rolling
around . . . and then they get married." She chewed
on the inside of her mouth. Maybe that would be as
far as she would go.

The shrink continued listening, didn't prompt her
with another question this time. She thought he had
a nice face. He was handsome, almost like a Kennedy.
She turned away to blow her nose, then looked over
at him to see if he understood. He didn't say either
way, so she had to go on.

"I thought he respected me, do you know what I
mean?"

He was sitting beside her; he gave a tiny shake of
his own head.

"Have you talked to him?" Heather Rose asked.

"Yes."

"What did he say?"

"Oh, I can't really tell you that; then you'd be afraid
that what you said would go back to him."

"You told me he said I had health problems. You
told me he said I couldn't have a baby. You told me
he had a girlfriend and had the baby with her."

"Maybe."

"Not maybe, you did. You see how he does things,
twists things around, tells people it's my fault when
it's his fault. He *couldn't* have a girlfriend if he wanted
to. He doesn't want anybody to know—" She closed
her eyes.

"Is he homosexual?"

"No, that's all I'm saying. I'm going home now. The lying is over for me."

"Heather, the police need to know if Anton beat and burned you. If you did it yourself, you need help. If he hurt you, it should come out. No one has a right to do that. You wouldn't want it to happen to someone else, would you?"

"You don't know him. It's not his fault. That's all I'm going to say."

A few minutes later the psychiatrist left. Heather used the phone in her room to call the Central Park South apartment where she had lived for six years. By eight-fifteen, no one was picking up the phone. When she and her parents felt certain that Anton had left for his office, they went home to get her things.

CHAPTER
37

Tick, tick, tick: 10:06 A.M. at the law offices of Pfumf, Anderson and Schmidt. Anton sat at his desk, staring at the screen of his computer and trying to ignore the subtle pulse of the expensive mahogany mantel clock whose heavy brass pendulum swung back and forth all day long to remind him that every second of his time was supposed to be paid for by clients. In the richest of tones it also chimed the same message on the hour and the half hour. The symbolic clock had been given to him by his father the evening of his first day at the firm. The whole family had been assembled for dinner and the ceremony: his grandfather, still alive then; his father, uncle, brother, and cousins; their spouses and children; his aunt, his mother, everybody, all dressed up for the event and the mountains of food the women had prepared. It had been a kind of unspoken celebration of his survival. The family had triumphed and he was now formally proclaimed master of the system, ready at last to give back in services all that he had received in support and loving care. Then, he had been proud. Now, he looked back on the occasion in the light of bitter remembrance; what a contrast it made to their less joyful response when he married Heather Rose. As so often happened in families, the price for their support had been high. Anton thought about that as he waited for word from his brother. Marc had phoned early that morning sounding upset—"Big trouble." Then he said he couldn't talk, he'd have to call back.

"Yeah, sure, whatever," Anton had replied. "I'll take care of it." He said the words easily, even though he didn't want to take care of anything for his relatives ever again.

For quite a while he'd been making no secret of the fact that dealing with every single problem of his highly litigious family was getting out of hand. Not only were his partners furious that he never billed relatives for all the time he spent on them, but also the cases brought by Marc and Ivan, and even the older generation, were often problematic.

"There's an argument for everything" had been his grandfather's motto. Anton had followed it and become adept at riding out untenable positions. The message of the elegant clock made him feel guilty with every tick. He'd paid his family back over and over and couldn't get out from under.

Gloomily, Anton thought of his wife's black eye. Oh yes, he had more than the looks of his partners to contend with now. They passed him in the hall; no one said a word. That was the way it was done uptown. No weeping and complaining and carrying on would do here. The surface had to be smooth: they had to do their work no matter what. Nevertheless, Anton knew his partners were talking about him behind closed doors. They'd never liked him, and now they had their chance to dust him.

He listened to the ticking clock and couldn't concentrate. Marc's voice made the knot of anxiety in his throat grow and grow until it was a lump so big he couldn't swallow. He wanted to know what had happened. Heather was crazy and uncooperative. Why had she done this? He just didn't get it.

The worst part was that he'd been such a jerk all along, so happy to accept the gift of fatherhood, so secure in the reality of having a family himself, that he hadn't bothered with the detail of his baby's birth certificate. If he'd bothered to line up a doctor and the forms and taken the baby down to the Health Department immediately, he could have done it legally. Or at least semi-legally. In any case, the birth records would now be where they should be. But he hadn't dealt with the legalities. Not doing it was against everything he'd learned about covering his tracks, covering his ass, and going by the book. Why hadn't he done it?

Okay, never mind, it was done now. He'd have papers by tonight. So what if the papers hadn't been on record until now? He could blame the clerks. He could blame the doctor, say he hadn't filed them promptly. He could say anything, negotiate anything. His brother had a lead on the baby. They'd get him back quietly in a day or so. He and Roe would get over it. He told himself this even as the clock ticked and he waited for his brother to call. He jumped when the phone rang.

It was one of the doormen at his apartment building. "There's a policeman here. You asked me to let you know."

"I'll be right there," Anton said. He grabbed his suit jacket and left the office without stopping to give instructions or tell anyone where he was going. Out of shape and angry at being called at his office, he stomped down the sidewalk, dodging pedestrians and talking to himself as he ran the four blocks home. He'd told those cops to stay out of it. Rage at the pile of misfortunes that had been heaped on him all his life, culminating in this final public hounding and humiliation, pumped him into a frenzy. By the time he got to his lobby he was gasping for air at the pain and unfairness of it all. But after all that rush, no police-

man, male or female, was in sight as he whirled
through the revolving doors and charged across the
lobby. He put a hand to his head and leaned against
the cold marble that framed the elevator.

"You okay, Mr. Popescu?"

Anton didn't look at the doorman. He knew the
man's name was Fred; he thought Fred was an asshole.
No, he was not okay. He was in agony, anybody with
a brain could see that. "Yeah," he muttered, catching
his breath.

"The cop's upstairs." He held out his hand for a
tip. It hung there.

"Oh shit!" Anton propelled himself off the wall,
punched the elevator button, and exploded. "Shit! I
told you not to let him go up. You're fired. Get out
of here."

The doorman was shocked.

"I said you're fired."

The man's eyes popped.

"*You're fired, asshole!* Don't be here when I get
back." The elevator doors slid open. Anton got in.
The doors slid closed. Mad for a fight, he counted the
seconds it took to rise to his floor. Then he marched
down the hall and let himself into the apartment. All
was quiet. He poked his head into the living room.
The first thing he saw was the detective with the expensive navy sports jacket comfortably ensconced on
one of his sofas going through a box of photos, the
only thing that had escaped scrutiny during the last
police search of the place. For a second Anton thought
he was losing his mind.

"What the fuck do you think you're doing?" he
screamed.

Anton saw the detective holding his special box, the
contents of which not even his own wife had ever
seen. The antique leather hatbox filled with photos
and mementos had been padlocked and put high up

behind a bunch of other stuff on a shelf. How had the box wound up in the living room? The fucking detective had gone through absolutely everything in his closets, that's how.

"Give me that." He plunged across the room and grabbed the worn leather.

The cop had the box on his lap and wouldn't let go. They jerked it back and forth a few times, finally tipping it so that photos from camp that awful year spilled across the floor. Anton saw the pictures of himself desperate, mortified, reaching for the cap that had been snapped off his egg-bald head by his archenemy, Brad. In the photo Brad held the hat high over his head so the much smaller Anton couldn't reach it. He could still hear the boys taunting him. The fury caught him in its tide, and he snapped. He punched the cop, catching him by surprise and knocking him off the couch.

But the cop didn't fall awkwardly and recover his balance slowly, as he should have. He rolled as he hit the ground. Before Anton had a chance to bend down and collect the painful images he'd kept hidden all those years, the cop was on his feet with a small pistol aimed at Anton's head.

"Put up your hands."

Anton turned his head and screamed again, this time at the sight of the gun.

"Put your fucking hands up," the cop demanded.

Anton grunted. The action of raising his hands was unfamiliar to him. He moved—but to argue, not to put them up. The gun jerked, eliciting another cry of alarm.

"Stand back and raise your hands." The cop bit off each word, really angry now.

"Are you crazy? Put that thing away!" Anton cried.

"You just assaulted a police officer, sir. You can be

prosecuted and sent to prison for that. Put up your hands."

"What are you talking about? This is my *home*," Anton cried.

"I'm telling you to do something. You don't argue with me. You do it."

Anton lived to argue. No way was he going to stop arguing just because some asshole told him to. "Don't give me that shit. I find a stranger in my home, going through my possessions. I had no idea you were a cop. Put that fucking thing down."

Now he was ashamed that he'd been afraid of the gun. The cop was not going to shoot him. He didn't know why he'd screamed. He glanced down at the scatter of photos on the floor. Let the cop hit him. That would be good. They'd have a hearing. He'd sue the city. He'd get millions of dollars and an apology for everything he'd suffered. It would be in all the newspapers. Roe would be by his side in court. They'd get rich in a hurry. He turned his back on the cop to pick up his pictures. It was then that he saw his wife staring at him. She was wearing jeans and a white sweater. The swelling around her bad eye had gone down. Her bruises were mottling now, but both eyes were open and staring at him as if she'd never seen him before.

"Hi, honey—" Then he choked on what else he saw. "What happened to your hair?"

The cop made a startled noise and looked surprised as well.

"She's dead," Heather Rose said, so softly Anton wasn't sure he'd heard her right. Then her mother and father appeared behind her. For once the bossy woman was silent. Soo Ling Kwan stared at her son-in-law accusingly. No words were needed to express her feelings. His father-in-law coughed and patted his tweed sports jacket, searching for cigarettes and a light. The dry cleaner from San Francisco looked everywhere but at Anton as he prepared to smoke. This was a pointed insult, because Anton didn't allow cigarettes in his house.

The shocking thing, though, was Heather Rose without her hair. He knew now that she knew about the pictures in the box. His in-laws were making faces at him, so they had to know, too. The cop had uncovered his secret. They all knew. Anton's injured pride demanded that he reassert his authority.

"Go to your room, honey," he told his wife.

Her head was round. Her cheeks were flat. Her hair was almost as short as his, but jagged, as if she'd hacked it off in a hurry. She looked different in other ways, too. Nothing like his worried little rabbit from before. Most annoying of all, she didn't move when he told her to.

"Honey, we'll talk about this privately."

She didn't move. To get away from all the prying eyes, Anton bent to pick up the photos. He saw that the cop had lined up on the table some of the very recent ones: Heather Rose with her gorgeous hair, bulging in a maternity dress at the family Easter party. He'd taken it for posterity to prove she had been pregnant, to show Paul when he was older that Heather Rose was his real mother. Another was a Heather Rose in bed in her long pink nightgown, holding the baby. That one had been taken a few days after Paul's birth, the day his family had come to see him for the first time. It all seemed a million years ago.

Another photo from the same batch of negatives showed Heather, slim, wearing a red cashmere sweater and reading a magazine. Where did that come from? Anton closed his eyes. When he opened them, the tableau was unchanged.

"What's going on?" he asked in as level a voice as he could manage.

"We need a photo of your wife."

"What for?" he asked.

"For identification. Your baby stroller has been located."

"What does that mean?"

Heather's father found his cigarettes. The pack crackled as he extracted one and lit it.

"The woman who has it said she saw a woman with a long ponytail give the baby to another woman."

"As you can see, my wife has short hair," Anton replied.

"She had long hair when I arrived here this morning."

"Are you so sure she had long hair that you would swear it in court?"

"What are you arguing about?" Heather cried. "That poor girl is dead."

"I'm not arguing."

"Yes, Anton. You don't even know what's going on. The baby is gone; no one knows what she did with him. A woman is dead. You can stop arguing now."

"Shut up, you don't know what you're talking about."

Furious, Heather shook her head. "You won't even wait to hear what's going on."

"This is unauthorized entry, unauthorized search and seizure. This so-called policeman came in here without anyone's permission and almost killed me when I caught him. You're a witness. You're all witnesses. You saw him hit me," he said stolidly.

Tears filled Heather's eyes. "I'm not anyone? I'm someone, Anton. I live here, too, and I authorized him to come inside."

"You're crazy. I don't know what you're talking about."

"That's true; you never know what I'm talking

about. But I'm someone anyway," she said softly. "I let him in."

"Shut up," Anton said coldly. "I didn't mean it like that."

"Are you ready?" the cop asked Heather.

"I didn't mean it like that. Don't be a crazy bitch—" He stopped, gaped at the cop, gaped at his wife, his in-laws. The cop pocketed the photos. Anton was stunned. He was tied in knots. He was wearing a suit, one of his best suits, which signified that he was an important person. But the cop had a gun. His low-class in-laws were gabbling in Chinese. His wife was gathering her things.

"Oh, no, you don't!" he cried to no one in particular, and to all of them. "You're not going anywhere."

His wife buttoned the light jacket he'd bought her, slung the expensive purse he'd bought her over her shoulder. He knew how much both those things had cost. He hadn't begrudged her anything. She walked out of the door first, followed by her mother and her father. The cop was the last in line. Anton, in all his wisdom, decided the best course of action was not to follow them at this time. Whatever she said later, he would counter with firm evidence as to her state of mind and her actions. He was certain it would be clear to anyone who saw her now that Heather Rose was insane.

CHAPTER
38

Mike left the medical examiner's office at 2:35 P.M.
with a set of photos of the dead girl taken at the
time of her autopsy and his conversation with the deputy ME fresh in his mind. In the department, homicide
news traveled fast. And Mike was always among the
first to hear about the new cases. If he wasn't on the
scene before the body was taken away, he liked to get
the medical details from the horse's mouth first thing.

The homicide in Chinatown interested him only because of April. He didn't like to admit it, but he'd
gotten used to working with her, being with her. Now
he didn't want to just sleep with her, then take off for
the day to deal with other things as if she had a different kind of job. They were still in the same world,
and though he didn't like to admit it, he wanted to
keep tabs on her and help her. Part of him knew this
was bad form. His girlfriend was independent and
wanted to make it on her own. He should back off,
leave her to come up her own way. She was a good
detective and didn't need him to follow her around,
giving her tips about how to handle her cases, worm-
ing his way in on them whenever he could.

He told himself this, but when the news of the dead
woman got to him, he was all over it. He'd missed
seeing the victim at the scene and missed the autopsy,

but the photos he'd acquired showed her on the table in the clothes she'd been wearing at the time of her death, also without her clothes, face up and face down on the autopsy table before she'd been opened up. There was little tension on her small, battered face. Her features were frozen in a dazed expression, only slightly distorted by her injuries. Although she had no body fat, there seemed to be loose skin on her abdomen. Mike didn't want to ask about that. He'd gotten the photos from Allan Gross, the deputy ME who'd done the autopsy. Dr. Gross told him the girl had been very sick at the time of her death.

"She didn't put up a struggle, so my guess is she was only semiconscious when she was being beaten. I'd be surprised if she could stand up at the time of the assault."

"What kind of person would beat up a sick girl?" Mike muttered.

"Someone who was very mad at her. Her skull is cracked like an eggshell. The hemorrhaging in her brain and the skull fractures suggest somebody banged her head, possibly on a crumbling cement wall, or floor, not once, but many times. Cement and other materials were deeply embedded in her hair and in her scalp wounds. I took a number of samples. Her clothes were sent over to the lab. Looks to me like this happened inside, not outside."

The two men were walking down the hall toward the elevator. Gross was shorter and stockier than Mike. He still wore blood-spattered green scrubs and a green surgical cap on his head.

"I'd like to see her," Mike said.

"No way, not this one," Gross said vehemently.

"Why not?

"You don't want to catch anything." The short ME was new to Mike so he wasn't sure if the doctor was serious.

"Like what?"

"I told you before. She's got tuberculosis."

"I thought you said pneumonia."

"She had tuberculosis. It's in my report." Gross was getting huffy. He pointed at the file in Mike's hand. "It's right in there. This is nothing to play around with. This is dangerous stuff. We can't take chances."

Oh, great. Now they had a missing baby, a murder, and a public health problem on their hands. Mike stared at him.

"Hey, you got the pics. You got a prelim. No one gets results like this faster than I do."

Mike nodded. Yeah, this new doc was very fast all right. Maybe too fast. He couldn't seem to get his diseases straight.

"You're gonna have to find everyone she came in contact with and see that they're tested for TB. There are some bad strains now. What about the baby? He might be sick. The baby's doctor will have to be notified right away. The woman had a baby. He might have it, too. You know that, right?"

"Yeah."

"And everybody who came in contact with the mother."

Mike was upset. This was a new twist on the baby. This pointed to there being a possible medical reason for the baby's return to its biological mother. It might not be a healthy baby. He made a mental note to check with pediatricians to see about cases of tuberculosis. There were requirements for reporting TB. This was a new lead.

"You going to get on it?" the ME demanded.

"Absolutely," Mike promised.

"Where'd she come from?" The guy was really involved with the health issues. He didn't want to let Mike go. "Somewhere in Asia. Hong Kong? Taiwan?"

"We're working on it."

"You don't know much, do you?"

"You're my first step on this one, doc. I have a few other things on my plate right now."

"Okay. Keep me informed. We've got more paperwork to do on this. And we've got to follow up in the community."

"Sure thing." Now it wasn't just a homicide. It was also a bug story.

When news of the new homicide came in last night, Mike had decided to put the follow-up of the Abraham case on hold. Mickla had been arrested. Now there was his indictment and subsequent appearance before a grand jury to look forward to. The arresting officer would be present for the indictment; so would the primary detective. But the grand jury might not call them. All the arrest papers were in order. The DA's office and Mickla's lawyers had taken over. No one liked the end game, the paperwork. Mike was glad to move on. He drove downtown, armed with the reports in the new case he'd horned in on.

CHAPTER
39

April slumped on the backseat of the blue-and-white taking them back to the 5th. Oh God, she was going to puke. Never in her life had she puked on the job. Hadn't even seen a dead body or anything, and she was going to puke. The backseat of the car was moving in a different direction from the front seat, was tilting off the edge of the world. God. She could feel it coming.

"Stop," she said suddenly.

Alfie turned around. "What's the matter?"

"Stop the car, for God's sake."

"Stop, you heard the sergeant," Alfie shot out.

The car stopped on Grand. April opened the door and crawled out. The sidewalk came up to meet her as she lowered herself onto the curb. "I can't do this in front of the lieutenant," she mumbled to herself. Can't do it. Can't heave in public, can't wimp out in the middle of a case. I can't.

"Hey, hey. You all right? Want me to call a doctor, huh? An ambulance?"

April concentrated on the water in her mouth.

"Talk to me, April. You don't open your mouth this minute, you're coming out of here on a stretcher. Got it?" Bernardino let her know who was boss. These men. Bullies, all of them. She swallowed.

"Sorry, sir. I have to make a phone call. Get him to pull up a little, will you?"

Alfie gave her a look she'd never forget. "Are you pregnant, sweetheart? Is that what this is all about?"

"Get outta here." April tried a joke, but nausea struck before she could say anything else. She managed to make it to her feet and lean over the back end of the cruiser just as her stomach turned inside out, emptying itself on the street. She had nothing to cover her face or cover her head or kill herself with except one of her own guns. The god of humiliation and losing face was working overtime. Mercy would be to let her die.

Luckily Alfie had seen a lot worse, and he had the manners to turn his back. He got back in the car whistling a little tune, pretending nothing was going on, thinking she was pregnant. April surveyed the shoppers looking for bargains on the Lower East Side. She was glad she wasn't in uniform, because that would have caused a street fair. When she was finished making an ass of herself, she scrabbled around in her shoulder bag for a moist towelette she'd picked up in a restaurant about two years ago. She finally found it and tore it open with her teeth. It was still moist. She mopped her face and hands, took a deep breath. Felt better and got back in the car.

"Everything all right now?" Alfie asked.

"Yeah, just had to make a quick call."

"Uh-huh."

They resumed the trip. No one said a word. April breathed in and out, trying to be Zen about this, clutching her cell phone as if it were a lifeline. When the car stopped, Alfie got out of the front seat and opened the back door for her. Another first. Behind gluey eyes, April tried to regain her tattered dignity. She took a second to count accessories. Shoulder bag? On her shoulder. Gun? One at her waist, one in the bag. Scarf? Hanging askew around her neck. Moist towelette, still in her hand. She used it to dab at her forehead. Cell phone? Still in her pocket. She was not about to call her mother to find out what was going to happen to her next.

Inside the precinct, it took a second for her eyes to adjust. In that second a handsome Chinese in uniform came out of the commander's office. It took April a moment to figure out that this was Chew, the commander she'd been wanting to meet for a year. She was confused. He looked too young to be an inspector.

Alfie introduced them.

"It's a privilege to meet you, sir," April said, bowing in spite of herself.

"The privilege is all mine." One whiff of her, though, and Inspector Chew took a step back. He said a few things behind his hand to Lieutenant Bernardino, then retreated to his office and closed the door.

April put her hand to her head, trying to brush away the devil. Oh, God, she was truly being punished.

Upstairs in the squad room, the gray-haired woman she knew as Annie Lee sat in the visitor's chair by her old desk. The woman was about the size and age of April's mother but the opposite in all other ways. Skinny Dragon was fleshless and dry, about as nourishing as last year's cornhusk. Her dyed black hair was crimped and curled. Annie Lee, on the other hand, was plump, soft, and damp-looking. Her thick gray hair was blunt-cut, in a bowl shape. She was dressed in black pants and a gray padded jacket. Underneath the jacket, begging to be seen, was a shirt of shiny material printed in a riot of colors. The outfit, face, and expression told April a lot. The woman was shrewd, greedy, and a sweet eater. She did not appear either frightened or nervous as she talked earnestly in Chinese to Madison Young. Like a good Chinese son or grandson, Detective Young was busy taking her seriously, nodding and writing down everything she said. When April came in, the self-proclaimed witness turned her head toward the door and saw her. Suddenly her mouth closed.

"How about your office?" April asked Alfie when she saw the reaction of the Chinese grandmother to the female Chinese detective she'd met before. "Mind if I sit at your desk?"

"Go ahead, just don't touch anything," Alfie said.

"There's nothing the matter with me. I'll be fine."

"Don't touch anyway."

Insulted, April marched into the glass office and sat at Alfie's desk. On another occasion this might have given her pleasure. Now it did not. Between her puking and fainting spells, she'd been wondering whether interrogating Annie Lee in the precinct was the right way to handle this. There was always a variety of ways to go. Sometimes it worked really well to take a frightened person out of the bosom of his family with all the neighbors watching, parade him down the street to a blue-and-white parked a hundred yards away so everyone had an excellent opportunity to see him. Then they'd parade him through the station house, let him visit the holding cell in the squad room and wait there for a while behind bars to think about what might happen if he never got out.

This didn't work with everyone. Sometimes the sight of the bars, the front desk, and so many officers in uniform made people angry and resistant. Sometimes just the experience of arriving at the precinct in a cruiser, before a detective even said a word, set them off. The nearness of the officers suggested the threat of a beating (which was strictly forbidden but happened sometimes anyway) and was enough to provoke resistance.

With every person there was always a choice to make: Be tough or be nice. The god of messing up made sure the cops didn't always make the right choice. Take Anton Popescu. A number of detectives had "spoken" with him. They'd investigated and surveilled him, canvassed his building, done a background check on his life, right from his date of birth. They knew he'd flunked his bar examination the first time he took it. They knew his wife "fell down a lot." They knew what his partners thought of him. But they hadn't gone far enough. Numbers of detectives were still wandering around in the fog of mystery. The result was that Anton had never gotten a proper taste of the enforcement side of the law. He hadn't taken the cops seriously enough. Error on their part. So many errors. April motioned Madison Young to bring the old woman to her. He did so with a great show of deference. This made the old woman's face wary and appeased April only slightly.

Annie Lee moved her dense body into the glass room and sat down in front of the lieutenant's desk. Her face was empty, so April knew she'd decided to go with stubborn. Suddenly the woman made some sniffing noises as if something smelled bad. April knew the bad smell was her. She ignored it. She plunked a black tape recorder on the desk between them, punched the button, and started speaking in Chinese. She gave her name, the date, the time of day, the location, and who was in the room with her. Then, with a sense of amusement at the annoyance this would cause the lieutenant, she conducted her interview with Annie Lee in Chinese.

"Would you state your name and your address for the record," April asked.

Annie stared resentfully at the black box, then looked around for Madison Young. He wasn't available to offer the support she craved.

"Didn't someone take your statement at the scene last night?" April asked her.

"Not with one of these. Why do we need this?"

"It's for your protection. So no one can ever claim you said something you didn't say." April gave her a fish-eye stare.

The woman stared back.

"I'm Sergeant April Woo." April took out her notebook and turned to a clean page.

"I Annie Lee," the grandmother conceded and gave her address.

"Where are you employed, Annie?"

Annie Lee let her face reveal how much she did not like a much younger woman (especially a ranking one) calling her by her first name. "Work at Golden Bobbin. You know that already."

"We need to hear it in words. How long have you worked there?"

"Twenty years."

"Twenty years. That's a long time. What are your duties?"

"I'm a supervisor." Annie sat up a little straighter as she said this.

April didn't look up from her note-taking. "How long have you been a supervisor?"

"What does this have to do with the accident?"

April's stomach started to churn again. "I don't know yet. Are you in some kind of hurry?"

April was counting the silent communications. Now she got silence number 14: *You are inconveniencing me by taking up my important time, but I will accept it without complaint.*

"How long have you been a supervisor?"

"Twelve years."

"And the eight years before that?"

"I worked on a sewing machine."

"What are your duties as a supervisor?"

"I'm charge of time clock. I open up. I count number of garments of each girl. I watch the girls. I watch the door."

"You watch the door. What do you watch the door for?"

Silence number 3: *You already know the answer to that question.*

"You have to answer me in words, Annie. Why do you have to watch the door?"

"So nobody disturb."

"Nobody disturb what?"

"Busy place. Bosses no like trouble."

"Nobody like trouble, Annie. But you have some. You told me you're a boss yourself, a supervisor. So you must know all the girls very well. Tell me about the dead girl."

Annie shook her head. "Don't know."

"Well, I have a copy of the statement you made earlier to an officer on the scene that a woman jumped out of a window in the place where you are, by your own description, the supervisor. You are the one who called 911, and this call was made at ten p.m. Let's get a few things straight here. What were you doing at the Golden Bobbin at ten p.m.?"

"Just passing by."

"You were passing by at ten o'clock? You said you live on One hundred and tenth Street. That's thirty-five minutes away by subway."

"I saw someone jump from window," Annie said stubbornly.

April let the notebook drop to the desk. She looked up at the ceiling as if trying to figure this out. "You were passing by where?"

"Passing by Allen."

"Annie, the girl was found in the alley. You could not have seen her jump."

"No see her jump from street, from building."

"I thought you were passing by."

"Yes, passing by. Then I went inside."

"How did you get inside?"

"The door was open. The light was on. I boss, so I worried."

"Annie, you've been working there for a long time. You have a lot of responsibility. You know all the girls who work there, you know what they get paid and what their stories are. You take care of things and watch the door. Do you like your boss? Is he good to you?"

Face impassive, Annie nodded.

"Is he so good to you that you're willing to go to prison for the rest of your life?"

"Not my fault. Stupid girl jumped. I see her jump, that's all."

"Annie, I'm going to tell you a little about how the law works. The law says if you kill someone, you go to jail."

"Not my fault."

"The law also says if someone else kills someone and you happen to be there and you tell lies about what happened, you go to jail for helping a murderer."

"No murder, accident," Annie insisted, clearly shocked. "I citizen," she added. That meant to her no trouble could come her way. She didn't care what the law said.

"Congratulations, but you can still go to jail if you break the law. Tell me the story of the dead girl. What's her name?"

"She very sick."

"In what way was she sick?" April asked angrily.

"Sick in head. Sick here." Annie banged her chest. "She like to stay there at night. Quiet."

"Oh, come on, Annie, that isn't going to work. What was a sick woman doing at the factory at night, and how did she happen to get her head beaten in?"

Annie looked startled for the second time.

STEALING TIME   289

"You weren't even there, were you?"

Annie opened her mouth to say something, then closed it.

"The girl was already dead when she went out the window. She was thrown out the window after someone beat her to death." April said this matter-of-factly. But her heart was racing, and she was furious.

"How do you know?" Annie asked.

"We know these things. We have the report from the doctors who examined her. She had head injuries that could not have been caused by a fall. You are the supervisor of this girl. Did you hit her and throw her out the window?"

Annie hung her head. "She was crazy girl. Sometimes you get a crazy girl."

"Did you hit the girl, Annie? I'm asking you a question."

No answer.

"I guess you have to be pretty crazy to jump out a window after you're already dead. But you didn't answer my question. Did you beat her and hit her on the head?"

"Not my fault if a girl is crazy."

"It's your fault if she dies in your factory."

"Not my fault. Talk to boss."

"Annie, I was just going to tell you that we *will* be talking to your boss. And your boss will not be talking to you again. So the next time you and I talk, you will not have him to tell you what to say. If you killed this girl, you will go to jail. If he killed this girl, he will go to jail."

Annie got a bright idea. "Someone else kill," she said.

"Okay, I'll bite. Who else?"

"Someone opened the door; that's why I went inside. I saw the door open. That's what I told them the first time."

"What were you doing downtown at ten o'clock?"

"I was visiting a friend."

"What's the name of the friend?"

Annie thought about it but didn't come up with a name.

"Annie, where's the baby?"

Annie had been confused but defiant. Now a shadow of anxiety crossed her round face.

"We know about the baby. We know Heather Rose Popescu gave the baby back to his mother. We know the baby was last seen in front of this building, and we know the dead girl was his mother. We don't know who the baby's father is, who beat her up, or where the baby is right now. But we'll find out. We always do."

Annie got another bright idea. "I don't know."

"What do you watch the door for, Annie?"

No answer.

"Where's the baby?"

"No baby. I don't know."

"As supervisor of this worker, you must know all about it. You're clearly not the father, but you could have taken the baby and done anything with it. You could have beaten and killed this poor girl. You could have thrown her body out the factory window, then called the police with a silly story."

"I do nothing wrong, only what my boss say," Annie repeated stubbornly.

"A judge might not feel the same way. That's enough. I have many people to talk to right now. But I need to know where that baby is today. And if I don't find out today, we're going to keep you here until you tell us. And you won't be a supervisor of anybody ever again."

"Don't know about baby. Talk to boss."

"I will, but I need the girl's address. You must know that."

"Yes."

Annie wrote it down for her. April got up from the desk quickly and ran to the bathroom to puke again. This time it was not her mother's medicine but the horror of the case and all the lying that had made her sick.

CHAPTER
40

On the Huas' Street in Garden City the garbage truck came on Tuesday and Friday. That morning it had come at 5:26. Nanci had been up most of the night talking with Milton and walking with the baby. Lin had hidden him in a laundry basket and Nanci hadn't even known he was there until she and Milton were halfway back to Garden City. She'd been worrying about the way she had behaved toward her cousin and the world ever since.

Just as dawn was beginning to gray the sky, she had seen the rust-colored truck rumble to a stop in front of the house. The baby, dressed in one of the expensive sleep sacks that had so baffled Nanci when she first saw them, slept in her arms. At the sound of the truck, she had been drawn to the window in the wild hope that Lin might somehow miraculously have arrived with the day. What she saw outside was a garbage man in a dark uniform and cuffed gloves almost as big as falconer's gauntlets. He walked behind the truck from the house next door and stopped at the green garbage can she'd so carefully placed right on the curb. He unlatched the clever hasp that foiled raccoons, tossed the cover onto the lawn, and effortlessly dumped three white plastic bags that had been her garbage collection since Tuesday into the truck's open jaws. Then he threw the empty can down on its side, far away from its cover, and waved his hand for the truck to move on.

This careless, almost defiant gesture reminded Nanci of herself. In the barely ten months since her cousin had arrived in New York, she had gone on with her life just like the sanitation worker, tossing the cans every which way, unaware of anyone's presence in the window. She'd worked in the library during the week, gone house hunting on the weekends. She and Milton had bought the house, moved in, and hunkered down for the last months of winter. All their short lives they'd been responsible, had struggled and saved their money for a house like this and the luxury of having a city-paid worker in his gauntlets to dispose of their private garbage from their private garbage can. And all this time, she'd scarcely thought about poor Lin.

At three in the morning she'd fed the gorgeous black-haired, blue-eyed baby, and put him back to bed. At five-fifteen she'd picked him up again. She'd sat in a chair holding him, alternately dozing and worrying. At seven he was still sleeping. She took him downstairs and put him in the plastic baby chair Milton had bought for him when they'd realized they did not want to give him back, and she made coffee. His tiny nose twitched at the smell of the coffee, and his tiny fingers moved against the satin edging of the blue flannel baby blanket that smelled of money and so perplexed Nanci when she first saw it. The baby's fancy layette didn't match her cousin's station in life, so she'd worried that even though the baby looked like Lin and also looked like her, it might not, in fact, be Lin's baby.

If anyone asked Nanci now whose baby he was, she'd say hers. He was in her dreams, in the rhythms of her day. He was serene and unruffled, and he filled her heart without even trying. She hadn't even known how much she longed for someone other than Milton to love and care for. Milton was a man; he had his own thoughts, his own world—his restaurant, sports, and his brothers. He no longer read as much as he used to when they were dating. He worked long days, from eleven to eleven sometimes, or from eight in the morning to nine at night. He was a householder; with the responsibilities of his job and the bills to pay, he was not always as patient and understanding with her as he used to be. Someone who relied on her and needed her, someone she could share her thoughts with and teach everything she knew was what she had needed to fulfill her life.

The baby's hold on her heart and the mystery of his fancy layette were so powerful a combination that even with her cousin in danger, Nanci had not been able to tell April the truth. If the baby was Lin's, she might have a chance of keeping him. At first she'd thought Lin might have had a boyfriend who didn't intend to marry her. If he *had* married Lin, Nanci would at least have had a chance to see the baby from time to time.

But the expensive clothes that came with him made Nanci think the baby might have been someone else's. She and Milton had been astounded when their argument on the ride home from Chinatown on Tuesday had been interrupted by a baby's crying. They had not known that Lin had been pregnant. When Nanci climbed over into the backseat and found the baby wearing such fine clothes, she couldn't imagine where he and they had come from. Until she spoke with April, she did not guess that the infant she and Milton had fallen in love with at first sight was the missing baby described in the newspapers, but she knew she didn't want to give him back. She had come to believe the baby was Lin's, and since the baby was Lin's, he was also hers to keep and protect. Under no condition could he ever go back to his adoptive parents. And in this way she and Milton, formerly among the most law-abiding people in America, became criminals.

From the moment they'd conceived of the idea of having Frankie and Joey talk to Annie Lee, she'd known it was a crazy thing to do. What if the woman got stubborn and refused to say where Lin was? What if she demanded the ransom and that was the end of it? What if she didn't really know where Lin was, after all? What could they do—bully her, hit her, threaten her with a gun? She'd known Frankie and Joey for ten years. They had not been the brightest teenagers in the world, and now they were not the smartest men—still unmarried, hanging around the old neighborhood, and looking for trouble instead of work.

Around 7:40 A.M. Nanci had the incongruous thought that she ought to go outside and bring back the garbage can lying on its side by the street. But she couldn't move. She was waiting for some word from the thugs. At a quarter past eight, she went upstairs to put the baby into the crib they'd borrowed from the next-door neighbors. He slept on. Then she padded into the bedroom to get Milton up. After his long hours at the restaurant, their speculation and worry over Lin and the baby, he hadn't gotten much sleep. Now he was out cold, his head buried in the space between two pillows. When she'd met him, he'd been a handsome boy with a lean and compact body, dreamy eyes, and long hair that fell into his eyes. Now he was an important restaurant manager, a confident young man who wore boxer shorts to bed and refused to stir when she tried to wake him.

Then the phone rang and she picked up.

"It's me. Let me talk to Milton," Frankie said.

"Frankie's on the phone," she told her husband's shoulder.

"Okay, I'm up." He roused himself and reached for the phone. "What's up?

"Oh, God, no." Milton turned away from her. "Yeah, okay. Yeah. Call me in a half-hour. Thanks."

Then he hung up without looking at Nanci and went into the bathroom to pee, still without looking at her. He didn't want to tell her what Frankie had said. She stood by the closed door, knowing she'd have to wait until he was ready.

CHAPTER
41

Anton fumed in the cab all the way downtown. Now he knew what Marc had called about this morning, but hadn't wanted to tell him over the phone: they had a dead girl on their hands. How could those two asshole relatives of his be so stupid? He knew he'd find them in the office at Golden Bobbin. Marc and Ivan wouldn't leave their clubhouse if it was under siege. And there they were. Marc opened up the building's outside door and pulled Anton inside before he'd finished knocking.

"Did anybody follow you?" he asked anxiously.

"What? No." As soon as they were in the office, Marc jerked his head, making faces at Ivan, who sat at his rolltop desk playing pinball on his computer as if he hadn't a trouble in the world.

"Hi, Andy," he said without looking up.

"Did you hear it on the news?" Marc asked.

"You guys are some fuckups."

Marc took Anton's arm and patted it. "Oh, man, it's so good to see you. I was getting pretty worried about all this."

"What's the matter with you, are you nuts? What are you doing here? Why aren't you in some lawyer's office working on a story?" Anton made a disgusted noise and paced to the other side of the room to examine the computer screen. "What are you doing, Ivan?"

"So our lawyer came to our office. What's the big deal?"

"You don't get it. I'm not your lawyer anymore. This isn't another public-nuisance case." Anton paced to the sofa. "You've got to get organized."

"How did you find out? Did it make the news?" Marc asked eagerly.

Anton stopped pacing and stared at him. "No, it didn't make the news. There's a cop at my house."

"Why? Do they think you had something to do with it?" Ivan looked up, surprised.

"You ruined my life!" Anton raged. "I could kill you both."

Marc nodded. "You know, that's what I told Ivan. I told him there's been a tragedy here. We've got to show respect, close up. But you know Ivan, he does whatever he wants."

"Fuck you," Ivan replied, glued to the computer game.

Anton moved to the desk, bunching his fists. "Marc, you ruined my life, you asshole. Get up. You've had this coming for a long time."

"Oh, this is great. Let's see a fight." Ivan grinned.

"See?" Marc said bitterly. "See what I have to deal with every day? You think this is a picnic, huh? A girl dies, he doesn't give a shit."

Ivan hit a few keys. His computer said, "Good-bye, and have a nice day." "How do the police figure you in this?" he asked Anton.

"Because of you, you idiot. That girl came from here, died here. They're not stupid. They're going to figure it out. You better get a very good criminal lawyer."

Ivan threw up his hands. "Oh, come on, don't give

me that shit. I'm not going to look guilty about something I had nothing to do with."

"What are you talking about, looking guilty?" Marc cried. "It was an accident."

"Jesus Christ, you're responsible. I want to kill you," Anton broke in.

Ivan shrugged. "Oh come on, relax. The way I figure it, she wasn't feeling well. She stayed over. I guess she must have—"

"She was staying here?" Anton cried.

Ivan shrugged again, glanced at Marc. "A crazy girl jumped out of the window."

Anton glared at him. "It isn't that simple. Questions are going to be asked. You were putting a lot of pressure on her to find out what she did with the baby. How do I know she wasn't pushed?"

"Hey, hey! Don't start that! Don't even think that." Ivan jumped up from his desk and crossed the room. "Don't start that."

"What do you think, I'm stupid? You think the police are stupid? Who are you kidding? I'm so fucking mad at you I could—"

"What, you want to hit me? Go ahead, hit me." Ivan jumped up and danced on his toes in front of Marc. Older, fatter, his stomach rolling over his belt, his dukes up.

"Oh, come on, you guys." Marc moved in to push Ivan away. "Come on, Anton, you don't mean this. Give me a hug. Huh? You're not mad, are you? Come on, we've seen worse than this before, right?"

"When are you going to wake up?" Anton cried. "This is the worst. There's nothing worse than this. It's you I want to kill. You're supposed to be the sane one."

"You see cops in here? They came; they looked around, they left. Don't worry about the cops. The girl was an illegal nothing. They don't care about this.

We got friends in the cops, don't we, Marc? Isn't your best friend a cop?"

"You ruined my life!" Anton cried. "Who's going to pay me for this?"

"Now don't talk that way. It was an accident." Marc rubbed his brother's shoulder. "Nobody ruined anybody's life."

Anton shook him off. "What was an accident? The assault on my wife? That was an accident?"

Marc glanced at Ivan. "Yeah, that was too bad."

"She wasn't going to tell who did it. She wouldn't even tell me, you bastards. But now that the girl is dead, she's a different person. I wouldn't count on her keeping her mouth shut about anything. I'm fucked, understand? I don't get over this, and neither do you." Anton punched the air. Marc stroked his shoulder. "I hate you."

"Her name was Lin," Ivan said softly.

Anton ranted on. "I don't give a shit. This was supposed to be so easy, a no-brainer. You knew a pregnant girl. Roe and I wanted a baby. And what do we have here—the biggest fuckup in history!"

"Hey, Heather didn't want him," Marc interjected fiercely.

"Heather wanted him." Anton pulled away from his brother and began punching the arm of the sofa. "I'm going to get him now. Where is he?"

Marc and Ivan exchanged looks.

"Where is the baby? I'm not kidding. I'll put you both away for this. I swear."

"We don't think it's a good idea," Marc said.

"What do you mean it's not a good idea?"

"Let it go. The girl had a cousin. The cousin has the baby." Marc looked embarrassed for the first time.

"It's funny, 'cause she didn't act like she had anybody." Ivan glanced at him angrily. "She was a scared little—"

Anton put up his hand. "Don't tell me. I don't want to know this. You both disgust me."

Ivan protested. "Oh, no, this isn't me. This has somebody else's signature on it."

"You always try to pin everything on somebody else. You won't take responsibility for anything. Damn it, you know I wouldn't hurt a fly," Marc protested.

"Same old story," Ivan rolled his eyes.

"Paternity is easily established these days, but I don't give a shit. I just want to know where my baby is," Anton said.

"He's not yours anymore. We have to distance ourselves from this thing." This from Marc.

"I have cops at my place going through my things. They think I'm a wife beater. A child stealer. I'm not going to let this go."

"Face it, Heather isn't the baby's mother. The thing is, this girl came on to both of us. She wanted it, didn't she, Ivan? There was no victim here."

Anton held up his hand. "I don't want to hear this. I don't care."

"It wasn't me. I like blonds," Ivan said suddenly. "And I can prove it."

"I don't give a shit. Tell a lawyer, tell the judge. It's not my problem. Just tell me where the cousin lives."

Marc looked uneasy. "There's a little bit of a problem with that."

"With you there's always a problem." Anton punched the air.

"Listen to me, this *is* a problem. She came from around here, but she's married to this well-off Chink. They're connected to the Mob."

"How do you know?"

Ivan laughed uneasily. "She came looking for Lin. That's how we knew where the baby was. She even left her number. Lin never told us. Annie got scared and told us last night after the girl was dead."

"Why'd she have to die?" Anton's face was white.

"She was sick. Who knows about these girls? Now we all have to get checked. It really bums me."

"Oh, God. You guys are pigs."

"Yeah, so? Anyway there are these guys watching us."

"Well, sure. The cops, the media, a lot of people are watching you."

"Uh-uh. These guys are I-tals. Buildings burn down around here. Things happen—you know what I'm talking about. You don't mess with those people."

"Oh, give me a break. I'm not going to worry about some pizza maker. That baby's mine."

"Not anymore. Your wife gave him back."

"Don't make me mad," said Anton.

"It's a fact. She gave it back," Ivan said.

"She changed her mind. Now she wants him back," Anton insisted.

"Too late. Lin gave it to her cousin. It's on Long Island," Ivan said.

"Shut up, you jerk," Marc snapped.

"How do I know that? How do I know he's alive? How do I know you didn't get rid of him? How can I believe any of this?" Anton raged.

"Guess you'll have to take our word for it."

"No, I refuse. After what happened, I can't trust you."

"You have to let it go, Anton. We don't want any more trouble." Suddenly Ivan was the serious one. "One of our girls got pregnant. We tried to do a good deed. It didn't work out. The woman gave her baby to her cousin, then jumped out the window of our factory. That's all we know. It's got to stop there."

"I did a lot of things for you, covered up your fuck-ups for years. You owe me."

"This is out of your control."

"You owe me."

Ivan heaved a sigh. "You don't understand, Anton. You don't know how it is down here. It's delicate."

"You killed a girl, and you care about 'delicate'?"

Ivan crossed the space between them with one leap and was pummeling his cousin before Anton could finish the sentence. "Don't you dare accuse me!"

"For Christ's sake, give him the name." Always the one to smooth things over, Marc went to the refrigerator. "Want a beer?" he offered the other two. No one answered. "Big deal, so all right. You want the name, I'll give you the name." He popped the top of a beer can, held it out to Anton. "There, happy now?"

Anton's nose was gushing blood, but he took the can. "Yeah."

CHAPTER
42

"You did what?" Lieutenant Bernardino glared at April.

A boss's anger always made her head swim. She could feel herself regress to the state of terror she'd endured in ancient times, back when Bernardino had been in charge of her life. "Gotta go," she murmured, avoiding his eye. "Is Baum back yet?"

"You're not going anywhere. You're going to stay here and translate that fucking tape. How could you do that to me, after I left you alone to do it your way, huh?" He really didn't like the Chinese interview.

April was back on the other side of the desk in the lieutenant's visitor's chair, reminding herself he wasn't her boss anymore. Fear of him receded quickly, but now the heat rose in her body again, beading up her forehead. The sweat and puking came in waves now. April checked her watch. She had to go.

"So, what did she say?" Bernardino demanded.

"She said her job was to watch the door. You know what that means." She picked up a file from Bernardino's desk and fanned her wet face. "Let her sit in an interview room for a few hours, then try her again. I don't think she was anywhere near the place when the death occurred. Her boss must have called her at home and asked her to come down and cover for him

after the girl was dumped. She didn't know the girl
had been beaten. When are you going to talk to the
Popescus?" Breathe in, breathe out.

"Soon."

Breathe in, breathe out. "One of them was probably
messing with her. Maybe both. When I asked Annie
what the victim was doing there at night, she said the
girl liked to sleep there because it was quiet."

"Oh, yeah? So these jerks were running a flophouse
for the girls, too?"

"This gives me an ugly idea." April closed her eyes.
She was feeling really sick.

"You want to share it?"

She shook her head. Give me a minute, will you?

He drummed his fingers on the desk. "April, you
with me?"

"Yeah." She swallowed.

"What if she gave birth there in the Popescus' building?" Alfie rocked his chair, thinking. "That might
play."

"Is Baum back? I gotta go," she said faintly.

"No way. You're not finished here."

"Alfie, I don't work here anymore. I'm looking for
a missing baby, that's all." She put the file down and
concentrated on rallying the energy she needed to
leave.

"Hey, I didn't go looking for you. You came down
here wanting my people to trace newborns. This is not
what we do here."

"Well, I truly appreciate your helping out."

Bernardino changed the subject. "April, you look
like shit. Maybe you should take the rest of the day
off." His hollow cheeks were corrugated with concern.
That meant he wanted her to take the day off from
Midtown North.

"No, thanks."

He continued to rock forward and back, exercising

his chair. His shrewd eyes went from hard to soft to hard again. "What's the matter? We're old friends—you can tell me."

"I know."

"You in trouble, kiddo?"

"Nothing long-term," she assured him. Unless it turned out to be fatal.

"What's with the—" He wiggled his fingers in front of his nose.

"Old family remedy. If I die, you can investigate my mother."

Alfie laughed. "What did you do to piss her off this time?"

April shook her head.

"Are you sure you're not—you know . . ." Alfie's hand curved over his belly.

"For Christ's sake, Alfie, stop pushing. I'm not going to tell you."

"I'm not a detective for nothing, sugar."

"Well, get off the idea. It's not that. When are you getting organized on this?"

"I'm organized. You might want to know your boy, Woody Tree, has Heather Rose Popescu and her parents downstairs. Heather wants to talk to somebody." Alfie frowned over her head at the squad room door. "You know this guy?"

April turned around as Mike pushed the door open without invitation. He swaggered into Alfie's glass box, looking very much the cool dude with his silky black hair and luxuriant mustache, in his uniform of cowboy boots and coordinating grays—pants, jacket, shirt, tie. And, for April, a shit-eating grin.

Her sweaty face lit up. "Never saw him before," she said.

"Mike Sanchez, Homicide. How ya doin'?" he said, advancing to the desk with his hand out.

April introduced Alfie. "My old boss, Lieutenant Bernardino, the guy who taught me everything."

"I thought *I* taught you everything," Mike countered.

"How ya doin, Mike? I got a call about you. You going to clear this thing up for us?" Bernardino shook Sanchez's hand with no apparent sign of rancor at this invasion from outside.

Mike lifted a shoulder, than sniffed the air, distracted. "Jesus, what's that? You got a dead animal in here?"

"This precinct always has dead animals in it, just like the O-Nine. What's in the envelope?" April changed the subject.

"Something should be done about that. It's disgus—" He sniffed closer to April.

Bernardino made some faces at him. "Let it go, Mike."

Mike frowned. "What's going on?"

Breathe in, breathe out. Too late. "Excuse me." April rose from her chair and bounded from the room. Half an hour ago there'd been nothing more to puke. But that was a half an hour ago. Now she rushed down the hall to the women's room and fell to her knees before the toilet that had become her altar. Her worst nightmares used to be job-related—having to be the one to find a dead body behind a closed door, having people shoot at her with assault rifles, having to subdue crazy killers who set fires or built bombs. Now she knew her worst nightmare was a lot closer to home. She flushed the toilet and got to her feet. At the sink she saw a wreck. Her hair was plastered to her head. Her eyes were red, her face bloodless. She was the color of window caulk, the palest she'd ever been. Almost a white girl. She wet a wad of brown New York City–issue paper towels and washed her face and armpits with the nasty green liquid soap on the sink. The paper towels disintegrated and the sponge bath left her feeling clammy all over. I have to go downstairs and talk to Heather Rose, she told herself. I have to find the baby. Got to check out the building where the girl died. There were a lot of things she had to do.

She resisted a powerful urge to sit down on the floor and rest for a while. Instead, she tossed the soggy wad of wet paper in the direction of the overflowing wastebasket in the corner. She missed. Then it occurred to her that she couldn't afford pride any longer. She had to get over whatever was making her so sick. She remembered the cell phone in her pocket, pulled it out, and dialed her home number. It rang and rang. Her worst nightmare, it seemed, was not answering the phone.

She slogged back down the hall to the squad room, where Mike and Bernardino were busy studying the dead girl's autopsy photos. When April came in, Bernardino said something April couldn't hear, and Mike turned around.

"*Querida.*" His tone stopped her at the glass door. He gave Bernardino a quick look and drew her out into the hall, taking her arm and sitting her down on an empty bench by the stairs. "What?" he demanded. "What is this?"

"I feel worse than I look." Tears came to her eyes. "And I stink."

"Don't worry about that. I've smelled worse. I don't remember when, though. What is it, some kind of Asian flu?" He put a hand on her forehead. "*Muy caliente.* How about I take you to the hospital?" He was being cool, a cop who didn't freak at anything. He chewed on his mustache, though, seriously worried.

"They won't know what to do. It's not a flu."

"How do you know?"

"Just one of those things. What did you find out?"

"April, you first. We've got to do something about this."

"What do you want to do? There's some poison stuff in me, but I didn't eat or swallow it. It was steam. I breathed it."

"You breathed something that made you this sick?"

"It's not a nerve gas. It's not biological warfare. She was cooking it on the stove. So I'm guessing it's some kind of purge."

"Who?"

"Mom." April swallowed.

"Your mother did this to you?" Mike looked stunned. "Why?"

"I don't think she meant any harm," April said stoutly, except that Skinny Dragon probably did.

"What is she, some kind of witch?"

"Let it go, Mike. I'll be all right." Maybe.

"Oh, yeah? When?"

Good point. "What did you find out?"

"Not much more than I told you. The victim had tuberculosis and herpes. That means the baby might be sick."

"Heather Popescu is downstairs with Baum. Maybe she's ready to tell us something."

"Let me get the photos of the victim; then I'll go down with you." Mike returned to the squad room.

April waited on the bench. Minutes passed. She got out the cell phone and tried her mother again. No answer. She dialed Jason Frank. He picked up on the first ring. "Dr. Frank."

"Hi Jason, it's April."

"Where the hell are you? I've been trying to reach you since last night."

"Sorry, something came up. What's going on?"

"I talked to the Popescus last night. Both of them. I'm not convinced Anton was the one who beat Heather up Tuesday, but I think he's been abusing

her for years. He's not the father of the baby—he's
never had sexual relations with anyone, including her.
Apparently, he has some kind of sexual dysfunction."

"Thank you." April watched an old man in a gray
cardigan slowly climb the stairs and pass her by, his
nose twitching. She took a moment to think about it.
Heather had married a white guy who abused her and
couldn't have sex. That added another layer of mystery to the situation. Why would she marry someone
like that? No wonder her mother was so unhappy with
the match. April thought Skinny Dragon's objections
to Mike were petty in comparison.

"April, are you there?"

"Yeah, just trying to figure it all out. Why would
an educated girl like her marry someone like him?
Why would they pretend the baby was theirs?"

"When she married him, she didn't know. I gotta
go, April. Call me later?"

"Jason, I almost forgot to tell you. We've located
the baby's mother. She's dead. Someone threw her
out the window of the Popescus' factory last night."

"Oh, God, April, that's bad."

"Yes."

"Do you know who did it?"

"We're working on that."

"Will you call me later?"

"I'll try." April was preoccupied by the mystery of
Heather's disastrous marriage. She hurried into the
squad room to pass on Jason's news. She was relieved
when neither Mike nor Alfie made a joke.

A few minutes later Baum was coming up the stairs
as she and Mike were on their way down. April made
the introductions. The two men shook hands, looked
each other over, reserved judgment.

"I hear you have Mrs. Popescu," April said.

"Yes, ma'am, and her parents." Woody beamed.

"I asked you for a photo of her. I didn't ask you to

assemble the family down here in the wrong house."
April wasn't happy about this.

"No problem—they found a room for us."

Yeah, but Heather belonged in a different case out
of a different precinct. Iriarte wasn't going to like this.
Hell, *she* didn't like this. "What did you bring them
down here for?"

"When she found out the girl was dead, she wanted
to come."

"How did she find out about that?" They were
standing halfway down stairs. April didn't want to grill
Baum, but she had to know.

Baum appealed to Mike with his eyes. Mike shook
his head. "The husband showed up while I was looking through the family photos. They happen to provide
the evidence we needed to prove he wasn't the baby's
father. Turns out he had cancer of the testicles when
he was a kid. Guy has no balls. When he saw that his
wife had let me in on his little secret, he assaulted
me." Baum couldn't help smiling at the way he'd handled it. The case was shaping up nicely, and he was
the one who'd filled in all the important pieces.

April was incredulous. "You got into a fight with
Anton Popescu? Are you crazy?"

"No, *I* didn't get into a fight. He punched me and
knocked me off the sofa."

"He hit you!" April was appalled. She was a supervisor now, the one responsible when her people did
the wrong thing. "What did you do about it?"

Baum scratched his head. "I unholstered my
weapon—but I didn't take him down," he added
quickly.

"Jesus Christ," April muttered. What a mess.

"But Mrs. Popescu had already decided to come
with me," Baum went on, helpfully.

"But what did you do about *him*?"

"I left him there."

"This guy—who might be a murderer—punched you, and you left him there?" The nasty green spots jumped in front of April's eyes again. "You didn't call for backup? You didn't take him to the house and document the incident? A possible suspect in a homicide gave you the leverage you needed to make an arrest, and you let him go?"

"Well, you told me to come back here with the photographs. I didn't know he was a suspect. Since when did he become a suspect?"

April licked her cracked lips. "You have to use your head, Baum. You have to be able to prioritize. Bringing me the photo of Heather Rose was not as important as documenting the fact that Popescu attacked you and bringing him into the station to probe the incident and his involvement in a homicide. Think about it: why would the guy freak out at your discovery of his family photo album? What was the meaning of it? Could he be a killer?" She was disgusted with herself for trusting Baum.

"Well, I have witnesses who saw him assault me. They can document that later."

"I don't want to hear any more." At the interview-room door, she stopped Baum with a look. She was going to make him pay for this.

With Baum put in his place, she rearranged her face into a benign expression that didn't change when she saw Heather's bad haircut.

Heather Rose was sitting at a table with her parents flanking her. "Hello. This is Lieutenant Sanchez," April said. "Mr. and Mrs. Kwan, Mrs. Popescu."

Heather's mother nodded. Her father stuck a cigarette in his mouth and lit it.

April smiled at Heather Rose. "Thank you for coming; it was the right thing to do," she said softly. "But we're going to have to go back uptown to talk. Have you had lunch?"

"He told us the baby's mother is dead," Heather said.

"Detective Baum told you?"

"Yes. Where's Paul? He has no one now. I want him back."

Uh-oh. "Does this mean you've reconciled with your husband?"

"No."

"Heather, were you aware that the baby was sick?"

"What makes you think he's sick?" she asked anxiously. "Did something happen to him?"

"His mother had tuberculosis and herpes. Did you have him checked out by a pediatrician?"

Heather paled. "Of course I took him to a doctor. He was fine."

"Blood tests and everything?"

"Yes, I think so. I don't really know what they do."

"I'll need the physician's name."

Heather Rose looked down at her hands. "I thought he was fine," she said faintly.

"Heather, you're going to have to tell me everything."

The parents made some angry noises. It wasn't clear whose side they were on. April was upset. There were too many people in the room and no place to put them all. Mike had the photos of the dead girl. Baum had the photos of Heather. Anton was now upgraded as a suspect in her mind. She decided she wanted to be the one to talk with all three Popescu males. She glanced at Mike, who wasn't saying a word. He was respectfully treating her like the primary, so she pushed away her nausea and took charge.

CHAPTER
43

Mike was preoccupied when he and April left the 5th Precinct. It was still a beautiful day, now over sixty-eight degrees, and the enticing aromas of Chinatown lunches issuing from dozens of restaurants charged the air with delectable temptations. Even as he prepared to go over the Popescus' building with a Crime Scene Unit, his mustache twitched at the odors of frying garlic and meats, baking pizza and calzone, and the outdoor fish and vegetable stands set up on the sidewalks. He wanted to get April fixed up and to eat something himself, but there was no arguing with her. April always had her own agenda.

The detective squad of the 5th had been responsible for a thorough crime scene investigation. The ME's death report made a mockery of the witness's statement and ruled out suicide or accidental death. Bernardino had caught the case, and the way it had been handled did not speak well for him. A more thorough search of the inside of the Popescu building was now a must. As was her wont, April was neither moaning nor complaining about what had gone wrong. In fact, she revealed no feelings about anything as she stared blankly up into the sun as if for guidance.

Mike had grown up with Latina girls who smiled and giggled, *mintiendo más que siete,* sending a con-

stant string of white lies up the flagpole for no reason
other than to practice for the whoppers. He always
got the feeling their intended purpose in life was to
beat one system or another every day just to prove
who was the real boss. Beating the system wasn't a
goal for April. She rarely giggled and never lied.
When she wanted to stay in control of a situation she
just beamed out a don't-mess-with-me message, the
way she was doing right now.

"*¿Como estás tu?*" Mike asked solicitously.

"*No me preguntas, mi amor.*" She was thinking in
not too favorable terms about mixed marriages and
the woe they could bring.

"Too bad, I'm asking."

She wasn't going to say how she felt about Baum's
handling of the order she'd given him, or about their
interview with Heather Rose and her parents, all three
at odds with the man she had married. The Kwans and
Heather were now being driven to Midtown North by
the overreaching Baum to hang around some more
while she took care of other things. Heather still
would not identify Anton as her attacker in the
kitchen.

"Where's the car?" April asked.

Mike pointed down the narrow street lined with
stores selling trinkets, toys, clothes, foods, spiritual ne-
cessities, important antique porcelains, and other an-
tiquities—all made yesterday in China, Taiwan, Hong
Kong, and Singapore. April saw the red Camaro
parked in front of the Chinese apothecary that her
mother used.

"You want to stop off and see your friend?" he
asked.

The pharmacist happened to be a well-known and
venerable member of the community who often advised the police about tradition and neighborhood
matters. Chan Wang was a wizened creature, hardly

four feet tall, with three or four really long hairs sticking out of a few sites on his face and not a single hair on his head. He smelled of star anise and had begun stating his age as a hundred years back in 1968. Mike had met him twice.

April ignored the suggestion. She marched down to the car, then stopped. "I think we should split up," she announced.

"No, go ahead inside, find out what your mother poisoned you with. I'll wait for you." He leaned on the car, preparing to wait.

"*Querido,* no one has talked to the people where the dead girl lived. I don't even have a name for her. I have to go over there." April looked past him, furious because he couldn't possibly understand what it meant to be her, with the parents she was trying to manage and the case she had to solve. Two of her countrywomen had been destroyed by men not of their culture, and her own mother would rather poison her than have her end up like one of them. How could she reconcile the love Skinny Dragon must feel for her with the destructiveness of her act?

"You have to take something," Mike insisted. He pointed to the filthy window display of nasty powders and roots. "One whiff and he'll know what to give you."

"I don't want any more nasty stuff. I'm going to get over it myself. I'll meet you on Allen Street." She gave him a look that dared him to challenge her.

"How are you going to get there if I have the car?" he demanded, wondering if this was the time for their first fight.

"I existed before you came along," she snapped. "I know how to get around."

He shrugged and got in the car, didn't say goodbye. Okay, he was hurt. Try to be nice and thoughtful and kind and what do you get? A smack in the face.

April's mother had tried nagging, tried whining, tried threats and dirty tricks; they didn't get her anywhere. Walking away was the only thing to do. He got in the car and didn't look back.

When he pulled up at the Popescus' building, the CSU van was already there, its back door open. Inside, Saul Bernheim, the skinny criminologist who claimed he never ate, was sitting cross-legged on the floor gnawing on a massive deli sandwich.

Mike pulled up behind the van, got out, and locked the car. "Hey, Saul."

"Mike, Mike man. You on this one? I thought you were working the *cojones* case. Mean." He shook his head over the mutilation.

"Nah, we got him."

"Him? Homo case? I thought as much."

"No, boyfriend-girlfriend. The wife went back to her husband. The boyfriend sent her his crown jewels."

"Doesn't ring." Saul shook his head. "Wasn't the victim with a he/she before he got wiped?" He took a bite of half-sour pickle and chewed.

"Yeah, but the he/she didn't do it."

"It wasn't the hooker? You sure?" He ate more sandwich and gave Mike more puzzled looks.

"No, it was the guy's business partner." Mike was salivating over the sandwich. "He sent her the guy's nuts. The package had a return address." Not a hard one to figure.

"Listen to me. Three guys, one a he/she? The other two fighting over a *woman,* and the winner gets his jewelry whacked. Come *on.* This is a homo thing."

"Thanks for your input, Saul. What are you eating?"

"Best pastrami in the world, right here at Katz's. Nothing else like it. Want some?"

Mike shook his head. "You been inside?"

"No, I'm waiting for Carmine. He went out for cannolis."

"Jesus, all you guys do is eat."

"This is an aberration. We never eat. Want to fill me in? I told them I don't like coming back after the body is gone. This is a big fuckup, a contaminated situation from the word go. But do they care? What are we looking for, anyway?"

Before Mike could answer, Carmine Cartuso trotted up, carrying a white bakery box by its string. "Hey, Sanchez, how ya doin'? You in on this idiocy?"

Saul eyed the box. "You know how long pastry cream will hold up in weather like this?"

"Ah, stuff it."

"You don't want to die of food poisoning. Come on, just one. Then you'll thank me for saving your life. How about it?"

"No way. This is for my wife."

Mike interrupted the banter. "Last night an employee in the building said she saw the woman jump. The ME's report says the victim had already been dead for several hours before the 911 call. Head injuries suggest her head was banged repeatedly against the wall or floor. She died inside."

"So we're looking for wall and floor samples. Okay." That was simple enough. Saul glanced at Carmine.

"Where was the body found?" he asked.

"In the back."

"Okay, let's take a look." Bernheim threw a knapsack over one shoulder. Carmine grabbed another, stowed the bakery box, and locked the van. The three men crossed the sidewalk. A chain-link gate, padlocked, barred entry to the narrow walkway between the old building and the high-rise next door. Mike glanced around quickly, then pulled a tool from his pocket and picked the lock.

"Thirty flat. Getting rusty," Bernheim remarked as they sauntered into the backyard, where there was nothing to see but some old junk and garbage. And the yellow police tapes, indicating where the body had been. It wasn't a nice place to end up. The men looked up. A body tossed from any window in the high rise would fall on the other side of the fence. The ground-floor windows of the Popescus' building had air conditioners in them. The windows on the next two floors were closed and shrouded in black.

Carmine made a face, hunkered down, and crawled around examining the broken surface of the concrete. Bernheim crammed the last quarter of his sandwich into his cavernous mouth, snapped on plastic gloves, then marched to the building, working his jaws. He tried the back door. Locked. Still chewing, he turned around and studied the ground, mentally measuring the distance between the building and where a body would have fallen if it had gone out a window. Finally he opened his knapsack and pulled out long and short metal measuring tapes, a drawing pad, and a pencil. Springtime had greened the saplings and weeds that rose through the cracks. Carmine's fingers probed the sprouts and scraped up samples of cement containing brown stains.

"You're repeating. They did this part already," Mike said. "I'm going inside."

"They sent me here, I'm doing it again. You never know."

"Sure, go inside, secure the area for us." Carmine and Saul laughed as Mike headed to the front of the building to see if anyone was home to let them in.

CHAPTER
44

April didn't let herself feel uneasy as Mike drove away. She had work to do. She was stewing over Baum's show of independence and disrespect after she'd singled him out to bring along. He should be driving her around, supporting her actions, not doing whatever he felt like. No one had instructed him to tell the Kwans that the baby's mother had been murdered or to bring them downtown when she wasn't ready to talk to them. Bad form on his part. On the other hand, a little breathing space and a walk weren't so terrible a prospect. Only two waves of nausea hit her as she hurried to Ludlow, then counted building numbers until she found the one where the dead girl had lived.

She hadn't told Mike the reason she didn't want to go into Mr. Wang's apothecary. The truth was she was ashamed of her mother and didn't want all of Chinatown to know what she had done. Besides, Mr. Wang had probably provided her mother with the poison in the first place. If Mr. Wang was responsible for selling her such deadly stuff, he should be charged with reckless endangerment and assault of a police officer. The thought almost made her smile.

The murdered girl had lived in an ancient five-story brick walk-up with no intercom and a primitive buzzer that didn't work. The front door was locked. This was pretty much the same setup as the building where April had grown up. It was meant to discourage visitors, thieves, and officials of all kinds, including the police. After pushing the broken doorbell a number of times with no success, April tried knocking. No one responded to that either, but there was a face in the first-floor window.

"I have an important message for someone here," April said in Chinese.

The ancient specimen wearing black glasses with thick lenses and a hot pink cardigan over her black peasant pants opened the door a crack. "No one here, everyone working." She gave the standard answer in Cantonese.

"Grandmother, I'm sorry to disturb you. I'm looking for the relatives of a young woman who lived in this building."

"People come and go." Frail as a twig, with failing eyes, the woman bravely defended the entrance.

"She worked at Golden Bobbin," April said.

"Something wrong?" The door opened a little more. April could see that she was missing all but two of her teeth.

"Yes. I need to find her relatives."

"What for?"

"Grandmother, this is confidential information."

"Ah, ah, maybe tell cousin."

"She has a cousin? I'd like to talk to her cousin. Where is the cousin, upstairs?"

"No live here."

"Where does cousin live?"

"Ah, ah, very rich."

April held on to the door frame, feeling a little dizzy again. "Where do they live?" she asked again. "Very rich" did not happen to be a place.

"Someplace. Long Island, I think. No, maybe New Jersey. Across the river."

At least she was sure about that, but of course every place outside of Manhattan was across a river. "Please let me come in," April asked politely.

The door opened some more. "I'm not supposed to open the door."

"I'm a friend of hers."

"If you're a friend, why don't you know her name or where she lives?" The old tabby was not the door-keeper for nothing.

"I'm a friend from work."

"Too many friends from work. Come every day. Too much trouble for an old woman like me," she complained, finally moving aside so April could enter.

"You have an important position in the building, Grandmother. What other friends came here from work?"

"Very old lady, even older than me. Take Lin to hospital."

"Lin?" April saw the brick falling, but she couldn't find a way to dodge it.

"You look for Lin Tsing, yes?" The old woman looked at her, puzzled because April didn't even know who she was looking for.

"Lin Tsing?" The brick struck with its full force. Lin Tsing was Nanci's Hua's cousin, the one who was missing, the one April was supposed to find. That meant Lin Tsing was the mother of the missing baby, and Nanci had been hiding that from her. April shook her head the way the puppy Dim Sum did when it was mad. How could Nanci be so stupid as not to tell her? Maybe both were dead now. Nanci, Nanci. Why keep the secret?

"What was wrong with Lin?" April demanded.

The old woman didn't have an answer. April pointed at a red-and-gold Chinese calendar in the hall.

A section of the Great Wall was the picture for May. "What day, yesterday?"

"No, no. Wednesday."

"Wednesday, are you sure?"

"Yes, yes."

"Thank you. What apartment?"

"Five in the back. Lin good girl. She okay?"

April made a noncommittal motion with her head and started climbing the stairs. "Thank you, Grandmother," she said over her shoulder. She knew the cooking smells, the creaks and moans of buildings like this, where only one lightbulb illuminated the hall, there was no carpet anywhere, and angry voices could be heard behind closed doors. By the time she reached the fifth floor, she was clutching her side. Oh, Nanci, how could you have been so stupid?

A youngish woman with a broad peasant face opened the door after April's first knock. "Something wrong?" she asked in Cantonese, visibly alarmed at the sight of a well-dressed stranger.

"I'm looking for relatives of Lin Tsing," April told her.

"Something wrong?" the woman repeated.

"Yes. I'm looking for her family."

"No family." She looked at April anxiously, then at the room, which contained three cots, neatly made up, some folding chairs, and a card table on which stood several open jars of oily-looking chili sauces, dirty plates, and other leftovers from lunch.

"I'd like to look around."

"Nothing to see. Not here. Went to hospital."

"Who went to the hospital?" April asked.

The woman looked wildly at the card table, edging closer to it as if she were afraid April might abscond with some of the food.

"Lin sick. Went to hospital."

April shook her head. "She's not in the hospital."

"Yes, boss said." Suddenly the woman was helpful. "Very nice lady. Come two three times, take to hospital."

"Did she take the baby, too?" April asked.

"No baby." The woman blew air out of her nose contemptuously as if the idea were ridiculous.

"Lin had a baby. She lived here. I'm sure you know that," April said severely.

"Lin young girl. No have boyfriend, no have baby."

"Yes, she did. I want to look around." April stepped toward the bedroom door.

"No, don't do that." The woman cringed when another irate voice responded to April's sharp rap.

"What's going on?" A middle-aged man came out of the room. A young woman on the bed inside covered herself with a quilt.

"Are you the leaseholder of this apartment?" April asked officiously.

The man turned his back on the question. "Get up, and get going," he told the woman in the room, and closed the door.

April opened it. Ignoring the naked woman, she marched in and gave the room a perfunctory look around. "How many people do you have living here?" she demanded.

"Three." Now the man was indignant as well as defensive. "What do you want?"

"I'm Sergeant Woo, with the police. I'm looking for Lin Tsing's baby."

"Ask them." He indicated the two women.

"No baby," insisted the one who had opened the door for April. The second woman, now dressed in a turquoise jacket, came into the room with a pale, troubled face.

The man scowled at her. "I told you that girl no good."

"What are you talking about? No baby!" the first woman insisted just as angrily.

"You should have made her go a long time ago. Why do you think she was so sick, ah?" The man was disgusted at their ignorance. "How could you miss it?"

Two flies buzzed around the condiments and dirty plates on the table. April felt the blood drain from her own cheeks as she thought of a pregnant girl stuck with companions like these.

"Are you her mother?" she asked the woman who'd opened the door.

"No mother. Lin just have stuck-up cousin. You better talk to her."

"You have the number?"

"Yes."

The woman took some minutes to find the 516 number. With great difficulty she copied it out for April. It was Nanci's. April was a cop. She made a big show of repeating everything the three people in the apartment had said, carefully writing it all down in her notebook. Then she took their names and told them what would happen to them if it turned out the telephone number for Lin's cousin was not the correct one, or if they had lied to her about anything else. They didn't change their story. But she'd known they wouldn't.

Finally she left the apartment and descended the stairs slowly, hanging on to the railing. There were only two options now: Either Lin had killed her baby when Heather Rose returned him to her, or she had given him to her cousin Nanci Hua, and the child was with Nanci on Long Island.

If Nanci had the baby, she'd made a big fool out of April, and April had good reason to be furious. But all she could feel was sorry that she'd snapped at Mike. It took her several minutes to stagger down all five flights in the unsavory building. The ancient lady with two teeth and a pink sweater was hanging out by her door, waiting for news. April bade her adieu without supplying any. When she emerged into the fresh air and spring sunshine at last, she was overwhelmed by a sense of freedom and escape from the claustrophobia inside. Then a vision of the nude photos of Lin's battered body on the autopsy table made her sit down abruptly at the top of the stoop. She was hit by a rush of sadness for the dead girl, whose fate could have been Sai Yuan's thirty years ago if she hadn't been so lucky as to marry Ja Fa Woo, or April's if she hadn't been so lucky as to be their child. What was she doing, thinking of marrying a foreigner herself? The edge of her jacket clunked against the concrete, reminding her of the phone in her pocket. She took it out and dialed Nanci's number.

Nanci answered warily before the second ring.

"It's April. I need to come out and talk with you about your cousin and her baby." She heard a sharp intake of breath on the other end of the line.

"My cousin's baby?"

"You lied to me, and you made a lot of trouble for a lot of people," April said wearily.

"You know?"

"Yes, Nanci, I do. You should have told me."

"I know. I'm sorry." Nanci's voice was so faint April could hardly hear it.

"Do you have the baby?"

"Yes." The voice got even smaller.

April didn't want to tell her she might have saved Lin's life if only she'd spoken up sooner.

"I'm coming out there. We have to talk."

"They all found out. Someone else from the police just called me!" Nanci cried.

This was news to April. "Oh, yeah? Who called?"

"Some captain. He said it turns out the baby wasn't Lin's. She got him by mistake, and *he's* coming out to take the baby away."

"What captain was that?"

"I don't remember his name. He just told me there's been a terrible misunderstanding about this whole thing because of Lin's unfamiliarity with the language. He said the baby Lin gave me isn't Lin's. The baby's real mother wants him back this afternoon, and he's on his way out to get him."

No police captain had told her that. April's sadness and dizziness vanished. Suddenly her head was clear. Nanci was crying now. "He said the parents want to prosecute me for kidnapping. I didn't kidnap him."

"I know you didn't. What did Lin do, call you to come in and get him?"

"Yes. It's my fault," she sobbed.

"It's not your fault," April snapped. She was getting tired of hearing her countrywomen take the blame for everything.

"He told me that keeping the baby without telling the police made the baby's real mother crazy with worry."

"Listen to me. He wasn't telling you the truth," April said firmly. "We can easily establish whose baby he was."

"But he told me Lin is dead," Nanci cried.

"What else did he tell you?"

"He said she jumped out of a window. I don't understand. Last night that woman, Annie, told me Lin was sick, and if I gave her two thousand dollars, I could have my cousin. But she never called me back. And now Lin's dead. It *is* my fault."

"Try to calm down and listen to me," April commanded.

There was a short silence; then Nanci blew her nose.

"Nanci, are you alone?"

"Yes. I called Milton at work, but he isn't home yet."

"When did you get that call from the man who said he was a police captain?"

"I don't know, a few minutes ago."

"Look, he wasn't with the police."

"He wasn't? Are you sure?"

"Yes, I'm sure."

"How do you know?"

"Because *I'm* with the police. Listen to me—I don't want you to let anyone in, okay? Wait for Milton to get there. Wait for me to get there. We'll go over all of this."

In the background April could hear the cry of a baby mingle with Nanci's panic.

"What's your address? How long does it take to get there?"

"Wait a minute. I have to pick up the baby."

"That's okay. I'll hold on. Don't hang up, Nanci."

There was static on the line as April waited. She willed the cell phone not to go dead. A wave of nausea hit, then passed. The baby stopped crying. A few seconds later, Nanci came back on the line.

"Don't give the baby to anybody. Keep him for now. He *is* your cousin's."

"Is she dead?"

"I'm sorry," April said softly. "Yes."

"Oh, God, it's my fault."

"No, Nanci, somebody hurt her. It's his fault, not yours."

"But why? Who would do that?"

"I'm not sure yet. Just stay inside and don't open the door. Give me your address."

"It's 355 Ring Road, Garden City."

"Okay, that's not too far. We'll have some people out there very soon."

"People? What people? Oh God, I'm scared." Panic traveled through the line.

"Just stay inside and no one will hurt you." April didn't think a Popescu would break the door down.

April hung up, then dialed Lieutenant Iriarte. He was not in a good mood.

"I told you to be back here by noon. Where the hell are you?" he demanded. "You got a fucking convention of hysterical Chinese waiting for you up here."

"You asked me to locate the baby, sir. I've located him. The dead woman's cousin has him at her home in Garden City."

"Well, great. Now get the hell up here and deal with these weeping women."

"Ah, I can't, sir. I think Popescu is on his way out to Garden City to reclaim the baby. I have to go out there."

"The hell you do."

"He may be a killer."

That got him. "What!"

"It had to be one of the Popescus who did the baby's mother. My guess is it was Anton."

Iriarte didn't buy the hypothesis. "Oh, come on. Why him?"

"It's complicated, sir. It may be because he has no balls." April really loved to shock her lieutenant.

"*What!* Are you crazy?" Now he was screaming in her ear.

"Lieutenant, why don't you call Jason Frank and ask him to talk to Heather Rose and her parents. He'll know how to deal with them."

"I know how to deal with them."

April could hear him swearing; she cut him off. "The cousin's name is Nanci Hua. I'll call you in an hour or so."

"You get the hell—"

April quickly tried to make some static noises with the saliva in her mouth. The sound was more like someone trying to choke her.

"Hey, April—"

Then she got an idea and pushed the channel button. Real static crackled on the line. After a few seconds the phone went dead. She dialed Jason. He picked up and started complaining right away.

"Where are you? What's going on? You promised to get right back to me," he chided.

"Sorry; I couldn't talk before. The baby's biological mother—her name was Lin Tsing—worked at the Popescu sewing factory. She was beaten to death in their building last night."

He was speechless.

"Jason, are you there?"

"Yeah. Jesus."

"It's a terrible thing. Did you meet his relations?"

"I met the brother in the hospital." He had nothing else to say about Marc.

"They'd been keeping Lin in a closet in the storeroom. I'm sure one of them got her pregnant. She probably gave birth there. That's why we couldn't find a hospital record."

"Jesus." Jason fell silent again, then asked after a moment, "What's Anton's involvement?"

"That's what I'm calling about. Some of the pieces are coming together on Heather's end. She's been identified as the person who gave the baby to Lin. Lin gave the baby to her cousin on Long Island. I'm on my way out there now."

"You don't think Anton's the killer of the baby's mother, do you?" Jason sounded horrified by this idea.

"Could be. I'm not placing any bets. I want you to talk with Heather again."

"But, April, I was with Anton at his apartment last night. There's no way he could have killed that woman."

"What time?"

"Between eight and nine."

"The 911 call came in at ten. But the death report puts the TOD at several hours before that. She could have died as early as five or six. The killer must have waited until the cover of darkness to move the body. It was light until nine last night."

"Couldn't have been Anton. I talked to him. I talked to Heather Rose. We know he couldn't have gotten the girl pregnant, and he didn't kill her. He doesn't have the profile of a killer. I'm sure of it," Jason insisted.

"You seem pretty invested in that theory," April remarked.

"I think Heather's protecting someone else."

"She's at the station house right now with her parents. She says she's ready to talk."

"So what to you want from me, April?"

"I'd like you to talk with her. We need to know who assaulted her."

"Why aren't *you* talking with her?" he demanded.

"I told you, I have to go out to Garden City."

"Why?"

"We have a situation. It's looking like Anton thinks if he recovers the baby, he can put his family back together again. He's gone out there to get him. The victim's cousin is a friend of mine. I don't want anybody else hurt."

"This whole thing sounds volatile." Jason sighed.

"You said Anton's not a killer," April reminded him.

"He may be unpleasant—grandiose and delusional. That doesn't make him a murderer." Jason sounded concerned, though.

"He could be the killer. He's certainly an abuser. You get Heather's testimony. I pick him up. Either way, we get him for something. I don't want this guy to slip away."

Jason sighed again. "Give me twenty minutes," he said.

CHAPTER
45

Get the fuck out of here. You can't come in without a search warrant." Ivan Popescu started screaming the moment he opened the door and Mike introduced himself as Sergeant Sanchez. Marc rushed to the door and held out his hand to Mike, who pretended not to see it.

"I'm Marc Popescu," he said. "Sorry about my cousin, Ivan," Marc went on. "He's upset. We're under a lot of stress here." Marc used the rejected hand to pat Ivan's shoulder. "Calm down, kiddo."

Ivan shook him off. "Don't kiddo me, you asshole." The two men blocked the doorway to the office, bickering.

Mike chewed on the ends of his mustache for a moment and watched them argue, wondering if this was collusion, or a party act, or both. The one called Marc rubbed and patted the one called Ivan, and the one called Ivan punched him back, insisting he wasn't a kiddo. It was diverting for exactly thirty seconds.

"Let's get started here." Mike pushed them aside and went into the office. The remains of pizza and deli, Cokes and Bud Lights on the coffee table indicated that the two men had been ensconced in the office for many hours. They broke apart and followed him into the room.

"What are you here for?" Ivan demanded.

"I just want to ask you a few questions."

"They already did that."

"We do it more than once."

"What are you talking about, you do it more than once? Get outta here."

"We still have a few things to clear up." Mike glanced around the room. At the front stood a sofa, and a table with fashion magazines and food on it; about a third of the way back were matching rolltop desks, one on each side of the room, one with a laptop on it. And finally, all the way at the end of the building-deep room, were the office computer, filing cabinets, and back door. It was the back door that interested Mike.

"It *is* cleared up. I don't want anyone else in here."

"It won't take too long," Mike said mildly.

"Shit, you're not listening to me. We already did this last night."

"There's been a little upgrade in the case since then."

"You in there, Mike?" Bernheim and Cartuso came through the front door, then sloped into the office with their open knapsacks slung over their shoulders.

Marc Popescu's jaw dropped at the sight of them. "Who the hell is this?"

"What are you talking about, 'upgrade'?" Ivan broke in.

"This is the Crime Scene Unit, Officers Bernheim and Cartuso. Messieurs Popescu, Marc and Ivan."

Marc's eyes popped. "Crime scene! She jumped out of a window!"

"No. She was murdered." Mike watched their reactions.

"Murdered! No way. We have someone who saw her jump out of a window."

"The witness is at the station now. She's changed her story."

"What?" Marc was shocked. Ivan didn't seem surprised.

"Maybe she jumped to escape her attacker." Ivan glanced at his cousin.

Bernheim and Cartuso ignored them both. "We're going up now. You want to clear out of here so we can get to work?"

"Fine, I'll take care of it and be right with you." Mike punched out some numbers on his cell phone, then turned around and spoke into it softly, requesting backup from the 5th.

"This is very puzzling. How could she have been murdered . . . ? Maybe the medical examiner is wrong." Marc seemed at a loss. He looked helplessly at the garbage.

"Well, Annie is nuts. She'll say anything for a buck," Ivan threw in.

"How can you say that?" Marc cried. He dragged the garbage can over to the coffee table. In the crisis he'd decided to clean up.

"Leave everything the way it is, please." Mike put the phone away and jumped on the bribery angle. "How much did you give her to say the girl jumped?"

"Hey, now. Watch your mouth." Ivan's voice cracked like a whip.

"Look, I'm not going to beat around the bush. We know everything that happened here. We know the girl had a baby—"

"Hey, that's no crime," Ivan said quickly.

"The baby was given away or sold or stolen; his mother was murdered. And the woman who had the baby was also assaulted. *Those* are crimes. So is bribery."

Three uniforms and Bernheim entered the room. Saul looked the room over, giving particular attention to the back door. Mike nodded at him. "Mike, you

want to come upstairs with me for a minute?" Bernheim said.

"Sure." Mike turned to the Popescus. "Gentlemen,
would you take a seat for a few moments?"

"What are you looking for?" Marc asked, almost
tearful now.

"Can I sit at my desk?" Ivan said sarcastically.

Mike glanced at the desk, then jerked his chin at
the three uniforms, noting their name tags. He didn't
want the Popescus leaving or touching anything. "Officer Lapinsky here will take your fingerprints."

Ivan's face reddened. "Hey, it's our building. Our
prints are everywhere."

"It's routine. We'll do them for everyone who works
here. Would you sit on the sofa, please?" Mike
stepped out without waiting for an answer. "What do
you have?"

Bernheim walked him through the place. On the
second floor he demonstrated how easily the windows
opened and closed and showed him the wooden props
used to hold the windows open when the weather was
warm. He also pointed out that the outside screens
hadn't been disturbed, nor had the large fans placed
in front of the windows. Even on a bright day, the
room looked ghostly and dark, filled with stilled sewing machines and overhead wires. Under one window
a sticky glue trap had recently claimed two mice and
a cockroach almost as big as the mice.

Then they climbed a more primitive staircase to
what looked like a messy storeroom. Up there Cartuso
was busy taking photos of the layout.

"Pay dirt," he murmured.

Two of the windows in the back wall had been
painted shut a long time ago, and the skylight was
padlocked.

"Take a look over there," Bernheim ordered. "See
how the paint has been chipped all around the frame

of the third window, and it was jimmied open?'' There were smudges in the dust that highlighted the activity. Mike moved in to get a closer look.

"I picked up some prints here." Bernheim pointed. "Two thumbs and the bottom half of one palm. Someone opened the window, leaned out, then closed it again. Now look out there."

Mike nodded. "Okay, I see it." The dirt on the outside of the sill had not been disturbed.

"If he had picked the body up, he would have rested it on the sill before pushing it out. The dirt would be disturbed on both sides. It's unlikely that he would have picked the body up, held it over his head, or even in his arms and then thrown it without touching the outside of the window, or dusting off the whole of the front side. You with me?"

Mike nodded.

"You can see he thought about it but decided against it. Check out the view."

Mike took in the view. Across the way was an apartment building. Two floors above them, a man wearing an undershirt sat in the window, holding up a newspaper, but watching them, not reading it. The ME's report said the skull had been fractured, but didn't mention broken bones. Now they had confirmation that the body hadn't gone out the window at all.

Saul let the window come down with a bang. "Now look at this."

Mike looked around at the abandoned furniture and sewing machine parts, and a folded mattress tied with rope. The floor had been swept recently, and parts of it had been washed. Cartuso flashed one more photo and put the camera away.

"Any sign of the mop that washed the floor? Any idea where she died?" Mike could feel the dead air crackle with the criminologists' excitement. The body was gone; to anybody else, this space might look like an unused attic. To them, it was a treasure trove.

"You're getting ahead of me. Look at this." Bernheim popped on a plastic glove and pointed out a line of ants emerging from the corner of the window and marching along the floor and up the tilt of the wall, where it slanted in to meet the roof. The ants disappeared into a straight crack in the wall. Bernheim prodded the crack with the business end of a chisel. As it shifted, the rounded side of two hinges came into view.

"Open sesame." He pushed the plaster board with the flat of his hand and the door to a walk-in cedar closet popped open.

In a corner the ants had converged on two shiny drops, which Cartuso quickly photographed. Then he scraped them up, ants and all, and put them in a plastic bag. He sniffed.

"Honey," he said with raised eyebrows.

CHAPTER
46

Two police cruisers and the Crime Scene van were parked in front of the Popescu building when April arrived with Alfie in his unmarked Toyota. April surveyed the party of vehicles, including Mike's red Camaro, which needed a bath, and gathered up her stuff. The driver killed the motor. Alfie hitched around in the passenger seat to look at her. "Thanks for the update," he said.

"Well, thanks for coming to get me," she replied. "I have to pick up Mike and get going."

"Too bad you'll miss the picnic—you okay to travel?" He gave her a second appraising look before getting out.

"Oh sure, I'm fine." April took a stab at pumping herself up for action.

"I mean for the trip to Garden City. You up for that?" Alfie regarded her so apprehensively she knew she must still look pretty bad.

"I wouldn't miss it for anything in the world. I want to nail that bastard." April said this with considerable force, but Alfie didn't appear altogether convinced. He leaned over to open the car door for her, then took her arm as she got out. She was impressed. "Just one quick look, and I'm out of here. I've called for local support. They'll be there waiting for me," she said.

They moved across the sidewalk like the team they used to be. Alfie greeted the uniform guarding the door, a tall, big-nosed blondie who'd propped open the front door with a shim. Alfie waved his hand for April to enter the building first. "Turn right," he directed her.

What she saw in the office was one middle-aged Popescu sitting on the sofa with his head in his hands. The other one, slightly grayer and fatter, was at a rolltop desk, seemingly unconcerned with the proceedings. He was playing a computer game on his laptop. The two uniforms, who'd been lolling by the door watching over them, came to attention.

"How's it going?" Alfie asked.

"No problem, we got them printed," Lapinsky said.

"Good, good." Alfie turned his attention to the suspects.

The one on the sofa stood up and started in on Bernardino in an aggrieved voice. "I don't know why you insisted on finger-printing, Sergeant. After all these years I thought we were pals. I'm really upset with what's going on here."

Alfie shook his finger at him. "You guys were holding out on me when I came in here yesterday. I don't like that."

"Wait a minute, you got it wrong."

"Don't give me that, Marc. What am I supposed to think, huh? I pay you and Ivan here a friendly visit, and the next thing I know, a girl dies in your place. This is more than careless." He took a disgusted look at the food, the beer cans on the table, and the full garbage can beside it. "And by the way, it's Lieutenant."

"Yeah, yeah. I knew that. When are you going to

get these people out of here? This is bad for our
image," said Marc.

"I can think of worse things," Alfie spat back. "Are
we going to have problems with you two, or are you
going to tell me what happened here last night?"

"I have no idea what happened. Ivan was the one
who closed up yesterday." Marc let tearful eyes wander over to his cousin at the desk. "I didn't want to
say it. I *hate* to say it. But truth is truth. Ivan knows
more about this than I do."

"Hey, wait a minute, asshole. I told you that's not
going to fly. I had nothing to do with this." Ivan shut
down the computer indignantly. "I told him to send
the girl to a hospital last week. See what happens
when you try to do a good deed?" he added bitterly.

"What good deed was that?" April asked.

Ivan spun around to where she was standing by the
door. "What's she doing here?"

"She's the one on Heather's case." Marc gave her a
hurt look, too. "What are you doing here?" he asked.

Before April could answer, a scraping sound on the
wall outside the door distracted them. Startled, Marc
turned to it. "What the hell is that?"

"Mice. The place is full of them," Ivan said,
unperturbed.

April popped her head out the door. Cartuso and
Bernheim were heading down the stairs, working the
tools of their trade.

"There's another one here." Cartuso was busy examining the wall and handrail with a magnifying glass
while Bernheim carefully dug out of the plaster and
aged paint the browning spots Cartuso indicated.

"Hey, April. Your boyfriend's waiting for you upstairs," Bernheim told her.

She left the lieutenant in the office to do his job
and closed the door behind her. "Hey Saul, you got
something?"

"You bet. Real geniuses, these guys. They left us the works. Looks like they kept her in a closet upstairs on the third floor. We found signs of habitation up there—cup, saucer, honey drips. Greasy food spots. Dirty towels. Blood and other stains on a folded mattress up there. We also got what we think is blood caked in cracks in the floor. The perp mopped up, but the mop only got the surface. The windowsills showed us that the victim didn't go out any window up there, so we checked out the stairway. Blood droplets on the treads." He swept his hand in a downward motion.

"You can see how they came down the stairs. There was a smear with a hair stuck in it on the wall. Must have bumped her head. Then two drops on the railing there, on the railing above it. And we have some more down here. My guess is that there wasn't that much blood, so he just carried her down the stairs, took her out the back door, and dumped her. You saw the door in there." He pointed at the office.

April nodded.

"We'll probably get something on the floor. There were a few drops outside on the pavement—not hard to pick up. He must have wanted it to look like a suicide. That's why he didn't wrap her in something. You'd think he'd have wrapped her up in something so she wouldn't drip all over the place." Bernheim shook his head at the sloppy work.

"Men don't think housekeeping. And these don't strike me as detail men. You think maybe they did it together?" April mused.

Saul shrugged. "Same thing, one or two. Neither of them wrapped her up." Saul seemed upset about this.

"Maybe it was a rage thing and they panicked when they realized they'd killed her," April speculated.

"Possibly."

"Is it okay if I go up?" she asked.

"Yeah, but keep to the middle and don't touch anything."

April met Mike in the room with the sewing machines. He was taking copious notes. "Feeling better?" he asked without looking at her.

"Okay. I'm sorry I acted like that," she murmured. "It upsets me when you get all protective on me when I'm in the middle of something."

He shook his head, still mad. She considered touching him, decided against it. "Forgive me? We've got to get moving here."

He turned a page in his notebook and wrote some more.

"Oh come on," she wheedled. "You're always bugging me to make the call. So this time I made a call. You can't be mad at me for that. I happened to be right. And time is passing here. I need you."

"You don't have to make the call when you're deathly ill," he said.

"I wasn't deathly ill," she insisted.

"Let's hope not. I wouldn't want to have to replace you." He turned another page.

Oh, God, she was in a hurry. This wasn't the time for a debate.

"When you love somebody, you're in it together." He was pushing every button.

"Okay, I'm sorry, but we've got a time limit here. This guy Anton is on his way out to Garden City, pretending to be a police captain."

"So I heard."

"He beat up his wife. For all we know he killed this poor girl. Who knows how far he'll go to get the baby back? *Caro,* we have to get going. What do you think, should I call for a bird?"

In the old days they were not supposed to call for the expensive equipment, like Aviation, unless there was a real emergency. These days, pulling out all the

stops and getting a chopper was not that big a deal.
April checked her watch anxiously. She didn't know
where Anton had started. He had a car in a garage
near Fifty-ninth Street; he might be leaving from
there. But if he intended to take the baby home with
him, he might well use a car service. April wanted to
get to Garden City before he did. She considered how
long it would take to get a bird. The helicopters were
on standby at Floyd Bennett Field. They'd have to
bring one over to Battery Park or South Street Sea-
port. It would take half an hour, minimum.

"It's all a matter of form, *querida.* Brushing me off
is bad form." Mike stood his ground, still on love. He
could be very stubborn.

April was thinking about a landing site. Where
would they be able to put the bird down? Somewhere
along the Southern State Parkway? That meant they'd
need coordination with Nassau County agencies for
the vehicles on the other end.

The minutes were mounting up. April did not want
to resort to groveling to get her boyfriend on the road.

"Fine. Don't bully, then. Do you want to drive, or
should I get Aviation into this?" She *really* didn't want
to grovel.

"Aviation will take too much time on both ends.
We'd do better on the road." He made the snap decision and eye contact at the same time. He was kicking in.

"Whatever. You finished here?" April figured she'd
won and smiled. He gave it up on the basis of the
smile.

"Yeah." He stuffed the notebook in his pocket and
took her arm as they hustled down the stairs. She must
really look bad, but miraculously, she was feeling a
lot better.

"Hey, watch that." An irritated Cartuso, now on the
bottom step, complained at the stampede for the door.

"Did you see everything?" Bernheim asked April. She shook her head. "I'll have to save it for later."

"No matter. It's not going anywhere."

They pushed past him, jostling each other for first out the door. Suddenly, after the delay, they were racing. April rushed out into the street and jumped into the passenger side of the unlocked Camaro, almost slamming the door on her foot. Mike dove into the driver's side and reached for the gum ball under the seat. He plopped it on the roof, turned the ignition key, and hit the hammer. His siren wailed all the way across the Brooklyn Bridge and kept wailing as they headed out on the Brooklyn-Queens Expressway.

CHAPTER
47

Ring Road did not run in a circle. It traveled parallel to Roosevelt Field, cutting a wide swath of comfortable, tree-and shrub-lined boulevard across a ten-block length of suburban city. Two lanes of traffic could travel each way, yet there was still room along the sidewalk for parking. Since every house had an ample driveway, few cars were parked on the street at any time of the day; even at peak traffic hours, a sense of quiet and order prevailed. By anybody's standards, it was an area not without its charm, even elegance.

After their long vigil on Allen Street and a frantic phone call in the early afternoon, Frankie and Joey arrived at the Hua house at 4:03. By a quarter past four they had settled in the living room and were heatedly reporting what they knew about the murder of Nanci's cousin.

"We saw those guys go in real early. Unbelievable, they were opening up as usual. These guys are something. They both have green Mercedes." Milton's friend Frankie had been marveling over the cars for hours now.

"We got there at seven-thirty. The two fat dudes showed up, like almost instantly," Joey confirmed.

"But then when the girls showed up for work, they

didn't let any of them come in. They stood at the door
and sent them all away. One guy went out for food.
Then a couple hours later, a pizza was delivered and
another joker turned up in a taxi. This one was wearing a suit, but he looked just like them. He left in a
hurry just before the cops got there. Then a whole
bunch of cops were in and out of there, are probably
still there. But your little Chink lady never showed—"

"Hey, watch that," Milton said sharply.

"What?" Frankie entreated Nanci with a what-did-
I-do expression.

"We're Chinks," she reminded him. "My cousin was
a Chink."

"Oh, give me a break. Can't you tell the difference?" He looked disgusted.

"No." Nanci stared at the window, too upset to
make an issue of it.

"Of course she didn't show up, stupid. Lin was already dead. That's why Annie never called back." Milton shook his head and glanced at his wife. "You
okay, baby?"

Nanci's teeth were clamped hard on her bottom lip
to keep it from quivering. She couldn't believe this
was happening, the sweet baby upstairs, crazy Frankie
in her living room, and the man who said he was a
police captain, coming for the baby. It was impossible
to imagine Lin dead and her murderer on his way out
to their little house to take away her baby.

She didn't have a chance to answer. Frankie was
back on track with his story. He'd never even met Lin,
but suddenly, describing the police activity around the
building where she had died, and the neighbors' feelings about the arrogance of the Popescu family, he
was as incensed as any blood relation.

Nancy wondered where April was. She'd said help
was on the way. But where was it? Where was help?
And where was the man who'd claimed he was a po-

lice captain? Nanci hoped he'd changed his mind. It occurred to her that the call might have been a cruel prank. Maybe no such person was on his way out there, and she and Milton had encouraged crazy Frankie and Joey to drive out for nothing. She hoped that was the case.

"Help is on the way," she murmured at Milton. He was sitting in a chair by the window. Like her, he had one eye on the street and one eye on his friend.

"Sons of bitches," Frankie was saying about the Popescus.

Nanci could see that Milton didn't like Frankie's being all pumped up like this any more than she did. Suddenly Frankie got up from the sofa by the fireplace and started walking around, waving his arms, all excited by the police investigation of a murder of someone he felt was closely related to him. If she hadn't known him for more than a decade, she would have been even more frightened. Frankie was not easygoing like Milton. He was almost nine inches taller than his friend, an angry-looking young man with a hooked nose and a big mouth who'd been a brawler from the day he could walk. Even in Little Italy, where a certain lack of impulse control among young men was not uncommon, Frankie was out there near the far end of the bell curve of aggression.

But of the two, his best pal, Joey, was generally regarded as the dangerous one. The only thing that could incense Joey more than the real cops he'd seen hanging out around Allen Street with their walkie-talkies and other cop gear was a cop impersonator. That really pissed him off. Joey never got tired of telling people of an incident a year ago when he'd been dragged off a subway by a man and a woman claiming they were police officers. The woman had been wearing a silver police shield around her neck; the man had on ragged jeans and sneakers. The two of them looked like a hooker and a doper to Joey, but they managed to pull him and three other people off the train at a deserted stop and rob them on the platform. Then they took off. As soon as they started running, Joey and the other men went after them. It must have been quite a sight: the two muggers emerging on the street with their victims in hot pursuit. Some passersby picked up on it and called 911. The woman got away, but when the victims caught up with the man, he turned on them with a lead pipe. In the ensuing battle, he managed to split one man's head open with the pipe before Joey took a good, deep slice out of him with his switchblade. Joey recovered his wallet and watch and was out of there before the police showed up. Nanci could see from the faraway look in his eye that he was thinking of the triumph of that much-discussed day, and of his wish to repeat it.

"We'll show this guy," he said, abruptly zooming in to focus on the present. It was clear that for Joey it had been bad enough to watch real cops at work that morning; the threat of being pushed around by a phony one was more than he could bear.

Nanci cast an anxious look at her husband. "Milton," she murmured.

"Okay, okay. Just calm down, will you?" Milton shook his head at the two, then turned his attention to the window. "It looks fine out there. Maybe you guys better take off."

Frankie sprang across the room, punching one fist into his open hand. "No way. Who's going to protect you if this asshole shows up with a gun?"

Nanci flashed to the last sight she'd had of her cousin, walking away down the street without looking back. Her eyes flooded.

"Hey, hey. It's okay." Milton jumped out of the chair, crossed the room, and took Nanci in his arms. He hugged her tightly.

"April said the killer threw Lin out the window," Nanci sobbed. "Oh, God, she must have been so scared." She held on to her husband. "Who could do something like that?"

"We'll get him," Frankie promised.

"No! Milton's right. You should go home. You've been great, but, please, we're okay now." Nanci got up and checked the street. There was nothing going on out there but the usual daytime traffic. She swiped at her eyes. "Get them to go, Milton."

"You're no fun," Frankie joked.

That really angered her. "This is not a game. Please, Milton, tell them we're okay now," she cried.

"Nobody has a gun, right?" Milton looked from one to the other. Now he was worried.

"Right," Frankie said seriously. "This isn't a game."

"You promised me no guns."

Frankie glanced at Joey. "I don't have a gun, do you have a gun?"

"No way, man." Joey got to his feet and backed out to the door to the kitchen. "I'm clean."

"There are real cops on the way out here, understand?" Milton got up, too. Now they were all on their feet. Nanci started trembling.

"You got a gun, you get outta here." Milton chose to advance on his friend.

Frankie struck a pose and held his arms out. "Go ahead, search me. You find a gun, I'll give you a thousand dollars."

Milton lunged across the room. "You're on."

"He doesn't have a thousand dollars," Nanci told him. She was so nervous she couldn't keep still. What was it with these guys? All of a sudden they were playing high school games, Milton wanting to be one of them. They'd forgotten all about Lin, about the man coming to the house. Frustrated, she blew her nose. She had to stop crying. It didn't help. She had to do something.

Frankie spread his legs and held out his arms. Milton started to pat him down. Nanci wanted to punch them all. Then she thought she heard a sound somewhere in the back of the house and froze. "Did you hear that?"

Joey charged into the kitchen for a look out the back window. "Nothing out here," he called.

"Stay there and keep watch," Milton told him.

Suddenly in her mind's eye Nanci could see the killer scaling the brick wall outside, hidden from their view, and carrying the baby she and Milton had named William out the window. What if he got the baby and took off without any of them ever seeing him? She ran up the stairs and into Will's room. The cherub was safe and wide awake in his borrowed crib. His blue eyes were open, and he was calmly trying to focus on the colorful figures in the mobile over his head. Nanci was transported.

"Hi, sweetheart," she crooned. "You're awake. How come you didn't call me, sweet boy?"

He gurgled up at her. She picked him up, her heart thumping as his tiny hand escaped the blanket and reached for her cheek. She kissed his fingers and the nose that didn't look Chinese. Then she took him over to the makeshift changing table they'd set up by the window to see if he was wet. It was from there that she saw the limousine drive up to the house. The car was navy blue and looked new. She gasped, couldn't move. She stood by the window, paralyzed, as a dark-haired man in a navy suit got out of the car and looked around at the quiet row of houses. Then he looked up, saw her standing in the window, and started walking toward the house.

"Milton, he's here!" she cried.

"Stay upstairs," he ordered.

She was scared. She saw the man move up the walk to the door, saw him raise his hand to the doorbell, heard the doorbell ring. She wanted to stay in the bedroom as Milton had told her to do, but she didn't know what the three men downstairs were doing. Three of them wouldn't let anybody hurt her or the baby, but they might hurt someone else or get hurt themselves. She moved silently down the hall, holding the baby close to her heart until, at the top of the stairs, she could see Milton's back as he talked to the front door.

"Yeah, who is it?"

"Captain Burke, NYPD. I called and spoke with your wife." The voice of the man outside was muffled, but they could all hear it.

"Show me your ID," Milton said.

"Open the door." It sounded like an order from someone who was used to being obeyed.

"I don't need to open the door. You show it to the peephole. I'll be able to see it fine."

"Oh, for Christ's sake, open the door. I'm not going to hurt anybody." Now he sounded irritated.

Frankie stood by the window. "That's the guy. That's the guy in the suit," he said. "The one who ran away when the cops came."

"You sure?" Milton asked.

"Of course I'm sure. What do you think, I'm stupid? This was the guy who showed up in a taxi, then took off."

"What makes you think he's the killer?" Milton said doubtfully, looking out at a prissy-looking guy in a fancy pin-striped suit.

"He's here, isn't he?" Annoyed by his friend's uncertainty, Frankie was using his logic.

"Open up," said the voice from outside.

"I'm going to open the door for a police shield, nothing else," Milton said.

"Come on, I'm losing my patience."

"I don't give a shit about your patience, you're not coming in here." It was then that Milton turned around and saw his wife at the top of the stairs. His voice softened instantly. "Didn't I tell you to stay upstairs, honey?"

"I want him arrested," Nanci said.

"Nanci, go upstairs. Don't be stubborn," Milton snapped.

His tone brought tears to her eyes, but she didn't comply. "She was my cousin. He's a murderer. Don't tell him to go away. Make him stay here so they can arrest him."

"Yeah, let him in, we'll arrest him." Frankie was psyched for that.

"Are you crazy?" Milton demanded, looking from one to the other.

"What'sa matter with you? There are three of us. Don't you think three of us can handle a stupid dick in a suit?" Frankie demanded.

Milton turned back to the peephole. "Oh shit. He's gone. Joey, you watching the back door?"

"No problem. I got it covered," Joey shouted from the kitchen.

Suddenly Frankie was on the move, hopping around from window to window, all excited. "Where'd he go? Where'd he go?"

"Thanks a lot. Maybe he got away," Nanci said.

"Nah, he didn't leave. The car's still outside."

Where were the cops? Nanci was so scared. She stroked the baby's soft head with one finger to calm herself. As the seconds passed, the baby became restless. His head started bobbing at her chest, searching for a nipple. It was feeding time. Nanci came down the stairs for a bottle.

CHAPTER
48

April and Mike were stuck in the middle of Friday afternoon traffic. April held the cell phone to her ear, waiting for someone to pick up. The red gum ball flashed importantly on the roof of the car, and the siren was very loud. Nervous motorists took a look at Mike's red car with tinted black windows and moved over even though the dirty Camaro didn't remotely resemble a police car. The cooperation got them up to about thirty-five miles an hour. After three rings an unfamiliar, croaky voice answered.

"*Wei.*"

The sound of a stranger on her parents' phone struck April with another wave of nausea. The hot, dizzy feeling swept over her, filling her mouth with water. The heavy traffic had been moving along at an even pace. Suddenly it was slowed almost to a stop by the yellow arrow of a street sweeper ahead of them, cleaning the roadway at rush hour. Her gut clenched. She grimaced and closed her eyes.

"*Wei?*" the voice said again, more urgently this time.

"Who's that?" April asked in Chinese.

"It's your mother, who you think?" Also in Chinese.

"What's the matter, Ma?" April asked, instantly feeling better.

Skinny Dragon Mother made a little crying sound. "I very sick."

"Too bad," April said, feeling better still. The dragon did sound pretty weak and pitiful, but April wasn't going to let it bother her.

"Come home right away. Maybe I die."

"That's terrible." April tried to put a little concern in her voice, but wasn't entirely successful.

"Come home right away. Need doctor."

Skinny hated doctors. She would never say she needed one without a very good reason. A reflex of filial thoughtfulness crept over April in spite of herself. "Is Dad there?" she asked.

"No."

"Anyone there?"

"Dog here."

"I mean someone who could help you."

"You police captain. You supposed to take care of me; mother comes first."

"Ma, listen to me. I'm chasing a killer right now. I can't come home and take care of you."

"Killer more important than me?" Skinny screamed.

"Be reasonable, Ma; you hurt me last night. That doesn't make me feel like caring for you." April found this surprisingly easy to say on a cell phone while Mike was driving the Camaro with the siren blasting. "You made me sick. I was sick on the job. I threw up and lost face in front of the whole department. I was on my knees because of you. You think I have sympathy now because you don't feel well?"

"What's wrong with you, ungrateful worm?" Skinny wailed.

"Gee, I'm not sure. Maybe my heart, maybe my liver. Maybe my brain. It's hard to know. Only the

person who poisoned me would know for sure." The
siren screamed, but so did her mother.

"Oh, *ni*, you bad girl," Skinny cried over the siren.

"If I'm bad girl, then a bad mother must have raised
me," April shot back. She heard a scream on the other
end of the line.

"I best mother!"

"Best mothers don't poison their daughters to get
their way."

"You were sick before, only try to help, *ni*. You
better now?"

"You made me sick because you don't want me to
be happy. You don't want me to choose my own husband, my own life." They passed the road sweeper
and sped up.

"What's going on?" Mike asked.

Sai attempted a death rattle on the other end of
the line.

April didn't answer Mike and didn't care what noises
her mother made. "Too bad. You got yourself sick
when you cooked up that poison in the kitchen. Just
because you didn't want me to be happy, you probably
smell and feel as bad as I do."

"Maybe I die. Then who take care of your father?"
Skinny countered.

Uh-oh. April wasn't up to a possibility as loaded as
that. "Better not die; he'll find another wife to take
your place."

Skinny made a clicking noise that April interpreted
as "Not a chance; you'll get him for sure."

"What was the shit in the kettle?"

"None of your business." But at the thought of a suc-
cessor wife she changed her mind fast. "Dragon bones;
sour herbs," she admitted.

"Must have been some low-quality, very sick
dragon. I bet those bones were black, huh. That's what
you get when you use cheap ingredients."

"You okay, *ni*? You learn lesson?" Sai asked, almost meekly.

What lesson? Skinny never even articulated why loving a non-Chinese was such a big deal. If she'd said, "Look what happened to Lin Tsing for messing with a Caucasian; look what happened to Heather Rose," then maybe she'd have a point that April could think about. They could have discussed it. Skinny could have gotten to know Mike and judged for herself whether he was a good man for a woman—of any culture. But Skinny was a wrathful dragon. She couldn't tell a good man from a bad one, was interested in her own prejudices, not facts.

"*Ni*, you come home and take care of best-quality mother," Sai Woo said in her most guilt-inducing voice.

"Drink lots of fluids. Call Mr. Wang. Maybe he knows what to do for bad dragon bones."

"*Ni*, you mad at me?"

"Yes."

"You coming home after you catch killer?"

"Not like before, Ma." April finished telling her mother off in Chinese and hung up the phone.

"What was that all about?" Mike asked, looking at her strangely.

"Oh, nothing much. My mother took some black dragon bones, and it made her sick."

"The same ones that got you?"

"Yeah. She wanted me to come right home and take care of her." April shook her head. Mothers!

"You want to take a detour and check on her, *querida*?"

"No way. You know we've got local people waiting for us. Let her wait."

"How are you holding up?"

"Me?" April took a deep breath, testing. "I feel great, just great." And it was true.

"Good, here's Ring Road." Mike slowed down and took a right.

"Nice area," April remarked.

"Looks like he beat us." Mike pointed out the long blue limo in the middle of the next block. The light turned red. He ran it.

CHAPTER
49

They were all crowded in the kitchen, peering out the window into the shady backyard with the two big oak trees and the dogwood that was still in bloom. Nanci had come in to get some formula for the baby. She took a bottle from the six remaining on the kitchen counter, twisted off the cap, and replaced it with a sterilized nipple. Anton Popescu walked around the house, searching for a way in. Frankie followed him from window to window, ending up by the back door, guarded by Joey. The top half of the door was glass, partially covered with a white, see-through curtain. The four people inside had a good view as Anton rattled the knob and rapped on the glass, his face distorted by rage.

"Let me in! What's the matter with you people?" he cried.

"Look at that asshole," Joey muttered.

"You're no cop," Milton said through the window.

"I just want to talk to you. What's the big deal?"

"You can talk when the cops get here," Milton replied.

"What cops?" Anton was undeterred.

"The cops are looking for you. So hang around, you'll get arrested," Milton said.

"I didn't do anything. Come on, be smart. Let me

come in and talk to you. I don't have any weapons. How could it hurt you to hear what I have to say?"

Seconds passed. Milton and Anton assessed each other. No one else moved.

"What's your problem?" Anton cried through the door. "I just want to talk."

"Let him in," Nanci said suddenly.

"Yeah, let's let him in. We'll make a citizen's arrest," Frankie agreed.

"Just keep your shirt on." Milton turned to Nanci. "Why do you want him in here?"

"I want to talk to the man who killed my cousin," she said, eyes narrowed at the man behind the curtain.

"Are you crazy?" Milton said. "Why?"

"There are four of us. What's he going to do?" she said.

"If he has a gun he could kill us all." Milton put his arm around his wife's shoulders. "Be reasonable."

"He came in a limo. Be reasonable yourself, Milton. What's he going to do, shoot us and get back in the car?" Nanci reached up and squeezed the hand on her shoulder, then kissed the baby's head.

"What can he do, scare us to death?" Joey laughed.

"Yeah," Frankie seconded.

Milton shook his head at them. "You're all nuts." Still, he went over and unlocked the door. Nanci was holding the bottle. The baby was bobbing his head at her chest, whimpering for food. She backed away to the living room entrance, her face pale.

"Go ahead, let him in," she whispered.

But Anton had heard the bolt turn in the lock. He plunged through the door before Milton had a chance to open it for him. Inside he stopped, squared his shoulders, and examined the four adults one by one. "I'm Anton Popescu," he said momentously.

Joey circled him, gave him a few little exploratory shoves.

Anton was solid; he didn't move. But his face reddened. He addressed Milton. "Who's the boss here? You?"

"Yeah, sure, this is my house. You wanted in, you're in. What do you want?"

"I want to talk, that's all. Why the gun?" He glared at Joey.

Milton's hands snaked out to Joey's pocket; he felt the bulge there and groaned. "Shit. Joey, I said no guns. Go outside." He pointed at the door.

"Aw, please," Joey raised his hands in supplication. "If he behaves, I won't touch it. How's that?"

"You can't be armed and stay in here with the baby. Go on outside, cover the back door."

"Go on," Frankie told him.

Joey gave his friend a hurt look and went out the door.

"Come on in here." Milton waved his arm for Anton to go into the living room. Then he whispered at Nanci to take the baby and go upstairs. Instead, she went into the living room, settled in the rocking chair by the fireplace, and teased the baby's lips with the nipple. The baby took it and started sucking. Milton frowned at her, but she was busy and didn't notice.

Anton made himself comfortable in an armchair before he began speaking. No longer upset by the thug with the gun in his pocket, he radiated confidence. "I want to thank you for taking care of my son Paul this week. He looks great."

"You barge in here saying you're a cop when you're not a cop. Now you say the baby is yours. You sound like a liar to me." Milton stood in the center of the living room. Frankie hung out by the front door. Anton seemed undaunted by the hostile atmosphere.

"I have to take him back now," he said evenly. "I'd be glad to give you some compensation for your trouble."

"He's not yours. He's not going anywhere," Milton said.

"I'm afraid he is, and I want to do this in as gentlemanly a way as possible."

Milton almost laughed. "You must be crazy. You're not taking our baby."

"I said I would compensate you for your trouble."

"How much?" Nanci asked.

"Nanci!" Milton flared up. He exchanged glances with Frankie. Frankie had already lost his patience. He was moving around nervously, a sign of imminent attack.

Nanci stopped chewing on her lip. She had two strong men in the room. She wasn't afraid of Anton's bluster. "I want to know how much the baby's worth to him."

Anton gave her a big smile. "How much do you want?" he asked affably.

Nanci glared at him. "No price. He's my own blood, my cousin's baby. How could anyone put a price on him? I just want to know how far you'd go."

Anton nodded at her, then at Milton. "I understand how you feel. I'm prepared to be generous with you."

"How generous?"

Milton took over. "Yeah, don't play games with us. What kind of offer are you making?"

Anton looked puzzled. "What do you mean?"

"For the death of my cousin," Nanci told him calmly.

"That was unfortunate." Anton rearranged his face to look sympathetic.

"It's more than unfortunate for me," Nanci murmured, stroking the baby's forehead with a finger as he drank.

"I'm sorry for your loss, but I didn't have anything to do with it. That's a separate issue."

"Not to me."

"What do you expect from me?" Now Anton's face was that of a negotiator. It looked open, flexible. He had his eye on the suckling baby.

Nanci had her eye on the hall clock. She still thought help was on the way. Milton moved from the center of the room to his wife's side.

"We want Lin's murderer punished, that's all."

Anton shifted in his chair. "Look, I can see there's been an unfortunate misunderstanding here. Paul belongs to me and my wife. She's his mother, I'm his father. There's no room for negotiation about this. I don't have any choice here; I have to take him back where he belongs."

There was a silence for a few seconds; then Joey burst in from the kitchen. "This guy is an asshole. Look at what he did to Nanci's cousin. I'm not sitting still for this. Let's take care of him." He appealed to Frankie.

Milton responded, "I thought I told you to stay outside."

"Joey, you're not related," Frankie put in. "It's not for you to say what punishment is correct."

Anton propelled himself out of the chair. "Hey, I just came for my baby. You touch me and I'll prosecute you," he said sharply.

Joey moved a step closer to him, threatening. "Oh, we're really scared of a guy who rapes and kills little girls."

"Okay, that's enough." Milton crossed the room and took Joey's arm. Frankie joined them. From far away there came the faint sound of a police siren.

Nanci let out the breath she'd been holding. April was there. Thank God, it was over. She cuddled the tiny baby who'd caused so much turmoil. He was feeding, unconcerned, in her arms.

With the three men in a huddle by the front door, Anton moved, in one step, to where she sat with the baby. "I'm sorry," he murmured. "I'm really sorry. I didn't expect it to end like this."

The other men had been threatening. This one seemed finally to be intimidated by the siren. He really appeared to be coming over to apologize to her. Earlier, he'd been aggressive but normal. He'd never acted like a killer or a rapist. He'd just acted the bully, like a lot of men did. And now he was deflated by the arrival of the police. Nanci didn't have time to adjust her grip on the feeding baby. In fact, she didn't think of it. She thought Anton was sorry. He stood beside her, leaned over her, and in a second he'd taken the baby out of her arms and was headed out the back door with him.

CHAPTER 50

There was something terribly serious about the blue limo, unlike anything else with wheels parked on this Garden City street. The car was long and wide, and even from a block away it was clear the thing had leather seats and a phone and a TV. The fancy car with its emblem and its shiny paint and its driver sitting inside made a clear distinction between the kind of people who rode around in conveyances like that and the kind of people who didn't. The car was a symbol of power that indicated how carefully and importantly those driving in it had to be treated. In the police department, these people held the ultimate rank the officers were taught to respect and fear.

As they drove toward the car, April couldn't help thinking of Anton's wife, Heather Rose, who had come from the same melting pot as she but had so much more promise as a child and such a different fate. By outward appearance, Heather Rose was superior to April in every way. Somehow, she'd been able to study during the years April had had to work. She'd been smart enough to go to a great university, fortunate enough to attract a man of wealth and influence. It occurred to April that she must be used to riding around in limos with her husband. But Heather Rose's marriage to a professional man, and the wealth April's

own mother so wanted for her daughter, hadn't ex-
empted Heather Rose and her family from torture
and shame.

The phone call to her mother had also made April
think of shame. All her life Skinny had shamed April,
made her feel like a worm. It was unsettling to think
that Mike Sanchez had done more for her self-respect
than her own parents, and even more shocking that
he was willing to take a detour to check on Skinny
even though she hated him. This made April ashamed
of her mother.

As the Camaro approached the limo, April started
to feel even more anxious. Half a block from the
house, Mike slowed the car and turned off the siren.
Instantly, all became quiet on the street. April swallowed, breathed in and out a few times, testing for
nausea and dizziness. She still felt all right.

"Maybe this'll be easy, and we can go check on
your mother soon," Mike said hopefully. She touched
his hand on the wheel.

"I have to admit, I didn't want you in this when it
started," she said slowly.

He brought her hand to his lips and kissed it. "I
love you."

It was the first time he'd said it in English. She felt
his mustache and his warm lips. Her anxiety intensified. The air in the car seemed to get colder, not
warmer as it should with the heat of their love. She
wanted to say she loved him, too, but instead she said,
"Do you feel that?"

"What?"

She frowned. "You don't feel it? Cold?"

"No."

"Maybe it's just me." She unholstered her gun,
checked out the 9mm, then cradled it in her lap. The
quiet lasted only a few seconds. Before they had time
to formulate a game plan, the unmistakable sound of

a shot came from behind the house. Mike braked
hard. April was thrown forward into her seat belt and
recovered her balance as Mike reached for his gun
and dove out of the car into the line of fire.

"Wait!" The word wrenched from her throat. It
wasn't what she was supposed to say.

"Cover me," Mike ordered over his shoulder.

She was supposed to do it without question. In the
middle of a power surge, though, April reverted to
type and rankled at the command. Their situation had
changed. He was no longer her supervisor. *She* was
the squad supervisor. He didn't outrank her. So who
was in charge here, who was supposed to take the
lead, be in the line of fire? All this in a split second.

What she was supposed to do was get out of the
car, position herself somewhere behind Mike, and
cover him. But she was overwhelmed with a sudden
feeling of inadequacy. "Wait," she said again.

But either Mike didn't hear her or he wasn't going
to wait. He was out of the car and across the sidewalk
before she could say anything else. He hit the edge of
the lawn as Anton appeared around the side of the
house, running toward his big shiny car. Clutched
close to his chest was a bundle wrapped in a blue
blanket, and the bundle was screaming. Behind him
more shots were fired. A young man with a handgun
ran out from behind the house and dove behind a
large oak tree.

"Police! Drop the gun!" Mike shouted. April heard
it. Anton heard it. Anton saw Mike's gun in front of
him and froze. The baby was shrieking. It wasn't clear
if the gunman ever heard him. Anton stood still on
the lawn as Mike moved forward to protect him. At
that moment more shots were fired.

"Mike!" April screamed as the first bullet ripped
through Anton, turning the bundle a sickening red as
he fell. The second bullet hit Mike. She could see him

miss a step as it slammed him. He fell to one knee, then struggled to get up again.

"Get down!" she screamed at him. She had her gun aimed at the tree. She fired, hit nothing. She could see the muzzle of the gun, but not the shooter.

She did not fire again, because other people ran from the side of the house, right out into her line of fire. Nanci was screaming, racing toward the bloody blanket. Milton and another man were trying to stop her, screen her from the sight of Anton, with half his head blown off. The gunman was behind the tree. April couldn't get a shot off with the three of them racing toward her.

"Get back!" April shouted at them. A second passed. Only a second. She wanted Mike down, everybody back. She had only a second. Mike wouldn't stay down. His gun was in his hands. He was up again, aiming at the shooter. His angle was better than hers, but Nanci kept coming. She was screaming, and Milton was screaming at her. And April was screaming at them to get back. Mike had a growing red spot on his shirt.

She was supposed to cover him, but she'd failed. He was supposed to get down, but he didn't. She knew what was going on in his mind. If he had to die, he was going to take the bastard down with him. Nanci and Milton were supposed to get out of the way, but they wouldn't. April had been in this kind of position several times in her life, the latest in enhanced computer-simulated training that was supposed to teach appropriate reactions to situations like this when there was no good line of fire and no easy solution.

Now her instinct was to dive out onto the lawn and make herself the target, to save Mike and the others with the shield of her own body. She knew that was not a good idea. Instead she moved right, intending to make the shooter turn away from the four of them

and toward her. She fired at the tree. The shooter
shifted his position and fired at her. Mike rushed him.
He turned to get off a shot at Mike, and April fired,
taking him down.

CHAPTER
51

Jason abruptly canceled his supervisory session just as Alison Peters, his attractive psychiatric resident, was coming into his office. In the elevator, as they went down to the street together, he explained hurriedly that he had to go to the police station. At first she was impressed; then she soured because he couldn't tell her when they'd be able to reschedule. In turn, he couldn't help being troubled by her selfishness in an emergency. By the time he hit the street, though, he was thinking of nothing else but Heather Rose.

He hailed a taxi and gave the address of the Midtown North police station. April used to be assigned to the 20th Precinct, only a few blocks away. Now he had to travel nearly twenty-five minutes into the traffic nightmare of midtown. As he sat in a dirty taxi, with a driver who couldn't speak English, didn't know the city, and hadn't had a bath in some time, he tried to digest the tragedy: another victim of the Popescus'; this one the teenage girl whose baby Heather had returned. Jason played over and over what April had told him and still it was hard to imagine the cruelty of a young woman forced to give birth in a closet, having her baby taken from her, and recovering him several weeks later, only to die violently in the end.

The silence among the family members surrounding all the catastrophic events of many years (possibly starting with Anton's cancer but equally possibly going back even further than that) was what Jason focused on. Anton's family was perpetually in denial about the permanent effects of his childhood illness. Heather Rose was horribly afraid to tell anyone that the man she'd married was impotent. In the hospital she'd made clear to Jason that she was afraid she was the crazy one. Her husband had kept her in line by intimidating her, torturing her, and isolating her from anybody who could help her.

The meaning of Heather's responses to her situation up to the time when she returned the baby, and of her responses to him in the hospital, was now clear to Jason. She'd given the baby back as atonement, and the punishment she'd received because of it had come as no surprise. Jason arrived at the police station, paid his fare, and got out.

Inside the precinct, he went to the front desk and asked for Sergeant Woo because he didn't want to deal with Lieutenant Iriarte. He waited for what felt like a long time before Detective Baum appeared, looking very upset.

"The situation's changed," he said, preempting Jason's greeting. "There's been a shooting."

"A shooting?" Jason frowned.

"It's not clear if Sergeant Woo took a hit. We do know that one officer and the perp were shot. They're on the way to the hospital. The third victim is dead."

"What? April was in a shooting? Are you sure? I just talked to her an hour ago." Jason was incredulous.

"Yeah, the local cops arrived on the scene immediately. I don't know. They were alerted earlier. I don't know. It's not clear what happened."

"I just talked to her. . . ." Jason was stunned. "What hospital has she been taken to?"

"Unclear. And we don't know it was her. Could have been Sanchez."

"Sanchez!" April's boyfriend, Sanchez? Jason tried to take it all in. "You said someone is dead. Who's dead?"

"Anton Popescu. It looks like the perp shot him when he took off with the baby."

"Jesus." For a moment Jason was speechless. Anton Popescu was dead? How could that have happened? It was staggering. Finally he recovered enough to ask, "Does his wife know this?"

"No. It just came in this minute. Do you want to tell her?"

"Where is she?"

"We have Mrs. Popescu and her parents separated. They've been here a while now."

"What, you left Heather alone? She has a history of unexplained injuries, she could hurt or kill herself in unguarded minutes." Jason spoke mildly, but thoughts of the shooting and all the bungling in the case made him furious. Suicide was an issue here. Now that her husband was dead Heather Rose would really have to be watched every minute.

Baum was taken aback. Apparently he hadn't considered this. "All she did was cut off her hair," he said defensively.

"She cut off her hair?" April hadn't mentioned that.

A commotion commenced at the front door when a well-dressed man wearing handcuffs was brought in by two uniformed officers. Detective Baum touched Jason's arm to move him out of the way as the cops hustled the prisoner to the front desk. The prisoner was complaining, and the two officers were trying to shut him up. They all had such strong New York accents Jason didn't understand a word. He tried to concentrate on Heather Rose's near-simultaneous loss of the baby she'd loved, who wasn't hers, and of her

husband, who'd hurt her and had never consummated
their marriage. It was a heavy load.

"How long has she been in there alone?" he asked.

"Several hours."

"She's been alone for several hours. Are you
crazy?"

"She's all right. We have an officer at the door."
Baum jerked his head for Jason to follow him up
the stairs.

Jason paused outside the interview room to take a
look through the window in the door. Heather was
sitting on a metal folding chair with her shorn head
in her hands. On the table sat an unopened paper bag,
presumably the lunch she hadn't eaten. She looked
frail in jeans and a summer pullover, with her im-
promptu haircut. With her hair less than an inch long,
the ugly scalp wound was clearly visible.

Jason felt a huge wave of relief, and another of
sadness for her double loss. And he wondered if
Heather was up to the questioning she would no doubt
have to endure. April had asked him to question her.
Now he had his own good reasons for doing so. He
composed his features and quickly went inside, chiding
himself for the mundane things he always said in the
direst situations. This time it was "Hi. Long time no
see."

Heather looked up, startled. "What are you doing
here?"

"I told you last night I'd be around for you. You
didn't think I'd disappear so fast, did you?"

"Who asked you to come here? Why are they keeping me here? What's happening?" Heather cried. She
reached up to her head in a characteristic gesture of
hair arranging, then realized her hair was no longer
there. The hand became dispirited and fell to her lap.
All the time she was anxiously focused on the door,
where Detective Baum stood behind Jason, waiting to

see if he'd be allowed to stay. Jason shook his head and closed the door.

"I thought you asked to come here," Jason said, taking a seat at the table.

"No, I told them everything I knew downtown. Look, I'm worried about my parents. What's happened to them?"

"They're okay. I'll check on them in a few minutes if you'd like." Jason cocked his head, considering Heather's appearance.

She hung her head. "I know it's horrible." She shuddered at how horrible it must be.

"No, you look different, younger, cute. That's all. Why'd you cut it?"

She kneaded a thumb nervously. "I guess it was pretty dumb. When I heard that Paul's mother had been—murdered, I just—I don't know—I just couldn't imagine anybody *doing* that, killing that poor girl— why? I felt so *bad.* I went into the bathroom to be alone for a minute." She closed her eyes as if to see herself from the inside at the moment when she'd heard the news. "All I saw in the mirror was the hair. . . . You know, he made me grow and grow it. He wouldn't let me cut it. It was the only thing he liked about me." She opened her eyes, appalled at herself for saying such a devastating thing. "I'm sorry."

"What for?"

"I should have left things alone and kept the baby. None of this would have happened if I'd kept him." She caught her bottom lip between her teeth to keep from crying.

"Oh, you never know."

Her eyes filled with tears. "Where is he? Is he all right?"

Jason nodded without knowing if he was. "You want to tell me what happened this morning?"

Heather shrugged. "Nothing. I checked out of the hospital and went home to get my stuff. I was leaving him to go back to San Francisco. He came home and was really mean about my parents."

"I remember. He didn't sound too happy about their coming. How did he deal with finding you there?"

"Oh, he did what he always does. He has this way of acting really nice sometimes in front of some people, really horrible in front of other people, then insisting the nice him is the only him."

"It's called splitting," Jason told her. "He didn't like his bad side, so he didn't acknowledge it as part of himself."

Heather Rose didn't pick up on the past tense. "He was furious when he saw the cop had his pictures. They got into a fight. Then we left. What are you doing here?" she asked again.

Jason stared up at the ceiling, calling for help from above. He was nailed. "You keep asking me that."

"Maybe I'll keep asking until you give me a good answer."

No help came from on high. Jason made a decision. "Okay, I'll be straight with you. I'm not acting as your doctor. But I'm not a policeman whose only interest is the law, either."

"What do you mean?"

"It's an unusual situation," he murmured. He was on the hook, struggling.

"If you're not a policeman and not a doctor, then what's your role?"

"Um. Sergeant Woo sometimes asks me to help her with assessments," Jason said finally, although none of his talks with Heather or Anton had been formal assessments. He didn't think it would be useful to explain further. Oh, he was really twisting in the wind.

"But you just said you don't work for the police department."

"That's right," he admitted.

"Then why—"

"Why do it? You're asking me good questions, and since you're not my patient, I don't have to hide from you. I'm going to answer you as fully as I can. Sergeant Woo was the detective on the case when my wife was kidnapped. She saved my wife's life." He looked at the bag of lunch and wished he were in it.

"Your wife was kidnapped!" Heather was shocked.

"Yes." Okay, maybe that wasn't such a bad thing for her to know. Bad things had happened in his life, too. Maybe that would help her. Jason changed the subject. "In your case, there was a history of unexplained injuries and a missing baby. It wasn't clear who was hurting you—you or your husband. And it wasn't clear whether the baby was still alive. Sergeant Woo asked me to talk to you. As I said, she does that sometimes when people don't open up to her right away."

Heather gave him a grim smile. "What did you find out?"

"It was clear to me that you were not a killer and that you didn't want to nail your husband as a batterer."

"He's not responsible for this," she said fiercely.

"For what?"

"For killing anyone." Her face contorted with the agony of saying those words.

"But you cut off your gorgeous hair when you heard," he pointed out. "For you it was an act of revenge, wasn't it?"

"No."

"What then?"

"It was my line in the sand. The girl was dead. I

drew a line in the sand." Her lip disappeared between her teeth again.

"A line in the sand." Jason looked puzzled.

"I always thought the worst had already happened."

"What was that?"

Heather was chewing on both lips, chewing, chewing. She was kneading her hands as if they'd lost circulation. Her breath was ragged. "Years ago when we were dating, he kept telling me how much he loved me, but he was very religious and didn't want to spoil our love with—you know." She glanced at Jason quickly, then away. "I don't know why I keep telling you these things. I've never told anyone this. It must sound crazy."

He shook his head. "Many people hide the things that make them miserable. Yesterday you told me your husband couldn't have children. You also told me he was impotent."

"We didn't have any kind of . . . physical . . ." She wrung her hands. "I feel so bad." She tried to sniff back her tears, but was caught by her sobs.

Jason gave her a few seconds. "You told me you had no sex life together."

"He was so mean—" She swallowed, gulped. "No. A lot of the time, he couldn't stand to let me sleep in the bed. He wouldn't touch me at all. Except when—after I . . ."

"When you were hurt."

She hung her head. "Yes. I felt so sorry for him."

"He hurt you, and yet you felt sorry for him. Why did he burn you, Heather?"

She tried to take a deep breath. It caught a few times. She looked away. "I didn't want to tell."

"It's okay. You can tell now. He can't hurt you anymore." Jason repeated it. "He can't hurt you."

"Oh, he can, you don't know him. My parents said they won't leave me alone with him. They promised.

But—he's very persistent. He always says if I'm really good it won't happen again."

"Heather, listen to me. Anton can't hurt you anymore. He's gone."

"Gone? What do you mean?" Heather was puzzled. She blew her nose on a badly shredded tissue.

Jason reached into his pocket and gave her his handkerchief.

She blew her nose and handed it back. He shook his head. "You can keep it."

"I'll have it washed—"

"Why did he burn you?"

"Oh, God." She gulped. "Oh, God. He got so angry. He just got so angry."

"What made him so angry?"

This was the question that opened the way for her. Physically, it was as if she were reliving the horror in front of Jason's eyes. She squirmed in the chair, almost writhed. Her bruised face suffused with blood. She pressed her knees together and gasped for air, like someone drowning. "He thought I was a—slut. I didn't want to be. I didn't want to be."

"He was jealous."

"His brother kept showing up all the time when Anton was at work. In the beginning he kept bringing me little wedding presents and telling me what to expect from the family. He said he'd take care of me and gave me advice on how to handle Anton and everybody else in the family. I hadn't known about Anton. I was so upset. I didn't know why he didn't want to—why he wouldn't touch me. And Marc was there all the time, being so nice about it. Saying it wouldn't do any harm. When I didn't want to, he got angry and told me I owed him for being good to me. He was so persistent. He just—Oh, my God. He kept touching me and hugging me and—I didn't even like him at first. But he kept saying I'd never have it my whole life and how I didn't know what I was missing and he'd, he'd—love me forever." She broke down and hid her face.

Jason sat very still, the anguished and helpless therapist, who always led people to the hurts they didn't want to face, always hoping to free them and take the burden of suffering on himself. And always aware how far away and tenuous that chance of freedom was. He let her cry for a few moments, trying to go there with her, imagining the terrible hold the two brothers had on her. He was waiting for the right moment to tell her that the reason Anton could not hurt her anymore was that he was gone from this earth.

She coughed back her tears, cleared her throat, and went on before he could say it. "I didn't know about Marc and the girl when I gave the baby back. I had spoken to Annie at the factory many times."

"Who's Annie?"

"Oh, she's the one who supervises the workers. Marc and Ivan don't speak Chinese." Heather sniffed. "When Marc told me one of the girls was pregnant and wanted a good home for her baby, I talked to Annie regularly about it. I didn't know the baby was Marc's."

"When did you find out?"

"He came over when he found out I gave the baby back to Lin. At first, I thought he just wanted to—" She closed her eyes. "When I said no, he started hitting me. He told me the baby was his. He said he'd gotten that girl pregnant for me, so I could have his baby. He was furious when I gave it back. Annie told him Lin took it and didn't come back. He didn't know where his baby was. He was so mad."

Jason felt the blood drain from his face. "So it was Marc who beat you."

"He almost killed me," she said softly, "because I didn't know where Lin had taken the baby. I didn't

know until that moment it was his baby. Anton still
doesn't know." She shook her head. "I hope to be
very far away when he finds out."

Jason decided this was the time to tell her that
Anton would never find out. First, he did something
therapists weren't supposed to do: he took her hand.
They were sitting in a grubby interview room in the
police station. He didn't know then that April had
gone to the hospital with Sanchez, who'd been shot in
the chest but saved by the cell phone in his breast
pocket. He didn't know that Marc's fingerprints had
already been matched with those found in Heather's
kitchen and had also been lifted from the very skin of
the dead girl, where he'd gripped her carrying her
down the stairs. He didn't know that the baby was
fine. All Jason could tell Heather at that moment was
that Anton was dead, and she was free.

She was puzzled, partly unbelieving, partly hopeful.
And after all the tears she'd shed, she did not have a
single tear in her eyes now. She and Jason sat silently
for a long while, holding hands, and Jason had the
feeling this was the beginning of the road for a strong
woman, not the end of the road for a weak one.

EPILOGUE

Four weeks later there was a confluence of three events in New York City that did not make the news but were nonetheless of great significance to April Woo. Weeks earlier, Marc Popescu had been arrested for the murder of Lin Tsing and the attempted murder of Heather Rose; now he was in jail, awaiting trial. But by June 15, Joey Malconi, whom April had shot in the chest, had sufficiently recovered from his injury to be indicted for the second-degree murder of Anton Popescu. On the same day Mike Sanchez, along with ten other sergeants, was promoted to lieutenant at a ceremony in the auditorium of One Police Plaza, otherwise known as the Puzzle Palace. And Jason's wife, Emma, gave birth to their baby.

April was not present for the indictment or the birth. At the time of Joey's appearance before the judge, she was sitting in the front row of Mike's promotion ceremony between Skinny Dragon and Maria Sanchez, Mike's mother, who was certain her son was receiving either the Purple Heart or the Congressional Medal of Honor. For the occasion, she was wearing magenta lipstick and a lime-green cocktail dress that showed off all her curves.

Skinny Dragon was attending the ceremony because Mike had personally invited her. On the phone he had told her that the police commissioner was presiding and especially wanted the honor of having her there. Skinny's rationale for appearing at Mike's promotion was that she did not want to offend April's top boss after she'd already caused April so much trouble. She maintained to April that Mike himself had nothing to do with her coming. Still, the Dragon wore an exquisite turquoise silk cheongsam with a matching quilted jacket, and nothing would convince her that "lieutenant" was not the same English word as "captain." It was the one thing on which she and Maria Sanchez were in complete agreement.

Also present at the ceremony were Nanci and Milton Hua, who were in the process of adopting Lin's baby, William. Since Mike had been wounded while attempting to save the infant, Milton had wanted to bring the baby to honor him. However, Nanci thought that little Will would be too much of a distraction from the heroes of the day—April and Mike—and vetoed the idea. Out of respect for April's boyfriend, Milton wore an expensive navy suit, as if he were going to a wedding. Nanci wore a blue-and-white polka-dot silk dress and a straw hat with blue ribbons hanging down her back.

April and Mike were also in blue. Cutting impressive figures in their uniforms, the two detectives held hands in front of their assembled friends and relatives. For the battery of cameras, Mike put his arm around his sweetheart, and both wore big smiles in all the photos. The commissioner mentioned them by name during his speech, and all present were moved by one of the few truly joyful intersections of job and family in this line of work.

Later that afternoon, after a festive lunch at one of the Hua family's Chinatown restaurants, April received an invitation from Jason to stop by Columbia Presbyterian and see his newborn. She wondered at this, but hurried over to the hospital before visiting hours began. One glimpse of her looking very much a top boss in her trim uniform, and no one gave her any trouble about getting in.

"Wow!" was Jason's reaction when he came down the hall to get her.

"Congratulations," she said, not hesitating on this occasion to give him a hug.

"Thank you for coming." Jason's own uniform of tweed jacket, gray trousers, and conservative tie was covered by a blue hospital gown. The shrink, a father for the first time at forty, was glowing all over. "I wanted you to be among the first to see her. After all, we named her after you. Come on."

Stunned, April followed him down the hall to the nursery, where ten rolling carts contained infants of varying sizes and colors, all tightly wrapped in receiving blankets. April Frank was in the middle of the front row. From the very first, April could tell that the sleeping Caucasian baby named after her, bald except for one tiny tuft of strawberry-colored hair, was triple-smart and a beauty already.

DEANIE FRANCIS MILLS

"Deanie Francis Mills stands beside the top
authors of suspense fiction." —Ann Rule

TIGHT ROPE

In south-central Texas, an imprisoned electronic
surveillance expert is granted an early release from
prison—with a catch. The FBI has arranged for her
early parole in exchange for her services as an
informant. Her job is to infiltrate the organization
known as Covertcom, a group which is suspected of
spying and espionage. She carries out her job, only to
be found out by the owner of the company. In the
blink of an eye, the woman's family and all she cares
for are in mortal danger. Now, she must stay one step
ahead of the ruthless corporation and the government
if she is going to protect her family.

0-451-18895-0

To Order Call: 1-800-788-6262

NEW YORK TIMES BESTSELLING AUTHOR

JOHN LESCROART

THE HEARING

Hardy's best friend, Lieutenant Abe Glitsky, has kept a secret from him...and everyone else. Hardy never knew that Abe had a daughter-until she was shot dead. It seems obvious that the heroin addict hovering over her body with a gun is the guilty party, and Glitsky has few qualms about sweating a confession out of him. But there is more to this murder-much more. And as both Hardy and Glitsky risk their lives to uncover the truth, others are working hard to stop them.

"A Riveting legal thriller." —*Booklist*

0-451-20489-1

To order call: 1-800-788-6262